Y0-EKS-472

Thanks for reading!

GODS
OF NEW ORLEANS

AJ SIKES

Copyright © 2016 by AJ Sikes

This is a work of fiction. Characters and events portrayed in this work are either fictitious or are used fictitiously. Any similarity to persons or events is purely coincidental.

All rights reserved.

No part of this publication may be reproduced, stored in a retrieval system, transmitted in any form or by any means without prior written permission of the publisher. The rights of the author of this work has been asserted by him in accordance with the Copyright, Designs and Patents Act 1988.

Cover Design by Eloise J. Knapp
www.ekcoverdesign.com

ISBN-10: 0997437510
ISBN-13: 978-0997437515

To Colin, for helping me get Brand's story on the airwaves
in the first place (anything that's happened since
then is entirely my fault)

HISTORICAL NOTE

Between the years 1936 and 1966, Harlem resident and US postal worker, Victor Green, published a slim volume of travel destinations under the titles *The Negro Motorist Green Book*, *The Negro Travelers' Green Book*, and, finally, *The Travelers' Green Book*. In the book were names, numbers, and addresses for locations where African-Americans using the nation's roads and railways could find lodging, food, and other needs and comforts.

From beauty salons to nightclubs, the *Green Book* lit the way for safe traveling during the worst years of Jim Crow and through the early stages of the Civil Rights Movement.

This novel is a work of fiction, and of alternate history. Here, the *Green Book* makes its appearance in New Orleans, in the year 1929, and with a different intended readership.

Readers interested in learning more about Victor Green's travel guide are encouraged to visit the New York Public Library's online archives of Public Domain titles:

http://publicdomain.nypl.org/greenbook-map/

. . .

The term *krewe* isn't specific to New Orleans, but is perhaps most commonly known to refer to groups and communities that support the annual Mardi Gras festival there. Mardi Gras does not appear in this book, but I do use the term *krewe*, and have taken more than a smidgen of poetic license in doing so.

Most of the *krewes* in Gods of New Orleans may be better described as gangs, though the word is not strictly used in that sense. A *krewe*, here, is any group of people united by a common aim, sensibility, or ethnicity.

CHAPTER 1

EMMA WRAPPED A HAND AROUND HER empty gut and took a good long look out the cockpit windows. The long wooden structure of the Memphis mooring deck stretched in both directions beside the airship cabin, but it was empty of anything like what Emma expected to see. Any mooring deck in Chicago City would have had a crew on it waiting to fuel up the first airship to get in line. But this place may as well have had a sign up saying NOTHING DOING.

Emma had been staring at the silent deck for the past few minutes from where she sat in the pilot's seat in the *Vigilance*. The airship's motors thrummed and rumbled behind her, close to using up the last drops of gas they had.

The fuel pumps on the deck below sat quiet and calm. Emma snugged her heavy wool coat tighter when she felt her gut turn over again, this time from fear. What if this was the wrong place?

She'd spotted the fuel station earlier than she expected. It should have been another mile to the west, right up against the outskirts of Memphis. Unless the map she had was out of date. That was possible, but something didn't smell right. She'd made two calls over the wire and still no answer.

Cracks around the cabin door let in another thin whisper of night air that stung her left shoulder, and Emma gave a cry as a shiver forced its way down her back. To her right, the windows over Brand's desk were buttoned up against the chill. The airship cabin still felt empty and cold.

Because it is.

But she had five other people on the ship with her. If something went wrong . . .

Emma tried to ignore her worry and checked the station house flag again, to make sure she had the right call sign for the deck.

"Memphis. WMR, sure enough. So what's with the silent treatment?"

The automatons on the deck hadn't moved a step. The mooring beacon glowed red in the gathering dusk, but it spoke more warning than welcome. The station house below had no lights on, and she couldn't see any movement in the small airfield adjacent to the deck.

Emma tried the radio one more time, muffling her voice in her collar like she'd done before. "Airship *Vigilance* requesting refuel on Farnsworth Wind and Water account." She gave the account number and drew in a slow breath. Maybe her father's account had run dry.

Been emptied is more like it.

The old man hadn't bothered to say good-bye the day he shot himself. Didn't even leave a note.

Didn't have to. He came back soon enough, from back there where the gods and monsters live behind the city.

Emma stuffed down the memories of her father dressed in a tramp's rags and fighting off the monster that chased her through Chicago City. That was all behind them now, her and the others on this ship. But there'd be nothing in front of them if they didn't get some fuel, and soon.

She reached for the radio again, but paused with her hand on the dial. A light flared in the station house and quickly went out. Then it came back and stayed steady.

The station house door cracked open, spilling a thin wedge of firelight across the threshold and into the gray light and shadows around the building.

Up on the deck, the two automatons came to life, stepped out of their shed, and clattered down to the mooring controls. As soon as she saw the gearboxes move, Emma felt her worry fade away like a ghost. She even cracked a smile while she waited for the gearboxes to work the ratchets and winches that would moor the *Vigilance*.

On the ground, two farmer types now stood beside the station house. The men shifted from side to side, shaking warmth into their boots even though they were bundled in heavy coats and hats. The station house door swung closed behind them and the dark night swallowed them up for a minute.

A small lamp glowed to life on a set of wooden stairs leading from the airfield up to the mooring deck. One of the men carried a lantern as he climbed up. The other man waited at the bottom of the stairs.

Up on the deck, the first man waved to Emma to indicate that the ship was secure. She thumbed her acknowledgment and silently hoped the guy wouldn't tumble to her being a woman.

Everything seemed fine; the gearboxes had connected the fueling hoses. Emma was prepared to unlock the valves when the man on the deck shouted an alarm. She thought something might be wrong with the ship and left her seat to open the cabin door. She froze mid-step when she saw the man holding a pistol in his hand. He had it pointed straight at her through the cabin glass while his partner climbed the ladder up to the *Vigilance*.

• • •

Aiden woke with a start, feeling a twisting in his guts that carried over from his dream. The darkness of the bunkroom threatened to choke him, and he quickly shuffled the blanket off his legs, untangling himself from the chair beside the bunk. His pa was up already and at the door. Aiden went to stand with him and drew up short at the sound of a muffled shout from inside the cabin.

In a flash, Aiden's pa rushed out of the bunkroom and made for the cabin. Aiden spared a look at his ma then. She lay on the bed, with her brown hair all around her head in a tangle. She was just staring up at the ceiling.

Aiden saw the rise and fall of her breathing, and he stepped back to whisper to her to stay hush, just in case someone rough had got on the ship somehow. Ever since they'd left Chicago City, Aiden'd worried they'd be nabbed by a patrol boat.

"Just going to check on Miss Farnsworth. Okay, Ma? Me and Pa. Okay?"

His ma didn't move or say anything in reply, but her eyes flicked at him for a moment, like she'd heard him but didn't care he was there.

Another muffled shout came to his ears, and Aiden knew that Miss Farnsworth was in trouble. Then his pa added his voice, and Aiden felt his stomach flip over with fright.

"Hey, how about just settling down? We don't want any trouble. We're just here for some fuel and then we'll be on our way."

Aiden bit his tongue when he heard a man reply and with a voice that spoke of hard times on harder streets. It was a voice Aiden heard plenty back in Chicago City, back when he'd spent his days delivering papers up and down the stem.

Tough birds and tougher crooks made a habit of snatching papers from him and only sometimes pitching a nickel back at his feet. The way they sneered when they said, "Thanks for the paper, kid," sounded just like the voice in the cabin now.

"I'll say it again, and this'll be the last time. Sit down and shut up."

Aiden went to the bunkroom door. He risked a look down the corridor and into the cabin. His pa was backing up against Mr. Brand's desk. Across the cabin, Miss Farnsworth leaned against something.

No. *Someone.*

Whoever it was had a hand wrapped around Miss Farnsworth's mouth, and the barrel of a pistol poked out next to her ribs, aimed at Aiden's pa.

The unseen man spoke again, with more force this time.

"I said sit down. Now hop to, buddy."

A rustling came then, followed by a third voice. Somewhere in his mind, Aiden felt a snag, like a memory wanted to come out where he could see it and hold it. He rubbed at his eyes and shook his head clear, thinking that if he could see the memory, he'd have a reason to smile again.

But Miss Farnsworth was screaming, and Aiden forgot about smiling and ran into the cabin.

• • •

Emma stayed put. The touch of cold metal from a gun barrel still lingered on her cheek. The guy hadn't wasted a second when he'd come into the cabin. He stuck the snub nose in her face and forced her to back up as he'd climbed into the cabin. Now Emma searched the cabin with her eyes for anything she could use to defend herself.

She'd been such a dope. This wasn't the Memphis fueling station; it *was* a pirate outfit run by two-bit tough guys, no better than the mobsters who'd rustled power off her father's plant for years.

She knew it sure as she knew they'd never make it to New Orleans.

The fight drained out of her like water from a sieve and Emma's knees buckled. She felt herself slipping until the gunman wrapped his hand around her mouth tighter and yanked her up. He pointed his piece at Al Conroy and told him to sit down. Emma darted her watery eyes around the cabin, as much as she could without her moving her head and giving the gunman an excuse to wrench her neck again.

The dark space of the cabin felt like a cave around her, empty of any help or light or safety. Even Al Conroy's eyes were bugging wide as he looked over Emma's shoulder. Another man's voice came into the cabin then, and Emma felt the gunman shift in place, like he was trying to pivot around to face whoever stood behind him.

Emma recognized the new voice and knew it was one she shouldn't be hearing. The gunman took his hand off her mouth and gripped her arm. He turned her around to face the hidden speaker and Emma felt the cabin floor dropping out from under her. The air of the room shook, rippling before her eyes. A thin film fluttered, like a curtain, and a dirty tramp stepped out of nowhere to stand in front of her.

"No!" Emma hollered, pushing back against the gunman and overbalancing him. He stepped to the side, holding the gun out in front of him, aiming at the scruffy, smelly tramp standing just inside the cabin door.

Emma's mind went in every direction at once.

He went out that door when we were over Chicago City. He can't be here. Not now.

Emma moved away from the gunman, frantic thoughts still weaving through her head. The Conroy kid rushed into the cabin and pulled up at the entrance to the bunkroom corridor, with his hair sticking out every which way. He slapped his hands over his mouth as he took in the tramp.

"Why don't you go out the way you came in, pal?" the tramp said from under his whiskers and through cracked lips. He stepped to the side, and lifted a hand to show the path to the door was clear. "Last time I was in this ship, I was the one holding the gat and facing a guy who looked a lot like I do now. Things didn't go so well for me, as you can see. So maybe you want to think twice about trying a stickup."

"You a . . . You some kind of ghost? What are you?" the gunman said.

Emma shifted farther away from the gunman, who'd forgotten about her as far as she could tell. She hoped he didn't remember all of a sudden. Emma kept backing up until she came up against the kid. They both edged back into the corridor.

The tramp stayed by the cabin door, but kept out of the gunman's way. Emma got look at both men now. The gunman was scruffy and thin, like he hadn't eaten in a month of Sundays, and he was nobody she knew. But the tramp—Emma took a good look. Good enough to know the madness she thought she'd left behind in Chicago City had followed her. Mitchell Brand stood before her, covered in grime and filth, looking nothing like the newshawk he'd once been and every bit as threatening as the last tramp who had come out of nowhere to stand in the airship's cabin.

"Brand?" she asked, holding a hand over her heart and keeping the other on the wall behind her, as if touching something solid might keep her from blowing away into the night outside.

"Yeah, it's me," the tramp answered, not taking his eyes from the gunman. "Looks like we meet again, and in this damn ship. You still got a grudge against me for Saint Valentine's?"

Emma shook her head in reply, not wanting to say anything to the man standing in front of her. As she stared at Brand, his face shifted, grew darker, more threatening. Was he going to turn into the monster now? Had he killed it only to become its replacement?

The gunman cut in on her thoughts by pulling back the hammer on his pistol.

"Enough chatter. I don't know where you came from, or what you are, but this operation runs on two rules: me, and this shooter in my fist."

Brand sniffed at him. "That's a low pair. Put it down and get out."

The gunman lifted the pistol and aimed at Brand's chest. "Fine by me if you want to die, friend," he said, and fired.

Brand jerked back with the impact, but kept his feet. He stepped forward and the man fired again. Then again. Each shot made Brand twitch like he'd been socked by a two-bit palooka, but he kept moving.

"Die, dammit! Die!" the gunman yelled as he emptied his piece, all six shots right into Brand's chest. Emma watched it all with her mind half in shock and half sure that she and Eddie would see New Orleans after all.

• • •

Aiden stared, struck dumb as a box of bricks, while Mr. Brand stepped close enough to grab the gunman. The guy flailed out, trying to bash his pistol into Mr. Brand's face. But Aiden's old boss sidestepped and brought his arms up and around the gunman's chest, lifting him off the floor. In a flash, both men disappeared from the airship cabin, leaving only a sliver of sparkling darkness that flickered and vanished like a curtain falling across a window.

Aiden's pa came to him, keeping his eyes on the space where Mr. Brand had just been.

"Aiden, you go on, get back with your mother. Make sure she's okay. I'll stay here with Miss Farnsworth and—"

"No, you won't, Al," Aiden's ma said from the corridor behind him.

"Alice—"

Aiden had words of warning for his pa, too. He'd seen how his father kept eyeing Miss Farnsworth the whole time the gunman and Mr. Brand were in the cabin. It wasn't just a look of concern in his eyes.

There was something pushing its way out of his pa, something Aiden knew himself because he'd felt it, and he knew it wasn't something his pa should feel for anyone but Aiden's mother. Before he could open his mouth, the cabin shimmered again and the space in front of Aiden shook. His pa leaned away, and put a hand up to shield his eyes. Aiden's ma crossed herself and began to pray. Miss Farnsworth stood back, too, but she kept her head up and her hands free.

A film pulled aside and Mr. Brand stepped into the space of the cabin, right next to his old desk like he'd been standing there all along, hiding in plain sight.

• • •

"Miss Farnsworth," Brand said to Emma but with his eyes on her feet. Now that she didn't have to keep one eye on a gun that might end up pointing her way, Emma left the corridor and stepped into the cabin. She spent a few breaths taking in Brand's appearance. His clothes had changed a lot from the last time she'd seen him. He looked like any bum, with a face full of whiskers and smears of who knew what. The rags he had on spoke of three rough and tumble days spent on the streets.

"Conroy," Brand said then, nodding at the kid.

"I'm— I'm Aiden's father," Al Conroy said, coming out from behind Emma and sticking out a hand. Behind them, in the corridor, the wife kept up her chanting and mumbled pleas to the empty sky. Emma wanted to whack her, but she couldn't bring herself to do it. It was the first time since she'd met Alice Conroy that the woman seemed to have something other than venom rolling off her tongue.

Brand shook Al Conroy's hand and Emma took the opportunity to get some questions answered. She stepped up closer to Brand and leveled a finger at his grimy mug.

"So you just pop up when you're needed? Like my father did? Is that how it works now? Because we sure could have used your help before that guy got in here and had his hands all over me."

She knew it wasn't fair, but she needed someone to holler at. It wouldn't do any good giving it to Al Conroy. The way his eyes kept roving, he'd probably just take it to mean she'd rather he was the one pawing at her.

"I got here when I could. If you remember, you let me out a few floors above Chicago City. Forgive me if I had some trouble catching up with you."

"So how is that, Mr. Brand?" the kid asked, coming into the cabin, too, and smoothing his hair with both hands. "I mean, you know, you went out the door, and that thing was with you. The—"

"Yeah, your pal, Larson," Emma said, remembering the other

tramp's name. At least the name he'd used when he wasn't a snarling beast with teeth and claws and covered in fur and blood. "What happened to him?"

"Turns out the gods don't like it when one of us flubs the job. I don't know the details, but the way I hear it, Larson had too many chances and didn't make the most of 'em."

"So are you—?" the kid started to ask.

"He's gone and you don't have to worry about him anymore. Or that thing he turned into," Brand said.

"But how'd you come back?" the kid said.

"Like I said, Conroy, I jumped from this ship. We all like to think we're in charge here, but you know same as I do it's the gods who run the show. So you don't like your cards and decide to fold, they just put you back in the game. Only thing is," Brand said, scratching at the whiskers on his cheek, "they figure it's best you stay at rock bottom from then on. You get turned into a mailbag with legs," he said. "And you hop to when you're told. Otherwise, you're on your own time, but you don't get much to work with."

Finished with his little speech, Brand pointed his eyes to the cabin floor.

"So what happens now?" Emma asked.

"I've done what I can," Brand said, taking a slow step to the cabin door. "There's nobody down there to give you any trouble, but I wouldn't bet on it staying that way. Gas up, but do it quick. And wherever you're heading, stay low and out of sight."

"Like we'd do any different," Emma said, moving to the cockpit as she spoke. "We're all on the lam."

"It's probably worse than that, Miss Farnsworth. The gods know what you did back in Chicago City. What all of us did. It's as much your head as mine that's on the block. That goes for your jazz man, too, and his pal."

Emma froze in a crouch, half sitting in the pilot's chair. She bristled inside but kept her teeth together. Turning to face Brand, she let her eyes tell him he should use Eddie's name the next time.

If there is a next time.

Brand peeled aside a filmy layer of air. Emma's eyes narrowed against the glimmering space it revealed.

"What's back there, Brand?" she asked, unable to stop her voice from quavering.

"Memories, Miss Farnsworth, and the only place I've got left to call home. Right here," he said, stepping to block her view. "Right here it's memories of every man and woman who's ever stood in this ship."

Emma reeled aside, ripping her gaze from the flickering images that had begun to take shape behind Brand.

"Conroy," Brand said, taking in the cabin and the airship itself, "take care of this pig for me, will you? Miss Farnsworth," he said, gripping his hat brim. "She's all yours." Brand looked at the kid's father then. "Mr. Conroy, a pleasure."

"Yeah, likewise, buddy. But—"

"Sorry, I'm out of time."

Brand whipped his hand and the curtain-like veil lifted around him. He slipped behind it and out of sight, leaving the others standing in the cabin. Emma stepped forward, daring against her beating heart to stand up and touch the space where Brand had been standing. She heard a thump behind her and spun around. At the entrance to the bunkroom corridor, Alice Conroy was lying flat on her face and out cold.

CHAPTER 2

AIDEN'S MA WENT DOWN LIKE A PRIZE fighter in the tenth round, just dropped flat on the floor. Her white dress was all smeared with dirt and stains from what they'd been through in Chicago City, and her hair was a rat's nest. She looked like someone else, someone he didn't know or had never seen before.

Aiden's pa went down on one knee beside her head and put his hands on her cheeks.

"C'mon, Alice. Stay here. Stay here with me. And with Aiden."

Aiden stooped and then kneeled next to his father, putting one hand on his ma's arm and giving a little squeeze.

"She okay, Pa?"

"I don't know," he said, shaking her gently as he rolled her onto her back. "Alice? Alice!"

She snapped out of it in a flash and heaved in a deep breath. Her fingers clutched at the air and Aiden's pa held her still with his hands on her shoulders. She bucked and shook on the floor. Her teeth clamped together and she whipped her head side to side as her eyes flashed open and seemed to stare at something far off in the distance.

"Get her feet, Aiden!" his pa said.

Aiden moved slow, like he was dreaming. He had to be. His mother didn't get fits. As he reached to hold his mother's feet, she kicked up with both legs, knocking him backward.

"Dammit, son, hold her still!"

Aiden rolled up onto his hip. Miss Farnsworth was at his ma's side already. She had hold of his mother's left leg while the other one kept swinging out and back in, like it was some kind of machine on a factory line. Aiden went forward again and got hold of his ma's right ankle just in time to avoid a kick in the teeth.

"Just hold her 'til she's through," his pa said. "Just hold her."

Together the three of them kept the rocking, flailing form of Aiden's mother down on the floor of the cabin. In a few moments, she went still and her eyes closed.

"Ma?"

"Alice? C'mon, honey. Come back to us. We're here," his pa said.

"Mrs. Conroy?" Miss Farnsworth asked, and her voice came out all nice and kind, something Aiden figured she didn't have in her. At least not where his ma was concerned.

Aiden held his breath until his mother opened her eyes. She looked at each of them, one by one, landing last on Miss Farnsworth's face.

"I'm . . . okay now. I'm just t— Sleep. I need to—"

"Okay, Alice. Okay now. We'll help you back to the bunk. C'mon everybody."

Aiden and Miss Farnsworth each held one of his mother's legs. His pa lifted her under her arms and carried most of her weight. They shuffled back to the corridor leading to the bunkrooms. There, Aiden's ma seemed to get her wind back and struggled to get her legs free. His pa said to let her go, so they did. Aiden and Miss Farnsworth stood back as his folks made a slow step into the bunkroom.

. . .

Emma waited for the door to close before taking the Conroy kid back to the cabin. They were his folks, and even if she didn't feel all that warm to them, they were all the kid had. She'd known enough of what it means to lose a family, and the whole experience had brought that pain right back into her heart. It was hell watching the kid's face twist through those same feelings.

For a moment, Emma let herself think about losing Eddie. He and Otis had been out cold since they got airborne back in Chicago City. She should go back and see how he was doing.

It'd just take a minute.

But they still had to get fueled up.

"Can you work the fuel lines?" Emma asked the Conroy kid. "Can you run the pumps, and shut them off when I give the word? The gearboxes down there put the lines into the ship, but without anyone to work the station house radio, we'll have to disconnect them manually. Can you do it?"

The kid nodded, but his head turned slowly back so he was facing the corridor again. Emma followed his gaze with her own and then, quick as lightning, she snapped her face back around.

Eddie's fine. He has to be.

"Kid, I'm talking to you here. I'm sorry about your mom back there, but I'm guessing you've already seen that vanishing act Brand pulled. You know what it's about, or at least you know as much as I do. My father did it a couple times back in Chicago City. So now Brand's in on the game. Fine. But how about we make good on the help he gave us and get this ship back in the sky?"

"O— okay, Miss Farnsworth. Yeah. Okay," he said, sniffling a bit and then pulling it in, holding his head up and looking her in the eye. "What do I do?"

. . .

A gust of wind came up as Aiden dropped off the airship's

ladder, making him hit the deck with a jolt. He stumbled sideways and just missed falling off the edge by hanging onto the ladder with both hands. The wind picked up again, but he was ready for it this time. He waited until he had both feet steady before letting go of the ladder.

Aiden dropped to a crouch by the posts on the edge of the deck. He fished the two restraining cables and pins loose from their clasps. Then he manhandled the ladder into position and drove the retaining pins home on each post.

The fuel pumps stood down the deck behind him; two great metal canisters attached by hoses to the storage tanks below the deck. Another pair of hoses extended past a set of stirrups beside the pumps. The hoses were joined to the fuel valves on the *Vigilance*. Aiden looked past the fuel pumps at the two automatons in their small, covered shed. They stood stock-still, like they were frozen. Something about the way they stood there worried Aiden. He'd always liked watching them work back in Chicago City. But these two . . .

He wondered if they were still powered up. He couldn't hear the clatter of their little two-cycle engines over the wind.

Miss Farnsworth's voice carried down to him from above and he cupped an ear to catch her words better.

"Go ahead and run the pumps, kid. The valves are open."

Aiden stepped up to the pumps and ran his hands over the gauges and buttons until he found the handle he was looking for. These pumps were older than the ones he'd used before, but the system was simple enough to figure out. Aiden rotated the handle in its slot until the arrow at the handle's end lined up with the word RUN. Aiden heard the fuel begin moving through the hose.

While he waited for Miss Farnsworth to give him the word to shut down, he let his eyes roam the surface of the pump casing. The metal was scratched up but good, and someone had painted all the signs and letters back on. The hoses joined the pump casing with new collars, though. The gleaming aluminum rings stood out like a set of city bracelets, making Aiden think about what waited for them in New Orleans.

Would they land safely? Would the coppers be there, holding out their jewelry? Or would they just shoot the *Vigilance* out of the sky?

Aiden listened to the fuel sloshing and bubbling through the hoses. He wrapped his arms around him and kept wondering how this would all turn out.

Miss Farnsworth's voice broke in on Aiden's thoughts.

"We're about full. You can shut it off."

He walked out from behind the pumps and waved up at the cabin, seeing her shadowy figure standing at the door. Back at the pump he flipped the handle to OFF and reached for the levers that would release the fuel lines. It took all his strength to move just one of them. When the second fuel line released, Aiden made for the ladder, but Miss Farnsworth reminded him they were still moored.

"Get us loose. You'll have to work the winch by hand. Can you do it?"

"Yeah, I got it," he yelled up at her, hoping his voice sounded more sure than he felt. The pump levers were a real doozy to work, and he knew the mooring winch took both gearboxes to operate. With the machines still standing pat in their shack, he'd have to manage it on his own. Maybe there was a trick to it though, like a—

"C'mon, kid! Get us loose! They're back!" Miss Farnsworth's voice carried down to him in angry fright.

Throwing a quick glance at the station house below, Aiden didn't have to ask who had come back.

"Move it, Aiden! Now!"

Aiden ran to the ladder without looking at the station house again. He'd seen the slim line of light in the corner of his eye. Someone had copped the sneak from the little building, trying to get the drop on him before he got back inside the airship.

A gunshot snapped through the windy evening air and Aiden heard the bullet zip past him. He dropped to the deck and crawled on his belly, just like he'd done with Mr. Brand when they'd run from the Governor's boys back in Chicago City. Memories of that awful night flooded Aiden's mind and his heart threatened to bounce him off the deck. The ladder was just a foot away now. He'd make it. He knew he'd make it.

Another gunshot snapped below him and a bullet *thwacked* into the deck beside his legs.

Aiden couldn't hold in the scream of fright, but he got his hands under control in two shakes. With a quick slap, he popped the retaining pins out from the base of the ladder and then he climbed with everything he had as another shot cracked the sky and then another.

The shots went wide, behind Aiden as he raced to the top of the ladder. Miss Farnsworth revved the engines and the ship gave a lurch as Aiden hoisted himself inside, sending him sprawling into the cabin.

"The mooring—" he started to say, but the whip-crack of the line snapping away answered his worry.

"That deck was just scrap wood, kid," Miss Farnsworth said. "This boat may not be much to look at, but she's got a team of Packards driving her. We'd be stuck on an honest municipal deck, but that old pile of sticks didn't stand a chance."

Aiden worked the levers to close the cabin door and draw up the ladder. As he did, he spied a bulky object swaying in the wind beneath them, hanging off the nose cone mooring line. It looked like a winch wheel.

"Won't that overbalance us, Miss Farnsworth?"

"Not too much," she said. "Like I said. That deck was mostly just sticks and glue, by the look of things. I wouldn't be surprised if that wheel is made of wood, too. We'll get it off the line next time we set down."

Aiden told her about the new collars on the fuel lines, but she swatted his worries aside.

"They probably stole the lines and pumps and everything else before they knocked the deck together out of whatever was lying around. New collars just means they're smart enough to make sure they don't blow themselves up."

. . .

The kid asked her a few more questions about the ship and she answered them as best she could. What she'd learned from the mechanics at her father's plant couldn't be passed along overnight, but she did her best to teach him the hows and what fors.

"That's your rudder pedal. This one here works the fuel. Step on it to give it more gas, lift up and it'll slow us down. The stick here works the flaps so we go up or down. And this valve," she said, working a handle counterclockwise, "this is your launch ballast for when you start out. This one," she said, aiming a thumb at a handle on the other side of the control board, "is for when you land at the end of the ride."

"Can I give it a shot?" the kid said, surprising her. She thought for a minute and figured it'd be good to have at least one more person on board who knew how to work the ship.

Breathing slow and struggling to keep her heart from beating out of her chest, Emma stepped out of the cockpit and let the kid get settled in the chair. His hands and feet went where they belonged natural enough, and Emma relaxed a bit.

"Keep us moving, but don't go for broke on the gas, okay?"

"Sure thing, Miss Farnsworth. And thanks, hey? For giving me a shot, I mean. My pa . . ."

Emma put a hand on his shoulder. She thought about saying something to make him feel better about his father, but the words got tangled up in her mind. Instead she just smoothed one of the tufts of his hair that still stuck out like a horn. Then she put a hand to her own head and felt the short curls and snarls she had left after their escape from Chicago City.

She'd have the finger waves she used to wear. Someday. She'd have to find a good cloche hat as soon as they got settled in New Orleans.

The kid shivered in front of her and Emma chided herself for worrying about having the right wardrobe. The cold night air came at them through a bullet hole in the glass, the hole that Emma had put there only a week earlier. She shook her head to clear the memories, but they forced their way in just the same.

Archie Falco, the guy who used to fly the ship, and the way he'd grinned like a wolf. Then the way he'd pawed at her like she was some kind of . . . and the way his head drooped forward on his neck while her ears rang with the gunshot.

Brand said the places he could walk now were filled with memories. Emma wished the ones she had of this ship would stay back there with him, out of sight and out of mind.

Swallowing a sob, she let Aiden fly them on, occasionally telling him to correct their course or let up on the gas a bit.

Doing this, Emma realized something she hadn't been wanting to admit. Her family was dead and gone, with her father's suicide only the most recent Farnsworth desertion from life. She'd made a name for herself in Chicago City as a murderess, so she'd lost her only home and community as well. Searching the airship cabin, Emma knew that this boat was all they had left. After what they'd all been through, it'd be a cold day in hell before Emma let any of them, ship or crew, come to harm.

She let the feeling sink into her chest and warm her. Then she remembered what she knew as well as anybody could. Making a promise is one thing. Keeping it is something else.

CHAPTER 3

B RAND STICKS A FOOT OUT, LETS THE OTHER
man fall on his face in the mud. Then he's off, running like
a scared chicken and knowing that's exactly what he is. The
other tramps behind him stop to help their fallen comrade. Brand
wonders if they do it out of some kind of bond, like what he felt
with the guys he helped out of the mud in No Man's Land.

Brand feels the tramps gaining on him. He risks a look back
their way. Sure enough, he sees more now. A lot more.

"Don't you guys ever get tired?" Brand hollers back at them. He
feels like he's been running since he hit the street back in Chicago
City. A five-hundred-foot drop from the airship cabin did a number
on his bones. The city's gods went one further and made him one
of their damn messenger boys wearing filth for the rest of his days.

The mud sticks to Brand's feet and he pulls his legs up like his
feet are shovels full of tar. As close as the other tramps get, they
never seem able to touch him. Brand hopes it stays that way, at least
until he makes it to New Orleans. That's where the others are going,
and something tells him he's got no choice but to follow them.

Brand died to save the people on the airship, and it hadn't been that hard. Then the gods traded out his newsman's standard for a tramp's rags and sent him on his way. They swapped out his shirt, slacks, and a tie, wrapped him in a set of dungarees and a greasy house robe, and only gave him one boot to run with.

He'd swapped that out himself, preferring two bare feet that could keep level on the pavement he'd landed on and sunk into like it was putty. He'd wound up under the streets, down in Old Chicago again, in the gypsy tunnels that connected their network of curio shops and hideaways and served as the railroad they had used to escape the Governor's army.

Once he realized where he was, Brand set to searching out familiar terrain, looking for a way back up to the surface to maybe connect up with the other Bicycle Men he knew in the city. That little journey lasted all of two minutes. The mud men showed up like they'd bought tickets.

How did they know he'd be there, and why do they keep chasing him?

"Clear off!" he yells. Only the third time he's tried it. *Maybe third time's a charm*, he thinks. Looks over his shoulder. They're still there. A clutch of bums, tangled in their own coats, all wrapped up like a mob fleeing a theater when somebody yells, "Fire!"

Now and then, when he looks back, Brand sees one get sucked under the feet of the others. Steamrolled and left behind, leaving fewer for Brand to deal with if they do catch him. And then, as soon as he's thought it, the guy who got trampled shows up in front of Brand, racing for him from the other direction so Brand has to time it right so he can land a punch that puts the man down as Brand runs by him.

On and on it goes. Brand runs. The tramps chase. The mud feels heavier now. Before, when he'd started running, it was easy enough to shake off.

He could feel Conroy thinking about him, remembering the night they spent running from the Governor's army in Chicago City.

Now, though, the mud has fingers. It digs into Brand's heels with every step, clutches just long enough to slow him down. And if Conroy's still thinking about him, it's only in dribs and drabs, half-formed memories that don't stick in the kid's head long enough to matter.

Behind him, the tramps struggle more with one another than with the mud. They move like the mud welcomes them, like it lets them move through it.

Because they are mud.

Brand knows why they chase him. It's his punishment for meddling in the gods' affairs in Chicago City. He knows what'll happen when they catch him. Brand thinks about going back to the airship, finding the others and seeing if they can help him. *A little reciprocation never hurt anybody*, he thinks.

Up ahead the tunnel opens into a cavern and a sliver of light cuts into the dark. The tramps behind him howl and roar. Brand chances another look back at them. The mass of the tramps' arms and legs and torsos looks like a steam engine with bits falling off every which way, but not enough to slow it down.

The light glows brighter up ahead now and Brand sees a doorway in the wall of the cavern, with a ramp of earth and cobbles leading up to the surface. The tramps shriek at him now, and they've caught up enough to catch at his clothes. He feels their clawing fingers on his collar.

Brand bats an arm behind him to knock them away, nearly stumbling as he does so. He swats at their clutching, angry hands, pivots back to face the cavern and focuses only on the ramp, the way out.

His feet sink into the muddy floor of the cavern, but still he runs, his feet sticking and slopping through the muck. The tramps fall to the floor behind him and are pulled underground, like the mud itself wants them and finally has a way of claiming them. Some thrash about, others go still and let the earth cover their faces.

Brand staggers backward, flicking his eyes left and right, looking for the doorway and the ramp. They've both vanished, and now the mud crawls up Brand's legs, cold and clammy. He stumbles against the wall, feeling for the doorway as he yanks his feet from the muddy floor.

The wall behind him gives way and he's on his back, with tendrils of mud slithering over his hands and arms. He wants to give up, give in, just lie there and let it happen. But an image of Conroy's frightened face comes to him, and Brand feels the kid remembering him again.

Brand forces himself up, wrenching his arms free of the mud and rolling onto his hip. He slides backward, farther into this space beyond the cavern wall, and he feels stone beneath his palms.

He looks down and sees a cobblestone. Then another. Frantic and charged, Brand scrabbles out of the reaching mud and bangs his hands and knees against the cobbles as he climbs the ramp. Up above, a half moon sends light down the tunnel. The sound of a horse and carriage comes to his ears and Brand climbs to freedom.

CHAPTER 4

AIDEN SAT IN THE COCKPIT, SWEATING UP
A storm even though the chill air from outside came
through the glass in front of him. It was something else,
being Johnny-on-the-spot like this, even if he'd only sat down because Miss Farnsworth let him. She wasn't too happy to give up the
pilot's chair, he could tell. But the way she was showing him how
things worked, it'd felt right to ask for a chance at the controls. And
sure enough, she'd said it was jake.

If only Mr. Brand was here.

Aiden let himself wish his old boss was standing behind him
and quick enough remembered that the man had been in the cabin
only a short time ago.

"Hey, Miss Farnsworth," Aiden said.

"Yeah, what is it, kid? Anything wrong?"

"I was just thinking about Mr. Brand. You know, how he came
in and out like that."

"Yeah, what about it? You've seen him do it before. I could tell
from the way your eyes didn't fall out of your head the way your
folks' did."

"Well that's the thing, Miss Farnsworth. I mean, your eyes didn't go dancing off your face neither, right? So—"

"So how come I played it so cool?"

"Yeah. I know you said about your pa . . . ," Aiden said, half mumbling the word because Miss Farnsworth's voice had dropped low.

"Brand was right. When you kill yourself in Chicago City, you don't check out for keeps. You get put back on the street like that. Like a tramp. I saw it happen to my father, and I wouldn't be here talking to you now if he hadn't pulled the same kind of stunt Brand did right when I needed him to. Figures the guy's about as useless as can be when he's alive, but then he goes and kills himself and turns into Daddy Dearest. I'd—"

Aiden sat up straighter and he kept his eyes on the night while Miss Farnsworth sobbed behind him. Her hand slipped off his shoulder and he heard her footsteps as she stepped back to Mr. Brand's desk.

· · ·

Emma let the tears come and go. She let the sobs shake her chest, round her back, and drag her forehead down to the desk. She stayed like that until it was done, until the sadness she'd pretended she didn't feel had its way with her and then left as quickly as it had come.

"So kid," she said, wiping a sleeve across her eyes. "What'd Brand get you mixed up in that you've seen that curtain business before?"

"Him and me, we were on the street," the kid said. "When the Governor's boys came in and started shooting up the place. Them and those Tesla men, with these ray guns in their mitts. Just lighting up the neighborhood. We got pictures, though, of all the people running away. The Governor had a guy in at the *Daily Record*, the paper outfit where me and Mr. Brand—"

"I know all about that damn paper, kid. Who was the guy?"

"Huh? Oh yeah. The Governor's guy, some bird named Crane. Heh, that's funny. You know I never put it together like that, but—"

"Okay, kid. You're here all week, and I'll try the fish. Get on with the story, hey?"

"Well, yeah, Miss Farnsworth. Sure thing," the kid said, his voice going glum.

"Hey, I didn't mean it like that. I'm sorry. But give a girl a break, okay? Just stick to the facts. You can pretend I'm a copper if it helps."

It didn't seem to help much at all, but the kid found his voice again and got on with it.

"So, this guy Crane, he had his ships, or maybe they were the Governor's. But they're over the city with these screens on 'em, like big picture shows, you know? And he was showing it like the people were making all the ruckus, just putting up pictures of them fighting back, like they were the bad guys and the soldiers are just doing their job. Keeping the peace and all.

"It was a real mess until Mr. Brand and me got those pictures, though."

"You keep talking about pictures. What pictures?"

"Oh, yeah. Like of the people. What was really happening, you know. We showed the real business from the street. People getting shot at and shot up, houses on fire because the soldiers threw bombs into 'em. All that kinda thing. Mr. Crane had it going pretty good, but then me and Mr. Brand, we showed 'em."

"You showed them," Emma said, remembering too well what had really happened on the streets of Chicago City. She and Eddie had run from the Governor's soldiers, too. They'd run through the underground, the tunnels of Old Chicago, and they'd met up with the gypsies and their trains leaving the city.

"You and Brand were on the front lines, huh?" A smile creased Emma's mouth for the first time in what must have been days and what felt like an eternity. She let a chuckle make its way out of her chest.

"What's funny?" the kid asked.

"Just . . . You and Brand, doing that while me and Eddie were running for our lives. You know what I was thinking about the whole time, when I wasn't worrying about getting nabbed or shot? Or worse."

"What's that?" the kid asked.

"I was thinking about the last time I'd seen Brand and something he'd said to me."

"What'd he say?"

"That he wouldn't put a picture of me on the front page even if he'd owned the *Daily Record* himself."

For a second she thought the kid was going to ask her why she'd been thinking that, but he kept hush and they flew on.

"But hey," Emma said, "that doesn't explain how you know about the vanishing act. That trick he pulled. Brand was still Brand before he went out the door with that monster."

"Oh, yeah," the kid said. "He, um … you know how he was saying about the gods and all? The ones who run the show."

"Yeah, what about it?"

"Well, I don't figure I know what's what, but when we were down there on the street, Mr. Brand went all quiet for a minute, and next thing I know it's like I'm standing next to the only person in town who knows what's right from what's wrong."

"How do you mean? Brand never had a noble bone in his body even if he did get us out of two fixes now. You telling me he got the lord's blessing?"

"Nah, nothing like that, but . . . it's like when you're in church sometimes and everyone's singing and you just feel it, you know?"

"Never spent much time in a church, unless you count being baptized."

"Well, yeah, I guess it's like that. You're just surrounded by this good feeling, like you're safe. That's what I felt. We'd been running through this park with bombs going off and the Tesla men marching around firing off those ray guns. Then Mr. Brand puts a hand on my shoulder and lifts up the city like a curtain. Next thing I know we're at the *Record*, standing there outside the radio booth and he's telling me I have to get the story out while he goes upstairs and makes with the picture show."

The kid told her more, about how he and Brand had fought with Crane and some fat guy named Suttleby, and how they'd seen a photo of what was happening in the scrap yard with Eddie, the coppers, and Emma standing there watching the noose go around her lover's neck.

"That's enough, kid. I don't need any more bad memories tonight."

They flew in silence for what felt like an hour before Emma thought she should take the controls again.

"You're doing really good, kid," she said.

"Thanks, Miss Farnsworth."

"I mean, Aiden. You're doing all right, Aiden," she added, realizing she hadn't, until then, thought about him by name. He'd just been *the kid*, but now here he was in the pilot's chair, keeping them on course just like she'd shown him.

"Hey, it's okay, Miss Farnsworth. I'm used to it," he said, like he could read her thoughts. "Mr. Brand always called me Conroy, though, and you can do that, too. If you'd like."

"Okay, Conroy. We'll see," she said. "Now give me the driver's seat for a bit. You can spell me again later."

They switched out and Emma took the controls again. Aiden sat at Brand's desk and in a few minutes she heard him softly snoring behind her.

· · ·

"Hey, you okay? Miss Farnsworth!" Emma snapped out of it and saw Al Conroy kneeling beside her with his hand by her waist. She was lying on the floor of the cabin. Emma pushed herself up with her elbows and Al Conroy shuffled back on his heels to give her space. She was happy about that. It meant she didn't have to ask the big dope to be a gentleman.

35

At least not this time.

"Hey, Aiden," she said. The kid was back in the pilot's seat. He looked back at her and smiled.

"What happened?"

"Well, you—"

"You just fell out of the chair," his father said. "I heard Aiden shouting. I didn't know my son could fly an airship, but I guess that's how it is. Are you all right?"

"Al," his wife said from where she stood in the bunkroom corridor. "Let her be. Your son could maybe use some of that tender, loving care. Or your wife."

"I'm fine," Emma said, getting up. She brushed herself off and snugged her coat tighter around her. "Just tired. We're all tired. If someone can stay out here and make sure I don't fall asleep, I'll keep us in the sky until we reach New Orleans."

"I'm not leaving you alone with my husband for a second," Alice Conroy said. Her voice rang a three-alarm fire and her eyes added a little more heat for good measure. Emma was about to tell the woman she had no intention of asking Mr. Conroy to do the honors, but the kid piped up first and surprised everyone.

"It'll be okay, Ma," he said, keeping his eyes on the cockpit glass. "I'll stay up here. Maybe there's some coffee in the galley. I can make it up and—"

"I won't have you around this . . . soiled dove, Aiden. Not you or your father."

"Look," Emma said, moving back to the pilot's chair. "I'm not up for a fight and I've got nothing left to fight with, anyway. We needed to refuel, and we did. Now it's straight on to New Orleans. Soon enough we can all go our separate ways if that's what you want. But I need someone to help me keep my eyes open, otherwise we might as well aim this ship at the ground."

"I'll get to it on the coffee," Aiden said and stepped aside to let Emma take the controls again. She watched him head off toward the galley at the back of the cabin before turning her attention to the night outside.

"We should have just stayed put in Memphis," she said, more to herself than anyone else in the cabin. Emma listened as sounds from the galley told her Aiden had coffee on order. A shuffling sound from the corridor got her attention then. She turned just in time to see Eddie come into the cabin, holding his ribs with one hand and using the other to hold himself to the wall.

"Oh!" The Conroy dame put a hand to her throat and stepped back, gluing herself to the space between the galley door and the corridor.

"It don't rub off him," Emma said. "I'm still white, ain't I?"

The woman pressed her lips together and flashed a look of horror at Emma as Eddie stepped slow and fell against Brand's desk. His swollen cheek and eye looked awful, and the way he held his arm around himself . . . His torn shirt and ratty looking pants made him look even worse.

Emma would have gone to help him, but Al Conroy stood all two hundred pounds of his bulk right in between them, and she didn't like the look in the man's eyes one bit.

· · ·

Aiden came out of the galley with the coffee in a pitcher and two steel cups on a tray.

"Only found the two cups back there. So who needs the java most?" he said, letting out a chuckle that fell flat instantly. One of the Negroes had come out to sit at Mr. Brand's desk and now the mood in the cabin was nothing but glum, and two kinds of angry to boot.

"Hey, um—" Aiden started, but clammed up when he caught his folks aiming a look his way. He'd wanted to greet the Negro man right, just like Mr. Brand used to do when they'd come around driving delivery trucks up to the newspaper building. They'd always have a laugh with Mr. Brand, and sometimes slap him on the back like they were old friends. And maybe they were, from back in the Great War.

Aiden had never figured whites and Negroes were much different, except colorwise. But his folks had their own feelings about it, and the airship was too small for those kinds of feelings to get loose.

"You want some coffee, Pa?"

"It's all right, Aiden. Go ahead. You *and Miss Farnsworth* can have the joe. Alice, c'mon. Let's get back to bed."

They stepped into the back together and Aiden watched them leave. He gave a little flinch when he heard the click of the bunkroom door.

In the corner of his eye, he saw Miss Farnsworth turn to look at him from the cockpit.

"You said something about coffee. Isn't that right, Aiden?"

"Sure enough," Aiden said. "Right here, Miss Farnsworth."

He moved toward Mr. Brand's desk and drew up when he saw the Negro looking at him.

"S'okay, kid. I ain't gonna bite. Couldn't do anyhow, even if I wanted."

"Eddie," Miss Farnsworth said. "You should be resting back there with Otis, not up here chit-chatting."

"Couldn't help myself," the Negro said. Aiden tried to think of him by his name, but the other word kept getting there first.

"Um, Eddie? I mean, Mr. Collins. Do you want some coffee?"

"Mister. Huh," the man said with a hint of a smile curling his bruised lips. "Name's just Eddie. And no, thank you, Mr. Conroy. I'm okay."

In the cockpit, Miss Farnsworth let out a chuckle, and soon enough the three of them were sharing a quiet laugh, the first piece of good Aiden had felt for as long as he could remember. As they sailed on, the airship lights pushing away the night, Aiden hoped the good feelings would continue in New Orleans. A second later he thought about his folks and had to kick himself inside for being such a dope.

His pa had always been a little hard to swallow, especially when he hadn't had a good night's sleep. But his ma . . . she was a sweet lady, always nice to him even if she did keep on him about finding work and making good on the family name. She'd been different ever since they left Chicago City.

Who'd blame her.

But still, something about his ma had changed. Maybe that fit she had when Mr. Brand showed up is what did it. Except Aiden had noticed it before they'd reached that mooring deck back in Memphis. His ma wasn't warm and kind anymore. Like when they left Chicago City, everything that made her sweet got stuck back there behind them, leaving just the sour parts for this trip to New Orleans. Aiden stared at the dark corridor for a moment, wondering if he'd ever see his ma smile again like she used to.

CHAPTER 5

EMMA SLID OUT FROM BEHIND THE CONTROLS and let Aiden take over again while she got some coffee in her. She stepped back to Brand's desk and stared down at her lover. "I still say you shouldn't be up, Eddie. Go back and rest."

When he didn't say anything in reply, Emma tried a different approach.

"Hey, it's me talking to you here. Your Lovebird. Remember me?" she asked, and instantly felt stupid for doing so. Eddie's battered face and body slumped into the desk's chair. His breathing was ragged and strained. Seeing him like this now brought a wave of guilt and regret washing through her.

If only she hadn't gone gunning for Nitti. If only she'd left her father's gun where she'd found it: in his lap, resting in his own bloodied hands.

Eddie coughed once and groaned. The copper had beat him badly, and every breath seemed to hurt him. He quivered with each inhalation and let it out slow and uncertain, like he wasn't sure he'd get another chance at taking in air.

"We've got Memphis behind us now, Eddie. Quick as we can we'll be in New Orleans."

"Okay then, Emma. Okay then . . ."

"What do you mean, Eddie?"

"I mean . . . I'm okay. You say we're going to New Orleans. Then we okay. I'm okay, too. Just wanted to see you smile again. Help me back there now, hey?"

"Sure thing, Eddie. Sure thing," she said, putting a hand out for him to grab and wrapping her other arm around his back. She pressed her hand to his side gentle as could be, and let him control every motion.

In the bunkroom corridor, she cast a nervous look at the door to Brand's old quarters.

They're in there. And they can stay in there for the rest of the trip.

Emma hated feeling like she had to defend her love for Eddie. She'd done enough of that in Chicago City, hiding from everyone that would have given her the business for daring to look Eddie in the eye without turning tail and running for the hills. And now she was stuck with people like that on an airship with nowhere to go for certain.

"We gonna get out of this, Lovebird," Eddie said. "You wait and see. We'll be fine."

"I know, Eddie," she said, helping him into the room across the corridor from where the Conroys were holed up. Eddie settled down on the bunk beside Otis and soon enough Emma heard his breathing relax. She kissed him on the forehead and pulled the blankets up over him.

Emma checked on Otis, too. He was still out cold and snoring deep.

Lucky man, she thought. Maybe the whole bunch of them would get lucky and New Orleans would have nothing but good news for all of them.

And maybe I'm the Queen of England.

Emma went back to the cabin to find Mr. Conroy standing at Brand's desk and looking out the window. He had a strained look on his face. Aiden turned and nodded at Emma, his eyes glistening in the cockpit lights. He stood up and said he wanted to get some shut-eye, so Emma took the cockpit again and thanked him for spelling her.

"Keep at it and you'll be a pilot someday, Aiden."

Mr. Conroy nodded at his son, like he meant to express the same confidence, but his face still didn't reflect it. Aiden's face fell a bit more. He stepped into the corridor and disappeared from sight. Emma turned back to the controls and kept them steady.

"Your son's not half bad, Mr. Conroy," she said.

"Yeah. You're right. Aiden's a good kid. He's got a lot to learn about how the world works, though. And call me Al, hey?"

Emma ignored the crack about Aiden, but she couldn't let the second line slide. "I think your wife might prefer it if we kept first names for the ones we love," she said, pivoting to face him. "I know I would. Okay by you, Mr. Conroy?"

A hurt look washed over the man's face before it was replaced by a weak smile. "Yeah. Sure thing, Miss Farnsworth. That works fine by me."

Emma's stomach relaxed and it wasn't until then that she noticed how tense she'd been. At least she'd gotten *Happy Pants Conroy* cooled off, or hoped she had anyway. She wasn't worried about having to let him down hard if he got frisky, but the last thing she needed was Conroy's wife getting more ideas about Emma wanting to cut in on their dancing.

"Look, Miss Farnsworth," Mr. Conroy said, his voice shifting into a peacemaker's tone. "I know we didn't start out all right with you and those—" He stopped short when Emma whipped her head around and gave him both eyes, dark with fury. "I mean, your friends . . . back there," he said, thumbing at the corridor.

"Go on," Emma said, half wishing he'd say the wrong thing so she'd have an excuse to haul off and belt him. She'd needed to strike out at the world for so many things for so long, and at the same time, she kind of wanted the dope to say the right thing. Anything that would lead to the calm and safety they'd all lost.

"Like I said, we didn't get off all right at the start. But you saved our lives flying this ship the way you did. And Al Conroy doesn't forget a debt like that. Whatever you need from us." He paused and gave a slow glance at the corridor to the bunkrooms. "From me, and I guess from Aiden, too. We're on your side. At least until we hit New Orleans."

Emma felt the stirrings of warmth in her chest, a hint of that calm and safety returning, even if just for a moment. Good ol' Al Conroy was right. She'd gotten them all out of the soup in Chicago City and had kept it going on this flight to New Orleans. Maybe they weren't much better off than before; they had nowhere but the airship to call home. But at least they were alive and didn't have to worry about soldiers popping up to lynch them or gun them down without so much as a *How do you do*.

"I'll stay up here," Mr. Conroy said, still waving the white flag with his voice. "Until Aiden wakes up again. Unless you think that'd be a bad idea."

"No, that's all right. You're the one has to explain it to your wife, not me."

The man grumbled at the comment, but he didn't press anything. Not yet anyway. Emma thought about telling him he could head back to the bunkroom, but she knew he'd balk. With one eye on the night and the other ready to look a dagger at Al Conroy, she kept them flying steady, much more alert than before.

• • •

Aiden's eyes roamed around the small bunkroom. Across the hall, he knew, the two Negroes were crammed into an even smaller room. This one used to be where Mr. Brand would sleep. Tucked into the near corner was an old camp chair. It had to be Mr. Brand's from the Great War. Even though the chair had seen some traveling, it looked like it could support Aiden's pa, and Al Conroy was no small-fry.

The bunk itself fit his ma and pa fine enough. There was even a bit of room against the wall for Aiden to squeeze in, but that would put his pa at the edge of the bunk and as likely to roll off as stay put.

"Your father is a good man, Aiden. I can trust him," his ma said from where she sat on the bunk, leaning up against the wall. She held a blanket around her and kept a pillow behind her back. Aiden didn't know what he should say in reply, so he just gave an "Mm-hmm," and hoped she'd drop it. It was good to hear her talking, though. After that fit she had, he was worried she wouldn't ever talk plain to him again. And he figured he trusted his pa, too, even though a heavy knot in his gut told him not to.

Aiden's ma shifted on the bunk. "You should try to stay warm, Aiden. It's been an ordeal for all of us. Here," she said, handing him another blanket from the bunk. He sat in the camp chair and pulled his legs up under him before he draped the blanket over himself. He felt like a tramp by a campfire, doing his best to stay awake while his ma talked into the room. Her old sunshine still hadn't come back, but it sure was good to hear her voice.

"Like I said before, Aiden, you have to carry your weight now. You had a job back in Chicago City, so you know what real work means. You know how to show up and get in line. But it will be different in New Orleans, Aiden. It—"

She cut herself off before another word got past her lips. Aiden looked up at her, letting the blanket slip from around his face a bit.

"What do you mean, Ma? What's going to be different?"

"You're—Why you're just a boy, Aiden," she said, tearing up and holding a hand to her mouth. "And we're taking you into that . . . that place. With nothing but—"

She didn't finish, but she didn't have to. Aiden could follow her gaze through the bunkroom wall and into the room across the way where Eddie and the other Negro were sleeping.

"Maybe it won't be so bad, Ma," Aiden said. She turned her red-rimmed eyes toward him, and her face sagged into a disappointed mask, like she doubted Aiden could possibly say anything truthful after what had just come out of his mouth. "I mean, Mr. Collins out there, he's been—"

"He's a Negro, Aiden," his mother said. "He isn't a mister, and you don't need to be calling him that way. He's just one of the boys down the block or across the street. They stay out of our way, and we stay out of theirs. That's how it was back in Chicago City and that is how it will be again."

"But Ma," Aiden began, until she gave him a look that would have had a weaker kid wetting himself down to his boots.

Aiden clammed up and looked at the canvas ceiling. Up above and to the back were the engine rooms. He remembered Mr. Brand saying there was a mechanic's cot up there.

Before he knew what he was doing, Aiden flung himself from the chair. Balling up the blanket and holding it against his chest, he wrenched the bunkroom door open. His ma called his name, but only half her heart was in it, and Aiden had lost his taste for hearing his mother's voice. Still, he paused on the threshold, giving her a chance to apologize or say something that was more like the woman she used to be.

Nothing came. No words of comfort, no apologies. Aiden left his mother sitting on the bunk and stalked down the corridor to the ladder at the far end. He climbed up, keeping the blanket pressed between his chest and the rungs. At the top, he flipped open a trapdoor to reveal a crawlspace above the corridor. Aiden pulled himself up, trailing the blanket behind him. The space was tight, and the dull rumble of the engines pressed in on all sides. Still, he felt better here than he had back in the bunkroom with his mother.

Hadn't she seen what happened during the Governor's attack? All those white and colored folks holding hands and running together, helping save the other guy's kids from the bullets and flames.

Chicago City seemed so far away now he could almost believe that what he'd been through was nothing but a dream. Some kind of crazy dream that he was stuck remembering like it was real. Like he'd really been there running through the streets with Mr. Brand while the Governor's army threw everything it had at them.

Aiden wrapped himself up in the blanket and tried to wish the memories away, but he couldn't get the images out of his mind.

People getting shot down by those Tesla men or the soldiers that lurked behind them. Bombs throwing wood and earth and concrete into the air. The dull ache in his ears that came after every explosion roared into the night and away again in a cloud of smoke and ash and falling debris.

Blazing lights in every house on every street. Lights that flickered and danced, sending screaming families into the night. And Aiden scrambling along beside his boss, feeling for all the world like a fish so far out of water he might as well be in the desert. What could he have done, though? What could he have done to stop any of it from happening?

A fitful sleep came fast in the close space of the mechanic's bunk. Aiden dreamed of monsters raging in the night, all claws and roaring and liquid fire that scorched the world.

CHAPTER 6

THE STREET IS COLD UNDER HIS FEET. BRAND shuffles in the early morning mists and tries to avoid frigid puddles of rainwater. His foot hits one, hidden by his shadow as he passes beyond the glow of a street lamp.

"Dammit!" he says, shaking the water off his bare foot. Brand hobbles to the sidewalk where he sits beside a rain barrel outside an abandoned storefront and tries to rub life back into his soles.

"What the hell do you people have against my feet?" Brand says, remembering the night Frank Nitti nearly toasted the skin from his soles in front of a furnace. Brand keeps up his hollering, waving an angry hand at the sky. "First it's the ice box on that street. Then Nitti gives me the mob's best remedy. Old Mother Nitti must have taught him that one, hey? And now it's the cooler again, is that it?"

If the gods are listening, they don't answer. But Brand isn't surprised at their silence. They haven't answered him yet, and he's been hollering like a madman since he left Chicago City. He rubs his sore, cold feet now and mutters into his collar, forgetting about the gods and their plots.

"I should go back in the mud tunnels maybe. See if I can't get a good coating on these dogs. Bake 'em up good in the sun next chance I get. Or ask Nitti's ghost to do the honors when I see him."

Brand left the tunnels an hour ago. Or maybe just five minutes. He doesn't know what time it is or why he's suddenly free to sit on his ass and rub his dogs without worry. When he first reached the surface, Brand did worry. The street was clear and clean—too clean. He thought about turning tail, going back the other way to avoid an ambush the mud tramps had laid for him.

And then he was stepping down the deserted street in a city that he knew had to be New Orleans, or somewhere nearby. He felt the cold shock of cobblestones under his naked feet, and he was alone, entranced by the night, the smells of the city, and the quiet.

The hum of an airship motor brings him out of it. He looks up and sees the *Vigilance* soaring through the dark night, only a few blocks away. He stands, sets out at a run, and nearly falls on his face.

His legs buckle and his feet feel like slabs of lead.

"So it's the slow dance up top, too" Brand mutters, catching himself on the rain barrel. "Fine. I know those steps."

Now he looks at the *Vigilance* where it hangs in the sky, aiming to the west. The sun grays the dark, pushes the night aside. Brand stands. He shakes both legs, wraps his arms around himself and trudges on down the street. At a cross street he turns and spies a mooring deck in the distance. The *Vigilance* hovers in a circle around the deck and gradually begins her descent.

"Hold her steady, Emma," Brand says, sending his hushed voice across the air with a cough. The cold seeps through his tattered clothes, and the scent of a lake comes to him on the morning breeze. He smells rot and sorrow, and remembers the trenches of No Man's Land.

Brand walks slow, but sure. He places his feet with care, making certain to avoid any more puddles. In this moment, Brand isn't sure he's still himself, the newshawk who got the scoop on the Saint Valentine's Day Massacre only to find out the story led down a hole deeper than any hole ever could.

Does he even remember the truth anymore? Does he remember anything but running through the mud, shuffling through the streets on bare feet, or the hunger that burns his gut, crying out at him to find something to drink. Brand doesn't know, and with each breath he finds it easier to forget. But deep inside, he keeps a fire burning. A little light that hopes that someone on that airship over there still remembers him.

CHAPTER 7

THE SKY GLOWED WITH THE CREEPING tendrils of dawn when Emma brought them over an airfield littered with junk. Around the dim landscape, she spied the shadowy hulks of wrecked or grounded airships, old trucks, wagons, and cars. To the north, the murky waters of Lake Pontchartrain lapped at the shore. Tumbled heaps of old rowboats, rafts, and barges haunted the shoreline. She would have thought they were piled for a bonfire except they all seemed to sink into the muddy earth.

A tingling shudder worked its way through Emma's neck until the sensation forced her to whip her head aside and turn her gaze to the mooring deck below. The deck stood across the airfield from the lake, looming there in the morning mists a hundred yards from the shore. Across from where she'd berthed the *Vigilance* two smaller craft hung on their tethers, bobbing and swaying with the dawn breeze.

The winch from the last deck had fallen off during the journey from Memphis. Thinking about their unlikely success in finally reaching New Orleans, Emma radioed to the station house down below. Soon enough, a pair of ornate automatons stepped out of their shelter on the mooring deck. They came forward and ratcheted down the lines that would hold the *Vigilance* in place.

Emma had never seen machines like these before. Instead of sleek limbs and a streamlined chassis, like the ones she knew in Chicago City, these two looked like suits of fancy armor with curling and scrolling waves of decoration on every surface.

Emma waited for radio confirmation before shutting down the airship's engines and locking the controls. She double-checked that the fuel valves were locked as well before leaving the cockpit.

The Conroys stood at the back of the cabin, looking like any old family except for Alice Conroy's ragged expression and her son's glum face. Only the father, Al, had anything like a spark in him, but even that was pretty well faded.

"We should probably, uh . . . maybe you should go on ahead, Miss Farnsworth. I mean—"

"Yeah, I know what you mean," she said and stepped around them to the bunkroom corridor. In their room, Eddie and Otis were sitting up on the bunk, playing a hand of cards.

"Where'd you find the lords and ladies?" Emma asked.

"Was up on the shelf here," Otis said, motioning to a slim strip of wood fixed to the bunkroom wall above the bed. An empty tobacco pouch and scattered cigarette papers decorated the shelf, along with a broken pencil and some crumbs. Emma noticed Otis kept his eyes on the door behind her, like he'd jump through it the first chance he got, or maybe that he worried someone else would be coming through it.

"You okay, Otis?" Emma asked.

"Huh? Oh, yeah. M'okay," he said, and dropped his eyes back to his cards. Eddie lifted his swollen face and gave Emma a questioning look with his good eye. She lifted her brows at tilted her head in Otis' direction. Eddie seemed to get it and went back to the card game, but Emma could tell he was watching their new pal extra careful.

Something ain't right, Emma thought. But whatever it was, she would have to wait until they had solid ground under their feet again to find out.

And maybe a hot meal in our stomachs.

"So we made it?" Eddie asked, with his eyes still on the cards in his hand.

"Yeah," Emma said. "Finally. If you're both up for it, the Conroys want us to lead the way, and I'm all out of words to argue with."

Eddie looked her way and smiled, his good eye shining with love. She tried not to look at the swollen mess on the other side of his face, or the way he still clutched one arm around his ribs with every breath. Otis packed up the cards and stuffed them into his shirt, still half looking like a scared rabbit. He slid off the bunk and Emma backed up a step to give him space. With careful steps, Otis maneuvered around to help Eddie down and together the two men made their way out of the room and into the cabin.

The Conroys had moved to stand beside Brand's desk. Emma nodded to them and went to the cabin door. She popped the catch and let it fall open. A cold wind blew in, rustling everyone's hair and putting a stitch in Emma's side. The cold went right through her, into her gut, down her legs, and up to her throat where it caught and doubled her over in a coughing fit.

Emma stood just as Eddie came up behind her and put one hand on her waist. He used the other to steady himself against the cabin wall beside the open door.

"I'm fine, Eddie. Just swallowed too much bad air I guess," she said, turning to face him but pointing her eyes to the side at the Conroys.

"We gonna be okay, Lovebird. Just go slow, hey? We made it to New Orleans."

Otis flinched as a gust of cold filled the cabin.

"Steady on, hey, Otis?" Eddie said. "You too, Emma. Steady on. Everything gonna be fine now."

Wishing she could believe him, Emma worked the lever to lower the ladder from the cabin. One of the fancy gearboxes clumped its way over and fixed the ladder in place. Emma waited until the machine had stepped back a few feet to stand beside its partner. Then she climbed down.

Eddie followed and took his time about it, using his arms to support his weight whenever he moved a foot down to the next rung. Otis came close behind. The Conroys stayed in the cabin, out of sight, until Emma shouted up at them.

"If you want to stick with us, now's the time to do it."

Al Conroy showed his face first, and soon enough the three of them came down the ladder, with the son bringing up the rear. He closed the cabin door behind him, and Emma felt a smile curl her lips. The kid … Aiden really wasn't half bad, and nothing as bad as his folks. But he was still their son and that meant Emma wouldn't have to worry about him much longer. The Conroys wouldn't be hanging around. Not if they had a chance to get away from the company she kept.

Good riddance to 'em.

Turning to Eddie and Otis, Emma nodded her head to say they should move down the deck to the station house. At the far end, a small shack waited with the door cracked open and a light inside, which cast warmth into the chilly air. For a station house, it wasn't much, but the deck was as sturdy as any she'd seen in Chicago City.

As a team, she and her two companions trudged down the worn planking, their feet finding ruts where carts had been rolled time and time again. New Orleans was supposed to be the biggest port city in the South, and Emma figured that had to be true enough.

But what gives with the junkyard down below?

Emma put her mind back on what was important. Getting settled in. Finding some digs, and fast. She and Eddie kept up their pace toward the station house. Otis limped along a few steps behind, casting his eyes in all directions, while the Conroys trailed at the back. Emma sniffed at their timidness, but she worried about Otis for a moment.

Why was he acting so cagey? He'd taken a few shots to the legs, but still . . .

A dark-skinned man pulled open the door of the shack when

Emma and Eddie were a couple yards away. The man wore a dark rumpled suit, and had long ropes of black hair framing his round face. He laughed long and deep and waved with his hands, beckoning, as if he could pull Emma and her crew faster down the deck.

"It's a cold day and the fire like to be growin' colder," the man called. "You berthin' with Mistah Celestin Hardy. So come an' pay your due."

The man laughed some more and clapped his hands before stepping outside the shack. He walked to meet them and Emma could make out the lines of his face now. His lips were thick and full, his cheeks narrow, and his eyes set deep beneath a wide brow. He smiled big when his eyes met hers, but in an instant his face slackened and went sour with anger. Before Emma or Eddie could move out of the way, Celestin Hardy brought the muzzle of a heavy revolver to bear on them, and they both froze mid-step, hands raised.

"You bring dat one with you as a friend?" he said, motioning behind them at Otis. Eddie turned first, looking back at their companion. Emma echoed the gesture and what she saw put a chill right through her.

The Conroys had stayed back and weren't up to speed on things yet. But Otis had a look on his face that said he knew all too well what was going down. And why.

"Didn't do nothin'," he said, backing away a step with his hands out. He still limped a little, but he made a showing of getting his strength back. "Didn't do nothin'," he said again.

Emma risked a look back at the man with the gat in his hand. Celestin Hardy's eyes burned bright red with rage, and something else, too. Emma'd seen enough to know the world held secrets she'd never guessed were there, but what she saw now made her feet put down roots. She and Eddie both stood stock-still as Celestin Hardy approached and passed between them, his arm outstretched and the gun still leveled at Otis.

"You comin' back now, boy? You comin' back and sayin' it wasn't *nothin*?"

The man roared his words, and as he did a crimson halo of

images swirled around his shaggy, dark mane. Emma flinched back in terror as miniature scenes of murder and torture swam in the air around Celestin Hardy's head. Bodies flung themselves to and fro, jerking against the impact of bullets or flopping down to lie prone on floorboards, sidewalks, and streets. The images kept coming, a steady litany of proof that Celestin Hardy was someone few dared to cross.

A red mist condensed around the man, surrounding him and protecting him. Emma felt a boundary form between them, further freezing her and Eddie where they stood. And still Celestin Hardy continued to march forward until his gun was pressed against Otis' chest.

Behind Otis, the Conroys had moved back by the ladder leading up to the airship. They cowered together like a flock of lost lambs. The mother looked ready to faint and the father kept eyeing the ladder. The kid had different ideas, though. He tried to muscle his way out of his father's grip, like he wanted to run off or find help. Or—

Emma didn't get a chance to think about what else the Conroy kid wanted to do. A gunshot split the cold air of dawn, just as the sun crept up high enough to cast a band of yellow-silver across the *Vigilance* and the other ships tethered to the deck.

Otis fell away from the end of Hardy's revolver and landed flat on his back. A dark stain spread out from the hole in his chest. Eddie swayed on his feet and Emma rushed to support him. The Conroy dame screamed her fool head off while the husband did his best to keep her hush. The kid went rigid, no longer held fast by his father. He just stood there, staring at Celestin Hardy like he would any man he'd met on the street.

The station master pocketed the revolver and turned to face Emma. He smiled and extended his arms to suggest Emma and Eddie lead the way to the station house. His face was a mask of calm now, and the haze of murder had vanished. Despite what he'd just done, Emma no longer felt the same sense of terror or violence coming from him, as if he'd snapped his fingers and cast a spell to make it all go away.

Emma looked back down the deck at Otis' still form. For a moment she let herself feel nothing, but it didn't last. She turned to the station master, pleading with her eyes that he let them go.

"I might could be troublin' to you, sure enough," he said to Emma. "But any man alive know you ain't familiar with dat dead man and his history in New Orleans." He turned and walked toward the station house, motioning with a hand for them to follow.

Emma let the man's words settle like a heavy coat around her. She knew Hardy wouldn't waste a second if she and her group caused him trouble. He'd just start blasting away because that was how Celestin Hardy solved problems. Emma was familiar with the idea, having solved at least one of her own problems the same way.

And look where it got you.

She held Eddie around the waist and together they made slow progress in Hardy's wake. Emma didn't look back to see if the Conroys were following. The mother had gone quiet, and Emma took comfort in that. But only a bit.

"Why'd you kill him?" Emma asked Hardy as they walked up to meet him at the station house door.

"He like to have business here once upon a time. Man been wanted many a year for things he did when last he lived in New Orleans. He takin' a certain somebody's property and claimin' it for his own." Hardy paused and smiled at them. "All you need knowin' is Celestin Hardy be workin' for this certain somebody, and *moi*? I would be remiss to be lettin' dat sonofabitch walk away from what he been havin' comin'."

Hardy flung a dismissive hand at the air, leaving his arm outstretched so that his finger wound up aimed back at Otis' body like the muzzle of a gun. "Not sayin' he could walk too good, mind," he said, chuckling as he drew his arm back to his side. "I might could ask you why da man been given a once over and then once more again. Where you comin' from?"

"Chicago City," Emma said before she knew the words were on her tongue.

"You travelin' long with this one?" Hardy said to Eddie, ignoring Emma completely. He looked straight at Eddie, sized him up, then turned questioning eyes back to Emma. "You do this to the man or you have it done to him? Chicago City no friend to da Negro man. Has no love for what he is or what he do. So tell me, Miss Lily White who flies an airship. Tell me now," Hardy said, stepping forward to confront Emma. Before she could explain, Eddie spoke up, defending her and letting the approaching man know where the lines were.

"She ain't done this anymore than I'll let you do half the same to her. Was a copper back in Chi. Bad copper. Now he's a dead copper, so now you know why we come down to New Orleans."

Hardy let out a grim laugh. "I guess I do now, don't I? Indeed. So let's get you settled in, and then you can be tellin' me about da three doves you carryin' with you." He stuck a thumb back at the *Vigilance*. Emma turned and saw the Conroys had climbed the ladder. The kid had his head sticking out the cabin door as he watched them follow Hardy into the station house.

CHAPTER 8

AIDEN THOUGHT ABOUT CLIMBING BACK into the mechanic's nook while his folks argued and shouted at each other. But without the motors running, their voices would carry anyplace in the ship. So he climbed down to the mooring deck instead.

The fancy gearboxes were standing to the side, a few feet from the base of the ladder. Another pair stood inside a low-roofed shelter across the deck. Their eye lamps still glowed, so they were ready for anything the station master radioed their way. Aiden wished for a moment that he'd never left Chicago City. Right before it all went bad, Mr. Brand had been hinting that he might have Aiden start working with the fix-it man at the *Daily Record*. He'd be learning to keep the automatons on their mooring deck running tip-top.

Woulda been.

Turning away from the gearboxes, Aiden cast his eyes down the deck. The dead man, Otis, was sprawled out on the wooden planks, draining his life out. Maybe it was memories of what he'd seen that night in Chicago City, or maybe it was just being tired of his folks acting like he was still just a kid, but something made Aiden feel like he should go over to the body. It's not like he hadn't seen worse.

The deck lengthened out in front of him in the wispy morning light, making the little station house at the far end look even smaller. Otis was lying midway down the deck, and Aiden thought he could see the pool of blood forming around the body, but it could just be shadows, too. The sun wasn't all the way up yet. Aiden took a few steps and waited, unsure now if he should keep walking or just go back up into the ship. His mother's voice came across the air from above, a frenzied shriek and then sobbing. His father's voice followed, pleading and comforting, or as close to comfort as Al Conroy could ever get.

Aiden took another step, then another. Shadows gathered around the dead man's face in the weak morning light. Aiden looked back at the airship above him. His folks had gone quiet. He half wanted to go back to them, but his mother's words came to his mind.

They stay out of our way and we stay out of theirs. That's how it was back in Chicago City and that's how it'll be again.

He turned away from the airship, leaving the ladder behind him, and walked down the deck toward the station house.

· · ·

Emma and Eddie waited against the wall just inside the door of the station house. A potbelly stove stood in the farthest corner of the room, giving off warmth that barely cut the chill coming in from outside. To the left of the stove, a long box draped in black cloth sat on a bench under a window. Emma let her gaze wander the landscape outside, and she felt a clutch in her stomach as the sun revealed a wasteland of ruined airships and vehicles by the lakeshore.

Celestin Hardy took his seat behind a heavy desk in the nearest corner of the cramped space, down the wall from where Emma and Eddie huddled together by the door. Hardy lifted a thick black book from a drawer and let it fall on the desk with a *thump*.

Hardy flashed a look at them both and opened the book. He flipped page after page, slowly enough that Emma could tell the book was a ledger.

Money.

What were they going to use to pay this man for berthing the *Vigilance*? Her father's name got them halfway here, and Brand had helped them refuel in Memphis. But this was different. Emma was almost ready to offer the ship in trade for help finding a place to stay, but the thought of being trapped didn't appeal to her. She couldn't shake the feeling they'd gotten in deeper than they'd ever been, and they hadn't been in town more than a handful of minutes.

Something about New Orleans clawed at Emma, raked talons over her skin. She fought the urge to run and felt her feet winning the argument. No matter how much Eddie had promised her it would all work out, Emma's doubt grew with every page Hardy flipped until he stopped and looked her in the eye.

We're sunk. We should have just stayed in Chicago City.

Hardy sat back in his chair and stared at them. His veiled eyes glinted with something like delight or glee. For a second Emma felt the world fall away beneath her feet, and then her old spark lit up inside. She'd stared men down before, and gunned them down when she had no choice. With a breath, she drew herself up and did what Emma Farnsworth always did when comfort went out the window and made room for nothing but tension.

"What kind of payment do you need, Mr. Hardy?"

"Oh, it ain't be paying Mistah Hardy you gotta worry about, Miss Lily White and Short Hair. You in Metairie now, and you say your destination be New Orleans proper. You gotta travel around, so you gotta pay up to Papa Lebat. Give him his rum, or his coffee. Maybe a cigar for smoking."

Emma gave a slight shake of her head without even trying. They had nothing.

"Well, you got a key? A cane? Something he can lean on when he walks? The man is old. He bein' older than New Orleans. But he still gotta walk around everyday, helpin' people make their way in and out. You come in. If you wanna go out, then be pleasin' Papa Lebat with what you offerin' up to him."

Hardy waved a hand at the cloth draped box and moved out from behind his desk. He crossed the small space in one stride and pulled the fabric aside. Emma gasped and put a hand to her mouth as Eddie's grip on her shoulder tightened. The fabric fell away, revealing a casket beneath it. Hardy opened the box and Emma steeled herself for the inevitable.

She let out a deep sigh and almost laughed when she saw the offerings jumbled together in the box. Cigars poked up from among the items. Here and there a small bottle or jar of amber liquid in amongst steel cylinders. Emma read the brands of coffee on the cans.

"Did you think we had the man inside, Miss Lily White? Did you think this box is bein' for you? Is that what goin' through your brain when Celestin Hardy show you the offerin' box?"

He leaned back on his heels and laughed deep and rich, like he had when he'd first greeted them.

"N-no," Emma said, letting out a nervous chuckle. Eddie stiffened beside her and she pulled herself up again, standing tall as she could against her lover, still sheltered by his embracing arm.

"Mr. Hardy, we don't have any of those things. We've just come from Chicago City, and—"

Eddie interrupted her with a squeeze of her upper arm, and she happily let him try to smooth things with the station master.

"Got family in the Easy. Gonna get back with them, but we ain't got your offering needs. Got nothing but that ship outside, and that ain't for trading. So what else we can do here to make our passage safe?"

Hardy stood back and regarded Eddie. Emma's eyes darted back and forth, watching the two men for signs that either would start swinging. Eddie still had one arm around her and the other held his sides. He'd be easy pickings if the station master wanted to play rough.

Tension hung between the two men, and Emma shifted her weight so she could jump in front of Eddie if Hardy threw a punch.

A knock on the door split the silence apart.

"Come on inside then," Celestin Hardy said, breaking eye contact with Eddie, but not before letting his grimace fall into a warm smile of greeting once more.

The door opened and Emma turned to see the Conroy kid standing there. Aiden's eyes said he'd rather be anywhere but New Orleans, and his hand shook as he held out a can of coffee.

"Um, I heard you all talking and thought this would maybe help. I hope it's enough, Mr. Hardy. It's all we had up in the galley. We'd have more if I hadn't made some up when we was flying down from Memphis, but we was all tuckered out, and . . ."

Hardy's smile had gone, and his face fell into a mask of suspicion. The kid trailed off and squeezed his lips together to keep them from trembling off his face. He turned and handed the coffee to Emma.

"Thanks, Aiden," she said. "Thank you."

Emma passed the can to Hardy. He accepted it with both hands and deposited it into the open casket. With a tender movement, he closed the lid and replaced the shroud. Then with a flourish of his left hand, Hardy produced three tin badges from a pocket or maybe thin air, Emma couldn't tell which because his hands seemed to move every way at once.

"These be your markers of safe passage in New Orleans," Hardy said, handing the badges to Eddie, then Emma, and finally Aiden.

"Put them on your shirts or keep them in your pockets. But always have these on your persons when you outside. On the street, day or night. You be found in the wrong part of town without Papa Lebat's blessin' token, and is nothin' can be done to help you."

Emma fumbled with the badge, trying to pin it to the thick wool of her coat, but gave up and settled for tucking it into her pocket. Eddie struggled to fit his into a pants pocket until she helped him out. Aiden managed to work the clasp and had his pinned just below his collar. Hardy chuckled and clapped his hands.

"You do fine here, little dove. Just you count on it. You do fine in New Orleans." He chuckled once more before he touched a hand to Emma's wrist and ushered the three of them outside.

The Conroys stood against the wall of the shack. The mother had been crying, and the father seemed about ready to snap out of his own skin with either fright or rage, Emma couldn't tell which.

Hardy came around her and aimed his welcoming smile at the white couple.

"You got nothing to be worryin' about. But . . ." Hardy paused to jab a cautionary finger into the air in front of their faces. He had warning eyes for Emma, too, before turning back to the Conroys.

"You raise your voice, lift a hand, or, blessed mama protect you, a weapon against a one of us, and the Devil hisself be a kinder man than any you will find in New Orleans. You be comin' down from Chicago City way, and that way is not our way. If you wantin' to survive, you believe me this is true."

As if on cue, a trio of men, two dark-skinned and one white, appeared a ways down the mooring deck. Emma couldn't tell if they'd been there all along or if they'd just popped into existence. Either could have happened, she knew, and that knowledge gave her no comfort at all. The three men strolled down the deck like they owned the place, and judging from the fur-trimmed coat the middle one wore, and the gold rings on his fingers, they probably did.

The man in the middle, one of the dark-skinned men, stood only as tall as Emma herself, but he made up for it around his waist. His footsteps thunked down onto the mooring deck with a force that Emma felt rattle her ankles. To either side of him marched one of his boys, big and making no mystery of the fact that they packed all the heat their boss would need. Emma had no trouble identifying them. A torpedo was a torpedo, no matter if you were in Chicago City or Timbuktu.

"Mistah Bacchus," Hardy sang out as the big man and his toughs approached. "A fine welcome to you on this mornin'."

"Celestin Hardy," the man said, his voice rolling across the air like a thunderstorm. "I do hope I am not intruding upon your business, though I must ask what business you find yourself conducting this morning. On my mooring deck."

The man finished with a chuckle that rumbled in his throat and shook his heavy mass. Hardy didn't speak right away. The two torpedoes stayed straight and narrow, eyes scanning the small crowd around Hardy. Emma watched the torpedoes' hands, waiting for them to snatch at their lapels to pull out a gat. She'd dive to the left, push Eddie out of the line of fire. The others would have to take their chances.

"Mistah Bacchus," Hardy said, finding his voice at last. "I was, in fact, just relievin' you of a problem from long ago. One problem by the name of Otis Martin, if you recall the man and what he do."

"I do. I do," Bacchus said, still smiling like the reaper come calling. "That, Celestin, is the reason for my visit, you no doubt have guessed. But I mean to inquire, again, as to the nature of your business with these pretty little doves." He stepped closer to the Conroys as he spoke, stopping within arm's reach of the parents. The kid stayed behind his pa, but kept his head out so he could see what was happening.

Emma watched the two heavies, who kept their hands in sight at all times. The next thing she knew, Alice Conroy was screaming blue murder and her husband roared like a lion.

Emma turned in time to see the wife shrinking away from the reaching hand of Mr. Bacchus, who had a lock of her hair entwined in his thick dark fingers. The husband leaped forward, knocking the gangster's hand aside. In a flash, Hardy had a knife in his hand, pulled from some hidden sheath in his coat. Emma screamed as the knife went through Al Conroy's hand and drove it back against the wall of the station house behind him.

The knife came out as quick as it went in. Hardy wiped the blade on Al Conroy's sleeve and replaced the weapon where he'd kept it hidden inside his coat.

"I warned you, Mister Big, White, and Dumb. I warned you. Don't say I didn't."

Emma reached for Eddie and held on to him, visions of their

last moments in Chicago City burning through her mind. Aiden went to his father's side and stood up straight, looking Hardy in the eye, but the kid's heart wasn't in it. His feet said *I dare you*, but his face just begged to be left alone. Al Conroy held his hand against his chest and whimpered as he fell into a squat against the station house. His wife went to him and shot a glare of tear-stained venom at Hardy.

From her right, Emma caught the beefy voice of Mr. Bacchus, telling his boys to go inside. The two bruisers did as they were told. Hardy moved to follow them into the station house, but his boss put a hand up and the man stopped.

"I believe we owe the man a book, do we not?" Bacchus said. His voice still scraped against Emma's eardrums, like a rasp on stone.

Hardy's face pinched up like he smelled something he didn't like, and Emma didn't miss the look the man almost gave to Bacchus. Then Hardy reached a hand back into his coat and fished around for something. Emma winced, half worried that *a book* was some kind of street talk in New Orleans for a bullet to the heart. But Hardy stepped fast into the station house and came out just as quick holding a slim book, like a magazine almost, with a green cover. He flung it on the deck at Al Conroy's feet.

"Dat book be savin' you a whole lot of trouble," Hardy said, looking at Aiden, who still had his gaze fixed on Hardy's own.

"What is it?" Aiden asked. The kid's mother squeaked in terror and flashed a look between her son and Hardy's hand that hovered over his lapels.

"It's *the book*, Little Dove. White folk who be walkin' and travelin' around New Orleans like to be havin' an idea of where 'tis safe to go. The book tell you dat. You read up and you tell your Mama and your clipped Pappy here. They know what's bein' good for 'em, they listen to you."

Hardy finished with a finger aimed at the kid's chest and a glare at Aiden's folks. Then he turned on a heel and stalked into the station house, leaving Emma and the others alone with Bacchus.

"Lest we move any farther down this path," Bacchus said. "I

hope all you doves remember what happened here this morning. And now I bid you good day. And welcome to New Orleans."

The heavyset man draped in fur and glittering gold took a short step back. He smiled before he slipped between shadows and early morning mists, leaving nothing in his wake but a fluttering curtain of air above the weathered boards of the mooring deck.

The Conroy dame gasped and snapped her eyes to look back at her husband, who kept his face bunched up to hold in his tears. The kid shuffled his feet and made like he wanted to help but just didn't know what to do. He reached for the little green book that Hardy had tossed on the deck.

"We should . . . we should probably get out of here," Emma said.

The kid looked at her like he would reply, but his mother got there first.

"Yes. You should. You should both go."

Emma wanted to tell her it wasn't like that. That she meant they should all leave together. But the lady's face said nothing doing. If those eyes of hers were gun barrels, Emma knew she'd be a fool to stare the woman down for another second.

Putting an arm around Eddie's waist, she helped him down the deck, leaving the Conroy family behind. She gave a glance back, just to be sure. The parents sat together in a heap, the father holding his hand against his chest and both of them sobbing like it was all they had left to do. The kid kneeled down by them, but he was watching Emma and Eddie leave. He lifted a limp hand to wave, like a bird with a broken wing trying its damnedest to fly from danger.

CHAPTER 9

BRAND HEARS THE GUNSHOT. HE CAN EVEN SEE the man who falls and knows who it is. Otis, the other Negro they'd rescued from Wynes' little lynching party back in Chicago City.

But Brand can't get up there, up those stairs and onto the deck where the *Vigilance* hangs heavy and dark. He can feel the ship watching him, but he also feels it pushing him back, like it somehow knows he's trouble.

"Gave you enough trouble already, hey?" he says, and decides to find someplace to hunker down and hide. At least he's above ground now, on the street and not *in* it.

Brand squats on his bare feet, puts his back against one of the posts of the mooring deck. Lake Pontchartrain kisses the shore a few hundred feet away. The sound of water lapping at mud comes to Brand's ears along with other sounds of a lakeside coming to life in the early morning. Coughing and wheezing startles him, and he jerks upright on his tired, naked feet. He sees tramps rising from around the airfield.

They come out of ruined cars and trucks, and the beat-up hulks of old airships. Brand ignores the tramps for a second, his eyes riveted to the wrecked airships, large and small, their frames like skeletons that have long since spilled their guts and sloughed off their skin.

A group of tramps shuffles away into the morning, then another. Stragglers come out like cattle to the farmer's call, lowing in a chorus of hacking coughs, spitting, and groaning as they stretch their legs and reach withered limbs to the sky. Spines, joints, and jaws crack and pop as the tramps stretch, and then they're on their way, all of them. All but one group.

The layabouts stay huddled under a piece of old canvas in the remains of an airship closer to the lakeshore. They've hung the canvas like an awning from the frame of the ship to the branches of a tree. Brand sees more canvas hanging from the airship frame.

Brand realizes the tramps aren't chasing him. The ones who left and these he sees now in their shelter. They aren't made of mud. These tramps here in the airfield are real men. Flesh and blood, just like he feels himself to be flesh and blood. Still. Even after what he's done to himself, he still feels alive.

No. That's wrong. What he feels most of all is cold.

His naked feet are freezing, nearly numb but still able to send knives of ice up his lower legs. Brand shivers and wraps his arms around himself tighter, watching the tramps by the lakeshore. They've lit a fire and Brand is on his feet now, walking across the mud with careful steps, watching out for every puddle, every slick patch that might hide a deeper pit beneath it.

He makes it close enough that the men notice him. He sees heads jerking his way, but the tramps' faces are still indistinct. Three men surround the small fire in the close space of the canvas shelter. One stirs a pot now, hanging it over the fire using a pair of blacksmith's tongs. The other two huddle together nearby, their dusky faces alight in the glow of the flames.

Brand is close enough to see that both of them have their eyes closed. The third, at the fireside, has his eyes closed also. When the man turns his face to Brand to greet him, opening his eyes, Brand screams and stumbles backward.

"Oh!" says the tramp with no eyes holding the pot with the tongs. "Do forgive me. It is long since the Three Blind Men have been approached by a fellow traveler beside the waters of Lake Pontchartrain."

"Who—who the hell are you?" Brand says, still on his ass in the mud. He stays there out of instinct. This isn't the first time he's found himself in such a position and happy to simply be alive to experience the sensation. At least this time it isn't the Kaiser's mortars that put him here.

The tramp by the fire stirs his pot and grins. His eyes are closed again, and Brand wonders why he doesn't just keep them that way since he's got nothing to see with.

"You got a name, pal?" Brand tries again.

"A name," the tramp says, setting the pot aside. He removes a mitten and wipes his thick fingers down both cheeks, like he's preening for a photograph. He smooths the snarled salt-and-pepper whiskers on his dark face, but they pop back up again, jutting out like some kind of fungus on the bark of a tree. "Surely I do have a name," he says, putting the mitten back on and taking up the tongs and pot again.

Brand is about to ask the man for his name a second time when the tramp speaks, his graveled voice carrying a hint of humor across the cold morning air to Brand's ears, like the man would laugh if only he could remember how.

"My name is Barnaby Augustine Fellows, and it is a tragedy that I have spoken so much at length but have not yet introduced myself to you. If I may ask your name now, sir, so that *acquaintance* can be a word we use with honesty."

Brand sits up and moves across the ground to accept the shelter of the canvas. He puts his back to the tree and chuckles at the tramp's talk, his fancy words and the airs he wears like medals on a dead man's chest.

"Name's Brand. Mitchell Brand. No middle name in there because Mother Brand didn't go in for that sort of thing."

"Well met, Mitchell Brand. And is it Mitchell, or do you accept Mitch as a substitute?"

Brand thinks for a second. His only friend in Chicago City used to call him Mitch, but they'd been in the war together, flying observation missions over No Man's Land in '17 and '18. His newsboys called him Mr. Brand, but that was kids talking to a man, nothing like this exchange between equals he's faced with now.

"Let's try Brand," he says. "And is it all right with you if I use Fellows? Only the whole thing's a bit of a mouthful, and I can't remember if you said Arbuckle or Augustus in the middle."

The tramp laughs out loud now, clearly familiar with the functions of humor. His laugh booms around the campsite like the shockwave of an artillery round. Brand feels his ears pinch inside, like the tramp's laugh is stabbing into his brain. Then all goes quiet and the eyeless tramp is stirring his pot again.

"Soup's almost ready, boys," he says, and then to Brand, "You may call me Barnaby, or Mr. Fellows. Though others may claim cause to truncate my given name, I do prefer full respect be given."

On cue, one of the other two tramps calls out, "You say soup was on, Barn?" The tramp sits up from where he lies and holds out a metal bowl. He has a spoon tucked between his fingers while his other hand keeps a scrap of canvas wrapped around him like an old woman's shawl. "Oh boy, Barn's famous Earl-eye in the Morning Chowder. Gonna get in on this, Finn?" the tramp asks, nudging a buttock into the face of his still-sleeping partner on the ground.

The other man barely stirs, but he too sits upright, almost as if the air itself pulls him to a sitting position. Posture is like a punishment that life will enact upon this man, Brand thinks, watching the tramp slip and slide where he sits until his spine is more or less straight, his head tilting only a few degrees to one side.

Brand watches as Barnaby serves the soup, not missing the lip of either bowl held out by his companions, and Brand knows now that the two on the ground are not of equal standing to the man who cooks and serves their food. It's the way Barnaby huffs and grunts while he serves the first one, the man who called him *Barn*. That man thanks him now, and begins eating like pig at the trough.

"Good chow, Barn. Good as good can get. Hey, who's the new guy?" the tramp says, tossing a nod in Brand's direction. The man's eyes are closed, and by now Brand has realized that none of these tramps has any eyes left to open. But they know he's here and where he is.

"Our visitor is none other than Mitchell Brand," Barnaby says, giving Brand a case of the frights that nearly sends him sprinting away across the cold ground of the airfield.

"You all know me?" he says, slowly rising to his feet, though the frigid pain coursing through his heels now threatens to keep him pinned to the spot with his back to the tree.

"Know you?" Barnaby asks, with hand held out, palm turned up. "No. I don't believe any of us have had the pleasure before this glorious morning." He puts his hand on his lap and goes back to sipping his gunboat slop.

"Oh," Brand says. "Just the way you said it there. It sounded like . . ."

The other tramp pipes up. "Don't go listenin' to ol' Barn now, Brand. Sure enough, he's a talker, and he'll talk your ear off. But he'll sew it back on a second later just so's you can keep on listenin' to what he hasn't got to say."

The tramp chuckles at his joke and sips the soup in his bowl. His partner keeps hush, and Brand wonders for a moment if they aren't setting him up to be caught by the other ones back in the mud.

The third one shuffles around on his backside until he's closer to the fire. He makes some gesture with his hands and Brand hears a scraping sound. Then he sees the tramp is using his spoon against the edge of his bowl to call for more chow.

Barnaby dishes it up and reclines against the frame of the ruined airship behind him.

"Brand," Barnaby says, "if I am not mistaken, and it is indeed a rare time when I am, in some small way, out of my depths these days . . . But if I am not mistaken, I would deign to suggest that you are a new arrival in New Orleans. Am I correct in this estimation?"

"Yeah, you got it right, pal. Look, sorry for dropping formalities, and I don't mean to be ungrateful, but I'm not in a position to waste a lot of time. I've got people looking for me, and something tells me you three are likely to know about them and maybe have some advice for how I can avoid making their, uh . . . what'd you say, *acquaintance?*"

"Well," Barnaby says. "Tell us of your troubles, and we will aid you as we can."

Brand sniffs and wipes a finger under his nose. "I don't know how you can help me. Suppose I'm a sap for asking. You haven't got eyes to see. Forget it."

"Mr. Brand," Barnaby continues, "you are no doubt familiar with the matter of communication as handled by those who sit in places of power. Yes?"

"You mean running messages for the gods? Yeah, I know about it. And I can add, pal. Two and two make four, and so does three plus one. Three of you and one of me, and we're all in the same business."

"Agreed, and applause for your acumen, Mr. Brand. Not every messenger knows what he's about when he arrives, but you seem possessed of a singular knowledge of our noble corps."

Brand waits, expecting a question. He isn't disappointed.

"So the question then becomes, how did you gain this knowledge? By hook or by crook? Or by some means as yet unheard of in the grand annals of hobo lore?"

"None of the above. A friend of mine threw himself off a building in Chicago City. He ended up like this."

"And yourself?"

"Well, I saw what a change it made in my friend so I thought I'd just follow suit, only I went one better and stepped out of that airship at five hundred feet."

"Impressive," Barnaby says. "But you say *that* airship as though

I can deduce which one you mean. And it is a known fact that none of these around us have tasted the kiss of clouds for many a year."

"Yeah," Brand says. "And why is that? What's with all this rust and wreckage? I haven't seen a pile like this since I was over there, and it was pretty obvious why those ships couldn't fly anymore. These here look like they just fell out of the sky."

"You are not so far from the truth, Brand," Barnaby tells him. "New Orleans has her problems, most of which are caused by those who call the city home. But there's one we can't change or fix or affect in any way except to let it come and hope it leaves us just as quick."

Barnaby aims his face to the south as he speaks at the sky. Brand figures it easily enough.

"Storms," he says. "You'd think people would know better than to fly airships around the place when it's storm season."

"You'd think they would," Barnaby says. "Then again, you'd think a lot of things, and ten'll get you twenty you'd mostly be wrong. But we've detoured, Brand, from my original question. Which ship did you mean?"

"That one up there, on the mooring deck. It just came in. But look, my feet are about to freeze off. Any chance you've got something around here I can wrap my dogs in?"

"Sure thing, Brand," the laughing tramp under the canvas says. "Give him yours, Finn."

The quiet man turns his eyeless face toward Brand, the dark skin of the man's cheeks stained darker with grime and his wide nose crusted with a mix of blood and snot, or maybe it's just the soup he's been eating.

Before the man can respond to his partner's encouragement to give Brand his shoes, Barnaby Fellows is talking again.

"Brand," he says, "you're a newcomer to the job of messenger, but with enough patience and the careful application of that most benevolent and yet insidious servant, alcohol, you shall find your way here. Of that I am sure. And lest you fear I speak falsehoods, why just look at whose lap you had the good fortune of dropping into."

"You mean you?"

"I mean all of us, Brand. The Three Blind Men. Myself, whom you have already met, and Reginald Welks, whom you have not yet met in name. And our final partner in crime"—Barnaby aims a hand at the quiet man—"Phinias Gardner, whom you have at least laid eyes upon but, alas, have not and shall not have the good fortune to speak with. Man's dumb as a post, but he's good company for it. I dare say his cohabitant, Mr. Welks, could learn a few things about the confluent actions of decorum and reservation."

Brand eyes the three men, their mangy hair and tangled coats, and the flaps of skin that cover the empty sockets beneath their brows. Phinias is handing over a pair of shoes now and Brand takes them without thinking. His feet have failed to register any feeling for the past few minutes, and he's certain that frostbite is growing on his toes.

"Thanks, pal," Brand says. "I mean Phinias. Thanks Phinias."

The quiet man simply nods, then hunkers back beneath the canvas. Reggie curls up beside him and the two of them are snoring in seconds. Barnaby waves to Brand, like he wants his attention.

"Yeah? What is it?"

"You still haven't told me what you were doing on that airship before you decided to wear the mantle of messenger. And if I guess correctly, which I so often do, those people who are looking for you are among the members of our *krewe* who have fallen as low as one possibly can while still remaining human."

"What do you know about it?" Brand says, dodging Barnaby's question about the *Vigilance*. "About them, I mean. The guys in the mud."

"The mud men, Brand, were once messengers themselves. They came by this station long ago, and in so doing, they became men with more purpose than any of them had in their former lives. Not so different from you or me really."

Brand turns away from the tramp and looks to the sky. Dim

light has washed over the horizon, bathing the airfield in a hazy glow. Brand thinks it's like looking through old glass stained with time and everything people do behind windows when they think nobody's looking in on them.

Brand thinks about the *Vigilance* and the people it carries. And he feels his backside forming a hollow in the mud where he sits.

"I think I've got more purpose than those fellas in the mud," Brand says.

"That you may, Brand," Barnaby says back, half swallowing a snicker.

Brand wants to ask what's funny, but the feeling that he's being watched from up above keeps his mind on the *Vigilance*. He nods at the ship and lifts a finger to his brow.

"Don't forget about me, hey?" he says to the ship hanging on its tethers above the mooring deck. The silver-gray bulk bobs in the early morning mists, like it's returning Brand's nod. He sniffs and turns to Barnaby.

"Got any slop left?" he asks. Barnaby sniffs now, and pulls a grimy bottle from his left pocket. He unscrews the cap and takes a pull before passing the bottle in Brand's direction.

"Ah, hell," Brand says. "Not like I'm a stranger to breakfast from the hip." He reaches for the bottle and feels Barnaby's mittened fingers brush against his own. A warmth passes between them, like the touch of friendship. Something Brand hasn't felt in a long time.

He takes a pull from the bottle and is surprised when his arm automatically stretches out to offer the hooch to Reggie and Finn. A hand snakes out of the canvas and retrieves the bottle, pulling it out of sight.

Brand's feet tingle and ache in Finn's off-size shoes. But the hooch warms him, and he laughs. Barnaby joins him, and soon enough they're a duet, hooting and chortling as the liquor does its work.

CHAPTER 10

AIDEN AND HIS FOLKS LEFT THE MOORING
deck on foot and took a streetcar into New Orleans.
Aiden's badge of safe passage was good enough for the
car man, but he told Aiden not to think it'd work all the time. His
folks would need to make their own offerings to Papa Lebat at some
point.

The streetcar got them down the river through some pretty
sad-looking parts of town. His ma's looked out every window at
every stop. She finally settled down when they got off in a place that
sat along the river. The car man said it was called Irish Channel, and
that actually put a grin on Aiden's pa's face.

The streets that ran around the Channel made it a narrow
neighborhood. And it seemed like a pretty safe place. Aiden didn't
see a single colored face anywhere on the streets.

Aiden's pa stepped out of the car, holding his bloodied hand
under his coat. He looked around the street and then went straight
into a tavern across from where the streetcar stopped. Aiden and

his ma followed, with her shaking her head the whole time and muttering things Aiden knew he was better off not hearing.

In the tavern, his pa sat at the bar while the barman wrapped a towel around his wounded hand.

"Marked you good, my boy," the gray-haired barman said. "Won't like to be finding work with a mitt like that on ya'. Sorry to say it, but it's the truth."

"Yeah?" Aiden's pa said back. "So I'm a charity case now, is that it?"

"Don't take the wrong tone, my boy," the barman said. "I'm helping you because you're our kind of people, part of our *krewe*; we have to stick together. But you get to thinking you're too good for being helped, well . . . I'm sure you know your way to the door."

Aiden thought his pa would say something else, but his ma cut in first.

"Please. We've just arrived and don't know where to go for help."

The barman smiled at Aiden's ma and brought a glass up from under the bar. He poured a swallow for Aiden's pa and talked to his ma. Aiden heard that word, *krewe*, again and again. After a bit he figured what it meant. Wherever they wound up in New Orleans, they'd have some people around them who they could count on. And who'd be counting on them in kind.

The barman gave a chuckle and Aiden turned to look. His ma had her head to the side, like she'd been nodding at him, and the barman's eyes were on him, too.

"You got a green book from the deckmaster?" the barman asked. "Well, you'll be knowing how to get there, then."

Aiden's ma had a few questions for the barman, and Aiden wanted to listen, but decided to watch the city life outside the window. He had to know this town somehow, and it wouldn't do no good missing out on a chance to watch it up close.

Before the town gets to watching me.

People moved through the dim mid-morning light just as they'd done in Chicago City. But the street looked older, like parts of it were frozen in time and you'd move in and out of history whenever you took a step. Across from the tavern was a bank, and next to that a general store kind of place. To the other side of the bank was a hotel, and a little post office sat next to that.

Aiden watched people leave the hotel, go into the bank, come out, and go to the post office. It was like those cuckoo clocks he'd seen where two people come out and walk along tracks to ring the bell with little hammers. Aiden felt like he could stay there watching the people all day, but a second later his ma marched him outside while his pa drank his lunch.

"I don't know what your father is thinking," his ma said.

Happy for the chance to talk to his mother again, Aiden tried to offer some reassurance. "Maybe he's just hoping we'll have an easier time is all. You know, like the barman told us? About Pa's . . ."

"Yes, Aiden. His hand. I'm sure that's why he's sitting in that bar an hour before noon swilling whiskey."

Aiden knew well enough when his ma was in the mood to talk and when she was in a mood to do all the talking. The way she stepped hard on the sidewalk let Aiden know which it was this time, so he kept hush and followed her down the street. He had the green book rolled up and stuffed into his pants pocket. He hadn't looked at it since they'd left the mooring deck, but figured they'd need it soon enough.

Like she'd read his mind, his ma told him to get the book out and make sure they were on the right street still.

Aiden pulled the little book out and let it unroll into his hands. The cover showed a picture of a white family, walking down a street, smiling and wearing sharp clothes. They looked like any bunch of folks Aiden might have known.

"Open it and look, please, Aiden," his mother said. Aiden felt her impatience as much as he heard it, so he was quick to flip the cover back.

The first page listed the contents. *Lodging and Restaurants* was first. Then came *Gas Stations, Barbershops and Salons,* and *Clothiers.*

"What're we looking for, Ma?"

"A place to stay, Aiden. What else? Oh, give me that," she said and snatched the book from his hands. He watched her leaf through the book while a burning ache filled his chest. It'd been a while since she treated him like some snotty-faced kid, and it couldn't be long enough before she did it again.

"Okay," his ma said while she looked around the street. She seemed to decide on something and closed the book, handing it back to him in the same motion. "Follow me."

Aiden stuffed the book into his pants pocket again and tried to stuff his face into his shirt. He knew things were going to be rough here, but wasn't ready for how his ma had turned out all of a sudden. He almost wished he'd gone off with Miss Farnsworth and her N— her jazz man, Mr. Collins.

Aiden kept up thinking about the two of them, and hoped he would see them both again someday.

Sooner the better.

"We're almost there, Aiden," his ma said a few blocks later as they came around a corner. She'd had him pull the green book out and give it to her twice while they walked, and each time she seemed to settle down a bit from before. By the time they hit Constance Street, he almost felt ready to talk to her again.

"There's our destination," his ma said. "Let's just hope they have a vacancy like the saloon owner said."

Up ahead, Aiden saw a shop window with dresses and bonnets hanging on mannequins and racks.

They'd come down Constance, passing rows of storefronts and houses. Before that they'd been on a cross street, Aiden didn't know which one, but it wasn't a main stem like Constance was. As they walked, he'd cast his gaze down every alley they passed, when he wasn't busy watching his shoes hit the pavement.

When he did look down the alleys, he found himself thinking about avenues of escape along the narrow streets that bent and juked their way through the Channel neighborhood.

One thing Aiden promised himself when they landed in Metairie was that he'd learn the streets of this new city. Same as his friend Digs had learned Chicago City and knew every way in and out of trouble there. Aiden would learn New Orleans like that, in case he ever needed to lam it and stay safe. And he'd make sure his ma and pa knew it, too.

"Aiden," his ma said, snapping his attention from the empty alley he'd been staring down.

"Yeah, Ma. I was just—"

"You were daydreaming, Aiden, and that's not a good thing to be doing in this city. It's not a good thing to do in any city. People will see you staring off into the sky and the next thing you know somebody's picking your pocket. Or worse. Now pay attention."

"Yes, Ma," he said, feeling the blush rise to his cheeks again and struggling to hold in the angry shame that burned him under his shirt.

"I'm going inside," his ma said, aiming a finger at the dress shop behind them. "You're to wait outside and stay alert. Keep an eye out for any . . ." Then she seemed to lose her way. Aiden was about to offer a few words to finish her thoughts, but she picked up again. "Any people who look like trouble. I'm sure you know what I mean, so I don't need to say it."

Aiden did know what she meant, but the whole time they'd been walking through the neighborhood, he hadn't seen a single dark-skinned person.

"Sure thing, Ma. I'll keep careful."

"Good," she said. Aiden watched her knock on the dressmaker's door before going inside. He figured it was okay to just go in, but maybe his ma was being extra polite so she could win the shop lady over. It probably wouldn't take much if the woman was anything like his ma in her thinking.

On the way to the streetcar stop back in Metairie, they'd passed other families, some with children in tow. Aiden's ma gave a smile and a nod to the white ladies they passed. But when a Negro family walked by, she kept her eyes straight ahead. Aiden noticed how the Negro ladies would look shocked, almost frightened, when his ma did this, like she was something out of a monster movie.

But she'd made it clear that her thoughts about dark-skinned folks were not up for questioning, so Aiden had kept hush. He did try to make up for his ma though, sometimes nodding or smiling at the Negroes they'd pass.

A few smiled back. Mostly the children, but sometimes one of the older Negroes would tip a hat or send a wink his way, like they knew he was trying to make good while his ma pretended she didn't see the dark-skinned people who stepped by them on the narrow sidewalks, with only inches to spare.

That word. *Negro.* It still bothered him, but since he didn't know any of these folks' names, he figured it wasn't a bad thing to think of them as Negroes. After all, they probably thought about him the same way.

Just some white boy nobody knows.

Aiden sat down on the sidewalk outside of the dressmaker's, leaning up against a post that supported a balcony over the storefront.

The street lived and breathed like any other he'd seen, but without the clockwork behavior he'd noticed earlier. While he waited for his ma, Aiden thought about his father sitting in that tavern, drinking and looking glum.

Aiden wondered how Miss Farnsworth and Mr. Collins were doing and if he'd ever see them again. They'd all been through a lot already and it was just their first day in New Orleans. As the sun pushed out from behind the clouds aside, Aiden felt like maybe everything they'd been through would stay behind them, waiting to be forgotten.

His ma stepped out of the dress shop behind him. He turned around as she came up to where he sat by the post.

"Come along, Aiden," she said. "We've got to get settled in."

"What do you mean, Ma?" he asked as he stood up and dusted off the seat of his trousers. He didn't miss his mother's glare or the way she heaved in a breath of shock as she watched him swatting at his backside.

"Young man," she said, "get yourself together." She took him by the upper arm. "We're in a new city. We don't know anybody. It is *important* to make good impressions on people." As she finished, she straightened up and put a hand to her collar.

"Sorry, Ma," Aiden said, shuffling to stand beside her and hating the way he felt inside. Like some kid, just a brat tugging at his ma's skirts, asking for a penny for the candy man.

"It's all right, Aiden. Goodness knows your father won't be setting the example this family needs."

"You aren't going to leave him in that saloon, are you, Ma?"

"Of course not, Aiden. What a thought to be having," she said and stepped around him, slow and sure but angry, like she wished every step she took would be her last, just so she wouldn't have to walk in New Orleans or even be in the city anymore.

Aiden felt like he should press it about his pa, like his ma might just forget about the old man and let him sink into a barstool and stay there. But the way her feet kept hitting the pavement, one after the other, like the way people walked at a funeral— Aiden figured it was better to just wait and see.

If she doesn't go back for him, I will, Adien told himself.

His ma led him down the sidewalk at her deathly pace and around the corner, to the alley behind the dress shop. "It's up to us to make sure people keep the right thing in mind when they hear the name Conroy. All right, Aiden?"

"Yeah, Ma. Sure thing," he said, staring into the alley. He heard a low humming like a machine working, and tried to get a fix on what was making the sound. It was close, whatever it was.

"What's that sound, Ma? And what're we doing back here anyway?"

"This is where we're going to live, Aiden. For now." She pointed to a staircase along the backside of the dress shop. The steps went up to a second floor balcony. Aiden could see a door up there, old and weathered with no glass in the window.

Aiden saw another door under the balcony, just to their right. The window was fine in that one. Through the glass he saw a few ladies sitting at tables with sewing machines running. The light inside was pretty dim, almost nothing really. And all the ladies hunched over their work, like their backs might curl over at any minute and they'd turn into a ball and roll away. Or just fall over.

His mother held a hand to her mouth and seemed to swallow a sob.

"I'll be working down here, Aiden. With these other women. The shop owner says the work is quite regular. So I expect to earn enough to get us into a proper home before too long."

"Are we all gonna bunk in there with you and them other ladies?"

"Oh for— Of course not, Aiden," she said. "We're to make do with the room upstairs. I'm sure it'll need cleaning. We'd best get started."

She went for the staircase, beckoning him to follow with a hooked finger. "When we're done, you'd better go and collect your father."

Aiden followed his ma up the staircase, thankful she'd at least mentioned going to get his old man. The worn and weather-beaten handrail left its mark as soon as he touched it. He reached the landing after his ma, scraping tiny splinters from his palm and keeping his arms in close to his sides in case the wall of the building decided to bite him, too.

His ma pushed the door open. A rat's nest of shredded paper and cloth greeted them, and the rat that lived in it squealed and lit out of sight. Aiden heard its scratching and squeaking in the walls. And he heard his mother's sobbing.

"It'll be okay, Ma," he said. "I'll find work, too. Honest Abe."

His mother chided him with her weary and teary eyes. Then she pulled herself up and stepped into the room. He followed her into the squat space. Dust coated the floor. To the right, the room opened into a single space with a small table centered under a lamp that hung from a hook in the ceiling. At least it was electric, Aiden noticed. He tried the switch by the door and the bulb warmed to life, casting a milky light across everything in the room.

A small kitchen space took up the left side of the room. The floorboards met up with a line of chipped tiles that spread across the kitchen. It wasn't anything like they'd had at home in Chicago City. Just a small sink, a tin basin it looked like. Some cupboards, all open and full of dust and cobwebs. A little iron stove stood on a square of bricks beside the kitchen. The stovepipe went up the wall, and it was covered in dents and bent to match up with the pipe coming from the roof.

Across the open space, blankets piled in a corner showed signs of squatters: newspapers the rat had been using as a nest; an empty wine jug; a pile of cigarette butts spilling from a metal cup lying on its side.

For a second, Aiden thought there might be a tramp hiding under the mess catching his rest before stumbling down the stairs and onto the stem to beg handouts and hooch. But he looked again and saw only blankets and junk. Trash he had to clean up. He walked over to the wine bottle and picked it up.

Thoughts of cleaning up, and of liquor, put Aiden's mind on his pa. They'd left him in that tavern sipping a drink before it was noon. *Why'd Ma let that go?* he wondered.

"I could go get Pa now," he said. "He could help a little. Nobody knows cleaning like him, right?"

"Just leave the man be, Aiden," she said. "He's nursing his wounds, both of them."

"Both?"

"There's nothing a Conroy hates more than wounded pride. Your father will help once he's had his little wake. Go down now and ask Mrs. Flannery for a broom and a mop. She said we could use them to get this place in order."

Aiden hesitated. His ma went to the little kitchen and pushed crumbs and dirt aside with her shoe. "I can get this place cleaned up faster with a broom, Aiden," she said and kept up the scraping and pushing with her toes.

"Okay, Ma," Aiden said, and went to the door. He took one last look at the mess before he went down the stairs.

He'd been right. He might as well forget all about everything he'd known in Chicago City. But what would replace it? Sneaking another glance behind him, Aiden saw the tattered rags hanging around the open door at the top of the stairs.

What if all we end up with is a whole lot of nothing?

CHAPTER 11

A WEAK SUN SLID BEHIND GATHERING clouds as Emma came into the cabin with Eddie trailing a few steps behind. She stopped at Brand's desk and leaned against it. Eddie came around her and she helped him into the chair. They'd left Hardy's deck at night, but only after they had caught a full day's sleep in the bunkroom. Hardy had said they could berth for a while, and as much as she and Eddie both wanted to get away from the man, they were both exhausted and needed the sleep more than anything. Now, Emma's eyes and mind were clearer than when they'd landed in Metairie. Her gut was none too happy with her, though.

"A whole day with nothing but coffee to eat. We can't do that again, Eddie."

"Ain't but scraps left in the galley there, hey, Emma?"

"Not even that," she said.

"That man, Hardy. He say we find some work here, didn't he?"

Emma cast a glance out the window at the mooring deck they'd come to. They were in New Orleans proper now, and tethered above a deck that looked more like what she was used to in Chicago City. All metal railings and concrete. No fancy ornaments or gearboxes that looked like they belonged in a castle or a museum.

"He said that, Eddie. I just hope he wasn't talking out both sides of his face."

Eddie grunted. "Only one way to find out, I guess. And we best be finding out. You look 'bout ready to fall over, Lovebird."

"Look who's talking," she said, letting a smile stretch her lips for a moment. Then she put a hand to her side to hold in the stabbing pain of hunger while she watched the last of the day's light fade through the cockpit window.

They'd made a deal with Celestin Hardy to berth the *Vigilance* at another deck in New Orleans proper. Eddie had asked about where he might get a horn, maybe play some music and make a little scratch to keep them under a roof instead of sleeping on the ship.

Hardy had said he had just the thing. Emma wanted to believe the man because if he was being true, then their troubles in New Orleans would be shorter-lived than she'd feared. But she couldn't shake the feeling that something more would be asked of them, something that would make up for her and Eddie knowing, first-hand, that Celestin Hardy had shot Otis Martin just that morning, like it hadn't been any harder than lifting a finger to point at the sky.

Emma looked out the window at the deck one more time. Four smaller craft hung above the deck. All of them two-seaters, like the little joyride jobs Emma had known in her youth. Little cabins, tight and close for couples to stand in, hung beneath the envelopes. The pilot's position was up front, with a ship's wheel to control the rudder and pedals to move the flaps.

Each cabin had a bench at the back, separating the interior from the small motor that propelled the ships. But since the bench was up against the motor housing, most couples went for standing side by side up front.

Before she'd met Eddie, Emma had gone for a ride with a class-mate from the school her father paid for. The young man was just like all the other young men she'd met at the school. Dashing, with a sharp suit, clear eyes, and a pencil-thin mustache. Too bad he had more interest in Emma's skirts than in her smile, much less a single word that might come out of her mouth. But he could fly, and that had her thinking he might not be so bad after all.

A couple of times around Chicago City airspace and she'd asked for a shot at flying them home. That's when Mr. Dashing turned to Mr. Damned. He'd recoiled in horror, standing at the pilot's position. His hands clenched the wheel as if he'd feared her suggestion would bring down a fiery bolt of retribution from above.

If only he knew what the gods were really all about.

Emma smirked at the memories and put her attention back on what mattered. Had they made a mistake coming to this spot? Would they be safe? Hardy said this deck belonged to him outright.

"Bought it off Mistah Bacchus myself. Free and clear, just like the two of you now."

He'd laughed at his little joke and then told them about the watering hole under the deck. A one-room joint with a piano and a little stage beside it. The tavern owner used to play the horn, Hardy had said.

"He might could have it still. Kickin' it around waitin' on the right mouth to come with the kiss of music."

Emma wouldn't soon forget those words of Hardy's. The man had kept his eyes on her mouth as he spoke, and for a moment she wasn't sure if she'd live to see her and Eddie get set up in a place of their own. Hardy's face said hunger. The bad kind. The kind that doesn't go away no matter how much a man puts on his plate.

But he let them go with a wave, while his other hand rested on his breast just above where Emma had seen him tuck the gun he shot Otis with.

"Think we'll make it, Eddie?" she asked. "Think we'll be okay?"

"Sure thing, Lovebird. Gonna be fine. Just you wait and see. Got real family down here now. Not like in Chicago City when it was just me and the band to lean on. We got a whole *krewe* gonna help us out once they know I'm back in town."

She turned around to see him straining to stay upright in the chair. His lips peeled back to show his teeth as he pivoted and put his feet flat like he would try to stand.

"Wait, Eddie—" she said, but it was too late. He lurched up and stood a for second. She was on her feet in a flash and went to him.

. . .

By some miracle Eddie stayed on his feet until Emma got him out of the ship for the second time that day. He'd even kept up beside her as they went down the stairs to the tavern beneath the deck.

The neighborhood was in an old part of town. Hardy called it Old Storyville. The street they'd flown over on the way to the deck was called Iberville and, except for the deck and tavern, it didn't have much along it. In all directions, a distant row of houses stood across an open area of freshly cleared land.

Emma could see the ruins of a few buildings here and there in the space surrounding the tavern and deck. Piles of brick and wood waited for workmen to come along and clear away the remains. Emma got a flash of fear as she remembered the scrapyard in Chicago City: the stacks of furniture, railroad ties and coils of wire, fence posts, buckets, chains and tools, and all that idle machinery. Most of it had been stolen from her father's power plant and everything in the yard was going to build the next World's Fair beside Lake Michigan.

Now, here in New Orleans, Emma wondered what would be built on the newly razed land around her and whether or not crime was involved.

She almost laughed at herself for even thinking it could be otherwise.

"Better get inside, Lovebird," Eddie said. She turned to see him staring into the growing dusk around them. The clouds overhead made the darkness fall quicker and dusk would soon become full night. Emma put an arm around Eddie and let him rest his weight on her for a moment.

The tavern not only stood beneath the deck, but inside of it, too. The scaffold holding up the deck framed the squat building, making it look like the tavern had sprouted from the ground and grown up into the scaffold like some kind of parasitic plant. Emma imagined a bottle being tossed off the deck one day and weeks later people coming by to see a roof sticking out of the soil, and then the second story windows. Finally the bottom floor would have risen out of the earth with its bright red door and soot-stained clapboards.

Emma stared at the peeling red paint on the door until Eddie prodded her with his hip against hers.

"Go on, Emma. Gettin' cold out here."

She opened the door and helped Eddie across the threshold. Inside, a half dozen faces greeted them as they stood in the door.

"Lettin' in the cold," the barkeep said. He was a white man in shirt sleeves with a shiny bald head and a little tuft of hair hanging off his chin. He stood behind a polished counter on the right side of the room. Glass bottles of all colors sat on a shelf behind him, against a mirror framed in dark wood. The barkeep picked up a pair of glasses and jutted his chin in their direction. "Go'on shut that door, Miss Emma."

Emma's face flashed in shock, but the barkeep settled her brow, laughing as he spoke. "Mistah Hardy say you comin' on. Now what'll it be?" he asked, setting the glasses down and turning to reach for a bottle. "First one on the house."

The barkeep's hand hovered in front of a clear bottle half full of clear liquid. It felt like a month of Sundays since Emma last had liquor cross her lips. She favored bourbon, but didn't want to give these men any thoughts about her being a chippy. Letting on she knew her drinking, and could hold it, would send the wrong signals around the little room.

"Whatever you're pouring is fine," she said, taking a careful step to the nearest table and helping Eddie into a chair. The other men in the place were all white, but none of them seemed to care much about Emma's choice of company. The two closest men kept eyes on her, but the others all went back to their drinks and conversation.

Amidst the hushed voices and occasional chuckles, Emma took in the rest of the room.

The bar ran halfway down the right side of the space. At the far end of the room, opposite the door, a small stage took up the rest of the wall. Tables and chairs filled the middle of the room, with a little square of space set aside as a dance floor in front of the stage. On the left, a set of stairs led up, and a door beside the foot of the stairs connected to what Emma figured must be the kitchen or the barkeep's rooms.

"Here ya' go," the man said from the bar. Emma heard the two glasses hit the counter. She checked Eddie, whose good eye said he felt safe. His mouth curled into a sad smile because of his busted lip, but Emma let herself relax just the same. She went to the bar and got the glasses. As she stepped away, it hit her that the tavern might have been operating out in the middle of nothing, but it was out in the open, too.

She turned to the barkeep. "Guess the law doesn't bother you out here, huh?"

The barkeep nearly split his sides he doubled over so fast, slapping a palm on the bar top along with a few other men who whacked the tabletops in front of them.

"Law, Miss Emma? Now that is a good one. Gonna remember that next time we hit a slow season and can't get music in here. Jokes like that one'd keep the crowd happy." He set to chortling again and winked at her. "Law don't mind what the law don't want to see no how. Sure enough, law don't want to be seein' this tavern."

"But why not?" Emma said, moving back to the table with Eddie and setting down the glasses. She had the full attention of the room and figured it was as good a time as any to get some answers about the new city she'd be calling home. "Hardy told you we were coming, so he must've told you where we came from."

"Oh, sure enough, Mistah Hardy did. And you'd be wise callin' the man mistah, too, Miss Emma. Folks down here take to politeness like bees to a flower. And they quick to sting you, case you forget."

Emma's mind flashed to the image of Hardy's knife slamming Al Conroy's hand into the station house wall.

"Sure enough," Emma said to the barkeep. "So you're all okay with me and Eddie here? We'd be strung up in two shakes if anybody saw us together on the street in Chicago City. I know New Orleans has her own ways, but how far does that go?"

"Not sure I follow you, Miss Emma," the barkeep said. Before she could explain, another man spoke up from across the room.

"She means are the two of them safe to walk the streets of New Orleans. She and Mr. Collins here are sure to be out and about and making their way in the Crescent City, and a woman wants to feel safe when she sets up a home. Thing is, she's already seen the worst New Orleans has to offer. Murder. In cold blood. Ain't that right, Miss Emma?"

The man wore a white suit and a fedora that he kept tilted down over one side of his face. Emma figured that was why she hadn't noticed him before. Other than Eddie, this guy was the only man in the place with colored skin. He'd been sitting by himself the entire time and as she looked at him, Emma got the sense she was in the presence of another character like Hardy—someone with a god in him. She couldn't tell which one though, and she knew it wouldn't come clear to her no matter how long or hard she stared at the man.

"Yeah," Emma said, half furious and half frightened at how clearly this man knew her mind. "That's exactly what I meant. Mind if I ask how you know it?

"Ghost knows a lot of things," the barkeep said, eyeing the other man with a look that echoed Emma's worries. "Mostly keeps to himself, except for them times when he feels like flappin' his lips a little too much."

The other man sniffed at that and threw back the rest of his drink. "Time I was gettin' on myself," he said, standing. He pinched the brim of his hat before striding across the room and up the stairs. Nobody spoke until the sound of a door closing came down into the tavern from above.

A man sitting at a table across from the bar was the first to break the silence. "Birdman gonna take the other one he goes mouthin' off like that again. You watch."

"Watch your own damn self, Jonas," the barkeep said. "Ghost has friends, too."

"Friends he may have," the man replied. "But he don't have near enough as matches the enemies that boy's found for himself."

"Which one is he?" Emma asked the room, halfway eyeing the man who'd spoken up.

The men ignored her. Some exchanged knowing looks, a few others just stared into their drinks. Emma kept at it. This wasn't the first time she'd got the silent treatment from a room full of men just for opening her mouth. "I asked which one he was, or do I sound too much like a little girl to get a question answered?"

Still nobody spoke up. Then the barkeep grunted and leaned over his bar again.

"Ghost, he's a riverboat gambler. Man like to be tryin' his hand at a game of cards more than he like to eat. He come and go easy as you please, like a few other men and women in New Orleans. Like Mistah Hardy, whom you have already had the pleasure of meeting. Ghost ain't that much different, but he different enough."

Emma wrinkled her nose at the barkeep. She got the sense the man would have that be the last of it, but Emma felt like he'd only put more questions into the air, and she'd as soon have answers as let another second tick by.

"I get why he's called *Ghost*. Any man wears a suit like that would be. But what's with the mind-reading, and how deep are we with Ha . . . Mister Hardy, I mean. What do we owe him for letting us set up on his deck? He didn't say he'd let on we were coming, but he did say someone here would have the skinny on the deal."

"Well," the barkeep began, "as concerns the man we call the Ghost, I've said all I'm willing to say. You'll have to wait until he decides to explain himself to you. Or one of these fools in here gets drunk enough to let his own lips do the telling. Course, most everyone in here, yours truly included, like to be seein' straight, so

I wouldn't hold your breath waitin' on more news about the Ghost from any of us.

"As for *the deal* . . . Mistah Hardy didn't tell me proper, mind. But these gentlemen around you can all attest to his fairness. Berthin' up above comes with a simple price. Just a little work is all."

"What kind of work?" Emma said, not liking the sound of it but ready to do just about anything to get something like solid ground under her feet again.

"As I understand it, Mistah Collins here"—the barkeep paused to acknowledge Eddie with a wave—"he plays a horn, is that right?"

"Sure is," Eddie said, and Emma could see him bracing himself to rise if he needed to. The safety he'd felt before was clearly a thing of the past now. She put a hand on his arm and tried to make her eyes show him she could handle things.

"Well, Mistah Collins, it just so happens that I have a stage, as Mistah Hardy no doubt told you. And I like to be having music on my stage from time to time."

The barkeep came around and leaned his back against the bar, crossing his arms and regarding both of them with the friendliest wolf's grin Emma had seen in a long while. "Usually," the barkeep went on, "music's good when the boys and girls come through from around the way. That's two, three times a week at most. Once the projects go up around here, though, we'll have a more steady flow. See more feet on my dance floor every night."

Emma let the barkeep's words settle into silence before she asked the question that had been burning on her tongue.

"That's it? Eddie plays his horn three nights a week and we can berth up top?"

"That's it," the barkeep said. "Sounds good to you, sounds good to me."

"Sounds too good," Emma said, and she didn't miss a few whispers and shuffled feet from the men nearby.

"Settle yourselves, boys. Miss Emma's got a worry bone, any man can tell." The barkeep returned his attention to her. "Don't you fret none. Mistah Hardy look out for them what do him right and proud, and Mistah Collins here gonna do the man very right and very proud. Now, why you still have that look on your face says you thinkin' like a rabbit?"

"What about me?" Emma said. "What do I have to do so Mister Hardy feels right and proud about my being here?"

A man who sat next to the one called Jonas spoke up and couldn't get half a thought out before laughing so hard he had to stop. Emma caught the last few words that fell off the man's tongue.

" . . . room upstairs," he said. The man laughed again, swallowed some beer from his glass, then wiped his mouth on his sleeve. Emma glared at him when he turned his wrinkled and boozy nose in her direction. "This Old Storyville, ain't it?" he said and laughed again, his cheeks going pink as the dawn.

Emma stood slowly, keeping one hand on Eddie's for support but also to make sure he stayed put. She reached a hand into her coat pocket for the gun that wasn't there anymore. These men weren't dopes, but it was her luck the room was dark and they'd all had at least a glass or three before she'd come in. She made as if to grab something in her pocket and lifted it slightly, aiming her finger through the fabric at the man who'd spoken.

"Any man tries it on with me and he'll find himself on the wrong end of a gat. Is that clear?"

The room went hush for a few heartbeats. Emma looked from the man who'd spoken to the one called Jonas, who scooted his chair a few inches away from the jokester. In the corner of her eye, Emma saw the barkeep had his eyes on her pocket like he believed good and well she had an iron.

"Don't need more shooting today," the barkeep finally said. "Old Clive didn't mean nothin' by it, Miss Emma. Did you, Clive?"

The old man with the wrinkles running across his forehead and a pope's nose settled in his chair and shook his head. "Just funnin' is all," he said. "Didn't mean it serious."

Emma sat back down and kept her hand in her pocket. The

empty space where a gun used to be felt cold against her palm, and she promised herself it wouldn't be long before she had heat on her side again.

CHAPTER 12

AIDEN KEPT LOOKING AROUND THE STREET like he'd been told by the man who gave him the box. The guy was in the dress shop when he and his ma went down for her first day of work. Aiden's ma asked if anyone knew where Aiden might find a job and the man seemed to appear out of nowhere, just popped up like a jack-in-the-box from behind the counter.

He'd handed over a shoe-shine box and said Aiden could find work up and down any stem in the city so long as he kept walking and carrying the box. When he was done at the end of the day, he was supposed to bring the box and any money he'd earned back to the dress shop and hand it in to the lady there.

That was a week ago. He'd come out on the street twice so far, trying to find shoes to shine, but no luck. Today would be different, though; he knew it. Still, it felt like hours had passed and he hadn't shined a single shoe, much less done anything but nearly put holes in his own.

Aiden pulled the green book from his trouser pocket and

unfurled it. The book fell open to the first map, and Aiden thumbed a few pages until he got to the 'East Carrollton' map. He found where he was on St. Charles Street and stuffed the book back into his pocket. He'd been thinking of trying his luck in the Hollygrove neighborhood, but he only saw dark-skinned folks walking in and out of the homes there, and not much that looked like a shopping district. The man who gave him the box told him to stick to streets with lots of storefronts, so that's what Aiden had tried to do.

He'd taken the streetcar down St. Charles and got off where the carman said he should.

"Over at Riverbend; you like to be finding shine work."

Aiden pretended not to hear the way the carman muttered about *doves fouling the nest.* Aiden just picked up his shine box and stepped off the streetcar. Now, he looked up and down St. Charles and saw nothing but crowds and storefronts in every direction. But which one should he aim for?

About as hopeless as a blind man in the dark.

"Hey, Shine!" Aiden spun around, but he couldn't see who'd hollered.

"I said, Shine! Dammit, son, you got mud in your ears? Shine!"

Across the street, a group of well-dressed men sat around a table outside a cafe. Aiden caught glimpses of them through the passing crowd. It looked like three of the men were dark-skinned. The other two he saw more clear. They were pinker than suckling pigs.

Aiden moved to cross the street when the traffic parted a bit. He got a good look at the fellas this time. They all had bellies that made Aiden think of livestock. One of the white fellas waved, so Aiden stepped fast across the street. He stopped at the sidewalk and nodded to the man with his hand in the air.

He was thick-faced and with a mustache that twirled up to meet his cheeks just below his eyes. When Aiden got close enough, the man lowered his hand and set it on the table next to him. The other four men all had smiles on their mugs, and Aiden caught a couple of them nudging each other in the ribs and whispering.

The man with the mustache snapped his fingers in Aiden's face then.

"Man yells *Shine* you bust tail and haul it over to him, you hear me?" the man said. His puffed-up cheeks behind the ends of his mustache made him look like a stage actor Aiden had seen once. Back when he was just a boy, a traveling show came through Chicago City right after the Great War. With all these Japanese folks with white paint on their faces, and these big manes of dark hair, looking like ghosts of lions.

The man in front of him now looked twice as scary, though, because he wasn't wearing a costume, and he was staring daggers straight through Aiden.

"I'm sorry, mister, I—"

"Mister? You hear that, gentlemen? This little Shine just called me *Mister*."

Mumbles of agreement rolled around the table, across the men's round bellies. Aiden spied gold watch chains glinting in the morning light. He watched the men's jaws work around their laughter. One of the dark-skinned men gave Aiden a stink eye he thought would never come off, and the other white man looked at Aiden with something between hunger and hatred on his face.

"I—"

"You didn't nothing, Shine," the man with the mustache said. "Now get on down there and do what you get paid for."

Aiden set his box down on the sidewalk and knelt beside it. The man stuck a leg out and propped his heel on the box before Aiden got it open, so he had to ask the man's permission to move his foot off the box. Then he had to ask if it was okay to set the man's foot down on the pavement again.

Aiden got his brush, rag, and polish out and barely had time to close the box before the man's foot landed on it again with a *thunk*. With a hard swallow that stuffed his anger down his throat, Aiden went to work, first brushing away bits of ash that had fallen on the man's shoe from the cigar he was smoking. As Aiden worked, more ash came floating down from above and onto the man's shoe again.

"You lean over the work, you won't have that problem, Shine," said the man. "You must be new at this, otherwise you'd have known that. Should be charging you tuition for what I'm teachin' you here today."

Aiden felt resentment and hatred curdling in his guts, but the thought of his mother sweeping aside rat droppings and dust kept him at his work. He leaned forward a bit and felt ash falling past his face, some of it landed on his ear and he had to fight the urge to brush it off.

The quicker he finished this job, the better. Whoever these men were, Aiden wouldn't soon forget their faces. Next time he was out looking for shoes to shine, he'd know to avoid this bunch if he spotted them. He'd just have to keep a good lookout as he walked to make sure they didn't get eyes on him first.

While he worked polish into the man's shoe, the other men around the table traded chuckles and hushed comments that after a while became less hushed and more like what Aiden remembered from the school yards back in Chicago City. There always seemed to be some group of kids, his age or older, who had something to say about how Aiden dressed or walked or talked. Pretty much anything he'd done had been cause enough for someone else to take issue with it, as if whatever Aiden did was bound to end up going wrong.

"Poor little Shine. Ain't got sense enough to do this job," said the other white man at the table.

"Must be trying to buy his momma out of Mister Bacchus's employ," said one of the Negro men. Aiden's ears pricked up at the mention of the gangster. He had to force himself to keep from shouting back at the suggestion that his ma was working for the guy.

It didn't take two seconds for Aiden to put together what the men around the table meant by *being in Mister Bacchus's employ.*

"How about it, Shine? Which house she work in?" the same man said.

"Now, Mister Clemmons," said the man with his foot on Aiden's box. "May I be so bold as to ask you to refrain from disrupting this young man while he's hard at work? After all, if his mother is *ad opus*, then I'm sure it'll be only a matter of time before we've all had the pleasure. Isn't that right?"

The men all set to laughing and Aiden couldn't take it. Before he knew what he was doing he'd torn the man's shoe from his foot and flung it into the street. The man nearly fell backward out of his chair he stood up so fast, but Aiden had his hands on the man's stocking foot and was yanking on that, too.

He felt a sharp pain in his gut and rolled onto his back into the street. One of the men had kicked him under the table. Aiden clutched his stomach and flipped over onto his knees. A small crowd had formed around the table.

Every man and woman in the area was watching Aiden, some with looks of horror on their faces, but most with a sort of half glee. Aiden saw bets trade hands between two of the Negro men at the table. The man whose shoe he'd torn off stood beside the table, shaking with rage and ready to kill.

Aiden felt heated enough himself, and he didn't back down. But he was wise enough to know when a fight was lost before it had begun. He skipped backward, onto his feet, and nearly stumbled over the man's shoe. With the crowd watching him, he leaned down and picked it up. The he tossed it to the man, who fumbled it against his chest.

Aiden had already dashed forward and grabbed up his shine box. He snapped up the brush in his other hand and stuffed it in his pocket before reaching for the polish. His fingers closed on the tin, but it slipped out of his hands as Aiden dodged a kick from the man.

Snarling, the guy lifted a foot like he'd stomp the shine box out of Aiden's grip, but Aiden was faster and twisted to the side, so the man's foot only nicked the corner of the box. Aiden ducked a swing from the guy's beefy mitt and snatched the polish tin off the ground. Then he wheeled around on his heels and took off down the street.

A few cheers let out behind him, and a couple of shouts, too. But Aiden didn't bother looking back. He just pumped his legs and slapped his soles on the street for all he was worth.

Two streets over he finally let himself settle down to a more even pace. Folks on the sidewalks all looked his way, most shaking their heads. A few pointed and chuckled. When he heard a voice calling "*Shine*" again, Aiden nearly jumped out of his skin. But it was just a Negro gentleman standing beside a horse and buggy across the street.

Aiden hotfooted over to the fellow and set his box down beside him.

"Yessir," he said. "You needing a shoe shine today?"

"Sure enough I'm not. But you look to be needing safe passage out of this street," the man said. "Probably like to be hopping up into my buggy, you know what's best for your skin." He pointed back the way Aiden had come.

Aiden whipped his head around. The big white man had both his shoes on again, and a couple of the other fellows had come with him. Their faces said they were none too pleased with the chase he'd given them, and Aiden didn't dare think about what they'd do if they caught him.

Without another thought, Aiden grabbed up his shine box and leaped into the buggy. The Negro gentleman stepped up behind him and grabbed the reins. He slapped them on the horses' rumps and they were off at a trot. Aiden risked a look out the side of the buggy and saw the big man and his pals spitting in the street and shaking their fists after him.

"That should be the last you'll have to worry about those fellows," the Negro said.

"Yessir. And thank you, sir."

"Don't mention it. Not everyday I get to help put a knot of trouble into the likes of those hogs. Damn fat cats living off the sweat of other men, deserve a little comeuppance from time to time. Now, you got a badge of transit, don't you?"

Aiden nodded, feeling in his pocket for the thin piece of metal he'd got from Mister Hardy on the mooring deck.

"Well go on then, Dove. Show me you got the right to be sitting beside me here."

Aiden pulled the badge from his pocket and held it up for the man to see.

"Good to go, Dove. Now best put that away lest someone who has to walk gets it in their head they'd rather be the one to ride in my buggy. You like your hand, don't you, Dove?"

"Sure I do, mister," Aiden said, pocketing the badge.

"Well then, best to be keeping that badge out of sight lest you need it. You go waving it around …." He trailed off and let his pointing finger finish for him.

Aiden followed the man's finger and saw a group of tramps huddled around a doorway to a saloon. Most of them had only one hand and nothing but a stump wrapped in raggedy bandages where the other used to be.

"Not everybody comes to New Orleans has the right payment for Papa Lebat. Some folks is like to be stealing a badge of passage off them what earns it proper. And some who does the stealing like to be adding an extra bit of punishment, as if to remind folks how easy it is to lose in the Crescent City."

Aiden choked back a sob as he remembered his father's hand and the knife that Celestin Hardy drove into it, pinning his pa's mitt to the wall of the station house.

"Excuse me, sir?"

"What is it, Dove?"

"You ever hear of folks just up and leaving New Orleans?"

"Some do. Sure enough, some do. But if you mean Doves like you what just come to town, it's only after a long hard day's work you gonna get free of this city's sweet embrace."

Aiden wanted to ask how the man knew he'd just come to town, but he figured it was plain as day. He'd just about lost his life over a simple shoeshine job.

Can't even get that right. Pa'd switch me good if he knew.

Thoughts of his pa being angry with him didn't help lift Aiden's spirits, so he let the buggy man's words find their way into his chest where he wrapped them up tight with his arms. He ignored the nagging worry that the man next to him knew more about Aiden and his family than he should. The fear that he'd just jumped from the pan into the fire burned behind his eyes, but Aiden closed them tight.

He'd done his crying, and he fought back the sob that tried its damnedest to squeeze through his eyelids. Aiden sniffed it aside and thought about his ma cleaning up their room above the dress shop. Then he thought about what the buggy driver just told him.

"Only after a long hard day's work you gonna get free."

Aiden's eyes snapped open, dry as a summer sky. He had to earn the Conroy family name, like his pa did back in Chicago City. It was long past time for him to work a real job, with real pay. The next time he set foot on the streets of New Orleans, he'd do it as a working man.

CHAPTER 13

THE LITTLE STAGE IN HARDY'S TAVERN HAD been set up with two stools, one for Eddie and another for Emma. A microphone rig stood in front of her stool with a long, snaking cable connecting the mic to a speaker box by her feet. Emma felt cramped up at the front of the stage, but she couldn't scoot back any. The stage had just enough space for a small trap set behind Emma and Eddie.

A young dark-skinned man sat behind the drums, tightening them up, tapping them one by one, tuning them with a little metal key he'd fit over each nut around the drum heads. Emma watched him while worry ate away at her insides. She tugged down the hem of her skirt as best she could. Hardy had come in and handed her and Eddie a new set of clothes each. Emma couldn't help but smile and thank him. Then she put the skirt on. It only just covered her knees, and she had to half sit, half stand against the stool to make sure she didn't flash the crowd more than they'd paid for.

The room had more people in it now. Many more. Trios sat at each table, and the barkeep kept up a steady rhythm of pouring while two dark-skinned girls carried drinks around on trays. A few men and their dates stood at the back of the room, framing the door and window. They had drinks in their hands, too.

Emma's throat felt dry and she glanced at the bar, hoping to catch the man's eye and let on she needed something to wet her whistle before she started in crooning.

No such luck, though. The man had his hands full keeping the paying customers' lips from drying out. At last one of the cocktail girls swished by the front of the stage and Emma called to her.

"Can you get me a bourbon, sister? Neat."

The girl looked at her like Emma'd just asked for her first born.

"You must be crazy," she said. "Didn't think Mistah Hardy hired on crazy white girls, but I see I was wrong. Let me just stop what I'm doing for the man and see to your needs now."

The girl's eyes rolled around like she'd see the back of her own head before Emma would ever get a drink out of her. With a sniff, the cocktail girl turned away and headed for the bar where she picked up another round for the trio at the table closest to the stage.

Two white men and a dark-skinned man sat there, each of them eyeing Emma. The Negro showed less interest than the other two, but only just. The weight of the trio's collective gaze held Emma fixed where she leaned against the stool. Given the choice, she'd never have worn anything like she had on now. But Hardy was clear as could be when he held out the costume.

"You dress right to sing on my stage, or you don't dress a'tall."

So Emma had put on the skirt that hung a good four inches too short, and the blouse that hugged her too tight no matter how she stood or leaned or stooped.

"We gonna get a song out of you tonight, Little Dove," said the Negro at the table in front of her.

Emma tightened her lips and held her chest steady as she could while she met his eyes and held his gaze. She dared him to look away knowing that if he did it would only be to let his eyes travel up and down her legs again. But he stayed put and even cracked a thin smile, the same kind Eddie had on when she first met him.

On cue, Eddie touched her hip. "Best be warming up those pipes, hey? How about we do 'Sugar Baby' first, then on to some of them Gershwin numbers you like?"

Emma glanced at the Negro at the table and saw he still had that same grin on his mug.

"Let's start soft and hot, Eddie," she said. "How about 'The Man I Love'?"

Eddie gave a short chuckle and said, "Okay, Lovebird. Okay." He put his lips to the loaner horn the barkeep gave him and blew soft and quiet. Emma saw how hard it was for him to play with his ribs still banged up and his lower lip swollen from the beating he'd taken. But the tones came easy and sweet just the same.

The drummer picked up a slow tempo with his brushes and the crowd went hush just like that. The room seemed to wait on every note from Eddie's horn, each beat, each brush and tap of the drums. Emma let the music fill her like air after being underwater, but still her chest felt tight and her lips wouldn't part.

The barkeep cleared his throat and Emma caught his eye bent her way. She drew in a breath and the first few lyrics came out like a spring breeze. Soon enough she was crooning alongside Eddie's playing with the drummer keeping time behind them and staying out of the way.

It had been over a month since Emma and Eddie had shared a stage, the last time being in a Chicago City speak after she'd skipped out on another of her father's parties. And like that last time, tonight Emma knew she'd done right teaming up with Eddie. Whatever they'd left behind them was where it belonged, and now so were they.

Emma let the memories of Chicago City fall away with each word she sang, like the lyrics were gusts of a welcome wind clearing the landscape after a storm. Around the room, couples danced slow and close, hands held hands and traced lovers' trails around necks and down backs. Emma breathed in the warmth and love she saw around her and sent it back out in the song while Eddie blew and blew on his horn, backing her up and carrying her at the same time.

The trio at the table in front of the stage had gone quiet, but now the Negro kept his eyes on Emma the whole time. He didn't seem to get that she and Eddie were a couple, so as she let the last few lyrics drop from her lips like honey, Emma reached out and touched Eddie's knee with her hand, light and sweet.

He blew the last note and the drummer tied it up with a bow, brushing a quiet finish across his snare.

The room lit up with applause and cheers, even the three men at the front table had glad looks on their mugs now. The Negro seemed to get the skinny. Emma saw him send a wink at Eddie, almost like he meant to congratulate him. Then Emma caught the smirk that held the man's eyes up and she knew he had more than congratulations in mind.

Ignoring the leers and wolfish grins from the front table, Emma hummed the opening line to another Gershwin tune. They played it and a few more numbers before taking their first break. The barkeep sent the cocktail girl over with a platter full of bourbon. Eddie passed, but said he'd take some water. Emma wanted to down his glass, too, but let the drummer have it instead. She sipped hers while she waited for the barkeep to signal their second set.

The time came before too long and Emma had to set down her bourbon only half finished. She'd forgotten to keep up her innocent act, and caught the looks the men at the front table sent her way.

Yeah, the gal can drink, fellas. What of it?

She only hoped they wouldn't hassle her after the show. She'd made it clear as day she and Eddie were a matched set, but it was just as clear that he'd be no good in a fight if it came to that. The guys at the table weren't all the way to wolf town, but that didn't mean they wouldn't get that way after a few more drinks.

Eddie blew a few notes to warm up. The drummer had gone off to hit the washroom and just as he came back the front door opened up. In walked a crew of three men, all tight together and looking like they could own the place if they didn't already.

Emma's heart skipped when she saw the man in the middle. All of him. The heavy form of Mr. Bacchus entered the room flanked by his two goons, the same ones who were with him on Hardy's mooring deck. Now Bacchus stood in the doorway spread out like a blanket to block whatever lamplight still filtered into the tavern.

Night had fallen right as Emma and Eddie had started their first set, and the darkness seemed to settle that much more with Bacchus and his heavies in the room.

"Mr. Bacchus," the barkeep said. "Wel-welcome, Sir. I wasn't—"

"No, you wasn't. And you won't," Bacchus said, lifting a palm and flicking his fingers in the barkeep's direction as if shooing a fly. The barkeep shrank behind the bar and went back to wiping glasses while a slick of sweat trickled down his brow.

The two torpedoes moved into the room ahead of their boss and made straight for the table at the front of the stage. The three men there didn't waste any time getting clear and soon enough Bacchus and his boys had front row seats for the show.

"I believe I heard that horn as we came in," Bacchus said, motioning at Eddie. "Was you just warming up for us, or did we interrupt a number? I do apologize if the latter. But please, play on, Mister Eddie Collins from Chicago City. I would be delighted to hear you blowing . . . on *my* horn."

Emma didn't miss Bacchus' jab, and she could see Eddie hadn't missed it either. They traded a look of worry before turning back to smile at the gangster. Bacchus swiveled his massive head in Emma's direction and gave her a grin that said he owned her as much as he owned the horn Eddie played or the hat he'd just taken off and set on the table in front of him.

"If you'd be so kind, Miss Emma, may I ask that you sing us a number? By request?"

Emma tried to nod once but her neck and shoulders shook enough that she was sure she looked like a marionette in the hands of a drunk.

"What—what would you like to hear, Mr. Bacchus?"

"How about a slow tune, something from up your way? We don't hear much Chicago City music down here in New Orleans what with travel restrictions being as they are. Indeed, one might suggest that nobody in this room has heard music from *up the river* in a good long time."

Emma didn't miss the stress Bacchus put on that phrase. She didn't miss the whispers and knowing looks that sprouted around the room like grapevines hanging heavy and ripe with gossip. She didn't know what to sing, but Eddie saved her by blowing the first two notes of 'Toddlin' Town'. It was an old favorite and one they'd sung every chance they got back at the Chicago City speaks where they used to meet every weekend.

But as she sang and Eddie played, the lyrics took on a pale, empty hue. Her lips went tight and thin, and each time she named the city they'd left behind, it felt like a knife was working around her insides.

Bacchus had relaxed into a comfortable slouch. His goons kept their posture tight and their hands close to their jackets, but the room showed no signs of trouble, at least none that Emma could see.

Except what's up here on the stage.

They picked a number about New Orleans next, as the crowd seemed to get that life *up the river* wasn't worth singing about. Looking out at glum faces wasn't going to do anything to improve Emma's mood, so she signaled Eddie to play 'Way Down Yonder'.

Through the rest of the set, Bacchus and his two torpedoes stayed put, with the boss's eyes on the stage and his boys' roving their gaze around the room.

It wasn't until the last number that Emma keyed in to what was going on. This was Hardy's tavern. The man may work for Bacchus, but that didn't mean he owed his boss anything beyond the loyalty of a servant. Hardy stood to make a lot of scratch off Emma and Eddie if tonight's packed room was any measure of how it would be in the future.

And Bacchus was here to jump Hardy's claim. Emma almost faltered on the lyrics, but she caught the lump in her throat and turned it into a cough between lines. The crowd whooped and clapped when the final song was done, and even Bacchus rose to join the standing ovation. Emma spotted Hardy's face at the back of the crowd, over by the stairs. He must have come down while she was singing. Or maybe he'd flickered in like a candlewick touched by a match.

Bacchus handed one of his goons a small envelope before he waved them both in Hardy's direction. They parted the crowd like knives through warm butter until they stood face-to-face with Hardy. Emma watched the man for some sign or reply, but he kept his lips tight and his eyes locked on some point out in the room, like he was forcing himself not to glare death at the two tough birds handing him a slim payoff for his golden geese.

Hardy stuffed the envelope into his coat, and for a second it looked like he'd pull his gat. Emma saw the red mist that had formed around Hardy on the mooring deck just before he shot Otis. It circled his head like a halo, and Emma had to force herself to look away. But in that instant, the mist seemed to flee from Hardy, leaving him looking more shell-shocked than when Bacchus' goons gave him the payoff.

The mist swelled into the room, above the heads of every man and woman in the place. Emma looked at the people all standing there with their eyes on Bacchus, waiting for him to let them go back to doing what they'd come here to do. Nobody else seemed to notice the red vapor that hung heavy in the air above them. Emma nearly choked when the mist gathered in a ball above Bacchus's head and then dropped like stone, washing over him and seeping into his skin until it vanished from sight.

Bacchus gave a loud grunt, startling the room back into action. People acted like they'd just woken up and noticed they still have all their arms and legs. Men checked their wallets, and then their women, while Bacchus gave a short, deep laugh and spoke up at last, breaking through the rustling of coats and jangling of beads.

"Well, now that matter is settled, my friends. Mr. Eddie Collins, Miss Emma," Bacchus said, nodding at each of them in turn, "would you kindly accompany me to your new lodgings? You'll find some new clothes in my car, and these gentlemen will see to your airship. She'll be berthing at a deck closer to home from now on."

Emma's heart skipped and she felt the floor fall out from under her. The room went sideways in her vision and the last thing she heard was Eddie groaning as he held her against his chest.

CHAPTER 14

B RAND FOLLOWS BARNABY THROUGH THE
streets of Metairie, marveling at the blind man's accurate
steps around puddles, piles of filth, and broken bits of pavement. They move through the near-ruined town past empty houses,
run down storefronts, and a stockyard complete with a ramshackle
abattoir that looks like as if it hasn't seen blood since before the
Great War.

All around them, men trudge up and down the streets, and
Brand sees only one accompanied by a woman. Women aren't
a common sight, Brand realizes, and he wonders why this is. In
Chicago City, he'd see guys and dolls on every street at almost any
time of day.

"Say, Barnaby," he says.

"Yes, Brand. What ails your mind and how might I provide you
the succor you seek?"

"Just a plain answer is fine," Brand says, hoping to avoid more
of Barnaby's long-tooth jawing. "Where are the women around this
town? Not that I'm looking for one, just it seems odd to only see

fellas on the pavement. It's morning. Shouldn't the missuses be out for the butcher's order or the baker's dozen?"

"Indeed, Brand. Indeed. It is a lonely sort of place, Metairie, but my companions and I find it—" Barnaby pauses himself and goes silent, not even letting his breathing disrupt the calm of the morning.

Brand is about to ask what gives when Barnaby continues.

"Forgive my moment of reticence, Brand. I fear we approach an unfortunate end."

"Where?" Brand says, shifting his eyes left to right. He sees nothing that doesn't look normal, and then mentally kicks himself for thinking anything like normal still exists in his world. Barnaby sets his mind at ease, though.

"It isn't the mud men, Brand, at least not yet. But neither is it our end of which I speak. See that one there?" Barnaby raises a finger and aims it across the street. "The gods are always watching those of us who find ourselves on the street. And they are quick to tempt us to the mud men's fate."

Brand follows the other man's finger and spies a tramp curled up around a bottle in front of an empty storefront. As Brand watches, the man sips from the bottle and slowly sinks, his body sliding into the street and down, like he's being pulled into a bath made of pavement. Then he's gone, leaving only an empty bottle behind to mark his passing.

"How'd you know he was there?" Brand asks.

"I smelled him," Barnaby replies. "As I always smell those who have fallen far enough to find themselves easy prey for the gods of New Orleans."

"They're a different bunch than the ones up in Chicago City, aren't they?"

"Oh yes, indeed. They are."

Barnaby leaves it at that, an odd moment of brevity from him that Brand welcomes. Still, the blind tramp continues deftly avoiding every loose cobblestone, every bit of waste and offal that litters the streets, and Brand finds himself struggling to keep up as they make their way through the city.

Metairie seems to decompose around them, and Brand wonders how this came to be. He'd only heard of New Orleans and its neighboring communities, but nothing he'd heard matches what he's seeing.

"What just happened to that bum, Barnaby? And what about this town? It looks like what we left behind over there, at the edges of No Man's Land."

"It does at that, Brand. It does at that. I, too, wore the uniform and traveled the muddy ways of trench warfare, back when I had eyes to see. It pains me to hear you compare these streets of Metairie to those tunnels and narrows from our war. But I cannot deny you are accurate in your assessment.

"The great flood of '27 did this to once proud and prosperous Metairie. Levees were blown. Old Man River took it as an offer to come visit. And visit he did."

Brand sees them now, the signs of flood damage. Water stains on the sides of every building, the persistent stink of mildew and damp.

"Two years gone and they still haven't cleaned it up?"

"I applaud your optimism," Barnaby says. "In fact, I am prepared to obligate myself to you, Brand, should you ever need my help. Myself and my companions, Mr. Welks and Mr. Gardner. The kind concern you express for fair Metairie warms my heart. But to answer your question: Who, Brand? Who would clean up Metairie now that it is merely a home for the messengers of the gods and no one else?"

"You mean it's just guys like me and you, like Reggie and Finn back there? That's who lives here? In this whole town?"

"Yes," Barnaby says and goes quiet. Not for the first time, Brand is happy for the other man's silence.

They walk on, and eventually Brand decides to ask his question again, the one Barnaby didn't answer.

"That bum back there," Brand says. "Sank into the street pretty as you please. What gives with that?"

"That, Brand, is what awaits us all," Barnaby says. "It is the fate of any man so stained by the street that he forgets who he is. And who but us should be so blessed as to feel the persistent stain of pavement and drink, a stain that smudges and conceals any semblance of the self?"

Barnaby raises his face to the sky, his eyelids fluttering like they might open. Brand can't suppress a flinch, but Barnaby keeps his empty sockets hidden. He's sniffing now, as if he expects a storm. Sure enough, Brand sees one on the horizon, coming in off the coast no doubt, stirred up by the same roiling weather that tried to wash New Orleans off the map in '15.

Brand hopes his visit to the city doesn't involve repeated history. His gut stirs with the feeling that he's about to be swept out of the world, and for good this time, regardless of what he does or where he is.

Barnaby turns his empty face in Brand's direction. The man's cheeks sag with time and regret, and the hangdog feeling settles into Brand, too. What surprises him is that he welcomes it, almost like a blanket against the cold.

Just so easy to let it all go, to forget.

"No time to get lazy, Brand," the tramp says. "You've got work. Your pocket there."

Brand sticks a grimy hand into his pocket and feels it. An envelope, slender but firm, like a heavy card. Brand pulls the letter out, goes to open it, but Barnaby has a hand on his wrist in a flash, the hangdog look on the bum's face replaced with one of horror, even though his eyelids stay shut. Barnaby's mouth is open, his lips drawn tight against teeth that barely hold back a scream.

"Never look," he says, aiming an accusing finger at his own face. "The Birdman has both his eyes, and you best believe the man is watching."

CHAPTER 15

AIDEN LEFT THE SHINE BOX OUTSIDE THE dress shop, just like the buggy man said. It wasn't there this morning, and nobody'd come up the back steps banging on the door for Aiden's blood. So he figured it was all square.

At least he hoped it was.

While his ma went down to her job at the dressmaker's, Aiden and his pa headed out early, looking for work. The old man would have stayed in that saloon if Aiden's ma hadn't gone back for him while Aiden kept up the sweeping and cleaning. They'd got the biggest stuff handled, him and his ma, and the little place above the dressmaker's almost looked like it might be a home someday. But not this day, Aiden knew.

Maybe not ever. he thought, wishing he'd just stayed curled up in the corner on the blankets the sewing lady gave his ma. They'd get a real bed soon, his ma said. But until then, they'd just wrap up in the blankets on the floor.

"Why we up so early, Pa?" Aiden asked without thinking.

"Best time to hunt work, son," his pa said. Aiden wanted to say how his pa should have spent the first day looking for work instead of swilling gin in that saloon. But he knew he'd just catch the back of the old man's hand for mouthing off like that.

"Sure are quiet this morning, son. What's the what, Aiden?"

"Just thinking about home, Pa. Back in Chicago City."

"Ain't home, Aiden. No more than this place is home. The Conroys are on the road now, taking it where we can get it and making sure nobody takes it off us. Won't be forever, son. Just a little detour is all."

Around them the Irish Channel came to life with doors and shutters slapping open against clapboards. Sashes slid in their frames and the sounds of morning chatter filtered out of quiet breakfast rooms and kitchens rich and warm with the smell of home cooking.

Aiden wanted to believe his pa about this city being just a stop on the road, sure enough he did. But how could he? New Orleans had only had them in its arms for a week now and already it felt like they were stuck tight with no way out.

Up ahead, the stem crossed another main road. A corner saloon had its doors open but it was just for the barkeep to carry his slop buckets out to the street. As they came up on the corner, Aiden caught his pa glancing into the dark room beyond the saloon's open doors.

"Think we'll find work, Pa? I mean paying work, like you used to have back ho—I mean, back when?"

His pa stopped walking and took a beat before he answered. "No," he said, and then, "I mean, no, not here. Not yet."

Aiden took another step, figuring the man just had his nose aimed at the saloon and was talking himself off the idea. When his pa grunted in disgust, Aiden stopped and swiveled his head to see what it was about.

Down the side of the saloon, all along the boardwalk, tramps rolled and shuffled and staggered to their feet. Some still slept with their feet sticking out of ratty blankets that were pulled up over their faces. Aiden stared at the tramps for a bit and then he saw the others.

Across the street, on almost every corner, tramps stretched and yawned, coughed, and spit. Some were up and eating cold stew from greasy looking mugs. Down an alley, Aiden spotted three others putting light to a small fire. Meanwhile the city rose around the hobo chorus like an angry crowd ready to leave and happy that the lights had finally come up. From all directions the city bumped and bustled, flooding the street with carts and buggies led by horses. Here and there, bicycles swam in and out of the growing flow of traffic. Aiden even spotted a few couples, arm in arm, strolling the boardwalks.

Nobody seemed to take notice of the tramps scattered about the place. Nobody but Aiden and his pa anyway.

"Jeez, Aiden. Would you look at 'em all?"

"Where'd they come from, Pa? I don't remember seeing them until just a second ago. Do you think—?"

"Don't much matter, does it?" his pa said. "Where they came from, I mean. Back there with your old boss and his gods, or just out of the gutter. They don't belong anywhere else, right?"

"Whaddya mean?"

"I mean they got nowhere to go, nowhere to be. Never did probably. Nobody knows these men and nobody probably ever did."

Something spun in Aiden's mind, a question that buzzed like a bee, and the words came out in a rush. "They gotta have somebody knows 'em, Pa. Nobody's born a tramp. Are they?"

"No, Aiden. I suppose not. But sometimes you just can't deny fate. Maybe it's destiny. But these men, they don't belong anywhere, or to anyone. They're just dregs, Aiden. Leftovers. It's only because God won't kill 'em off that any of 'em are still alive. Course they'll be dead enough someday soon. Half dead now. Only the drink … keeps 'em going day by day."

Aiden's gut clenched around his pa's words. The man had his nose aimed at the saloon again.

"C'mon, Pa. We gotta find work. Don't look like there's much around here, hey?"

Aiden's pa kept his face turned away, toward the saloon door.

The barkeep had dumped his slop buckets in the gutter and was heading back inside. A few of the tramps went over with their mugs and dipped them into the flow of syrup and grime that flowed into a nearby drain. Aiden nearly brought up his breakfast and had to spin away from the sight.

"Yeah, Aiden," his pa said, finally looking down the street instead of at the saloon. "Let's go find some work. Somewhere …."

The longing in his pa's voice was like a slow jazz tune. Aiden tried to forget it and just focus on looking for shops with HELP WANTED signs in the window.

· · ·

They trudged through the Channel for what felt like an hour, following Constance Street up into the Garden District. They didn't spot anything like a place to find work, but Aiden's pa kept his eyes on every saloon and tavern they passed. Aiden didn't see more than two places that he'd know were bars just by looking at them. But his pa kept pointing at little buildings beside houses or tucked in between shops in a row.

"There's one. Another one up the way there. Jeez, this town sure does have it in the bag. They don't even bother hiding their speaks like we had to back in Chicago City. Whaddya make of that, Aiden?"

"I don't know, Pa." He wanted to say more, to tell his pa they weren't out looking for places to drink. But Aiden kept his mouth shut. His old man just had a nose for any joint that sold hooch and that was that. It didn't mean he'd end up sleeping outside the saloon and drinking spilled slop from the gutter.

"Where do you think we should look next, Pa?"

"Why don't you pick it, son? Up or down at the next corner. I think Magazine Street is up and Laurel is down. That's what your mother said. I knew I should have brought that book with us."

"Which book, Pa?"

"The green one, son!" his pa hollered and then seemed to change his mind. His face went soft and he swiveled his head side to side, looking at the street and anybody on it who might have heard him yell.

"The green book, Aiden. The one you got from—"

Aiden didn't need his pa to say where he'd got the book from. He remembered well enough. And his pa remembered, too. The old man tried to tuck his wounded hand into his pocket, but the bandage made it so he couldn't. For a second, Aiden thought his pa would just up and quit right there on the street. He'd never seen his old man so far down.

Down ...?

When that buggy driver had dropped Aiden off at the dressmaker's, with the shine box, he'd suggested Aiden look for work "up on the Magazine." Aiden didn't know if he could really trust that man, but anything was better than following his pa's nose to the next saloon.

"Let's go up, then, Pa. I hear Magazine's got lots of work."

"You hear, huh? From who?"

Aiden gulped. He hadn't told his folks about the buggy man, or about the whole mess with the shine box, either. "Um, this guy in the dress shop," he said, hoping his pa wouldn't press it.

He didn't, but Aiden didn't miss the look on the man's face that said he knew Aiden was having him on.

They went up to Magazine with a tight silence around them. Aiden hadn't ever spent this much time with his pa outside of being at home with him on weekends. They reached Magazine Street, and it hit Aiden that he didn't really know much about his pa, except for that he'd had a job cleaning up the Field Museum at night and slept most of the day because of it.

"What kind of work should we look for, Pa? Cleaning up like you did back home?"

"If we can find it, Aiden, sure thing. But that's if we can find it. More likely we'll find work that's dirtier and doesn't pay as well."

All around them, Magazine Street was alive with activity. Women led children by the hand up and down the sidewalks. Small carts filled with fruit and vegetables stood like lampposts in front of every house, welcoming people up to the stoop. Girls with every color skin possible sat on the steps, smiling and waving at everyone who passed them by.

"C'mon up now. Beets, beans, and collards," said a light-skinned girl across the street, waving at Aiden and his pa. Then she seemed to notice something and switched her attention to a young woman pushing a baby carriage. The girl's mood shifted so fast and harsh that Aiden wondered if he wasn't supposed to be looking at the girls, or if he should do something like wave back.

"Late oranges comin' in here," said another girl, with darker skin. She sat on a stoop nearby and Aiden could almost catch a hint of sadness in her voice. He looked at her as they passed and she turned her eyes away just as fast and sharp as the other girl had.

"Just keep walking, Aiden," his pa said. "Don't pay 'em no mind."

Aiden walked beside his pa, playing out what he'd seen and wondering what he'd done to put the girls off him and his pa so bad.

Up ahead, a dark-skinned gentleman came toward them. He wore a fine suit and porkpie hat and carried a walking stick that tapped a steady rhythm on the ground as he stepped. Aiden picked up on it first because his pa wasn't looking at the man, but it was clear the guy meant to block their path and to do it quick. His feet and stick hit the sidewalk, clicking and snapping like typewriter keys. Aiden tugged on his pa's sleeve in time to get his old man's attention before they collided with the guy marching toward them.

The man drew up sharp and proper, with his stick between his toes and both hands on its head. His eyes met Aiden's and he spat out a question that made Aiden's skin crawl.

"May I ask just what in the name of Jehovah the two of you think you might be doing walking down this street?"

"We was—" Aiden's pa started to say.

"I am speaking to the boy," the man said, not looking at Aiden's pa.

"Now hold on," his pa said. "I'm the father here, and I'll speak for my son. We—"

The man's hands moved like lightning, bringing the tip of his stick up under Aiden's pa's chin just like that. Aiden spotted the little knife that extended from the stick to poke at his pa's gullet.

"You'll do no such speaking," the man said, his eyes rounded with something like rage. "You'll keep your fool Dove mouth shut unless you want another hole in your person. And this one won't just mark ya. It'll kill ya." The man's eyes rounded big and bright white, and full of what Aiden could only call hate.

Aiden's pa stepped back as fast as the man had brought his stick up, so the knife point was left hanging in midair. The man slowly lowered the stick and did something with his hands on the stick's head to bring the knife back inside.

"I asked you a question, Dove," he said aiming a finger at Aiden while he kept his eyes locked on Aiden's pa. With a quick glance, Aiden saw his pa looking ready for a fight but not so ready that he'd risk actually starting one. All around them the street seemed to go still. The calls from the stoop girls had stopped and only shuffling feet or cart wheels came through the air to Aiden's ears.

"I am growing mightily weary of waiting for my answer, Dove," the man said, turning his head to stare at Aiden now.

"We . . . like my pa—" Aiden started. His voice seemed to have snuck back into his throat, though, and the words wouldn't come out unless he forced them. "We was . . . just out. Looking for work."

"Work?" the man said, his eyes flashing open with a mix of fright and fury. "For the likes of you? A little Dove and his clipped pappy. And you like to be finding work along the Magazine? If that ain't the best story I've ever heard."

"It ain't a story, mister—"

"Oh no? Well go on and tell me the long and short of it. I'm just dying to hear it."

"Well, okay . . . ," Aiden began, feeling his voice taking over now and getting the words back where they belonged on his tongue. "We just got to town and settled in over on Constance Street. My ma works the dressmaker's shop there, along with the other sewing ladies. Me and Pa, we set out trying to find our way now, so we can help keep the home, too. Like a real man does, you know?"

The Negro seemed ready to slap the words right back into Aiden's mouth, and for a second Aiden thought he would. Then the man's face split open in a grin and he let out a belly laugh that shook Aiden to his feet.

"Well now, Dove. That is a story, indeed. And it's one I'm like to believe. But tell me now, how do you propose to find work when you got a man like this by your side? He's been clipped, and surely you know what that means."

"Clipped? You mean how he got stabbed? That was all because some guy had his fingers in my ma's hair. Ain't that right, Pa? Tell him, will ya? How come I gotta do all the talking here?"

"I . . . ," his pa started to say. "I can't, Aiden."

"Whaddya mean you can't? You're talking to me, ain't ya'? Jeez, Pa. Help me out here. C'mon."

The dark-skinned gentleman spoke then. "Your pappy knows, Little Dove. He clearly knows what clipped means, and he knows better than to speak out of turn again. Ain't that right, Dove?"

Aiden looked between the two men, his pa and the man with the walking stick that hid a knife in the tip. As he watched the two men face off, his pa's face softened and fell, and a tear crept out of his left eye.

"Yeah," Aiden's pa said. "I know what it means. Or I can figure it well enough I guess."

Aiden waited for his pa to finish, and he could see the man with the stick was waiting, too. He tapped a foot and rolled the fingers of one hand across the back of the other that held his walking stick steady.

Aiden's pa started up again, and said something that made Aiden's blood go cold in his veins. "It means I can't work in this town, Aiden. That's right, isn't it? Sir?"

In that instant, Aiden remembered what the barman had said when they first got into New Orleans.

"Won't be finding work with a mitt like that on ya."

The man they'd met on the street nodded at Aiden and his pa, and then he said, "Yes it is, Dove. That is right."

He reached a hand into his coat and brought out a slim metal case, like for holding cigarettes. He held the case out, toward Aiden, and flipped it open to reveal a small stack of visiting cards.

"Go on and take one, Little Dove. You apply at the address thereon and you'll like to be finding yourself . . . some work, I daresay."

Aiden lifted a card from the case. It was a thin cream-colored piece of paper, but heavy, not like the newsprint he used to read when he worked for Mr. Brand. The card had a name and a street number on it, and a little note.

Chez Jambord et Pomet
45 Lafitte Street
For seekers of employment in New Orleans

Adien read the card while the man with the stick closed his little metal case and put it back in his coat.

"Now if you'd be so kind as to get this clipped bird off my street," the man said with a smirk in Aiden's direction. "I believe I can be wishing you a good day. And if you dilly or dally a second longer, I'm like to forget my offer and have the both of you run out of town on a rail."

Aiden's pa didn't waste a breath. He turned and stepped fast down the sidewalk so that Aiden had to scurry to catch up with him. When he did, he thought of asking his pa what it was all about and how come he went quiet and got soft back there. But the look of shame on his pa's face said enough.

CHAPTER 16

EMMA WRUNG OUT ANOTHER WET RAG IN THE bucket beside her. She let it hang off the rim and sat back against the wall. The house Bacchus gave them wasn't much to look at, even after three days straight of nothing but scrubbing and polishing. The walls were clean at last, and the few furnishings that'd been in the place were no longer coated in dust. A carpet in the front bedroom had to be thrown in the dustbin out back. There was one chair in the back bedroom that Emma swore had bloodstains on it, but she'd scrubbed it clean anyway, telling herself not to notice.

Just get it clean. Clean as can be is all we need.

The bathroom and kitchen were the easiest of all, since they had tile floors. The wood floors through the rest of the house, however, needed more work than Emma could do on her own, and Eddie was still in no shape to bend or get down on his knees.

Bacchus had sent them to a sawbones he said they could trust.

"Man works for me. So he works for you. When I tell him he does."

Emma couldn't suppress the shiver that whipped through her when the gangster put a hand on her waist and escorted her into the doctor's clinic. Two of Bacchus' toughs had helped Eddie in and the doctor didn't spare a moment when he saw how bad Eddie'd been hurt.

"Lucky he's still breathing . . . ," the doctor had said as he peeled Eddie's shirt off and exposed the bruises around his ribs. Emma had cried long silent tears while the doctor and one of Bacchus' boys wrapped bandages around her lover's middle.

Right where my arms should have been, she'd thought to herself while the tears rolled down her face.

But now they were home together, and Emma had cleaned the place up as nice as she could. The work wasn't finished, but she was. And she knew Eddie wasn't ready to take over.

Of course, the man just couldn't let things lie. Emma jerked up from where she sat when he crawled into the room with a rag in his hand.

"Eddie, you'll just make it worse," Emma said, giving him a bent eye and reaching for the rag. He didn't miss a beat and slopped the rag in the bucket, splashing Emma with some of the sudsy water. She gave a little squeal when it soaked through her skirt.

"Can't have you doin' all the cleanin' up now, Emma. Wouldn't be right."

Emma wanted to argue, but at the same time she didn't. Eddie was the reason they had a home of their own, and she knew it. But that didn't make it easier to accept how quickly she'd gone from calling the shots to following them.

Eddie had kept the horn he'd gotten from the barman at Hardy's place, and there wasn't any protest from either Hardy or his bartender. When Bacchus brought them to the little shotgun cottage over on Dumaine, he'd handed them the keys and told Eddie to "keep an eye on her for me."

Emma hadn't been sure if Bacchus had meant the house, the horn, or her.

With Eddie making lazy passes with his rag along the floorboards,

Emma scrubbed as fast as she could, trying to get the lion's share done so Eddie wouldn't have to work too hard. She knew he'd need his strength to play later that night. It would be his first show without her, but it would also pay in cash.

Their gig at Hardy's place had paid in room and a little board, if you count two heels of bread and a wedge of dry cheese. They'd eaten proper that day that Bacchus came to collect them, but Hardy said it would have to come off their pay for the night anyway. And sure enough, it had been slim picking since then. Now, even with Bacchus lording over them, Emma didn't know when she'd see something like a decent meal again.

When they'd arrived, the icebox in the back of the kitchen had some provisions in it. Nothing too fancy, just some cabbage, collards, a few apples, and a bottle of milk that was already going off. They'd eaten all of the food in the first two days, adding it to a steak Emma bought from a nearby butcher's. Bacchus had given Eddie a few dollars.

"To get you and Miss Emma in good order before your big night."

But that money was gone now, and even with the promise of a cash gig on the horizon, Emma still felt the bite of worry in her gut.

"You think you'll earn enough for us to get some more food stored up, Eddie?"

"Huh?" he said, like she'd woken him from a dream.

"Tonight. You're playing that gig for Bacchus tonight. He said he'd pay you in cash, and I'm wondering if you know how much it's gonna be."

"No idea, Lovebird. But you know, it's got to be better than what we been earnin' this week. Sure would like to know who's gonna pay us for all this cleanin' up we been doin'."

Emma couldn't help but laugh. Even in the worst moments, Eddie's funny bone could tickle her into liking their chances again. She slapped her rag into the bucket and a spray of water fanned out and covered Eddie's flank.

"Hey watch out now, girl," he said, laughing, and then flung his rag at the bucket. He turned away to avoid the splash and Emma did the same, but they both ended up with suds on their backs and in their hair.

Emma turned back to see Eddie holding his ribs and wincing. She went to him right away.

"I told you to take it easy, Eddie."

"I know, Lovebird," he said. "I know. Help me to the bedroom, hey? I need to lie down a bit before tonight."

Emma put a hand under his arm and stood. She supported his weight as best she could as he pushed himself off the floor on shaky legs. Together they stepped slow down the hall and into the back bedroom.

Eddie moved carefully to the bed and kept his weight on Emma's arm. He turned so as to lie down on his back and Emma leaned to hold his weight and let him down onto the mattress easily. She caught the grin on his face a second later and then they were tumbling to the mattress, his hands around her waist and their lips pressed together.

"You sneak, Eddie Collins," Emma said, playfully batting a hand on his chest. "Playing possum. You better not've been holding back all along. This girl's been on her knees scrubbing and scraping for three days now."

"Hey now, Lovebird. Just makin' sure I rested, so you can put all that strength you been buildin' up to good use."

Eddie wrapped his arms around her and they gently rolled together across the bed. Eddie winced as she moved with him, but soon enough they were into that rhythm from before. His hands, her hips. Her lips to his lips. His fingers through her tousled hair, still ratty and short from when she'd cut in to hide with the gypsies in Chicago City. The bandana she'd tied around it slid down around her collar, pushed by Eddie's anxious fingers.

Their shirts ruffled up as they pressed and slid against each other. They tangled their hands, pushing her skirt aside and his slacks down and out of the way. The bed creaked. Emma's ears followed the rhythm of the groans and squeaks of the old metal four-poster. And she caught every moan and gasp of pleasure from Eddie. His voice mingled with her own, like his music behind her singing. Only this time the stage was in the bedroom of their little shotgun shack in New Orleans.

She'd flown them over a thousand miles from home, and the whole way it had felt like she was leaving it all behind. As she held Eddie against her, the feeling of loss slipped away and New Orleans became the place she was always meant to be, a haunted place that surrounded her, held her close, and kept her warm and tight.

When they were done, they lay together in a quiet embrace, Emma's hand on Eddie's chest. She watched the rise and fall of his breath. Soon enough her eyes drooped and the dark of New Orleans rushed in to claim her fully this time.

• • •

Emma and Eddie snapped awake to a hammering on the front door. Eddie didn't miss a beat and shoved Emma aside so he could slide off the bed and get his clothes back right. He gasped and put a hand to his side as he stood, and Emma didn't miss the look of pain on his face.

"Eddie, you—"

"I'm fine, Emma. Fine. You just get yourself right. I'll go see who it is."

Eddie finished tucking his shirt into his pants and struggled into his suspenders again. Emma shimmied to the foot of the bed and straightened her skirt and did up her blouse again. Her hair still wasn't much to speak of on a good day, so she just slipped the bandana off her neck and retied it while Eddie went to see who was out front. Emma's hands froze tying the bandana when she heard the door open and let Bacchus's angry voice into the house.

"I do hope," the big man said, his heavy tread following his words into the house. "I said, I do hope, Mr. Collins. Do you know what I hope?"

"N-no, sir. No sir, Mister Bacchus, I don't."

"What I hope, Mr. Collins, is that you were not exerting yourself overly much. I see the way you hold your hand to your ribs. I'm counting on your horn tonight, and if you know what's good for your silly black ass, you'll be blowing as fine as you did the first time I heard you play."

"Yessir, Mr. Bacchus. I can play just fine."

Emma waited for it. She could feel the air shift, like every move Mr. Bacchus made was a heavy stone thrown in a lake.

"Let's hope you don't need your legs to be tip-top, then. This is for just in case," the big man said. A second later Emma heard a *thwack* and Eddie cried out. A second strike followed the first and Eddie's muffled cry echoed down the hall to the back bedroom where Emma stood shaking with terror.

"Now, Mr. Collins. You'd best be able to blow that horn tonight. And if you can't, those little taps are gonna come a whole lot worse when I deliver them a second time. Or I might like to call on the Birdman to ensure you see *straight*. Do we understand each other?"

Emma heard Eddie stifle a sob and then say, "Yes . . . yessir, Mr. Bacchus."

"That's good. Now go on and get ready. Streetcar is coming by in about thirty minutes. And it's a ten-minute walk to the stop on a good pair of legs."

Emma clutched her hands over her mouth, waiting for the sound of another strike, but none came. The door closed a second later and she heard shuffling sounds from down the hall. She dared to peek around the doorjamb and saw Eddie on his knees, one hand still held to his ribs. The other was holding him up off the floor.

She ran to him, and helped him up. She supported him all the way down the hall, back to the bedroom where they were both careful to sit on the bed at the same time, mostly so Eddie could lean on Emma.

"Eddie, what are we gonna do? We can't stay here. Not if he's going to hit you every time he feels like it. We can't—"

"We gonna be fine, Emma," he said. "Don't you worry. Boss just upset is all. Gotta keep the man happy. We'll be all right. You'll see."

"But what does he have to be upset about? We were just having a little fun." Emma felt her chest rising and the outrage she'd once felt for every man in Chicago City climbing up her throat. "Does this mean we can't love each other like we used to because Mr. High-and-Mighty won't like it? Is he worried that you'll come into his room smelling like another woman? Is that it? He doesn't want his high rollers and fat cats thinking the jazz man is getting it better than they are?"

Emma's anger flooded out of her in a rush of accusations and demands, until she couldn't even hear the words she was saying anymore. Her voice became a torrent of fire. Eddie backed away from her, but she kept at him, ignoring the look on his face and the way he held up his hands.

"Emma! Emma, please!" he said at last, his face twisted with confusion and fear. "Girl, I gotta go play tonight. And you heard what Mr. Bacchus said. Streetcar on its way, and I gotta walk with this knee he just gave me. Ain't doing us any good you tearing into me like that."

Emma felt her face soften, but her chest still heaved with the same heavy feelings of betrayal and torment. Eddie put a hand on her knee and looked her in the eye.

"Save it for when I get home if you have to. But please. Let me get ready and go, hey?"

She held up her chin and closed her eyes, letting her breath go, long and slow and deep like she'd been holding it in for a year. "Okay, Eddie," she said, opening her eyes and nodding. "Okay. But—"

Eddie put a finger to her lips. "No *buts* right now, Lovebird. Just *okay*. Just *I love you*. And you know I do."

He leaned in and kissed her. Emma took the kiss and gave him a little of her own. But she felt herself keeping back the little part of her heart that she'd always held from him, at least until earlier in the day when they were making smiles with each other on this very bed.

Whatever happened between that time and this, Emma wasn't sure. The fear she'd felt was real, and the anger, too. But where the anger came from, she couldn't say. One thing she knew, though. That little piece of herself would go back to hiding out until she knew for certain she and Eddie really had a chance in New Orleans.

CHAPTER 17

I T'S SOME HOUR OF THE MORNING, BRAND doesn't know which and knows he can't even try a guess if any-one bothers to ask him. Barnaby and the other fellas are snoring over there under their canvas. Brand pushes his tattered blankets aside and stretches his limbs, trying to ignore the cracking and popping noises.

What the hell did I do last night, he thinks.

He made his delivery, that's what. He got the envelope to the god it was meant for. Some guy in a white suit with a patch over one eye. Dark skin, tall and lean like a beanpole, but tough. Brand could tell. Guy carried himself like he'd whip out a hand and take your eye if you dared use it to look at him wrong. Called himself Ghost even though the letter Brand gave him was addressed to *Chance.*

Brand tries to remember something else about the guy, but his head feels ten times the size it should be, and Brand figures that's why he thinks he's knocking his skull into everything around him. He shuffles away from the camp and makes his way to the mooring deck, reaching for the pillars supporting the platform like they'll tether him as soon as he lays his hands on their cold metal skin.

Behind him, in the campsite, Barnaby snores on. Brand imagines Reggie and Phinias are doing the same. The Three Blind Men have practice, Brand thinks. They've done this so many times it'd take a whole barrel of hooch to get them drunk enough to wake up sick.

Brand moves to return to the camp, maybe find some sleep in there somewhere after all. Rest his throbbing noggin enough it might stop beating him to death every time he tries to use it.

Then he feels it. A weight dragging on one side of his coat, just enough to let him know he's got work to do. Another envelope fills the pocket.

"Guy can't catch a break no matter how hard he tries. C'mon then," Brand says to nobody in particular. He wants someone to be there, a pal, one of his newsboys, or just anybody who cares enough to look him in the eye. But Brand knows he's alone, so he lifts a hand and peels back the air by his head, revealing the world of memories and the torment of regret. "Time to deliver the mail," he says, and steps through.

• • •

It's dark, like always, and Brand's feet stick in the mud. He slogs, not bothering to run, because he knows the mud can't have him when he's on a job.

"You fellas just hold down the fort while I'm gone, hey?" he says to the mob of muddy coats, grimy skin, and tangled whiskers rolling along behind him.

The mud men moan at him, angry and confused, like they know something isn't right and are ready to rain hell or high-water on whatever's getting in their way.

"I said cool it back there," Brand shouts at them. "You know what happens if I flub this job, don't you? It's the mud for ol' Mitchell here."

And I'm not going out like that.

They moan at him some more, but eventually they hush up. Brand slogs through the muck and grime for a while more until he finds the cobblestone road leading up to the city streets above.

"Be seeing you, fellas. Maybe next time around the dance floor I'll let you lead."

Brand climbs the stones with heavy legs, feeling the weight of the city bearing on him now, his back curling until he thinks he must look like a walking question mark. And what else should he look like?

"Not like I have anything left to give the world. Might as well give them a reason to wonder what happened to me."

He's walking on cobblestones still and then he's on a street in a neighborhood somewhere. The buildings all have a look about them that says they belong to another time and place, but they've been put here to remind people of that place.

Old New Orleans, then. Okay.

Brand wipes a sleeve across his mouth and whiskers again. He thinks about how people move through the world, going from one place to another, always taking with them something of memory, something that tells them all is not lost and they may yet find where they belong. Immigrants flooded through New York with bags and belongings. Conroy and the others on board the *Vigilance* brought only themselves to New Orleans.

"And I followed you all because I thought I belonged with you, too."

Around him people have begun their daily routine. Down the street he sees a cluster of tramps unfolding from where they'd holed up in the ruins of a burned-out building. Their sooty clothing and filthy skin make them look like silhouettes. All around the street, signs of life begin to show. Windows go up and shutters open, rugs flutter over stoops and let dust fly into the air.

"Some people just can't give up on hope," Brand mumbles, fingering the envelope in his pocket with one hand while he smooths his whiskers with the other.

A woman on a nearby stoop says something to him as he passes her by, but Brand ignores her. Whatever she's got to say can't be anything as important as finishing off this mail run so he can get back to—

"Yeah? To what?" he asks the morning around him. "What'm I gonna get back to? Whole lotta nothin' is what."

Brand can hardly believe his ears, but it's his voice saying those words, and his head that catches the echo of their portent.

Brand wanders the streets for a while, following his feet that seem to know where they're going. He stops finally and looks through the dissipating mists of the New Orleans morning. Across the street he sees a long sedan parked in front of a rich hotel building. The facade is all ornament and filigree, stonework with the weight of authority carved into it.

A figure steps out of the sedan, a heavy man who holds a cane. Brand sees a glint of light off the tip of the cane, and more pinpoints reflecting off of rings on the man's fingers. He's like a chandelier with legs, Brand thinks and chuckles to himself.

For a while, Brand watches the gold-tipped man across the street. He doesn't seem like he's going to move and slowly the street fills with wagons and bicycles, horses, and even a motor car or two.

"So I have to dodge traffic to do my job?" Brand says, shaking his head and tossing a sneeze at the idea.

Brand lifts his hand slowly and puts it in his pocket. He feels the envelope there and he removes it, remembering Barnaby's warning just as he looks at the name on the envelope.

To Vice C/O Mr. Bacchus.

Brand lifts his eyes and he's face-to-face with the walking chandelier. With a start, Brand stumbles a few steps backward and nearly goes over on his ass, but he keeps his feet at the last second.

The man standing in front of him now is easily a head shorter than Brand himself. But his girth is twice Brand's own, if not more. He's dark-skinned, with heavy, drooping jowls that frame a mouth set in a grim smile that's a few steps along the way to being a sneer.

The man wears a fur-trimmed coat draped around his heavy bulk, and holds his walking stick across his gut with both hands.

"I believe you have my mail," says the big man with the rings and stick.

"Yes, Sir. Here it is," Brand says, holding out the envelope. The big man nods his head to one side and a servant Brand hadn't noticed before appears at the god's shoulder. The servant is a white-skinned man in liveries that match the big man's own suit. He wears a black tailcoat and blood-red vest over a white shirt. Woven into the vest are threads of silver and gold.

The servant takes the envelope and produces two coins, which he extends, pinched between his fingertips as though he would drop them rather than hand them directly to Brand.

Brand cups his hands and catches the coins as they fall. He looks at them as they sit in his palms. The two discs of glimmering yellow metal give off a warmth that spreads through Brand's hands and arms. He looks up to thank the big man and finds the street empty.

Doesn't stick around, does he?

Brand figures the big man for a gangster. That's easy enough for him to put together without help. Brand's been face-to-face with gangsters before, he remembers. And this one owns most of New Orleans, same as Capone used to own most of Chicago City. Only *Mr. Heavy Black Lightshow* here has something Capone didn't.

"There's a god in him, though. Bet it's a big one. Wonder how many more they've got down here," Brand says. He pockets the coins and feels their weight for just a moment before they vanish like sand through a sieve. A man in a sharp suit strolls through the early morning and dodges around Brand at the last minute. Brand waves a hand after the guy like he'd brush him away. But the guy's already gone, his back to Brand and his eyes on the road ahead.

"Gods're all the same. Same as always," Brand says. "Get you to do their work and give you nothin' back for it."

On cue, Brand feels the weight of the coins in his pocket again, and then realizes it's an envelope. He pulls it out. When he sees what's written on the front, he puts a hand to his mouth and holds in the scream that's forming in his throat.

To Innocence C/O Aiden Conroy.

Brand chokes back his scream and reads the address again.

"Conroy? They're after you, too," Brand says and turns his face to the sky. "Well let 'em try. You hear that?" He's shouting now, ignoring all the looks and stares and glares he draws from the people on the street.

"You just try it!" Brand the Tramp hollers at the city around him, waving the envelope like a bailiff holding a court summons.

CHAPTER 18

AIDEN'S PA WAS NONE TOO HAPPY ABOUT it, that was clear enough. He sat across from Aiden, with his back to the kitchen where Aiden's ma paced around like a gearbox gone haywire. She kept stepping close to his pa and then spinning off to go some other direction. The way Aiden's pa clutched the bottle against his belly said it all.

That day on Magazine Street, his pa had stopped them off at the same saloon he'd been in when they first hit town. His pa had gone inside and told Aiden to wait, then he'd come out and told Aiden to come in. The guy at the bar had aimed a thumb at a door in the back of the room, and Aiden went. He wound up in a little kitchen with a sink and a whole lot of dirty dishes.

Aiden scrubbed and soaped up the plates and glasses while he pa held down a stool. The barkeep said he'd done a real good job, more than enough to earn his pa a glass a hooch. The guy had said he was sorry he couldn't pay Aiden for the work. Then Aiden's pa had said *"How about a bottle to take home?"*

The last drops of the liquor made a little pool in the bottom of the bottle now. Aiden tore his eyes off it and looked at his ma again, but not straight on. Meeting her eyes wasn't any better than staring down the bottle in his pa's lap.

Behind his pa, the kitchen was still a dingy little corner, but now the cupboards had tins and jars of food put up for keeping. The family's dishes sat stacked on a shelf above the tin wash basin. On the other side of that, their new green icebox stood by, keeping cool a roast his ma had gotten that morning. When she'd come home with the roast, Aiden's eyes had lit up. Then he told her about the work he'd finally found and they'd all three of them ended up like this.

The way his ma kept pacing around the kitchen made it look like the set of a Punch and Judy show.

Aiden wanted to tell his pa to put the bottle down; he could feel the words on his tongue. But the old man's hangdog mug let just enough of the Conroy fire through. Aiden knew better than to say anything of the kind. Besides, the work he'd got meant pay. Real pay. and a lot better than the shoe shine gig.

Maybe his pa would put the bottle down on his own once they got things sorted out and Aiden showed up with money for the family.

That's gotta be worth something.

He'd thought for sure it would. He went to the address on the card he got from the man on Magazine Street. But when he'd told his folks about the gig, his pa sat there looking glum as can be. And his ma didn't like it no matter how he sliced it. She almost bounced around the kitchen now, with her arms crossed, and still not getting too close to his pa.

"It's five dollars, Aiden. *Five.* And that's just to buy the cart and, what did that colored man say? A book? It sounds like gambling to me, and you know how I feel about gambling."

"Alice . . .," his pa started. For a second, Aiden thought his pa would take over where his ma left off, just tell Aiden to forget it. Then the old man surprised him.

"It's like any job the kid's gonna find now. He's got nothing …

no credence. He doesn't belong here and neither do we, but we're here. So he's got to find work where he can. People down here. They don't care his old man used to run the cleaning crew at the Field Museum. Might as well tell 'em I was King of Siam all the good it'll do him. Al Conroy's name is mud in New Orleans. The kid got work that pays. We should be thankful."

"Thankful?" his ma said. "Al Conroy, did you just suggest—"

Aiden's pa went to take a slug from the bottle and Aiden didn't miss his ma sending a bent eye in the old man's direction. If his pa noticed, he didn't let on, but he stopped with the bottle in front of his lips. Then he let it sink back down to his lap where he held like a newborn baby.

The distance between Aiden's parents didn't feel anything like normal, but he couldn't pretend it felt wrong, either.

He had some more words in his mouth and thought he should say his piece, maybe try to bring the family back together around him finding good-paying work. Get his pa to stop slugging hooch. The words pushed at his lips, but a tightness in his throat kept him quiet.

Aiden's pa lifted the bottle again, and this time he didn't stop. Aiden closed his eyes so he wouldn't have to watch.

His ma's shoes clapped on the wood floor, echoing against the hum of sewing machines in the room below. Aiden opened his eyes, thinking she'd come close enough to snatch the bottle out his pa's hands. But his parents just kept up their dance like they'd been doing the whole time.

His mother's mood still went in every direction, like she was being forced to follow steps she didn't know. She seemed to stagger from place to place in the small kitchen: over by the sink, then the counter, back to the sink and away again. Her feet landed firm and steady each time, but her face said it clear enough.

She doesn't know what to do.

Aiden's pa didn't seem to mind, or notice if he did. Aiden hated watching it, but he knew that opening his mouth would just get him hollered at.

Getting hollered out only counted in his book when he'd earned it. His folks were on a roll, and he had no choice but to leave them to it. His pa made sure he wouldn't get a chance to speak anyway.

"It's just five dollars, Alice. That's what? About a day's pay for you? Okay, it's a lot, but—"

"Al, I barely bring in enough for us to keep food on the table, and what little I have left seems as likely to end up in a bottle as anywhere else."

That was what Aiden had been waiting for, but he didn't know it until the words left his ma's lips. Aiden's pa clammed up tight, set the bottle on the ground beside his chair, folded his arms, and stared at the wall behind Aiden.

"Ma," Aiden said, testing the waters. She didn't reply, but she didn't holler at him neither, so he kept on. "I think it's straight, this cleaning job I got. The fella I talked to showed me the other guys' books and it's just keeping records. It don't look like gambling."

"*Doesn't*, Aiden," she said, her eyes finding his now. "Doesn't look like. Oh for— Do you remember what I said about keeping the Conroy name in good standing?"

Aiden nodded, and he didn't miss the look his ma aimed at the back of his pa's head.

"Yes'm," Aiden said, doing his best to just keep his eyes on his ma and pretend not to see the way his pa's face squeezed up like his head would pop any minute. His ma was staring at the old man's head now, and Aiden knew she was talking to his pa as much as to him.

"People in this city value proper etiquette, Aiden. The people that matter anyway. That means speaking clean as much as it means acting clean. Don't forget that, or the people we care about and want to like us will start thinking we belong with the—" She stopped, but Aiden knew what she had in mind to say. He didn't want to give her a chance to get the word out, so he piped up and did his best to make like he cared about 'speaking clean,' like she'd said.

"Yes'm," Aiden said again. "It doesn't look like gambling. Not a bit, Ma. Honest."

His pa kept hush, but Aiden still caught the grunt that came up into the quiet that followed his words. His ma's face darkened and she went to lean against the sink.

"It doesn't sound honest, Aiden. The people you'd be working for aren't our kind of people. They aren't honest people."

Aiden didn't know what to say to that. He'd hoped she wouldn't mention it, because he knew what his pa would say about who Aiden would be calling boss. But he remembered how Mr. Brand would shake hands with the dark-skinned delivery men, and how he used to huff and puff about having to wait for another white man to be finished using the can instead of just using the one marked COLOREDS when it was empty.

"They're just people, Conroy. A colored man can die in a war same as any other man."

"They're just folks, Ma. Not like you and me and Pa here, sure, but they're still folks. They've lived here good and long, and we're the new guys in town, hey? I figure them offering me this job is like getting a welcome mat. Kind of," he added when he saw his mother's face hang with doubt.

"Kind of," she said, almost mocking his tone. "Aiden I don't *kind of* want you working around those people, and even though he's too drunk to say it himself, I'm sure your father doesn't, either."

Aiden was about to add a few licks of his own, because the way his mother said *those people* had started to eat at him. But she beat him to it and what she said surprised Aiden even more than it burned.

"I suppose your father is right, though," she said, her eyes going soft and the snarl dropping out of her voice. "If you're going to earn for the family, you'll have to take work where you can find it. How much did you say they'd pay you?"

Aiden almost missed the cue. "I … the man said I'd get fifteen cents a day, but only three days a week. Unless they have extra work, and that can happen pretty often, the man said." Aiden went on, doing his best to parrot back what he'd been told.

"Which man, Aiden? The one who threatened your father or another one with a knife hidden in his walking stick?"

"The one at the workhouse, Ma. Like I said. He was a dark-skinned fella, sure, but he was wearing suspenders and carrying a mop and bucket. No knife on him that I could see."

"That you could see. That's just the point, Aiden. You won't see it until they're sticking it in you."

"They aren't like that, Ma. They're not all hiding knives and trying to kill us because we're white."

Aiden had heard the words but didn't believe they'd come from his mouth until the look on his mother's face told him she'd heard him loud and clear.

His ma took a few breaths to cool off, and Aiden figured he should do the same. His pa just picked up his bottle again and took the last swallow. He set the bottle back down and looked at the wall some more.

"Well, Aiden," his ma said. "Why don't you tell me again what they were like. Apparently I've been misinformed by the twenty-seven years I've spent living with colored people free to walk the same streets as I do."

Aiden wanted to fix his ma, put her mind right about things, but he didn't know how to do it. And every time he thought he had the words to send back her way, she'd come up with something worse for him to deal with. He just couldn't see how to change her mind, so he gave up trying and stuck to the facts.

"I just went around the back of the house there, with the guy carrying the mop. He showed me a couple of colored folks, a man and a woman, and they were all dressed up in glad rags. They'd been talking, but went hush when we came around the corner of the house. The guy with the mop told me, 'Go on,' so I did. I asked about work and the woman gave me the rundown on the gig."

"And what was that, Aiden? The rundown."

Everything felt all turned around in his head now, where he'd be working, how much he'd earn, and what he'd have to do. But he remembered how his heart got light when the color— When the lady told him he'd be cleaning up houses.

"I'll be cleaning floors, just like Pa used to do back at the Field. Sometimes it's washing out a kitchen sink I'll be doing, and sometimes washing walls, too. Mostly just floors, they said."

"And where are these places you'll be cleaning up? What do they do there?"

Aiden had to think a second, and he realized he didn't have an answer for his ma's question. Not a ready one anyway. The people he'd met hadn't told him anything about *what would happen* or why the houses would need cleaning. Aiden figured it was just because houses need cleaning.

Houses get dirty, right?

"The lady—"

"The *colored* lady, Aiden," his ma stuck in.

Aiden swallowed what he'd thought about saying back to his ma before he went on with telling her about the gig.

"Yeah, her. She called 'em *workhouses*, and I didn't think to ask her on it. She said something about watching out for the mothers, but . . . it just sounds like cleaning up houses. I figured . . ."

The look on his ma's face went from soft to cold. She narrowed her eyes and glared at Aiden's pa, almost like she she was thinking he could have found better work for Aiden. But she'd heard about what the man said, up on Magazine Street. Aiden's pa was out of work for good.

The old man had the bottle in his lap again, even though it was empty; and his eyes drooped low like he'd fall out of his chair any second.

"Aiden," his ma said. "You'd better hope that whatever you've gotten mixed up in doesn't lead to trouble. I'll give you the money. But you keep track of your dollars and cents, young man. Every time you get paid, you make note of it in that book. Every time somebody charges you something, you make note of it.

"Don't let *those people* take a cent out of your hands without a good reason, and don't think for a second that they won't try."

"I won't, Ma," he said, even as he wished he could have said something to send the words back into his ma's mouth. Her voice went sour in his ears, like a wrong note on a piano that won't stop ringing. He nodded, trying to shake the feeling out of his head.

"I'll be all right, Ma," he continued, bringing his eyes up to meet hers again. "I'll be fine."

"Okay," she said, with a twist to her lips that said she only half heard what he'd said. "Do me a favor and brush your hair now, Aiden. I need to go— Oh, I can hardly believe I'm doing this," she said, stepping to her left and taking a can of coffee off the shelf.

"Doing what, Ma?"

"I need to *make an offering* at their so-called *church*, so I can get one of those pieces of tin that says it's okay for me to walk on the street or ride the streetcar. I'd use yours, but you'll need it to get around town yourself, since you weren't able to find work in *this* neighborhood. And then *I'll* need to confess all of this to Father James before mass. Since your father's in no state to do much of anything, you'll have to walk with me."

Aiden nodded and stepped over to the mirror by the kitchen. He raked their one comb through his hair and slicked his cow lick down as best he could.

"Here's the money, Aiden," his ma said, holding out a five-dollar bill to him. He took the fin slow and careful, to show her he knew how big this was for her to be doing.

"We'll eat lean for the rest of the week now. If you earn what you say you can … we might get some bread again in a couple of days."

Aiden pocketed the five and took his mother's hand at the door. They both turned to look at his pa, who had fallen asleep where he'd been sitting. The empty bottle slid to the floor and rolled off to the side, up against the bundles of rags that Aiden's folks called a bed.

For a few breaths, he and his ma watched the old man sleep. Before they left, Aiden's ma whispered a prayer. Aiden closed his eyes and thought about what he'd do with his first day's pay.

CHAPTER 19

AT THE ENTRANCE TO THE ALLEY, AIDEN hopped down from the wagon and tipped his hat to the driver.

"Thanks for the lift," he called up to the heavy jowled Irishman holding the reins. Aiden waited while the man pawed through the little box by his right hip and came up with Aiden's badge of transport.

"Here y'are, me boy. Walk safe now, mind."

Aiden tucked the badge into his coat pocket. He nodded and tipped his hat again before stepping back. The driver cracked his whip on the nag's rump, edging her along the alley and around the far corner. The street beyond had just woken up, and the bums' usual chorus rang out in fits and starts, covering up the sound of wagon wheels on the cobblestones.

Aiden counted the coins in his pocket one more time as he walked down the alley. Two days after getting the gig, he'd received his first day's pay. The cleaning cart he'd used to earn it was safely stowed back at the workhouse. It was a big house, with lots of rooms inside, all emptied out mostly, except for a little stage in one room downstairs and a piano in almost every room except the two smallest ones upstairs.

Every other night, Aiden was supposed to come by around eleven o'clock to start work. He'd scrub scuff marks and shoe black from the floors in the workhouse. Then he'd put a polish of wax in the biggest rooms and make sure the pianos were dusted, too. And if it needed doing, he'd wash out the bathrooms when he was done. An old white man worked the job with him this first time, but told Aiden he'd be on his own starting next week.

"And you got lucky there ain't much doing on your first night. Usual, you gonna find them mothers in here, watching you work, making sure you do right. They come, you stay out their way. You hear me?"

Aiden had said he heard just fine and nodded fast to make sure the man saw he meant it. The old man chuckled and said something about doves learning to fly. He then sent Aiden off home around four o'clock in the morning.

When he'd told his folks about his schedule, his ma said she didn't like him being out during those hours. But his pa backed him up.

"Same as I used to do, Alice. Isn't it?"

Aiden's ma pretended she didn't hear the man, and that worried Aiden more than their little feud around the table when he came home with news about the job. His folks just acted more like different people every day.

Their little place above the sewing shop waited a few paces down the alley, all splintered siding and rusted hinges, windows swelled shut, and a door that stuck tight anyway because it was hung wrong.

He dodged a pile of freshly dropped horse manure and went to the back door of the building, beneath the stairs. He could hear his ma and the other ladies working inside already. Their sewing machines made a constant *pitter-patter* and *click-clack*, like a drummer taking it easy on the jazz stage, waiting for the crowd to get onto the dance floor. Only Aiden knew there wasn't any dancing going on where his mother worked.

Nothing but long days and sore thumbs. Fingers tender from getting stuck with needles time and time again. And backs stooped, hunched over, and rounded.

Maybe she wouldn't have to work so hard now he'd gotten work that actually paid. Maybe now that he was earning real money, his folks could go back to acting how they used to. Or maybe his ma would keep on worrying because of who was paying him.

Aiden knew the stuff his ma and pa said about Negroes wasn't even half true. But every time he thought about the way that man Hardy's knife went through his pa's hand and the way his pa screamed and hollered . . . . Aiden shook the image from his mind and turned the knob, opening the door to the sewing shop.

The ladies and Aiden's ma all paused for a moment, some of them looking shocked before their faces slipped into a grimace. They all went back to work like nothing had happened, except for his ma. She gave him a look, too, but he could tell she was trying to smile behind it. She set her work down on the low sewing table in front of her and stood to come greet him at the door.

"Aiden, you're supposed to knock before coming in. You put fear of the Almighty into these women. And your mother," she added, wrinkling her nose at him. "Now what is it?"

She still wasn't the warm and kind lady he remembered from before, but Aiden's ma was in a better mood every time he saw her at work. At least he thought she was. It could be she was just happier than his pa, but then again he could say that about almost anyone.

"Sorry, Ma. About the door. It's just . . . see, I got paid today. I wanted to come tell you first before . . ."

Aiden's ma put a careful hand to his cheek. She knew before what. Before he went up the stairs outside, the rickety wooden ones that ran up the wall of the building like a staircase to the gallows.

"That's really good to hear, Aiden," she said, and he could see she was holding something back. He wanted to ask what she meant to say, but he caught some of the other ladies behind her coughing into their shirts and working their machines extra loud.

"I have to get back now, Aiden. You go upstairs and tell your father the good news. When he wakes up."

Aiden's eyes found the floor before he knew it. "Sure thing," he said and stepped back so she could close the door. Overhead, the dawn sky rolled aside and made room for a weak ray of morning light in between the clouds.

"Tell your father the good news."

"Just like when I got the *Daily Record* gig," Aiden said to himself. "Me and Digs, working for Mr. Brand."

Back then, in Chicago City, his pa took it right when Aiden told him about the job. Clapped him on the back, told him he was a real Conroy now, earning good money for good work. He even poured Aiden a splash out of the bottle he sipped from when Aiden's ma wasn't around.

Good news.

Aiden stepped slow to the staircase and put his hand on the bannister. He looked up at the door to their place. The weathered frame looked like it might fall off the wall any minute. His ma had sewn rags together to stuff into the cracks around the frame, to keep the little heat they had from sneaking out to get swallowed up by the cold.

The front of the building had a nice view of Constance Street, and a sign that read Duffy Dressmakers. The people who went in the front door would never set foot in the alley behind. Only Aiden and his folks and the ladies his ma worked with used the backdoors.

With careful quiet feet, Aiden climbed the stairs, half hoping his pa *would* be asleep when he got in. At the top of the steps, Aiden stopped outside the door, thinking if his pa was awake, maybe he could convince him to go looking for work today.

Aiden knew he was thinking crazy even as the idea went through his mind. What the barman had said was true as could be. Aiden's pa wouldn't be finding work in New Orleans.

The last time the man had gone hunting a job, which was the only time he'd gone out after that day on Magazine Street, he'd just come home silly drunk. Aiden's pa had slipped when he was only halfway up the stairs, and he'd come to rest in a puddle of horse piss. Since then, he'd mostly just been drunk, when he was able to sneak a few coins for hooch, and he hadn't been anything like silly.

It didn't help that the one place his pa probably could find work in a heartbeat was the last place he'd ever think about taking a job. Even though it would mean working side by side with his fellow Irishmen.

"The docks are integrated, Aiden. Like parts of this neighborhood, Negroes and whites side by side. Damn Dagos, too. I know they aren't supposed to care about this," he'd said, holding up his bandaged hand. *"But I don't know about working with coloreds, and I don't want to know about it."*

Well, Aiden figured it was time his pa knew about something other than drink. With hope in his heart, Aiden reached for the door, ready to share his good news, and all the while knowing that nothing he had to say would help his pa feel anything but low. If the man was sober enough to hear a single word.

Aiden's pa was just where he figured he'd be, slumped over the little table with an empty bottle on the floor at his feet. A trail of liquid bled into the floor, adding another stain to the wood, alongside all the others from spilled food and who knew what else.

Looking at his pa now, Aiden got the feeling the room hadn't changed much at all since they'd moved in, and maybe it was to blame for how things had gone for them. Maybe if they'd found nicer digs to start off his pa wouldn't be such an old soak.

"Pa?" Aiden said, stepping up to the man. "Hey, Pa. I got paid, Pa."

It took all his strength, but Aiden kept his hands loose and relaxed while he waited until his old man stirred.

I should give him a sock on the jaw to wake him up.

As quick as the thought came, Aiden swatted it aside. Even

drunk, his old man was bigger and faster than he was, and a fistfight wouldn't solve anything anyway.

Finally, after what felt like a hundred heartbeats, Aiden's pa shifted in his seat and raised his head off the table. He turned a pair of red eyes Aiden's way and let out a sigh that reeked with the stink of old booze.

"Jeez, Pa," Aiden said, unable to control himself. He staggered back and put a hand up over his mouth and nose. "You gotta get cleaned up."

"Huh?" his pa said, glancing around the room like he was looking for the ghost that was tickling his ear. His eyes finally settled on Aiden's face again and they seemed to droop lower than Aiden thought possible, like his old man was just going to melt into his clothes and slide off the chair to disappear between the floorboards.

"That you, son?"

"Yeah," Aiden said, struggling to keep his stomach. Every time his pa opened his mouth, a fog of stink rolled out and filled the room. "It's me, Pa. C'mon and get cleaned up, hey? I'll get the water warming."

Aiden stepped to his left, to go around his old man, but his pa stuck out his good hand and grabbed Aiden by the arm.

"Just . . . a sec, son. Just a sec. How does a guy like you come in here? All cheerful, like it's Christmas day?"

Aiden didn't know what his pa meant exactly, but the sound of his voice said the old man was itching for a fight.

"I-I don't know, Pa. I got paid, though. I got fifteen cents for—"

"*Fifteen cents!*"

Aiden just about jumped out of his skin and stood there shivering while his pa shook and fumed where he sat.

"You got fifteen cents, did you? A whole fifteen cents? And how'd you get it, huh? What'd you have to do for them damn coloreds? Huh? You call yourself a Conroy and you're working for the dark man like he's the boss and you're the flunky. Is that what's got you so happy?

"And you come in here asking me. Me! Al Conroy! You ask me

what's going on. What's happened to your old man. Well I'll tell you what's happened."

"Pa, what's this all about? I just said you should get cleaned up a little. Before Ma comes up for a break. I didn't mean nothing by it, Pa. I just—"

"Yeah, you just. You just. It's your job, son. That's what happened to your old man. You work for them now. Them and the way they live. The things they do. It's like I always knew would happen."

"Whaddya mean, Pa? Like what would happen? I got work, and sure, yeah, it's working for the—well, for colored folks. But they treat me fine, Pa. Their money spends same as yours or mine. And now it's mine. See?"

Aiden reached into his pocket and pulled out the coins, holding them for his father to see, but the man's eyes didn't waver from the distant stare that had fallen over his face.

"Pa? C'mon, Pa. You see . . . ."

But he could already see it in the man's eyes. The way they aimed low and drooped in his face, falling like his heavy cheeks that sagged around his tired mouth, all stubbled and worn from crying and moaning day in and day out. Aiden spilled the three nickels onto the table, then reached out to grab his pa's mitt that hung down by the side of his chair.

His father's hand felt cold, stiff like a dry branch that was ready to snap.

"I'm still here, Aiden. Sure thing. I'm still here. Shouldn't be— Shouldn't have to see me . . . Should be somewheres else. Just forget about me, son. Just forget . . ."

"Pa?" Aiden said, letting go his free hand and reaching for the man's shoulder. For a second, he felt something there, the meat and bone of where his dad's arm joined up with the rest of him. And then Aiden's hand dropped to his own knee, falling right through his old man's body.

Aiden didn't scream. He didn't cry out or whimper. He just let the tears fall as his pa faded into nothing and disappeared from sight.

CHAPTER 20

B RAND LOOKS UP AT THE RICKETY STAIRCASE. Barnaby and his pals all told him to go on and do it, to deliver the mail. Then they shambled off to Metairie and he hasn't seen them since. Brand wants to do the job, but he can't. For two days straight he couldn't do it, and now he's here at the bottom of Conroy's stairs with the envelope feeling like a lead balloon tied around his hips.

Upstairs, Al Conroy is going out like the worst of 'em. Brand feels the old man slipping into the street, down into the pathways of mud. And he can feel the kid up there, too. Waiting.

Does he know? How can he know? I didn't know when the god came for me back in Chicago City.

Brand puts a hand in his pocket and touches the envelope. He wants to open it, but Barnaby's face shows up like a ghost in his mind, flapping its eyelids over those empty holes, and Brand swears he hears the flapping of feathers, too, like some great mythical bird about to come down and rip out his liver. Brand takes his hand out of his pocket and puts it on the railing. He lifts a foot to the bottom step.

A dull hum comes to his ears from the room below the stairs. The kid's mother is in there. Working hard and earning what she can. She's doing right by her son, sure enough. Any dope can tell she loves the kid and doesn't want to see him hurt.

But Brand remembers the woman. He remembers the time she came by the *Daily Record* to "meet Aiden's employer." The way she looked at the delivery men who'd come in with the rolls of newsprint and the barrels of ink. Ink as dark as the skin on some of those men, and the kid's mother skewing her eyes any way she could so she didn't have to look at them.

Brand shakes his head and stares up at the door on the landing above him.

He heaves a deep sigh into his chest and lets it out. Halfway to empty, Brand doubles over and starts coughing. He has to step back into the alley and lean against the wall to keep from falling over. Down the way, at the alley mouth, a horse and buggy stops and the driver sends a bent eye and a few sideways words in Brand's direction.

"Go on then, fella. Spit it out," the driver says and laughs as he whips his nag to move along.

Brand does spit, but he's careful to wait until the driver can't see him do it. He knows his place in New Orleans, same as it'd be if he was back in Chicago City.

Bottom of the barrel. World's got no use for old war dogs. Even ones like me who showed the world what war really is and finally got 'em to call it quits.

Brand takes a deep breath to clear his head and his chest. He remembers the men he photographed in the trenches. He remembers their stories, the ones they told him before going over the wall and into the meat grinder.

The creak of a door breaks him from his stupor and Brand spins around to see the Conroy kid aiming a pair of red-rimmed eyes at him from up on the landing. He's standing there in the morning air in his shirtsleeves and with no hat on his head.

It's just like Brand figured it would be. The kid stands there with those ghosts of the god circling him and he doesn't even know it. Brand stares at Conroy for a solid silent minute, which he counts in his head while he watches the god make its way into the kid's chest.

He has no idea how bright his eyes look now, Brand thinks.

"How'd you know we was here, Mr. Brand?" the kid asks. Brand runs a hand down his face and pulls on his whiskers before he answers.

"Same as I knew where you were back in Memphis," he says. "You remember me. As long as that's still true, I'll be able to find you when I need to."

The last few words don't get past the kid's ears. "What do you mean, *need to*? What'd we do now? Is this about Pa going out? You know where he is, don't you?" he says, making Brand think he should've just dropped the envelope and ran off.

But you gotta to stick around. Do the job right if you're gonna do it at all.

"Easy, Conroy. Easy," Brand says. "Yeah, I know about your old man. But it's not what you think. At least—"

"Well what is it then?" the kid asks, coming down a few steps. He's got one hand on the railing and the other on the wall, but Brand sees the kid's careful not to hold on too tight on either side. The wood's rough, and Brand figures the kid's gotten more than a few bites from splinters and old nails. He's learned to watch out for his own skin.

"It's—" Brand starts to say, but can't get the words out yet. The envelope is heavier now, even heavier than yesterday, and it's going on three days since he got it. But it's not so heavy that Brand can't move his feet, and so he does, backing away from the staircase where the kid's standing like he's ready to take a swing at anyone or anything that gets near him.

"Well what is it?" the kid says. "What d'you know about my old man, Mr. Brand?"

"I know your old man's not the same man he used to be. He hasn't been the same since the night he fell down the stairs and got himself stained with the street."

Brand can tell the kid's hot under his shirt, even in the chill morning. There's a fire burning in Conroy's chest, and if Brand isn't careful, that fire'll come out and burn them both down.

"Stained? What do you mean?"

"I mean he's one of them now. Or will be soon."

"One of who? You mean like you? But he ain't killed hisself. He just vanished," the kid gets out. Then the tears come, and Brand can tell they've got twice as much behind them as they did before.

"I'm sorry, Conroy," Brand says. "I couldn't stop it, and even if I could've, that would've just made it worse on all of us."

"Why?" Aiden says, still shaking and shivering with his sobs. But that fire's still burning hot inside him, so Brand plays it slow and even. The envelope feels like a block of lead, dragging him down, so he leans against the wall and tries to forget why he's really here.

"Your old man . . . he was marked," Brand says, jabbing a finger at his own hand to remind the kid about his pa getting stabbed. "I've seen it in the other fellas. And they've told me as much. After a man gets marked, it's only a matter of time before he goes wrong, starts doing things to make other people forget about him because he can't bear to remember himself."

The kid looks at him with something like confusion on his mug, but his eyes are shining now, bright with flame that dries up the tears in a flash.

"Yeah? And what else? You know it all, is that it? Because you're one of them, so you get to know everything about how it all works. Is that it?"

Brand wants to tell the kid to cool it, just like he used to back on the mooring deck in Chicago City, when the kid and his pals would pitch a fit over who got the best-paying beat for the morning edition.

"Look, Conroy, I'm not—"

"How about Aiden? My name's *Aiden*. I think you can remember that, can't you? Can't you?" he asks, and the tears are coming again, but slower this time, more like Brand figures they should come. Steady and strong, but only because the tap's been left open and the kid just doesn't know how to shut it. Not yet anyway.

"Okay, Aiden. Sure thing, I can remember your name. Just like I remember your pals from back in Chicago City. Pete Gordon and Ross Jenkins. Remember them?"

The kid sniffs and wipes a hand over his face. He takes a few more steps down, so he's almost eye level to Brand now, but still a little above him.

"Yeah," he says. "I remember Digs and Ross. They were good guys."

"Ain't that the truth, hey?" Brand says, feeling a smile creep up his face, but only letting it get halfway there. The kid's not ready to smile yet, or at least isn't showing signs of it.

"My pa didn't like me working with Jenkins. He said he was mixed. Passing white, but wasn't really. Is that true?"

Brand can't hide his surprise. The kid is hot all right. Hot and sharp and ready to cut through anything.

"Yes. It's true, Aiden. But you knew that already. And so did Digs Gordon. You both knew it, and you didn't say anything to anyone."

The kid shakes his head. "No. I didn't have to, though. My ma figured it and I heard her telling Pa that night, after she came by the *Record* to meet you and the other fellas. She told him and then he told me he didn't like it. Just like he didn't like the gig I got now."

Something lights up in the kid's face. It isn't fire this time, but more like a lightbulb going on.

"That's why, isn't it? That's why he's gone. Because of the gig I got. But I had to get work, Mr. Brand." The kid's face goes plain and in a second it's like he hasn't been crying at all. His eyes get sharper, and his mouth stops shaking like it'll jump off his face. "I had to earn something so we could make it here. Ma's only getting a fin a week down in the sewing shop, and she spends all day in there, sun up to sun down."

"You and your folks got it rough," Brand says, nodding and aiming his eyes at the kid's feet now. "No question about it. And yeah, maybe your pop didn't care much for the job you're doing. But that alone wouldn't have done it."

Brand lifts his eyes, testing the waters. He can tell the god's working its way into the kid, making him into whatever it needs him to be. So far so good, though. The kid's still in charge of himself and won't go lighting into Brand like a flamethrower if he makes a bad step.

"Your old man went on a bender a short while back. Some of the other fellas were there. Saw him do it. Then he landed himself on the street, slipping down those stairs you're on. The gods figure the street is where he'd rather be, and today's the day he got set up with his own little corner of New Orleans to call home."

"The gods," the kid says and throws a sniff at the sky. "You mean the ones you work for?"

"That'd be them," Brand says, wondering if now's the time to spill it, but he holds the words on his tongue and finds new ones to share. "You know, it isn't like I can send word up the chain that they should do things different by your old man."

"Where is he now?" Aiden asks, his voice raising with each word. "Where'd he go? Where's my dad?"

Brand feels his face go glum as can be. "He's on the street, Aiden. Probably down a few blocks and over a few more. Could be anywhere, but usually a fella starts out near enough to where he goes out. Least that's how I've heard it. If your old man plays his cards right, he'll be in the same place everyday unless he's running messages. Just like me and the other fellas."

"Well how come you're not out there, too? How come my dad has to sit in the gutter, but you get to—"

Brand watches the kid stew and chew on whatever's going through his mind. It's clear enough he expects an answer, so Brand thinks for a second, trying to put the words in the right order. "I came here . . . so I could be with you when it happened. No kid should have to watch his old man slide into the street on his own. I'm sorry I was late," Brand says, hoping the kid'll buy it straight. He doesn't, though.

"C'mon and spill it, hey? What else?"

Brand puts his hands at his sides and looks Aiden in the eye. "I'm sorry, Aiden. I shouldn't have waited, but . . ."

Brand takes a step back at first; he can feel the kid wanting to take a swing at him. "You know how I earn my keep now. Playing the mailboy. Right?"

"Yeah. Like the fellas back in Chicago City. Only you're not gonna turn into a monster, are ya?"

"No, Con—Aiden. No, I'm not. But . . . Well, maybe you'll think differently after you see this." Brand reaches into his pocket and feels the heavy envelope. He pinches it with two fingers, but it's like a brick and he has to put his whole hand in to lift it free.

Aiden closes his mouth as Brand lifts the envelope out of his pocket. "This . . . this is for you," he finally says, holding out the message.

Aiden's eyes round in fear, and then grow tight with rage. He flings himself down the stairs and shoves past Brand on his way down the alley. Brand tries to catch at his coat or scarf, but his fingers only grab empty air. At the alley mouth, the kid stops short, with one foot aimed forward and his trailing leg fishing around for a place to land, like he wants to come back but has to force himself to do it.

"You should tell your ma, at least," Brand says to the kid's back.

"You tell her," the kid says. "Tell her I went to the church to pray for my pa."

And then the kid's gone, out the alley mouth and down the stem, leaving Brand with an envelope in his hand and the taste of bile in his mouth.

CHAPTER 21

EMMA WRAPPED HER COAT AROUND HER TO keep the chill away, but it didn't matter how much she pulled or tugged. The evening air off the Gulf was still cold and sly enough that it found a way in and set her shivering. Another mixed couple sat a ways down the streetcar on the opposite bench, and a lone man stood at the far end, near the conductor's box. The other couple chatted while the car sliced and scraped on the rails as they went around corners and took curves.

New Orleans slid past the windows, a blur of brick and stone and ramshackle wood. Eddie's arm went around Emma. She leaned against him, careful not to put too much pressure on his chest or side. He'd healed up pretty good in the two weeks since they left Chicago City, but he was still sore in places, and it was almost a sure thing one of his ribs didn't knit right.

Good luck earning enough for a sawbones to fix it right.

Bacchus set them up with his doctor that first night, but he'd made no further offers for another visit to the man's clinic. He'd given Eddie work playing with a band at shows in the Ninth Ward, leaving Emma on her own at home for a week of lonely nights full of worry. Then last night Bacchus came by and told Eddie to spiffy up for his next gig. He even gave Eddie a new suit and shoes.

"Gotta look the man when you in my gala house, Mr. Eddie Collins."

They were on the way to the gala house now, for a heel kick like they used to have back home. Emma didn't know what was so special about the house or the dancing that it had to be called a *gala*. Bacchus was big time in New Orleans, but so far she hadn't seen him do anything that rivaled the mayor's events back in Chicago City.

"Gig like this bring real money in," Eddie said as they sat in the rocking and swaying streetcar. "Not like them little shows I been doin'."

Emma just nodded. So tonight they'd find out what real money was in New Orleans. The thought gave her only a little comfort.

Until now, Eddie had been playing for whatever change he could get. It was okay money. Eating money. Rent money, for their place and for the mooring deck Bacchus had moved the *Vigilance* to. The tavern where Eddie usually played in the Ninth Ward was just like Hardy's place, standing beneath a mooring deck. The *Vigilance* still hung there. Emma could see the ship in her mind, bobbing on its tethers like it wanted for all the world just to fly again.

As the streetcar rolled on, Emma thought about the airship and the first time she'd set foot in it.

The first time she'd ever shot a man down.

The ghosts of her life in Chicago City had begun eating at her in the past week. Eddie had work. They had a roof, and they could eat okay. But everything Emma could claim now came from Eddie, and rich man's daughter or not, she wasn't used to being so dependent on someone else for survival.

The one thing she'd sworn not to do was to let her and Eddie's love turn into the kind of thing she'd seen happen to so many girls back in Chicago City:

The guy comes along and it's nice for a while. And then it's back in the house while he's out in the world earning his keep and yours.

"Eddie," she said, half asking and half demanding his attention.

"Yeah, Lovebird. What's what?"

He was happy. Dammit, why did these questions come to her mind when he was in a good mood? It'd be easier to challenge what they had if he showed some sign of discomfort, too.

"Eddie, what about me finding some work? I mean tonight. Do you think Bacchus—"

"You like to asking the *krewe* boss? You're crazy, girl." He grinned as he said it, but Emma couldn't ignore the sincerity in his voice.

"What's crazy about it?" she said. "I'm sick of warming the home fires while you're out every night. If you're afraid of upsetting the man, why not let me ask him? What's the worst he can do?"

Eddie's face went hangdog dark. "Emma, you don' wanna know what's the worst he can do. Look, Lovebird, lemme get us on our feet again, hey? Get something under us, like we used to have."

"When did we have something under us? When I wasn't on the run for killing Archie Falco? Or for loving you?" She kept her voice down, but the last words came off her tongue with more force than she'd expected. Eddie's face showed it, too.

"I'm sorry, Eddie. I didn't mean . . ."

"I know, Lovebird. Don' mean nothin'. You just tense is all. Come on join the dancin' tonight. You can hear me play and dance with whoever you like. Just remember whose lips are for kissin' and whose for sayin', 'Thank you for the dance.'"

He laughed and stroked her under the chin with this finger. Emma laughed, too. Inside, she still felt that same bubbling joy of love for him, and his touch never failed to remind her of the way it had once been. In Chicago City, their love was a secret saved for late nights after speakeasy sessions, and it had been fabulous. Fun and forbidden. But fabulous. Sure it wasn't perfect, but the city streets were only dangerous if they were seen together.

Now, in New Orleans, they could cuddle and kiss on a streetcar in plain view and nobody'd bat an eye. But was it better than what they'd had before?

The streetcar slowed and rolled to a stop in front of a high house with tall windows and a set of steps leading up to an open door that spilled light and laughter into the night. A heavy in a suit waited by the door with his hands clasped in front of his belt.

"Our stop," Eddie said. "Come on in with me, Lovebird."

"I can't, Eddie. Not tonight. Maybe next time."

Emma looked away from his eyes to take in the nearly empty car. Up front, by the conductor's box, the lone man stepped off.

The other couple stood and made their way to the exit doors, too.

"Gotta go now, Lovebird," Eddie said. "You sure you don't wan—"

"I'll walk you in, Eddie," Emma said, feeling her gut go tight all of a sudden. Her mind flashed to a memory of the last words Mitchell Brand had for her.

"When his pals down here find out you're around, it's as much your head as mine."

Emma let a shiver run through her and take those memories with it.

"You okay, Emma?"

"Fine, Eddie. Just a little cold I guess," she said, and hoped he wouldn't see the fear she felt behind her eyes.

Together, she and Eddie rose and stepped off the car through the same door the other couple had used. The gala house rose before them like the greatest mansion in the city, but the shotgun shacks to either side of it said different. They'd come to an older portion of the Central City district. Across the way, shopfronts stood in a row, decorated with hand-painted signs and sandwich boards proclaiming all sorts of finery for sale.

Gaslight glowed from within a few of the shops, but most had the steady warmth of electric lighting spilling out of windows and doorways. Emma wondered why the shops were open at first, but soon enough a parade of couples emerged from every nook and cranny. The women wore gowns and seemed to perch on the arms of their male companions. Some couples were dark-skinned but it was mostly mixed couples moving among the throng.

As the crowd approached, Emma had to stifle a gasp. The women weren't women at all. Just girls, and not one of them could be much past age yet. They were close, sure, but it was clear enough from their wide eyes and tight lips that these girls were on the town for damn near the first time in their young lives. And the men. They were all of them easily twice the age of any girl in the bunch.

Each of the girls wore a corsage on her wrist, and the men all had boutonnières pinned to their lapels. The flowers looked fresh and sparkling clean, like they'd just been bought across the street. As the last couple passed by and went up the stairs, Emma's breath caught in her throat and she spun to the side.

That man.

She knew him. He was a banker from New York City. He'd been at a party her father hosted for the mayor back home, almost a year before her debutante. The Great Lakes Governor had been there, along with the governors from the Southern Territory and Eastern Seaboard, too.

That man came with the Eastern Seaboard group, and when her father had introduced them, the man shook her hand for a good long time. Long enough for his eyes to take off every piece of clothing she'd had on.

"Eddie," Emma whispered as the couples lined up with the doorman, waiting to get into the gala house. "What is this? They're just debs. And the men—"

"Just how they do things down New Orleans way," he said. "Mr. Bacchus run the balls down here. Debutantes come out with daddies and uncles. Big brothers, too. Learn a few steps 'fore they go findin' a man of they own."

"Eddie, most of those men are white."

"I know, I know. And how do you think a white man calls a Negro girl his daughter or his niece? You ever look at me and you in a mirror, Lovebird?"

Eddie smiled and kissed her. She let his lips press against hers and she pushed back to make sure he didn't mistake her feelings, even though she wasn't so sure of anything she felt at that moment.

They separated and Emma waited while Eddie straightened his jacket and smoothed his slacks. With a quick jerk, he shot his cuffs and, Emma noticed, only winced for half a second or less.

He is getting better.

Then Eddie looked Emma in the eye. He kissed her again and went up the steps to speak to the doorman.

Emma let him go even though she wished he'd stay. She couldn't ignore the stabbing worry building in her gut like tangled barbed wire.

Maybe it was like Eddie said. Just how things were done down here.

But that man from New York . . .

Lights glowed behind sheer drapes in every window and silhouettes moved in rhythm to a soft lilting piano played somewhere deeper in the house. The tinkling strains of the music came to Emma's ears as if on a breeze that sighed and sang at once, melancholy as can be.

Emma stepped back onto the streetcar. Other passengers boarded at the far end, by the conductor's box, each one flashing a badge of passage to the little gray-haired man who drove the streetcar. The couples looked like they'd just left the gala house, some of them stumbled and all of them laughed, even the girls. Emma felt her heart relax, but her gut kept up its twisting and turning.

Up on the steps, Eddie was going inside. Emma called out to him.

"Good-bye, Eddie. Good luck tonight."

Her heart grew heavy in her chest when Eddie stepped through the door and disappeared inside, not even turning to look back and wave.

CHAPTER 22

MAMA SHANDY, THE HOUSE MOTHER, shook her head at Aiden, who stood in the middle of the dance hall, feet sopping wet and his pants soaked up to his knees. He had his eyes on her knees, but she was a lot shorter than him, so he could still see the way she snarled her dark face. She narrowed her eyes at him. Behind her little gold-framed glasses, those eyes looked like knives she'd stick him with if he put one toe out of line.

"Boy, you need learnin' you wanna keep this job. Who the hell taught you to work a mop that way? Your momma? Your daddy?"

Aiden held his tongue, forcing the anger to stay in his chest where it belonged. Earlier that same night, he'd seen what happened to boys who spoke out of turn or "gave sass" to a house mother. But he couldn't deny everything he felt, and a few tears of rage leaked out.

"Oh, you gonna cry on me now, boy? Damn if you ain't worth half the money I paid for you. Now get on with the moppin', an' don' you go addin' them tears to the bucket. Ain't no good cleanin' a floor with tears, boy. And you think twice before raisin' them eyes to me, Dove. Damn Birdman gonna take one of 'em. You can count on that."

Aiden kept his eyes on the floor until the house mother left by the far door.

Back and forth he worked the mop, slow and careful, like his pa showed him the few times he'd gone to the Field Museum to watch the man work. His pa had been gone a week now. His ma worried herself to sleep every night, and Aiden didn't know how to help. When he'd run out on Mr. Brand he'd gone to the church, hoping Father James would offer up a hand. Instead, the man sent word to the house mother, who came around lickety-split, almost like she was waiting in the vestry.

Or maybe she was one of them. Like Mr. Brand and the man who'd marked Aiden's pa. Or like Aiden himself? But he knew that was crazy as crazy can get.

What if Mr. Brand wasn't fooling, though? What if he meant it, about the letter?

Aiden didn't feel any different, though, and he sure as heck couldn't slip in and out of a room like a ghost. If he could, he'd have disappeared the minute Mama Shandy came stepping into the church with a hand on her hip and trouble on her tongue.

Father James had offered words of comfort to Aiden and held him while he cried. That must have been when the priest had made a signal at the altar boy who was there. Because that boy came back in with Mama Shandy in tow.

She'd handed Father James a few coins and some folding money, then waltzed out the door wagging a finger for Aiden to follow.

"C'mon now, Dove. You work for Mama Shandy now."

The priest offered Aiden a quick prayer before he spun on his heel and disappeared out a side door. With thoughts of his father lying drunk on the street like a no-good tramp, and his mother drifting around their little room like a ghost herself, Aiden did the only thing he could do.

He'd followed Mama Shandy out of the church, stepping lively to keep up. Even as short as she was, she moved fast and too strides that made Aiden have to step fast to stay with her. Now, instead of fifteen cents for cleaning the workhouse for that colored couple, Aiden would earn eight cents from Mama Shandy for cleaning the floors in her gala houses.

Nobody'd told him, but Aiden put two and two together. The workhouse he'd cleaned that first night was like a practice joint where musicians would work up their acts for the gala houses. The couple who owned it was probably in debt to Mama Shandy. The gala houses she owned weren't like the workhouse, either. They had something special that went on, something different. Aiden didn't know how different, but he knew enough not to ask Mama Shandy to explain it to him.

Aiden cleaned the floor with even strokes, just like he'd seen his pa do, all the while thinking of how much he'd like to take the mop to Mama Shandy's head. He quickly pushed that thought away, because if anything he did would lead to him to a bad end, *that* would be it.

When he'd finished, Aiden hoisted the bucket of grimy water onto his cleaning cart and rung out the mop until it was dry as could be. The floor didn't sparkle, but it was clean.

He'd earned another eight cents at least, maybe ten if Mama Shandy felt generous. Aiden sniffed at the idea. Like Mama Shandy would ever feel generous toward a white boy like him. A white boy she'd had to buy off the church. He'd meant to tell his ma all about what happened, but he figured it was better to save it, or just pretend like nothing had changed at all. His ma didn't need more worry to bend her back.

Aiden snugged his wool cap down tight, buttoned his coat, and patted the pocket where he kept his badge of passage. Then he opened the pay box outside the door. Aiden felt around in the box and came up with . . .

Six cents.

He swallowed his anger and pocketed the coins. Then he pulled the now ripped and tattered little green book out of his pocket and checked his way home. He'd learned the streets well enough, but still needed to know for sure he was going the right way.

Once he'd settled his mind, Aiden stuffed the book down into his pocket again and wheeled his cart down from the house to the street. A block along, Aiden poured his mop water into the gutter and watched it race away toward the river, wishing he could move half as fast.

Just another ten blocks to home.

A whisper caught his attention when Aiden passed an alley a little ways on. He peered into the dark space between two shotgun shacks and spotted a collection of houseboys, just like him, except they were all Negroes. They were bundled in coats and caps and huddled around a window. Their carts stood in a tangle, jumbled together behind them.

"C'mon, Dove," said one of the boys who spotted him. "C'mon, now." The boy smiled at Aiden right enough, and waved him forward, like he was a friend.

Aiden knew he should just push his cart home. But Mama Shandy's words echoed in his head.

"They your krewe now, Dove. All them houseboys workin' this town. They the only friends you got, so you better learn to keep 'em."

He'd nodded and said, "Yes'm." But he hadn't needed Mama Shandy's lesson. The word *krewe* told him well enough where he belonged. This bunch of dirty, rag-bare, underfed kids who pushed mops for pennies were his *krewe.* Whatever they didn't have, they were still the only friends he had in New Orleans.

"C'mon now, Dove," the boy said again, coming closer to the alley mouth. He smiled big and waved Aiden forward again. Looking once more down the street in the direction he should be going, Aiden wheeled his cart around and followed the boy into the alley.

Leaving his cart next to the others, Aiden joined the huddle. The boys all circled the space outside the window that let a glow of warm light into the alley. Craning his neck to see, Aiden got a view inside the room. A single man wearing a white jacket and trousers sat at a table shuffling a deck of cards. The brim of a white fedora hid the man's face.

"Who is he?" Aiden asked.

The other boys all chuckled and broke into a fit of laughter.

"You ain't heard 'bout the Ghost, an' you a houseboy?" said one.

"Ain't been out in the dark long enough yet," said another. "Dove got skin still white like rice. Maybe he a ghost, too."

A third boy, the biggest of the bunch, laughed loud and long, his voice ringing rich in the alley like the sound of a man shouting into a barrel. "Oh, Dove. You best fly away home now 'fore you get plucked."

Aiden shook, both from fright and anger. He'd gotten used to being called a "dove," but the way these boys used the word it felt like being socked in the gut and slapped across the mouth.

"I ain't no damn *dove* and I ain't a gambler," he said, turning on his heel to go. The first boy, the one who'd called him in, grabbed him by the wrist and pleaded with him to stick around.

"C'mon now. Ain't like that, Dove. We don' mean nothin' by it. Just what you called, you know? You new in town, any fool know that. We just tryin' to learn you how it go round New Orleans."

Aiden felt his heart settle its rhythm, but he still had nothing but angry eyes for the bigger boy who'd warned him about being plucked. The first boy let go of Aiden's wrist and held out his hand instead.

"Name's Julien Durand. Call me Jules if you wanna. Call me Julie an I take your eye quicker'n the Birdman do it." The boy still smiled at Aiden but with a look in his eyes that said he wasn't fooling.

"Aiden. Or Conroy, if you want."

"Conroy. All right. Hey y'all. This here's Conroy. Greet him up."

One by one the boys looked up and waved, some extended hands that Aiden shook. They all said names that Aiden heard but couldn't keep stuck in his mind. Aiden did his best to keep up with them; he could tell they were all younger than he was, and some younger than Julien, too. But try as he might, Aiden couldn't focus on the boys around him. His eyes kept going back to the man with the cards.

The boys all seemed to understand, or at least didn't care if he caught their names or not. Finally the big one who'd talked about plucking Aiden's feathers came up and stuck out a hand, and Aiden was forced to draw his attention from the man in the white suit.

"Theo Valcour," the older boy said, his voice heavy and rich as before, but with less of the malice Aiden felt the first time. They shook hands and then Julien put a hand on Aiden's shoulder, turning him to the window. The other boys had settled back into position around the patch of light that came into the alley. Inside, the man stayed rigid, almost like a gearbox that had been turned off.

"What're we watchin' him shuffle cards for?" Aiden asked, nudging Julien.

"Man called the Ghost," Julien said. "He used to be way up in Bacchus's *krewe*, but now he down low. Ain't nobody seen him around for almost two months gone."

"Where'd he go?"

"Nobody know. Ain't the first time he go missin' like that, though. Birdman take his eye back when, right about New Years time. Then Ghost come back and win Mr. B's debutante game. And he let the girl go. Least that what everybody sayin' he did. Then he go away again, and that was two months back. People sayin' he off earnin' for some other *krewe*, but me, I think he off with that girl he won."

"Girl? What—?"

Before Aiden could ask the rest of his question, the big boy, Theo Valcour, piped up.

"He playin' pyramid. Look."

The boys all crowded closer around the window, peering into the glowing room. Aiden stood on tiptoe and put a hand on the wall to balance himself over the smaller boys beneath him. The white-suited man in the house had laid out a pattern of cards in a pyramid shape, and now sat with his hands on either side of the display. About half the deck of cards stayed stacked up at the bottom of the pyramid.

Theo Valcour's deep voice broke the silence again. "Who says he make it in one? How 'bout it, Dove?"

Aiden knew well enough what he was being asked, even if he couldn't put together a reply with the same words. He also knew that gambling away the six cents he'd just earned would be the dumbest move he could make. He shook his head.

"I'll just watch," he said.

The boy looked like Aiden had just claimed to be the lord and savior of all mankind. Then all the boys began talking at once, and Aiden's heart skipped as the din swelled around him.

The smallest boy, the one right in front of Aiden, stuck a hand out at Theo Valcour. Aiden saw a nickel pinched between the boy's fingers. "I got five say he make it in one."

"Takin' it," came Theo's reply.

"Two say he make it in three," another boy said.

"Fool's bet. I'm takin' that," Theo said back.

And on it went, bets placed and answers given in a pattern like a dance that Aiden had never seen, but he could feel the rhythm of it, and he promised himself he'd learn the steps someday soon. When it was done and all the boys had gone quiet, Aiden felt his lips moving before he knew it.

"Six says he makes it."

A crush of faces turned on him, some wearing questions, others something between a question and disgust. Julien helped Aiden out of the jam he'd stepped in.

"Make it in how many? You gotta say how many you think he gon' make it in."

The other boys sniffed and went back to watching the window. Some chuckled, and Aiden caught Theo's muttering.

"Dove gon' get plucked."

All around the circle came whispers and nods of agreement, except from Julien who kept his eyes on Aiden like he was waiting for an answer.

"Two," Aiden said, only half knowing what he'd just bet would happen. Nobody replied to take his bet, but he didn't think that much mattered. Somebody, somewhere, would call things to account. Aiden didn't know how he knew that, but it wasn't up for arguing in his mind.

"He'll make it in two," he said, nodding his head with a sudden confidence he felt in his chest.

The instant the last word left his lips, the man in the house moved his hands on the cards. Starting at the bottom he paired up sets and removed them. Sometimes the man would draw a card and pair it with the one previously drawn. Other times he'd draw three or four in a row before making a match. At last, with only two cards left to be drawn, the man paused.

The playing field still showed at least a half dozen cards, and even though he didn't know the rules to the game, it was clear enough to Aiden that the man wouldn't be "making it in one."

Theo and a few other boys shook their heads, all of them except for Julien and the one boy who'd bet on "three." The others stomped away from the window. Theo and one boy shuffled their feet, talking quiet as they left the alley. Aiden listened to the scrape and clatter of wooden wheels on stone as the boys pushed their carts along and into the night.

Soon enough the alley went silent, all but for Aiden and Julien's breathing. The other boy had his hands in front of his mouth and a look on his face that said he thought he'd struck gold.

The man inside picked up his thin stack of cards and made his final draws. One more set was matched. The man took the stack of drawn cards, flipped it over, and drew through again.

After the first five cards the game was over. The man had finished removing all the face-up cards from the table. He shuffled the deck together again and set the cards aside.

The third boy shouted and threw a punch at the night. Tears spilled down his face and he ran out of the alley, coming back seconds later to grab his cart. Aiden felt his heart hammering in his chest. He worried the boy might try some kind of knockover, make a grab for Aiden's money.

The guy just kicked at the ground, though, and screamed at the night. He took off, slamming his cart against a waste bin by the house across the alley. Then he shoved his cart into the street and followed it, and Aiden heard his shouting and hollering fading into the distance, like a train whistle going down the line.

Julien's voice snapped him out of it. "We won, Dove. Me an' you bet he'd take two. An' he did."

"Yeah," Aiden said, looking at the man in the house. "But so what. Theo and the others all left, so who's gonna pay up on our bet?"

In that instant, Aiden knew he'd been a sap.

There ain't no house, so who's gonna make the payouts?

He was shaken from his thoughts when the man looked at him and Julien. His face beneath the brim of his fedora looked ashen white, pale as the full moon, but Aiden saw that was just the way the lamplight glowed against his pale brown skin. The man turned his head some more and the fullness of his color came clear to Aiden.

But the only thing Aiden could focus on was the patch that covered the Ghost's right eye.

"Ghost don' mess around," Julien said from beside Aiden. "He used to be way up, like I say. Then he lose his eye to the Birdman, but he don' end up in the street."

"Who's the Birdman?"

"Ain't time for a history lesson now, Dove. You bet. You gotta put in."

"Huh?" Aiden asked, then noticed Julien had an old can in his hands. He shook it and Aiden heard the rattle and clink of coins against the sides.

Aiden fished into his pocket and drew out the six pennies he'd *earned* from Mama Shandy. With his heart beating and sweat burning on his neck and under his shirt, Aiden dropped the coins into the can. Julien smiled and huffed a little laugh. Then he reached to the wall beside the window and opened a small iron door Aiden hadn't noticed before.

"Ghost probably gon' cover us. Or maybe nothin' happen, we jus' get our money back. But I'm thinkin' he gon' cover us."

Julien put the can in and stepped back to close the metal door. Inside the house, the man in the white suit stood up and came to the wall. Aiden heard the squeak of small hinges, and the sound of coins *plinking* and *plunking* into the can. The hinges squeaked again and the Ghost went back to his table where he fished a cigarette case out of his jacket.

Aiden watched the man light up while Julien opened the metal door on their side of the wall. The can was still there. Julien reached for it and hefted it from the box. Aiden could tell right away that it held more than they'd put in to begin with.

Aiden felt himself grin, big and happy as Julien shook the can, and he saw Julien's face light up just the same.

"Hah! My momma's gon' be happy to see me come home tonight," Julien said.

Aiden silently thought about his mother and what her face would look like when he told her how much money he'd brought home, and then how it would look when he told her he'd won it gambling.

"How'd you know?" he asked.

"Know what, Dove?"

"About the can. And that he'd pay up."

"Ghost don' mess around, like I said. He say he gon' do somethin', he do it," Julien said, pointing at a sign tacked up on the wall beside the metal door. Aiden hadn't spied the sign before, and reading it now he felt his heart skip a beat.

ALL BETS PAID, GUARANTEED
HOUSEBOYS ESPECIALLY ARE ENCOURAGED TO PLAY
100 TO 1 ODDS

"Hold out your hands now," Julien said. Aiden did as he was

told and his eyes nearly fell out of his head when a torrent of coins spilled from the mouth of the can and splashed off his fingers. Julien kept up his pouring and the coins kept up their jingling and jangling on the pavement at Aiden's feet.

CHAPTER 23

BEING CAREFUL NOT TO PRESS TOO TIGHT, EMMA slid her hands down Eddie's body to rest at his waist. He'd healed up good, sure enough. But she still caught him moving slow now and then, and he winced whenever he leaned to the side. Emma let her eyes drift to the window. Rain fell in sheets outside.

A good old fashioned Gulf Coast downpour.

Emma thought about the rain like it had been brought in just for them. Just for tonight.

"You don't have to go again, do you Eddie? It's pouring down outside, and you're still—"

He stiffened and placed his hands on her arms. His touch was soft, be she felt the pressure to release him all the same. Too late she realized she'd clasped her hands to his sides. He gave a short cry and breathed in sharp.

"I'm sorry, Eddie!" she said, leaving her hands where they were even as she relaxed her touch.

It was worse when he was up on stage. The music inside him

had to come out, and if he wasn't playing, he'd sway and tap his feet to the rhythm. After that first gala house session, the *krewe* boss had given Eddie a new horn. He'd started playing on the side of the stage, but tonight Eddie would be out front, like he was the band leader. Emma was happy he had his music again, even if the demands of playing caused him pain, and she couldn't let herself feel anything but guilt about that.

"Gotta get on, Lovebird. Krewe waitin' on Mr. Collins to bring his horn to the show. Can't disappoint, you know?"

Emma knew, and she kept her fear and resentment hidden behind a thin smile. Ever since the *krewe* had adopted Eddie as one of their own, he'd been more and more ready to fly from their nest on a moment's notice. That first time he'd asked her to go with him, and Emma had believed he truly felt torn between staying home with her and heading out to play with the band.

That hadn't lasted long. One week and three shows later and Eddie was champing at the bit to leave her alone on the wettest night she'd seen since they arrived.

"I know, Eddie," Emma said, looking around at the mildewed pile of sticks they called a house. "We'll never get a better place around us if we don't have the scratch to buy one. But—"

Emma was interrupted by a heavy knocking on the front door.

"Guess the *krewe* got tired of waitin' on me," Eddie said, pushing her arms away and turning to open the door. Emma bit her tongue and kept her hands hovering in the air in front of her.

Eddie opened the door and froze. When Emma saw who was standing on the stoop, she went still, too, only moving her hands to smooth her skirt.

The *krewe* boss rapped the end of his gold-tipped stick on the threshold and opened his wide mouth in a toothy grin. Another glimmer of yellow metal adorned his waistcoat. Emma held her breath as the man who all but owned her and Eddie's lives lifted a dazzling pocket watch and checked the face.

"About forty minutes left, my very good man, Mr. Collins. Forty minutes. Before the very big show."

"Yessir," Eddie said, stepping aside so the bigger man could enter. "We was—I mean, me. I was just on my way now, Mr. Bacchus. I was just—"

The *krewe* boss waved a hand, his gold-flecked eyes glowing with reflected gaslight. "Never you mind about what you was just, Mr. Eddie Collins. Never you mind. Tonight you ride with Mr. Bacchus in his chariot."

Eddie's eyes rounded in surprise tinged with worry, and Emma felt her eyes being drawn into the same tight circles. The *krewe* boss pursed his lips and then erupted with laughter that shook the house. Emma's feet tingled with the motion in the floor and her ears rang deep with Bacchus's bellowed gusts.

"You two," the big man said between laughs. "You two got no reason to fear. Mr. Bacchus means you no harm. Not an ounce, not a sliver."

The *krewe* boss snapped his thick fingers and rapped the tip of his stick on the floorboards. Two liveried white servants appeared, both dripping wet. One entered and quickly snatched up Eddie's horn in its case before exiting just as fast to stand on the stoop. The man opened an umbrella he'd held by his side and used it to keep the instrument case dry.

The second servant entered carrying a paper-wrapped bundle in his arms. He held it out and carefully peeled back the wrapped so that Bacchus could lift the contents in one of his thick mitts. With a quick shake, he unfolded a heavy fur coat, nearly as fine and fancy as the one the gangster wore draped around his thick frame.

"Miss Emma," Bacchus said. "To keep out the cold, I thought this coat would suffice. May I?" He gestured as if to drape it around her and Emma felt herself turning her back to the man, like her body knew what it wanted even as her mind screamed at her to run out of the room.

The coat sat heavy on her, and the warmth instantly came through to her bones, filling her with comfort like she hadn't known since she was a child in Chicago City. Her father had given her a coat just like this one for her sixteenth birthday.

Heavy, warm. And nothing like what she'd really wanted.

"It's . . . it's very nice, Mr. Bacchus," she said. "Thank you."

"You are welcome, Miss Emma. Very welcome. Now, if you will accompany me," Bacchus said, extending his hand as if to usher her and Eddie outside.

The servant stayed just inside the door with an umbrella in one hand, held outside to cover the stoop. Emma watched droplets of water fall from the man's clothing to mark the dirty wooden floor beneath his feet. In a flash, faster than his bulk should have allowed, Bacchus whipped a hand out and across the servant's face, sending him stumbling out the door.

"Damn stupid white boy," Bacchus said. "Getting wet on the floor inside Mr. Collins' home. The very ground he walks on is worth more than the two of you put together."

Emma's face went stony as the scene before her recalled a childhood memory, and the coat felt more and more like a cage she couldn't leave. On that same sixteenth birthday, her father had taken issue with a member of their household staff. She cried when her father hit the man. She'd never known what he had done, but she saw the same look of resignation on the white servant's face now, and it burned a hole inside her heart.

The *krewe* boss turned to face Eddie. "I do apologize for my boy's behavior, Mr. Collins. But let us not delay. We should all be going," he said, his eyes flashing on Emma as he finished his statement.

"All?" Emma said before she knew the word sat on her tongue.

"Oh, yes. Miss Emma," the *krewe* boss said. "We all have work that awaits us. In fact, I have a proposition for you in particular. And should you accept, then this"—he motioned around the room with his gold-tipped stick—"all this will be but a memory. A new home has been prepared for Mr. Collins and his . . . companion. If, as I said, you accept the proposition." He ended with a question in his eyes, and a set to his mouth that told Emma she'd better just nod and play along like a good girl.

Emma regarded the *krewe* boss with the only expression she felt safe showing the man, something between awe and admiration. Even if all she truly felt was terror.

"Well, yes, Mr. Bacchus. Yes, and th-thank you."

"Very well, my Lily White," he replied. "Very well. Now shall me depart for a venue more . . . befitting your new found station?" He offered Emma his arm and she moved slowly to accept it, watching Eddie for signs of objection. But he'd seemingly fallen under the same spell and had his eyes on the rain outside.

The servant holding the umbrella over the stoop walked Eddie to the car first, then returned and held the shelter over the *krewe* boss while the other servant used his umbrella to shield both Emma and Eddie's horn. As they walked, Emma forced herself not to look at either of the sodden men beside her, and she was both surprised and horrified to find it didn't take much effort to ignore them. As much as she hated what this 'new station' meant about the people around her and what she knew would be expected of her, she couldn't deny the relief the familiarity brought.

Comfort, care. Authority. The trappings of her life in Chicago City. And she didn't miss a beat as the word *trappings* went through her mind.

But it was the life given her at birth, and the life she had let fall away without much thought to the consequences. Now, after just two weeks of playing second fiddle to Eddie's life, she was ready for anything if it meant she'd be stepping into the world on her own two feet again.

At the car, a long sleek Duesenberg, Emma wondered if Bacchus knew who she was. Had he found out that she'd once been a society gal in Chicago City? The thought stung Emma's gut. She'd escaped the city of her birth, leaving behind nothing but the ruins of her family name. As much as she wanted to blame her father for all of it, she couldn't deny she'd played her role just as well as Josiah Farnsworth had.

He'd lost the family's money and killed himself. She'd killed two men, and one of them was a copper. A filthy copper who'd had a noose around Eddie's neck, but a copper just the same.

"Won't you precede me into the vehicle, Miss Emma?"

Nodding, and accepting the hand Bacchus offered, Emma put a foot on the running board. Eddie sat inside on a rear-facing seat. His half smile showed he was just as unsteady as she felt, but in that moment Emma's mind quickly skipped away from fear and worry. The car was like a piece of her childhood come back to her, all welcoming with warmth and luxury.

Smooth leather and polished wood decorated every surface and seam, with shining brass trim around the windows. A decanter of glimmering amber liquid stood on a tray suspended from the wall of the car just inside the door. A leather strap held the glass container in place along with two glasses.

Emma leaned forward, reaching for Eddie's hand so he could pull her inside. As their fingers touched, Emma's foot slipped on the rain-slicked metal surface and she fell back a step.

The servant to her right put an arm out to catch her, but in doing so he dropped the umbrella covering Bacchus. Emma steadied herself and saw the servant fumbling with the umbrella on the ground. He hoisted it, covering the *krewe* boss again, and stood upright, staring straight ahead. But the damage was done.

Bacchus swiped at the rainwater that had pelted his fur-lined coat. He removed his hat and shook it to release a spray of droplets in the servant's face. Emma thought she should just get into the car, but she stayed rooted in place. Something inside her forced her to wait for Bacchus's reaction, to witness it because it was due to her mistake that the servant would be punished. Her eyes went wide when she heard the gangster's words.

"Ain't got time to be callin' the Birdman in. Give me your hand, boy," the *krewe* boss said as he replaced his hat.

The servant hesitated a second, and Bacchus snatched up the man's free hand even as he was lifting it from his side. Emma saw tears fall down the servant's cheeks, mixing with the rainwater that Mr. Bacchus had spattered onto his face. Then the servant's face twisted with pain and he let out a howl as Bacchus drove a knife through his palm.

The umbrella wavered in the air over Bacchus's head, but it continued to cover him as he withdrew his blade. Emma felt an urge to comfort the servant, wrap his hand somehow. But she had nothing to use, and the look on Bacchus's face told her it would be unwise to do anything but watch.

So she watched. And she felt that old agony burn anew inside her. Servants treated like filth. A man beaten because the color of his skin didn't make him a full man in his attacker's eyes. The servant took his beating on his feet, all the while holding the umbrella above Bacchus's head as the *krewe* boss's stick cracked against the man's shins and ribs.

Finally it was done and Bacchus again extended a hand for Emma to enter the car before him.

"I do apologize that you had to witness that, Miss Emma," he said, shaking his heavy jowls. "Discipline. It is a nasty business, but sadly a needed one." As he ended, Bacchus stared daggers at the servant who now stood shuddering and sobbing, clutching his crippled, bloodied hand to his chest, but still holding the umbrella above the *krewe* boss, sheltering the man from the rain.

Wanting to voice her objection, but knowing better than to do so, Emma stepped up into the car and joined Eddie on the rear-facing seat. At first, she thought Bacchus would have the other servant precede him as well, but the *krewe* boss instead took a step forward and turned his back to the car door, obscuring Emma's view of the injured servant. Bacchus spoke then, and his words sent fingers of fear across Emma's scalp.

"You made one mistake too many, I am sorry to say. Good bye, boy. Maybe your next employer will take pity on you and end your miserable life."

Bacchus arm made a swift pushing motion as he backed into the car. He moved like he was made of air, billowing into the space without actually stepping a foot up to the floorboards. He took his place on the seat opposite Emma. She and Eddie both recoiled from the man as the ghosts and phantoms began swirling around his head.

Wispy images of knives and gun barrels swam in the air, flashing out to strike, or exploding in blasts of remembered crimes. Then Bacchus seemed to dissolve where he sat and all that was left was the red mist that she had seen in Hardy's tavern, just like what Emma had seen hovering around Celestin Hardy himself that morning they'd arrived.

That morning he shot Otis.

Outside, the injured servant lay in the rain-soaked earth around Emma and Eddie's front stoop. Mud stained his livery in great splotches mixed with blood from the stab wound in his hand. Emma felt herself leaning out of the car, like she would help the man.

Bacchus's voice broke Emma's concentration and she spun back into her seat, facing the gangster and clutching fast to Eddie's shaking hand. The red mist had vanished and Bacchus was there again, whole and made of flesh. He called out to the other servant. "Close the door now, boy. Chill is coming in, and I am not given to having the chill on my skin."

The man lifted Eddie's instrument case into the car and set it on the floorboards in front of Emma's feet. Then he stepped back to close the door, revealing once again his fallen companion on the ground. Emma's breath caught in her throat as the man sank into the ground. The mud came up around his shaking form, swallowing him like a black soup come from hell itself.

The door closed before she could see any more of what happened. As the driver started the motor, Emma looked out the window at the place where the injured man had lain in the mud. She only saw the broken remains of an umbrella, its spines snapped and bent as if by a storm.

Emma sat against the leather seats, fear and sorrow fighting inside of her. She glanced at Eddie, whose face was soft but set with fear as well. Bacchus sat with his eyes closed, his hands on the head of his gold-tipped stick with the shining point stabbing into the floorboards between his feet.

For a brief moment, Emma forgot everything she had just seen.

The interior of the car again fit around her like a glove and she remembered being a young girl riding with her father, and then racing around Chicago City with her friends. Then she remembered her father striking their servants, berating them for simple errors, and threatening them daily. And she remembered the red mist in the shape of Bacchus's body, like a ghost of all the blood he'd ever spilled.

The driver moved the car into the street, and the remaining servant stood on the running board beside Emma's window. The man clasped tight to a cold metal handrail mounted beside the doors. In that instant, any hint of familiar relief that remained in Emma's heart was washed away in the torrential rain that shivered the servant and soaked him to the bone.

CHAPTER 24

"HEY JULIEN, WAIT UP," AIDEN SAID, PUSHING his cart along the street behind the other boy.

"Oh hey, Conroy," Julien replied. He turned to greet Aiden with a handshake, but kept his eyes on the ground.

"What gives?" Aiden asked. "Thought you'd be all smiles after that pull down with the Ghost the other night. You and me came out on top, hey?"

They had come out good. Aiden was worried it had been a dream, or that the money would disappear as soon as he tried to spend it, like the fairy gold in the stories his mother used to read to him. But the coins were real when they hit his hand and they stayed real all the way home.

"What you do with your loot?" Julien asked, his face sagging so bad Aiden thought he might trip over his own chin.

"Gave it to my ma. Most of it anyway. What about you?"

"M'daddy took off with most of it. Went off to Old Storyville. Damn fool ain't even my real daddy," Julien said, sucking back a sob that Aiden pretended he didn't notice. He could see Julien's anger was just under the boy's skin. "Why'd you give it your momma anyway? That much dough, oughta like to buy you some new shoes or something."

Aiden mumbled a reply, wanting to agree with the other boy because Julien was the only friend Aiden had in the whole city. And the only person he'd met so far who had dark skin and *didn't* make Aiden think his mother might be right about Negroes after all. Of course, she'd first accused Aiden of stealing when he came home with the money, and then, when he'd told her he won it, she went on another tear about the 'dark influence' of New Orleans.

"Gambling, Aiden! And with . . . those people."

She had settled down a bit when he showed her the pile of coins he'd collected. Even the idea of ill-gotten gains didn't stand a chance against a stack of loot like that. He'd lied and said the boys all played a hand of cards in the gala house after they were done working. Something told him that the Ghost wasn't someone his ma would want him knowing about or having anything to do with.

"What about your daddy? You find him yet?" Julien asked as they rounded a corner to the street where they'd be working for the night.

"No," Aiden said, not wanting to say much more and knowing that he wouldn't have a choice in the matter.

"You say he just disappeared, huh? Ain't seen nobody go out like that before. Usually a guy gets the knife, he end up in the street that same day. But your daddy he took a while to slide down. Funny."

"What's funny?"

"I mean it's funny he didn't just go right there when Hardy put that knife in him. Usually that's how it go down. And you say Mr. Bacchus hisself was there. Man like that don' let you get away with just a stabbing. He put you down. Dat's how it happen to every man gets the knife or lose an eye."

"You said the Ghost lost his eye, though. To the Birdman. So what gives?"

"Ghost different. He ain't like all them other fools end up on the street."

Aiden bristled, but found it easier to take the remark when Julien said it. It didn't feel like he was naming Aiden's pa direct. In the past two weeks, Aiden had also made his own kind of peace with things. His pa had crossed a line somewhere and now he was on the wrong side of life. Aiden chuckled as he remembered what his father used to tell him when he was a boy, before bedtime.

"What you laughin' at, Dove?" Julien said.

Ignoring the name, Aiden told him. "My pa used to say if you wake up and your feet hit the floor, then that's a good thing. It means you're on the right side of the grass."

"Shoot," Julien said, "any fool know that. But I guess you gotta find somethin' to laugh about with your daddy down in the street now. Maybe you find him soon and show him all them coins you won off the Ghost."

"Who'd he hit?" Aiden asked, still wondering about the mysterious man in the white suit with the patch over one eye.

"Huh? Ghost ain't hit nobody. He lose his eye to the Birdman over some kinda trouble with the gala houses. I don' know the story more than that. But hey, here go our house for tonight. Better get in and start workin'. We finish up fast, maybe go make some more money off the Ghost. An' this time that fool calls hisself my daddy won' know about it neither, 'cause I ain't gonna tell him."

The boys struggled to navigate the narrow walk up to the front porch. A pair of boards had been left standing next to the steps. Julien went to these and set them down to form a ramp for their carts.

"Mama Shandy mus' be in a good mood she leavin' them boards out for us."

"What do you do if they're not there?"

"Same as you always do, Dove," Julien said with a laugh. "Break your fool back lifting this cart up the steps."

The door was locked, so Aiden went to the paybox to fish out the key. He had the job down now, knew how it all worked. He still had trouble with the way the house mothers all called him 'dove' like it was a word for something they'd found on the bottom of their shoe. But Aiden's ma was always quick to remind him it wasn't just dark-skinned folks who could use words that way.

Inside the gala house, the goings-on upstairs echoed around the upper halls and down through the stairwells. Aiden started in the kitchen, doing the tiled floor first because it was the easiest, and at this time of night nobody'd be using the kitchen anymore, so it was a sure thing he wouldn't have to go over his work twice because some dummy tracked mud through the room after he was done. Mama Shandy did that to 'teach a lesson' the night she hired him.

Bought. She bought *me.*

Aiden remembered the look of relief on Father James's face as the money changed hands, as if the priest was getting free of a burden. Aiden had gone in asking the man for help, a little money so him and his ma wouldn't have to live so rough anymore. It was all he could think to ask after his pa vanished. And what'd that priest go and do? He'd put the money Mama Shandy gave him straight into the donation chest, without even looking at it. But Father James had wrung his hands, too, like he knew somebody would call him to account someday. He'd wrung his hands good, just like Aiden was now wringing out the mop.

Speckles of water dotted his pants again, but he kept most of it in the bucket this time. He was learning. Maybe someday he'd learn how to get away from Mama Shandy. Or maybe he'd just go on cleaning floors like his pa had done back in Chicago City. If a man could make a living doing it, the work really wasn't half bad.

"What you standin' there dreamin' for? You damn fool dove!" Mama Shandy's voice whipped across Aiden's neck like a switch and he spun around to face her.

The house mother stood in the doorway to the kitchen, staring at him across her eyeglasses. She had them down on her nose, the gold frames reflecting the moonlight coming into the kitchen window and the one gas lamp Aiden had lit to help him see the floor better.

Mama Shandy crossed her arms and twisted her lips at him in a half pout, half sneer, like she'd as soon smack him one as say another word to him. She reached one hand to lift her glasses up in front of her eyes. Those glasses were worth ten times as much as Aiden had won from the Ghost the other night. Little strings of pearl and gold looped from the frames to drape around her neck.

"You and your partner best work good tonight, boy. You work fast and good, you maybe earn somethin' extra. Somethin' special. You work slow or bad, you get the foot. Or maybe," she continued, uncrossing her arms, raising one, and stepping closer to Aiden, "maybe I give you the foot anyway, damn dove, make sure you know what you supposed to be lookin' at and what you ain't!"

Aiden dropped his eyes immediately, expecting a swift kick or a swat around the ears. You weren't supposed to look at the house mothers unless they told you to. And he'd been staring straight at her eyes while she spoke. Aiden waited for the pain that he knew would come. He had to force his hands to stay by his sides, even though every soft part of him cried for protection.

"Here, boy," Mama Shandy said. The echo of her voice told Aiden she'd turned around to talk to someone in the hall. Julien must have come up behind her. Or maybe he'd been with her the whole time?

"Yes'm, Mama Shandy," Julien said. Aiden caught a hint of fear in the other boy's voice, but nothing like what Aiden felt himself.

"You get in there teach that damn dove how to behave. I don' wanna have no more sass from him, you hear? And dammit, boy, but get you some new shoes on your feet and quick. I know I pay you right and proper, not like that dove you let tag along with you. Ain't no reason you need to be walkin' around in a pair of beat-up old cow hides like what you got on now. Dammit all, if your momma didn' earn so good for me, I'd send you and that dove a'yours waltzin' in the mud."

Aiden's ears stung with the word, but worse was the sense that he was being threatened with death and that he didn't know why or what he could do to change Mama Shandy's mind about him. He felt even worse when the thought came that maybe he couldn't. Maybe this was how he would be treated in New Orleans, at least by the house mothers and some of the other houseboys he worked with.

Everyone except Julien.

Mama Shandy stepped into the hall and away. Aiden followed her footfalls down to the other end of the house and up the stairs before he dared move from where he stood. Since Julien hadn't budged either, Aiden figured he was doing the right thing.

Aiden caught the sound of a door opening upstairs, and a few thick laughs like from a big man who sounded like he'd had enough hooch to last him a week of Sundays. The door closed on the sounds of celebration. Julien came around the corner, his eyes wide and rimmed with something between fear and sadness.

"What'd you do, Dove? The hell you do to get Mama Shandy riled up like that?"

Aiden told him how he'd been staring at her eyeglasses. Julien hauled off and slapped him. Aiden raised his fists, but he was staggered by the other boy's shift to violent anger, and he only put up a weak guard. Julien had stepped back, though, and had his hands on his cart.

"C'mon. We still gotta do the brass and the window glass. Let's get done so we can get on home."

Aiden followed Julien down the hall, keeping a distance between them. Along the way, they stopped at every gas lamp and polished up the fixture. Julien did the more delicate parts, leaving the easy work for Aiden. At first he thought it was because Julien felt guilty for slapping him, but he found out he was wrong soon enough.

"I let you do the hard parts, you like to make a mess of things. Set Mama Shandy on another tear, and this time she make good on her promise. Put us in the mud. Like your damn fool daddy."

On and on they went through the house, wiping down brass and cleaning window glass. Now and then Julien would come out with another line about Aiden's 'damn fool daddy,' and eventually it was enough to set Aiden on the attack.

"Look, I don't talk like that about your pa, so lay off mine, okay?

He didn't start out a damn fool, even if he ended up one when we got here. It ain't his fault no how, so just shut your yap."

"Sure enough, Dove," Julien said, half smiling. "Like seein' you get somethin' in your back that hold you up. Had me worried you was just another cripple white boy. You prove me wrong all right. Truce," he said as he stuck out a hand.

Aiden looked at Julien's hand for a moment before reaching out to shake it. They finished the job in silence, closing the front door an hour or so later. Aiden's fingers and wrists ached from all the wiping and rubbing he'd done. His back and neck were sore from the way he had to stoop to get at some of the brass surfaces Julien left for him to polish, giving him another reason to wonder how much of a friend he had in Julien. The other boy had done the more detailed cleaning, but he'd also done it standing up and looking straight at his work.

"So hey, Dove," Julien said as they pushed their carts back down the street.

"Make it Conroy. Please."

"Okay then. See, you got them bones in your back, just like I said. Sure enough, Conroy. Okay then, so back in the kitchen there. With Mama Shandy."

"Yeah? You gonna say sorry for smacking me one?"

"Huh? Don' go growin' too big for your britches now, D—I mean Conroy. No, you earn that one, so I gave it to you. Be thankful you don' work with Theo Valcour. He knock out teeth when he teach a lesson."

Aiden was happy enough not to have seen or heard from the larger boy since the night outside the Ghost's window. Hearing Julien's words now just made Aiden more hopeful he'd never see Theo again.

"Okay, so if it ain't *Sorry* I'm gonna hear, what is it?"

"Rest of the lesson, fool. Listen, you gotta keep your eyes on the floor when you workin'. The floor where the work is at, so don' go gettin' distracted by them pretty things and fancy stuff you be seein' in them houses. Shoot, Mama Shandy's eyeglasses? Ain't half as pretty or fine as stuff you gonna be seein'. And get this, when you see your first girl in there, you don' look at her no way. You hear?"

Aiden nodded and figured he should leave it be, but the way Julien said the word *girl* nagged at him. Something in the other boy's voice sounded wrong, like he didn't want to think about the girls they'd be seeing or wanted to forget about them.

"What gives, Julien? About the girls?"

"Huh?" the other boy said, and then he let on in a steady run of words, fast and angry as a freight train heading off the rails.

"Damn *krewe* got my sister in them houses. Gonna put her on the block someday soon. My momma ain't got money to bid her out. And that damn fool call hisself my daddy. Man's about as useful as a sandwich made of soup. But damn, Dove, ain't you hear me? I mean it. You wanna keep both eyes in your head, you pay mind what I'm sayin' to you about them girls. Forget about 'em."

After Julien's breathing went back to calm, Aiden asked the question he'd had on his mind the whole time. "Who does it?"

"Does what?"

"Takes the eyes. You said the Birdman does it, but who is he?"

"I don' know. He s'posed to be around, though. Always is, just where you can't see him 'til it's too late and he on you with his bird and takin' your eye."

"Why does he do it? I mean, what else do I gotta worry about not doing so I don't lose an eye?"

"Pretty much everythin' I guess. Like I said, just keep your eyes on the floor and don' go lookin' any higher than somebody's belt if they talkin' to you. 'Specially not a house mother."

Aiden nodded and pushed. At the next corner Julien left him with a wave and a promise to meet up at the Ghost's window next time they got work.

"Gotta get a few more pennies in my pocket, and 'specially now. Mama Shandy short us both tonight for you pullin' that starin' contest in the kitchen. I only get ten cents thanks to you."

Aiden tried not to think about the nickel that he pinched between his fingers in his pocket. He watched Julien wheel his cart away down the near empty street. A streetcar waited outside another gala house half a block along, and Aiden saw another houseboy pushing his cart in the opposite direction from Julien. The two met in the middle of the street and exchanged some kind of greeting, some fast talk. Then they separated, each to the opposite side of the street and pushing their carts along home.

When the boy came abreast of Aiden he stayed on his side of the street and kept his eyes on his path. Aiden thought about calling to him, trying to make some sign of friendship with this boy who did the same job as him. But the boy's step said he wanted no part of any greeting, much less a conversation, with someone who had Aiden's color of skin.

CHAPTER 25

EMMA SAT IN THE PILOT'S CHAIR OF THE *Vigilance* and looked out the windscreen at their new neighborhood. The two-story brick house they lived in sat a block away. Her view of it was centered on the bullet hole in the cockpit windscreen.

The *Vigilance* hung above a nicer mooring deck now. It was even nicer than Celestin Hardy's deck, and Emma liked that about it. She felt she and Eddie deserved something for their troubles, even as she wondered how long she'd be able to hold out as part of Bacchus's *krewe*. That night he'd taken her and Eddie away from their little house, Bacchus offered a job. At first, Eddie seemed like he might object, but he sat back in his seat when Emma opened her mouth and said she'd do it.

Bacchus hadn't even told her what it would be before she was nodding her head and saying *Yes*, but something in her had known the work would be honest. Not the kind that has a girl looking at the ceiling. And she was right.

But even with real pay for real work in her pocket, Emma

couldn't deny the truth. Bacchus scared her. Plain and simple. He terrified her, and not just because he was a gangster, no different than Frank Nitti had been. The way Bacchus moved and talked, the weight of everything he did, it all settled onto her like the coat she couldn't refuse and didn't want to because being unprotected in New Orleans wasn't something Emma dared to dream about.

The thought of the coat brought Emma's hands to her collar to clutch at the fine wool of the new garment Bacchus had provided her. The closets in their new house were packed full of clothing, all new and all very fine. Emma had to admit she'd liked that about the arrangement, and even found herself given to smiling at Bacchus after he opened the second closet and showed her the dresses and shoes he'd *acquired* for her.

"You should look every bit the part when you step out in these fine things. Don't you think so, Miss Emma?"

She did think so, and she'd said as much to the man right then as his fingers danced a line across the hanging dresses and skirts, brushing them like a spring breeze through tall grass. Emma did think she'd look good in the clothes, and she'd turned to Bacchus and grinned like a schoolgirl.

And now I hate myself worse than ever, don't I? Smiling at that monster like he was my own father.

Bacchus was a walking horror in glad rags. But he was the reason she and Eddie had this nice neighborhood to call home.

Emma stared at the mooring deck, and that put her at ease. That comfort of familiar luxury had come back when she walked up the staircase to the platform and stepped along the deck to where the *Vigilance* berthed. The deck had the same fancy looking gearboxes as Celestin Hardy's. But it had a brass and steel railing along its length, broken here and there to accept gangways leading up to tethered ships. A manor house like Emma used to live in stood beside the deck, and more nice homes crouched in the night in every direction.

Maybe this is home at last.

The radio crackled beside her and Emma gave a sharp cry of surprise.

"Lovebird, you in the ship? I gotta get my suit on. Need some help. Now c'mon."

Emma fingered the radio handset before pressing the button to open a channel back to her and Eddie's place.

"Be there in a minute, Eddie," she said.

Outside, the late evening sky said spring rain was coming again, but the last fingers of sunlight still shone through the gathering clouds. It had been a fine day, Emma thought as she picked herself up and left the cockpit behind.

• • •

Eddie moved slow as they got his jacket on. Emma held it out so he could slide his arm into one sleeve and then the next. He gave a careful shrug to settle the jacket into place and tugged the lapels to keep them flat.

"How I look?"

"You look good, Eddie. Real good."

"You ready to do your part? Mr. Bacchus say this a big job, good money we don't mess nothin' up."

"Yeah," Emma said, forcing herself to hold Eddie's gaze. "I'm all set, Eddie."

Eddie lifted his horn in its case, with only a slight wince this time, Emma noticed. He was getting a lot better, healing faster now they had a good roof and plenty of food on the table.

Food she cooked. In a kitchen she kept clean.

It wasn't the work she resented. It was knowing that particular work would always be there and that she'd be the one doing it.

They walked to the mooring deck in silence and into the *Vigilance*, side by side. Eddie sniffed from time to time, like he had a cold, but Emma knew he was just trying to get her attention. He was healing up really well. So well he'd started drinking again after his shows, and sometimes came home smelling like he'd been washed in a tub filled with gin.

"Where's your show tonight, Eddie?"

"What—? Oh, new place, Mr. Bacchus told me about. Called the Sun, out by the riverside."

They'd reached the *Vigilance*, so Emma let it go and helped Eddie get up the ladder. She had a feeling there was more he could tell her, but the set of his jaw told her it'd be a waste of time to ask. Just like when she'd asked him again about all those younger women and girls accompanying older men to these heel kicks. The girls she now flew around the city at all hours of the night.

She'd asked and Eddie'd told her, the same as had before.

"Girls gotta know how to walk and talk, gotta know how to dance proper, not like how you see in the speaks. These girls learnin' the waltz and more like that. Real dancin', for special occasions. Debutante, that kinda thing."

Emma knew when she was being lied to, just like any girl knows when a man tells her something he thinks she wants to hear. He always makes it sound like something she *needs* to hear. But that's not what Eddie sounded like, and as much as she doubted his words, she didn't doubt he believed them to be true.

Emma thought about the sound of Eddie's voice as she got settled in the cockpit and radioed to the gearboxes on the deck to cut them loose. She stayed hush while she got the *Vigilance* into the sky and thought about everything they'd seen and done since they got to New Orleans.

"Hey, Lovebird," Eddie said from where he sat at Brand's desk. "Was thinkin' I'm a fool let you work like this, but I gotta admit. This a lot better than ridin' some old streetcar out there in the elements."

Emma gave him the only thing he deserved in response: a simple grunt of acknowledgement that he'd opened his mouth and put some words into the space between them. She couldn't argue though. Flying was a *lot* better than riding the streetcars. For one thing, she didn't have to show her badge of transit anymore.

That's worth more than a dozen of Eddie's ham-handed attempts at being sweet.

They would have taken a streetcar if it weren't for Emma's new job for Bacchus. He had her lined up to fly girls to shows like the ones where Eddie played.

Maybe someday I'll get to fly Eddie to a show and see just what goes on behind those doors.

Emma shook her head to chase the thoughts away and paid attention to the city skies around her. She heard Eddie open his case and take out his horn. In a few short moments, the airship cabin filled with notes that danced and juked as Eddie warmed up for the night.

The ride was easy. No other air traffic as a spring storm came in. It was a quiet one, though, only a few minutes of heavy rain and then it was gone, blown off for some other patch of land.

And wasn't that just New Orleans, Emma thought. A place for storms to show up for a while, leave their mark, and then move on.

Emma brought them in above what passed for a municipal deck down in the riverside districts. She'd thought that for the happening part of town, New Orleans would make a better showing. But the city must have other uses for its money. The deck looked to be ten kinds of falling down, and only had one gearbox on it.

Eddie stepped fast to the door once the machine had them moored and the narrow gangway in place. They were down the street from where Eddie would be playing, so Emma stood to accompany him to the show before she went to do her part and pick up a group of girls who'd be dancing at another house.

"You go ahead, Lovebird. I'll be all right."

"You sure, Eddie? You're still hurting. I can tell. Let me—"

But Eddie had already opened the door and set foot on the gangway. "I'll be fine, Emma," he said, his smile wavering just a touch. "This a big job you doin' for Mr. Bacchus. Remember? Go on now. I'll be fine."

And then he was down the gangway and stepping off down the

mooring deck to the staircase that would take him to the street. Emma closed the door, went to the cockpit and started to pull the ship away before she remembered it was still moored. She settled herself with a deep breath, and then another, before radioing the gearbox to release the *Vigilance*.

• • •

The house mother's boarding place was across the river, over in Algiers. A lighthouse beacon swept the water from the point by the oxbow. Emma spied a few ships moving out downriver. The sky had darkened while she had flown Eddie to his gig. She'd be picking up the girls under the full cover of night.

Something still smelled funny to her, but she couldn't tell if it was the job itself or just the idea of finally having work to do instead of living off her father's money. One thing she had to admit was that it felt good to be flying and earning some pay for doing it. Even if she wasn't sure about the people she worked for.

Something was going on with the girls she flew to and fro around the city. Or maybe Eddie was telling the truth, not just what he believed was true. Maybe these dances were just how people did things down here. And could she honestly say it was any different from how things were done in Chicago City?

Since Bacchus had set her and Eddie up in the French Quarter, she'd flown three unpaid jobs for him. The first was just taking him around the city so he could look at his 'sovereign domain.' The second job was more of the same, but Eddie had come with that time, and the two men had talked about the gala house shows.

"Play your horn, Mr. Eddie Collins. Play your horn so my guests can make merry. And make merry yourself if the mood strikes you."

Emma had pretended not to hear what the gangster had said, but she had to bite her tongue to keep from complaining about the two men talking like she wasn't right there in the airship with them. Eddie didn't say much that Emma could say was out of line, but he didn't say anything against the words coming out of Bacchus's mouth either.

It still gnawed at her guts that she hadn't asked Eddie if he was staying true to her. But then, in a way, it gnawed even more to suspect that he wasn't.

The third job she'd done for Bacchus was ferrying a group of young ladies to a social event. The women had all been stern-faced and solemn while they stood in the cabin on the flight. And only one of them acknowledged Emma with a wave of her hand.

The others acted like Emma was just hired help, and not particularly good help. She'd overheard whispered comments about 'doves fouling the nest' and somebody needing to 'find a new jellyroll.' In the moment, Emma told herself the women were talking about someone else. It wasn't until they'd left the ship that Emma let her heart key in. She had flown home looking at a city stained with tears.

Now, coming down over a mooring deck off Delaronde, Emma swallowed back fresh tears inspired by the memories and forced herself to keep a good face on for tonight's job. She hated to admit it, but Eddie wasn't the only one worried about keeping Bacchus happy.

The boarding house was supposed to be nearby, and Emma reached for the radio to let the house mother know she'd arrived. As Emma opened the channel, she spotted the chaperone climbing the stairs to the deck with the girls in tow. A dozen at least.

As the group approached the gangway, Emma unlatched the door and opened it. The chaperone ushered her charges forward and followed in their wake. The girls stepped on uneasy legs, all of them with mixes of worry and wonder on their faces. Maybe it was their first time in an airship.

Or maybe it's where this airship is taking them.

Emma couldn't shake the feeling that something was wrong, but as the chaperone came up the gangway she forced her face into a weak grin.

"I'm Emma Farnsworth," she said, but kept her hands by her sides.

"Good evening to you, Miss Farnsworth. My name is Adelaide Roche. You may call me Miss Roche."

Emma nodded and bent to work the lever to close the door. Miss Roche took a seat at Brand's desk while the girls milled around the cabin space.

"Washroom's in back, just down the hall," Emma said to the girls.

"They won't be going nowhere's," Miss Roche said. "Not if I can' see 'em. And you don' need to be talkin' to 'em anyway. Just fly us on, if you will."

Feeling that familiar burn of resentment mixed with fear, Emma settled herself into the cockpit and radioed the gearboxes on the deck. Moments later they were airborne and sailing through the New Orleans night. Emma's mind swam with worry for the girls. They were mixed, with faces running from light-skinned to dark and all points between. The girls looked about the same age, and not one of them more than two years passed coming into season.

Emma remembered her own innocence. She also remembered the way her father's friends and the men at the power plant would look at her once womanhood began to peek out from behind her child's face. And when she'd turned sixteen, dammit if some of those men hadn't tried to do more than look when they knew nobody else was.

Eddie hadn't asked her if she would come join him tonight, after she was done with her job. But Emma knew the next time Eddie opened that door and she could spare the time she'd be walking straight through. Whatever went on with these girls, she'd find out about it. And then she'd decide if staying in New Orleans was still in the cards.

CHAPTER 26

DAYS AND NIGHTS FELT NICER ALL AROUND FOR Aiden as springtime had come to New Orleans. He had heard from Julien that was the best season in the city. Plenty to see and do, and the storms wouldn't come in for a couple months more. Of course, they still had to clean the gala houses for Mama Shandy.

"Girls be 'round the houses more now, so watch your eyes, Dove Conroy. Don' go lookin'. Not 'less you wanna give half what you see with to the Birdman."

Julien took to calling Aiden "Dove Conroy" after Aiden's latest win at the Ghost's window. Julien was still down on his bets, but he'd won a couple recently. Aiden, however, had a solid winning streak. That didn't sit with the other boys, especially not Theo Valcour. But for Julien it was like Aiden was doing some magic trick. The guy even stood up for him, telling the others, "Don' go hasslin' Dove Conroy" and "Leave Dove Conroy be."

Now, after a long night's work and a bigger than usual win at the Ghost's window, Aiden was pushing his cart down the street, heading home. The air felt thick and warm around him, and he shrugged out of his coat to let the night air tickle his arms. He enjoyed the quiet small hours, and hoped the coming day's sunlight would be just as nice. Of course, he'd be missing the first half of it.

He'd brought in enough dough to get him and his ma a real bed at last. It was just a mattress for now, but the rest would be coming soon. He just had to bring home tonight's winnings. Since they got the mattress, Aiden had taken to sleeping until around lunchtime. Then he'd grab a plate of hash at the nearest sandwich counter and pick up something for his ma, too. They'd eat sitting on the steps leading up to their room, or inside at their little table when a cool breeze made the shivers race up and down Aiden's legs.

His ma still had worry on her face every time he looked at her, but she'd been kinder to him since his pa went missing.

The old man did something right when he went down the neck of a bottle and then just plain vanished.

Aiden wouldn't let himself think about that day now. He'd figured he could keep earning dough for him and his ma and things'd turn out better than they'd had in Chicago City. His pa was gone and that was that. Nothing he could do about it.

Mr. Brand sure seemed to think different that day he came by.

And so what? So his old boss was some kind of ghost tramp now and could dance around the place like a breeze through the trees. The guy looked half crazy the last time Aiden'd seen him, and the way he held that letter out . . .

He still hadn't told his ma about it, and he had no plans to. She was down in the mouth about him working for a Negro lady as it was. Add some talk about his old boss telling him he's a god and Ma'd blow her top.

Better to just keep bringing in the dough. They'd already got some new dishes, a few new pieces of clothing, and a whole new sewing set for his ma. He still wasn't bringing home enough to help her buy her own machine, and half of what she earned paid rent on the one she used now.

But still, he'd done something to make living in New Orleans a little easier on them both. Even if he did have to work the night through, he'd made good on the Conroy name, and doing the same as his father used to do for a living. If he got lucky, he could keep on doing it.

As he trundled his cart down the streets, Aiden wondered if Julien and the other houseboys were talking up the rumors going around.

Mama Shandy had competition coming to town, people were saying. She'd been acting real sweet lately, not giving Aiden half the trouble she usually had. Julien joked with him that maybe she was sweet on him and wanted to make him her "little prize dove." That had to be what Theo and the other boys were jawing about when Aiden left. The way they laughed, it couldn't've been much else.

"Damn near a dozen blocks to go," Aiden said to himself. He shook off the urge to leave his cart where it was and just head home without having to shove the thing up every little incline along the way. He'd cut through an older neighborhood to save time and wondered if it was a good idea. After the third little hill he had to climb, he was starting to think he'd made a mistake.

The street leveled out again and Aiden pushed his cart toward an intersection of streets with brick houses with hedges on one side and dark storefronts on the other. He stopped when he heard a whistling sound from behind him. It echoed around the intersection and he turned in circles trying to pinpoint the source.

The whistling returned, this time from back the way he'd come. He looked back and saw nothing. The whistling continued, an almost happy tune, but the way it echoed around the empty night gave Aiden the shivers, so he set to pushing his cart along again.

Theo Valcour stepped out from behind a hedge across the way and waved at him. The large boy was whistling a greeting, too, and then sent his tune diving to the depths of threat.

Aiden spun his cart to the side and took off running down the main stem. He didn't usually take this street to get home, and he knew he could end up taking a wrong turn if he wasn't careful. But going this way put him the farthest from Theo as he could get, so he ran and he followed the street into the darkness.

Behind him, the whistling continued, and Aiden looked back the way he'd come. Theo stood under a gas lamp a few steps down from the last corner. Aiden slowed for a second, but picked up his pace again when he saw the larger boy take off at a good clip, coming straight for him.

Aiden put everything he had into making tracks, but he knew it wouldn't last. He banged his shins against the back of his cart, and he nearly stumbled.

He thought again about leaving the cart behind. Just grabbing the mop and running, so at least he'd have a weapon when Theo caught up to him. But then he'd need to buy a new cart for Mama Shandy, and he couldn't bear to imagine the beating he'd get from the toughs who worked for her if he told her he just left the cart behind.

And what else am I gonna tell her?

Side streets disappeared in the corners of Aiden's eyes as he ran. Theo's heavy footsteps kept coming, kept pounding into the street behind him. Aiden spun his cart to the right and launched down a side street. He got about a dozen steps in when he drew up short and halted his cart from nearly running over a man lying in the street.

At first, Aiden thought the man might be dead, but a heavy snore rumbled out of the man's chest, and a second later Aiden caught the stink of old liquor wafting through the air. He looked around the street for somewhere to hide, all the while listening to Theo Valcour's footsteps grow closer and closer. Aiden was about to push his cart around the sleeping bum in the street when his breath caught in his throat.

The street looked like a flophouse turned inside out. Tramps lay all around him on the pavement, on sidewalks, up against buildings, half in and half out of doorways and alleyways. Some on their feet, sleeping standing up, others spread out like they'd been stepped on by a giant and left to lie there until the undertaker came to haul them away.

Aiden heard a chorus of snores and sneezes, raspy breaths and wheezing coughs from throats burned raw with hooch and cigarette smoke. Aiden coughed himself when he breathed in the thick smell of unwashed skin and ratty hair mixed with a day's worth of filth and the remains of last night's booze.

Was this where his pa had wound up? Every one of the bums bristled with matted, scraggly hair and a tangled beard. As Aiden stared, some of them began to moan and roll around on the street, like big hogs put over on their sides for the night. Others staggered away from the walls that held them upright. These moaned, too, and their lowing and grunting made Aiden's gut twist. He began to back up but remembered Theo Valcour was on his tail. Aiden pushed his cart to the side, meaning to move across the open street and back out to the main stem.

He'd waited too long, though. Theo came rushing around the corner and nearly crashed into Aiden when he pulled to a stop. Aiden looked the big boy in the eye while the tramps made their clumsy way in the two boys' direction.

Theo gave Aiden a shove and laughed as he stepped back a few paces to stand at the mouth of the street.

"Go on, Dove. Go on down the way. Take your chances with the mud men. You lucky, you just get a little dark on you. But I'm thinkin' you ain't gonna be lucky, Dove. I'm thinkin' you had your run of good luck today already."

Aiden didn't move, and Theo came forward again, grabbing at Aiden's pocket. Before he could stop the bigger boy, Theo had a handful of Aiden's winnings from that night in his mitt.

"Hey, give it back!" he shouted, but Theo wasn't playing ball. He stepped up and shoved both hands against Aiden's chest, nearly toppling him over his cart. "Go on," Theo said. "Get in there, white boy. Or come out here and pay the piper with the rest of what you got in that pocket."

Theo Valcour backed up, away from the tramps and their street.

He pocketed what he'd nabbed from Aiden and balled his fists. He made to stand guard at the end of the street, waiting for Aiden to run past him.

Aiden turned to see a team of three tramps standing near him, mouths hanging open and hands reaching, palms up, as if they expected Aiden to give them something. Money or hooch, either way he had nothing to offer to these filthy gutter rats, even if one of them might be his own father. So on shaky legs, and glad to be free of Theo Valcour, Aiden pivoted his cart and moved away from the trio of bums.

He took a winding route through the others that had come staggering into the street with their beggars' hands out to him. But the tramps were ready for him. As he moved around one pair, another swept into the space he aimed for, so he had to bump them with his cart and push his way through to a clear section of the street.

Soon enough, though, tramps had boxed him in on three sides. They rose up from where they'd lain or peeled away from a dark patch of shadow next to a building. No matter where Aiden aimed his cart, they got into his path somehow.

Aiden shivered with fear and cold, and then did the only thing he could think of. He ran, using his cart as both a shield and battering ram. He dodged the tramps when he could and pushed past them when he had to. Finally, he slammed into one and knocked the man out of the way with a shove of his arm.

The street didn't empty before him, though. A pair came up from his left, almost rising straight from the ground it seemed, and then two more on his right. One of the pairs got hands onto Aiden's coat. For a second he felt trapped in their strong grip. But he wrenched free and felt both tramps fall to the ground in a tangle behind him. The street was clear for a few feet and Aiden darted forward. Then, just as fast as he could move, a trio rose up from the street and blocked his path. Aiden's heart beat a mad dance and he aimed his cart at the rightmost one.

He struck the man with his cart and reeled away from the blow, using the momentum to shift his path toward the edge of the street.

If he could get onto the sidewalk, he might have an easier time escaping.

But they swarmed all around him now, and still moaning, begging him for who knew what, but Aiden knew it was something he didn't have. He checked to see if the one he'd hit had gone down. He saw that one and two other men fighting with one another, rolling in the street. As they struggled, the street itself turned to mud beneath them. The thick sloppy muck spread out in a halo around the wrestling tangle of grimy coats and greasy hair. In a flash, the edges of the mud pool raced to either side of the street, capturing all the tramps it touched.

They all fought now, with each other and to free themselves from the growing pool. Aiden pushed his cart, aiming himself at the sidewalk because he could see it was still solid.

Theo Valcour's deep laughter echoed across the night to Aiden's ears, and at that moment, Aiden felt the wheels of his cart dip forward into the slime. He overbalanced, tumbling headfirst into the mud. His bucket tipped and a cold, greasy spray splashed over his hands and arms as they sank into the mud.

Aiden screamed. He fought with the mud and he screamed and cried, thrashing out with one hand just as the other arm sank into the black ooze up to his elbow. The tramps came to him then. They came across the mud somehow, moving in it, like they were a part of it.

Forgetting his cart and looking only for a clear path to the sidewalk, Aiden ripped his arm free of the muck and fought against the clutching and grasping hands. He swatted them away, kicked out with a leg and got his feet under him. The mud beneath him felt firm, but went soft the longer he stayed put.

Four tramps circled him now, mouths open, eyes hidden by bushy brows and floppy hat brims. And their hands were all reaching for him. Aiden flung a hand out to swipe at a tramp that came too close. His fingers caught on something and pulled. At first he thought it was the tramp's coat, but then he saw the night air of the street fluttering like a curtain. And he saw the space behind the city, the mix of night sky and half remembered dreams. The tramps closed in, all of them groaning angry and violent in his ears. Aiden stepped into the hole he'd opened.

With that first step, Aiden learned he probably was supposed to take that letter from Mr. Brand, but he couldn't figure how knowing that was supposed to help him now. All around him the tramps came through the curtain, flowing like water through a sieve until they filled his vision like an ocean. Aiden spun around and saw an open tunnel ahead. He ran as more tramps filtered through from the street and into the world behind the city.

Whatever Mr. Brand had wanted to show him, Aiden knew it couldn't have been this. No way his old boss would do him this way. The tramps kept coming, and Aiden kept running. His feet didn't stick like they had on the street outside, but he worried they would if he stopped for even a second.

So Aiden ran, and he thought about Mr. Brand. And when he got enough wind in him to do it, he yelled the man's name and begged him for help.

CHAPTER 27

EVEN THOUGH EDDIE WAS PLAYING MORE shows than ever, Emma still hadn't made it into a gala house since going to work for Bacchus. Tonight's run was a full load of the girls and their chaperone. And Emma's worry over where she was taking them had grown with each passing day. She'd tried talking to Eddie about it, but he denied or dismissed or just got angry as she'd ever seen him. The conversation never got beyond her telling him something smelled wrong.

"Ain't nothin' you need to worry about, girl. Mr. Bacchus pay us right. Set us up in this fine home. What you wanna ask trouble in for? What's trouble gonna bring but more trouble?"

Tonight she thought about bringing trouble of her own and just waltzing into the gala house and checking things out herself. But Eddie'd warned her off that idea, too.

"Won't let you in if'n I'm not playin'. Doorman got a list."

Promising herself to find a way in somehow, Emma brought the *Vigilance* in slow above the gala house's mooring deck. This one stood right beside the house itself, and calling this building a house was almost an insult. Lawns spread out around it on three sides, and the fourth backed up against a copse of oak trees. Wrought iron railings bordered the yard with lamps hanging from posts every so often, glowing bright and warm.

Emma had to force herself to stop staring at the mansion with its warm windows and the parade of guests in their finery and lace down at the front steps. The scene looked bright and cheerful, but Emma knew better. And she couldn't deny the dread she was feeling as the gearboxes locked the mooring lines in place. After a short whirring and clicking, the airship bobbed against its tethers.

This deck was the nicest Emma had seen around New Orleans, nicer even than the mayor's deck back in Chicago City. Just like the railing around the manor yard, gas lamps lit up the whole length of the deck, sending halos of warmth around the late evening. The planking looked polished and smooth, and a glimmering gangway swung out as the gearboxes maneuvered it into place with a set of levers.

Emma went to the door and worked the lever to fix the gangway to the outside of the cabin, waiting for the gentle bump that told her it was in place. She popped the door open to reveal brass hand-rails illuminating a golden path from the cabin to the deck below.

Along the deck itself, stanchions of brass and steel and velvet ropes made for waiting areas. As Emma stared in awe, the radio popped with the familiar cadence of tones that meant the *Vigilance* had the "all clear." She could unload her passengers.

Emma went to the cockpit and confirmed. She fiddled with the radio headset for a bit, unsure if she should keep hush or try to help. The first chaperone she'd worked with, Miss Roche, hadn't accepted her help.

This one answered Emma's unspoken questions with a note of command in her voice.

"You just wait on me to come back, Miss Emma," the woman said, standing up from Brand's desk and motioning to the girls who were huddled against the rear of the cabin. "I won't be but a minute getting these girls to the dancing hall."

"Sure thing," Emma said to the woman's back, watching her parade the six girls out of the cabin and onto the gangway. It was the same group as she'd flown the first time, and Emma didn't miss the signs of fear and worry they still wore under their thickened eyelashes and rubied lips. One of the white girls even lagged behind, leaning against the wall by Brand's desk. She caught a cuffing around the ear from the chaperone.

"You get on now," the woman said. "And don't give me none of that sass like you did back at the boarding house."

The girl moved to the cabin door. Before she put a foot outside, she turned worried fearful eyes to Emma. Before Emma could say anything, the chaperone came between them and took the girl firmly by the arm. With a look of warning in Emma's direction, the chaperone pushed the girl before her and marched down the gangway.

Emma sat tight for a second, then jumped up and went to the cabin door. With its brass rails glowing golden in the gaslight, the gangway looked for all the world like a path to the heavens. Emma didn't miss a beat thinking it was aimed in the wrong direction.

The chaperone stayed true to her word, coming back up the deck only a few short minutes after leaving with the girls. The chaperone's eyes rounded with intent as she stepped along the planks toward the gangway. Emma backed into the cabin, fleeing that accusing gaze just as she felt guilty for letting the younger woman intimidate her.

What did Emma have to fear? She'd done as she was told, and Bacchus had already paid her for the flying, even fueled up the airship for her on top of the pay.

Emma's hand found her coat pocket and she felt the roll of bills she'd tucked in there, money the *krewe* boss himself had given her, from his hand to hers. Not through Eddie like the times before.

The chaperone stepped into the cabin and held Emma's eyes. The other woman's lips pressed tight together and then flared open as she spoke.

"Don't you never go looking at them girls like that again. You hear me? Never. Les' you want the Birdman to come an' *take* your eye." The chaperone snatched at the air like she'd pluck Emma's eye out herself.

Emma's chest heaved and she nearly spat back at the woman standing in the cabin doorway, like she could push her out with just the right words. But the words didn't come, and wouldn't come no matter how much Emma willed them to. She again clutched the money with the hand in her pocket and nodded, feeling the shame rise to her cheeks when she realized her bottom lip was trembling.

The chaperone moved into the cabin. Emma went to the door and worked the levers to release the gangway and pull the door closed.

"Good," the chaperone said. "Now get us on back the boarding house." She stepped to Brand's desk and took her seat there again, yanking open the bottom drawer as soon as her tailbone hit the chair.

The woman made a disappointed grunt and slammed the drawer shut. "Ain't got a bottle in there? What the hell it's for then it don't hold a bottle? Half useless, like a few other things round here."

Emma ignored the taunt and sat in the pilot's chair. She kept her eyes on the controls and signaled the gearboxes she was ready to go. The radio crackled and gave way to the usual series of chirps Emma had grown accustomed to. The gangway withdrew and the mooring lines released. With another series of chirps and clicks, Emma had confirmation that the ship was free and clear. She turned her attention to piloting the craft away from the gala house.

Down below, gaslight glowed from every window down the long side of the house. Inside, twirling silhouettes danced round and round the floor, like music box dancers cascading past the windows in a quickening flurry. Emma held the ship in a steady rise but still angled so she could watch the gala house through the cockpit windows.

"Why you keeping us aimed this way?" the chaperone demanded. "Mama Fontaineau's boarding house off east, same as when we left to come out here."

Emma held her tongue and turned the ship to the east. The gala house disappeared from view out the left window and Emma let it go. The feeling that she'd just delivered a flock of lambs to the slaughter didn't leave her, though. It stayed with her the whole way back across the city.

She left the chaperone at the deck by Mama Fontaineau's boarding house without so much as a "So long, sister." The fury had built and continued to build as they flew, and the chaperone hadn't done anything to change Emma's mood, at least not for the better. By the time she had the *Vigilance* moored in her and Eddie's neighborhood, the ache of anger in her chest had wilted to a dull sorrow, pressed beneath a heavy dread.

Emma walked down the street to their home and went inside, struggling to keep from folding over where she stood.

Settling into the chair in the front parlor, Emma fell asleep, dreaming of little lambs stripped of their downy wool and let to run through a nightmare of dark houses that erupted with flames from the windows.

• • •

Brand stands under a tree across the street from the Rising Sun and watches the jazzers and flappers having their fun. Light flares out of the building and the rumble and stomp of a good heel kick come to Brand's ears across the night from the open front door and balcony windows. The two-story building looks solid and strong even in this run down riverside stretch of New Orleans. Somebody takes care of it, Brand knows. And that somebody is the man he met on the street the other day. His first delivery.

Vice.

Bacchus owns the Sun, and a whole lot more of this town. Brand's figured that out in the short time he's been on the street. Wasn't that hard, really, what with every mud man from here to Lafayette telling him that was how things were. Bacchus owns this gala house and plenty others.

He probably owns the people inside them, too. They just don't know it yet. Or they don't care.

Miss Farnsworth's jazz man is in there with them, hooting it up and blowing on his horn in between sips of sherry or brandy or whatever else they're pouring inside.

Looks like he's having a glass of Janet and one of Josephine, too, from where I'm standing.

Brand winces when a pang of hunger rips into his guts and stirs them up good. Worse than he's felt before, even in the trenches. It's been a long night of watching this jazz house glowing like a lighthouse by the riverside, and the night's just getting longer. But Brand has nowhere else to go. Nothing to do but wait it out under this tree with his collar up and his hands wrapped in his frayed sleeves, while he hopes Miss Farnsworth's jazz man is sober enough to carry a letter home in his pocket.

Since Conroy spurned him, Brand figures he's got one of two plays with this new gig of his. He can deliver the mail like he's supposed to, and slowly go crazy in the process until he's sucking down mud for breakfast, lunch, and dinner. Or, he thinks, as the jazz players slow down in the house across the way, he can find a patsy, someone who can do it just as good as him.

He doesn't know how the gods will take it, him handing letters to the wrong people. But if he makes sure the patsy doesn't do something stupid, like opening the letter, well, maybe Brand can go back to doing the only thing he feels good about doing anymore.

Wherever Barn and the fellas took off to, I'll find 'em. And then we can talk about what's left in the bottle.

Drink. That's what he's come to, Brand thinks. A man and his drink. All he needs is someone to take over for him, someone to play messenger boy for the gods. So long as the person can walk a line to a destination and listens good enough to know they shouldn't tamper with the mail, well . . .

Brand sniffs and wipes a hand over his face. The jazzers are all quiet now, putting their horns away. The flappers are smoking and giggling, someone in there is almost cackling. And sounds from an upstairs window tell Brand that two people are having more fun than he's had since who knows when.

Soon enough, everyone but the pair upstairs is spilling out of the Rising Sun and taking over the street outside. A couple of jazzers strike up a song and dance with a pair of flappers. They all fall down in a heap with a groan and a screech. Somebody's hurt, but Brand isn't paying attention to their pissing and moaning. He's worried about Miss Farnsworth's jazz man, what's his name again . . .

Collins. Somebody named Collins. Brand tucks himself tighter against the tree and scans the crowd slowly filling the street. They're all circling around the tangle of bodies on the ground. Someone in there is sobbing now. Brand thinks for a second he can help, and then remembers the weight like a lodestone in his pocket.

Conroy's letter. And now one for Miss Farnsworth, too.

Then Brand sees him. Her jazz man. *Eddie Collins.*

He's got his horn in its case and he's walking down the street. Stumbling down the street is more like it, Brand thinks as he watches Eddie fetch up against the side of the building with a thin, pale flapper trailing after him. She's calling to him and pawing at his collar. Eddie turns around, plants a wet one on the flapper's mouth and gets back as good as he gives. Brand waits it out while they have their fun. Soon enough the girl acts like she remembers where she is or who she's supposed to be with. She turns away from Eddie and heads over to the circle of people in the street.

She gets there and disappears into the group, swallowed up like a shadow of a shadow until she's just another pair of flapper's legs in the mix of bodies. They're all standing around the group that took a tumble, two men and two women, now huddled together like they're sheltering from a storm.

Brand doesn't see any blood on the faces or hands in the mix. But it's dark as can be at this time of night, and it's only shadows that Brand can see really.

Shadows and more shadows. Brand peers around the street, trying to remember why he's standing there, and then he sees him. Miss Farnsworth's jazz man is still trying to walk his silly drunk ass home. This is the guy Brand is going to trust with Miss Farnsworth's letter?

What'd the gods think they were doing naming Conroy and Miss Farnsworth as the latest and greatest?

"Don't you have someone else you can drape your laurels on?" Brand mumbles into his collar.

Nobody answers and Brand doesn't bat an eye or lose a second wondering why not. They never do. He's used to it now. The constant silence of New Orleans nights that never answer him.

He steps out of his hiding place, careful to stumble like a good little tramp, and ignores the cries of surprise that follow him from the group in the street. He staggers down the way, keeping Eddie Collins in his vision as best he can, and gets himself ready to jump in case Eddie Collins starts to slide into the street.

Sure enough, at the first intersection, Brand has to rush across the way and grab hold of Eddie. Brand hooks his hands under the black man's arms and pulls for all he's worth until Eddie's legs come free of the mud with a sickening *Pop*.

"Let's get you home," Brand says to the now sleeping jazz man. Brand lifts a hand and peels back the night, revealing a tunnel to the French Quarter. "I guess I'm stuck with this gig after all," he says and then hauls Eddie Collins into the world behind the city.

• • •

Emma woke with a start when Eddie came home. He was covered in sweat and the stink of cigar smoke mixed with perfume and sweet wine, like a cocktail poured from the Devil's own decanter. And his pants were covered in mud up to his knees.

"You ought to wash up, Eddie," she said to him as he put his instrument case down on the love seat and flopped himself next to the case. He turned weary eyes to her, above a grin that was half wolf and half sloppy hound dog.

"Oh, Eddie," Emma said, her voice falling to the floor. "You're drunk."

"C'mon here, Lov—" Eddie started to say and then spilled the night's revelry into his lap. Emma reeled away from the scene and the sounds, flying from the chair and stepping fast down the hall. She closed the bedroom door behind her and leaned against it.

How many nights? How many times had she cleaned up after her father when he'd been on a tear with the men from the power plant? Or the mayor? Emma had lived a servant's life around the men she'd grown up being told to admire. The petty yet powerful of Chicago City's elite. Nothing but a gang of drunks at the end of the day. And Emma had been their cleaning lady.

May as well have been their nursemaid, cook, and mother while she was at it. Not half of them had wives at home. She'd taken that as a sign that no woman should stand by a man with one hand in hers while the other clutched tight to the neck of a bottle.

Now Eddie's gone over the falls, too.

Emma stopped herself there. Had she really thought that about him? The man she'd risked her life to rescue from the lynch man's noose. The man she'd set out with on this adventure in starting over. She had no delusions about life in New Orleans being easy, no matter what the city was called. But it wasn't supposed to be like this. Eddie wasn't supposed to wind up just as bad as the men she'd turned away from.

A grunt and the dull thud of his instrument case hitting the floor told Emma that Eddie was moving around the front parlor. Shuffling footsteps and thumps against the walls and floor signaled his slow progress to the washroom. Emma breathed a sigh of relief that she wouldn't have to clean him up like she had her father for all those years.

• • •

The next morning, Emma stood outside the washroom. Eddie had slept in the bathtub. His clothes sat wadded up on the floor, reeking of his misery. Emma turned her head and breathed deep before going into the washroom and snatching up the soiled clothing.

She fast-stepped down the hall to the auto-wash and tossed the whole mess into the basin.

Emma worked fast to get the machine ready. With a sniff of disgust, she hit the switch. The machine started up with a jerk and whirred into a steady rhythm.

In the kitchen, she made breakfast for herself and ate it in silence while Eddie snored and sometimes coughed in the bathtub. She thought about waking him, but figured he'd hate himself enough without the look she was bound to give him.

Outside, New Orleans slowly came to life. Emma washed the dishes, and still Eddie slept. She thought again about waking him up and had decided to do it when the wall beside the kitchen door shimmered and lifted away like a translucent drape, revealing Brand in his tattered coat and beat-up hat. He stepped into the kitchen, letting the gossamer wall fall into place behind him, making the kitchen whole once again.

Brand had the same weather-beaten look on his mug. His suspenders sagged lower than a gambler's bottom lip after a bad day at the track, but his eyes were still bright as ever, alive and full of warning.

"You got a minute, Miss Farnsworth?"

"Looks that way, whether I like it or not. You don't exactly give a girl a chance to tidy up for guests. Do you?"

"I'm sorry," he said, taking off his hat and running the stained fingers of one hand through his now-thinning hair. "I'm doing this as a favor. If that makes you feel any better."

"It doesn't. So what's it about this time, Brand? More hocus-pocus and abracadabra? I'm not saying I mind, but if it's all the same to you, I don't see what's in it for me. All this talk about gods and—"

"That's just it," he said, as the hint of a smirk crept around his lips. He put his hat back on and motioned a hand to a chair by the kitchen table. "Okay if I sit?"

"Go ahead," Emma said, standing back from the table a step farther. His stink wasn't that bad, but he looked every type of dirty there was, and Emma'd had plenty with cleaning up after Eddie.

"So?" she said as Brand got settled. "What's the scoop, Brand?"

"Your jazz man," he said, tossing a look down the hall to the bathroom. "Got himself good and sauced last night, hey?"

"What business is that of yours? Look, I'm not up for chit-chat, so—"

"You want to hear this, Miss Farnsworth. You don't have to like it and you probably won't no matter how I tell it, but you'll be thanking me when I'm done. Your good-time guy in the bathtub is only alive because of me, and I risked what's left of my neck making sure he got home last night. If I hadn't, he and Al Conroy would've been bunking together in the street. A couple of mud men with nothing better to do than hit the sauce and lie around waiting for the boss to call."

Emma leaned back against the counter, finding the rim of the sink with her twitching fingers and holding on to the enameled metal with all her strength. A grimace worked its way across her mouth and up her face until she felt her eyes watering.

"What the hell is this, Brand? The gods followed us from Chicago City?"

"No, but you'd be better off if it was just them we had to worry about. *Industry* and his pals are still fighting the bad fight, or the good, depending which side you're on."

"Then what—?"

"The ones down here don't care as much about taking over and making the world run by their rules. *Vice, Corruption*, even *Innocence*. They just take you in soon as they've got half a chance to do it. Last night, *Corruption* had her sights on your fella. Eddie nearly hit the street with a belly full of hooch and ten kinds of lady paint on his collar. He—"

"What?" Emma shouted, her tears forgotten. Now she felt nothing but a burning hatred. "Get out, Brand. Get the hell out!"

Brand stood up slow, but as she advanced on him he seemed to get the message. He stepped back to the kitchen door.

"I-I'm in a jam here, Miss Farnsworth. I did you a favor and figured you'd do me one back, hey?"

"A favor?" Emma said, hoping Brand felt the word stab him in the guts like she meant it to. "You call bringing Eddie back a favor? He should be out there making a hot mess of himself instead of making another mess for me to clean up in the house."

"It's the kid," Brand said. "Conroy. He needs help, Miss Farnsworth, and his folks aren't good for helping him anymore."

Emma had another knife on her tongue, ready to stick in him, but the mention of Aiden put her back on her heels.

"What about the kid? What's going on with him, and why does he need my help?"

Brand didn't answer right away. He stuck a hand into his coat pocket and lifted it like he intended to bring his hand back out with something between his fingers.

"Before I show you this, you gotta promise me you'll help him. He's the only one I've got left out of the three of 'em," Brand said, choking up on the words. "My three newsboys. That damn monster the gods sent after us took care of Jenkins and Digs Gordon back in Chicago City. Conroy's the only one left. I can't let him down."

"So why don't you help him? You've got the magic tricks, Brand. What's the matter?"

"I tried," Brand said, sucking in the tears and wiping his face with his free hand. "Aiden . . . he didn't want the kind of help I have to give."

Brand pulled his other hand out of his pocket and Emma's eyes went narrow with doubt when he held out two envelopes.

"Go on," he said. "Please. I need to give it to somebody and the kid's nowhere I can find him. I've looked."

"Isn't it your job to deliver the mail, Brand?" Emma reached for the letters and her fingers closed on them, but she didn't tug like she wanted them yet. "What happens to me if I take these from you and I'm not the right person to read 'em?"

"Just be sure you only read the one addressed to you and it'll be jake," Brand said, letting the letters go. In a flash, he'd lifted the curtain beside his head and stepped through it. Before Emma could holler at him to wait, the hallway dropped back into place and Brand was gone.

Emma's eyes wanted to go every other way they could, but she forced herself to look at the letters.

Innocence C/O Aiden Conroy

Vigilance C/O Emma Farnsworth

Emma put a hand to her brow and rubbed the knot of worry that formed between her eyes.

"The man's got to be crazy," she said.

Eddie stuck his head out of the bathroom then, his eyes bleary and weak, and his mouth hanging open like he'd just had another round of reliving last night's fun and games.

"Get me some coffee on, Lovebird. Gotta—"

"Get it your own damn self," she said, and stepped past him down the hall to the stairs, holding the letters to her side. She walked up the steps fighting to prevent her mind from lingering on memories of the lipstick and perfume that had decorated Eddie's clothes

CHAPTER 28

IF HIS OLD BOSS WAS ANYWHERE AROUND THE mud tunnels, Aiden had no idea how to find the man. He'd screamed until his throat felt raw and ragged, worse than the first time his pa handed him a slug of hooch and told him to drink it down in one go.

The mud didn't stick as much now at least. And the tramps seemed to have forgotten about him. He saw only two behind him now. One of them stopped moving as Aiden looked at him. Then the man opened his mouth to speak. His voice came down the tunnel like rushing water.

"*Figger . . . figger we losht . . . losht thish'n.*"

Then the man's partner pulled up and gave Aiden a hard look. He had words for Aiden, too, and they weren't much better than what his pal had to say.

"*G'on, dove. G'on back to mammy. Get you both someday. Now g'on.*"

Aiden's heart jumped as the first one who'd stopped just fell sideways into the wall, slipping into the dirt like it wasn't even there.

The other tramp seemed to notice he was alone and turned around to look back down the tunnel. A second later, that one gave a shrug, too, and did the same trick as the first.

Aiden spun around, double-checking he wasn't getting set up for an ambush from behind. The tunnel sat empty, cold and murky and nothing but dirt as far as he could see. Aiden waved a hand in front of his face, trying to pull back the curtain again like he had on the street. Nothing happened. So he stuck a hand at the wall like he'd move it aside, too, and the next thing he knew he'd stumbled into the alley outside the place he and his ma called home.

Aiden gave himself a quick once-over, making sure he hadn't brought the tunnel with him all stuck to his clothes. Except for a little smear on his shoes, he looked like he'd just stepped out of a gala house after working his shift. His pants were a little wrinkled up and wet around the ankles, but that was it.

Figuring he had one chance to fix things, Aiden stepped up the stairs quiet as he could. At the landing, he took his key off the chain around his neck and undid the lock, wincing when the tumblers clicked sharp in the night.

His ma had always slept straight through the small hours when he got home. Tonight she was up, sitting at the edge of the mattress in the far corner. She had a blanket wrapped around her and her feet were stuffed into a pair of old slippers she'd just gotten from one of the sewing ladies downstairs.

"Hey, Ma," Aiden whispered, standing in the doorway with one hand on the knob and the other on the frame.

"Close the door, Aiden. You're letting out the heat."

"Yes'm," he said, stepping inside. His eyes went straight to the kitchen shelf and the can where he kept his earnings. Hoping his ma hadn't noticed what he was looking at, he moved into the room more and made to get ready for bed.

"How much did you earn tonight, Aiden?"

Feeling a dope for letting his eyes give him away he shook his head and put together the best lie he could.

"About the same."

"And how much is that?"

"Eight-eight or ten cents, Ma," Aiden said, hoping he still had that much left after Theo Valcour went digging and came up a rich man at Aiden's expense.

"Let me see it, Aiden," his ma said, and Aiden felt his guts start rolling around. He tucked a hand into his pocket and collected the coins he felt there.

Bringing his hand out, Aiden knew it'd be jake with his ma. He had at least one dime left in his pocket. He brought the coins to his ma who held out her hand for them. Aiden's ma looked like a ghost in the weak light that was coming in through the window in the door. Her face looked gray, like ash, and her hair hung around her head like old wet straw.

"You okay, Ma?" he said, handing over the coins.

"I'm fine, Aiden," she said. "I just wish you could tell me the truth. This is sixteen cents, Aiden. Sixteen. Not eight. Not ten."

"Oh, yeah," he said, fumbling for the next lie that might get him out of this fix. Or sink him lower. "I guess . . . I guess Mama Shandy—"

"Oh, I wish you wouldn't call her that, Aiden. She's no momma to you and never will be. I'm your mother, young man." Aiden's ma stood up, bringing the blanket with her so she stayed wrapped up in it. She glared at him, and Aiden was sure he felt her eyes digging into him somehow. Her mouth looked different, too, meaner than he'd ever seen it.

"That woman who pays you to clean her floors is nothing but a-a two-bit, lazy old—Oh, dammit, Aiden." His ma stomped a foot and then seemed to wish she hadn't. She looked down at the floor, like she could see through it.

"Mrs. Duffy is probably still sleeping, Aiden. You should get some sleep and don't make any noise. Here," she said, holding out the coins. "Put those away with your other ill-gotten gains."

Aiden took the coins back and tried to ignore the look in his ma's eyes. She'd had tough words for him before, but never like now. Something changed in her voice just there when she was talking about Mama Shandy, right before she cut off. Aiden knew what she'd meant to say. He could hear the word ringing in his ears, with his mother's voice filling it with all the anger and hatred she'd ever felt for anyone or anything.

With quiet steps, Aiden went to the kitchen and slowly added the coins to the coffee can on the shelf. One at a time they slid down the side of the can to *chink* against the others in there.

Hope it's enough to buy me a new cart.

• • •

His ma got up at dawn, like always. She made herself breakfast and left the tea kettle on the stove for Aiden. Like always. But she didn't bother setting his place at the table. Aiden tried to make it even out, like she was doing it to show him how hurt she felt. But he couldn't find it in him to make that work. His ma was acting ten kinds of mean, and Aiden knew he'd only earned two or three at most.

After scrambling an egg and eating it with toast and a glass of milk from the icebox, Aiden went to the shelf and got his can. As soon as he lifted it, he knew something was wrong.

She took my pay!

Sure enough, almost half the money he'd had in there was missing. But a note had been left in its place.

Dear Aiden,

You'll recall I gave you the five dollars you needed to buy the cleaning cart in the first place. It's time you learned about repaying a debt, young man. The two dollars I took this morning are the first payment. I expect you to pay the remaining three dollars within the next month.

"Not even a 'Love, Mom,' hey?" he said, eyeing the note like it might burst into flames the longer he held it. He flung it to the ground and snatched up the can, pouring the coins out into his pocket. The tinkling of metal on metal wasn't half as loud as it should have been. With two dollars gone, he knew he didn't have enough for a new cart from Mama Shandy. Maybe he had enough to start paying for one, though. The house mother wouldn't be any nicer than his ma about paying off a debt, and was as likely to be much worse. But what choice did he have?

Where else could he get a job in New Orleans? The docks? He'd heard about guys his size working out there. They didn't last long. Usually ended up face down in the water if they got found at all.

With his earnings in his pocket, Aiden set out down the stairs. He stopped when his feet hit the alley because his mother's voice came to him from the sewing room door.

"Where are you off to, Aiden?"

"I'm going to see about getting a new broom. For Ma—the lady I work for. I broke the other one."

"And you didn't think to mention this last night? You should be more careful, Aiden. That money has places to be, including your mother's pocket. You wouldn't have it without me giving you that five dollars anyway, and I hope you remember that from now on."

"Yes'm," he said, tucking his cap down and waiting for his ma to go back inside.

When she'd closed the door, Aiden lifted a hand up by his ear and felt for the curtain he now knew was there. Sure enough his fingers dragged against something that felt like fabric, but light and easy to move. He tugged and the memories of the alleyway opened up beside him.

Aiden risked a peek behind the curtain, hoping to see more than a muddy tunnel this time. Or a mob of muddy tramps come to claim him as their own.

The tunnel was there again, and it was empty. But instead of just a dark muddy passage, Aiden could see outlines of doorways, openings off the sides here and there, and a little more light than before, too. The doorways and side passages all had cobblestone floors.

Figuring he didn't have long to spare, Aiden thought about

hot-footing it to Mama Shandy's. Back in Chicago City, when Mr. Brand had taken him behind the curtain, they'd skipped halfways across town in a few heartbeats. Maybe he could do the same thing here.

Aiden tried a few steps in the mud, then thought about Mama Shandy's place, where she did her business and kept her books. He knew about it because he'd had to follow her there the first time, when she'd bought him off that priest.

The tunnel stretched out in front of him, long and empty, with hollow patches in the walls where doors stood waiting. One passage, far away and up ahead, began glowing. Aiden made for the side passage and was surprised to find himself standing in front of it after only a few steps.

"Just like Mr. Brand did," he said, feeling a smile working its way onto his face. That smile fell when a voice shocked Aiden like a two-thousand-volt seat cushion.

"You, uh . . . you needed to see me?"

Aiden spun around and saw his old boss standing there, half in and half out of the wall behind him.

"Mr. Brand? Jeez, you put a guy off his legs all right. Where'd you come from? And how'd you know I—?"

"It's how it goes now. You need me, I show up. Comes with the territory, I guess. You're the boss these days. I'm the messenger boy." he said, stepping into the tunnel. Mr. Brand took off his hat and held it in front of his stomach.

Aiden thought about what he'd said and it added up in his head all right. "Well, yeah. I mean, you were right. About the letter. I guess I'll take it off you now," Aiden said, holding his hand out. Mr. Brand already had his face aimed at the ground, but whatever parts hadn't found their way down there sure looked ready to join in now.

"Yeah, about that letter. It's with Miss Farnsworth. I don't know where she is and doubt she'll let on any time soon. She seemed happy to see me go, kinda the way you did when I tried to hand the letter to you the first time. I'm not counting on her calling me back again, though."

"Calling you—Miss Farnsworth is . . . she's like this, too? Like me?"

"And then some, yeah. You've got *Innocence* in there," Mr. Brand said, looking up and pointing at Aiden's chest, but dropping his eyes just as fast. "Miss Farnsworth, heh . . ." Mr. Brand let his laugh trickle off like water from a leaky tap.

"What about her?" Aiden asked. "She's one of the good ones, ain't she? I mean, I figure that's where things are at with me, hey? *Innocence* is a good thing, isn't it?"

"I wouldn't know about that," Mr. Brand said, and Aiden knew the man had just ducked the question without missing a beat, and would keep on ducking it no matter how many times Aiden asked.

"But Miss Farnsworth. She's good. Right?"

"She's who she is," Mr. Brand said. "And right now she needs your help. Mine, too, if there's anything I've got left to give that could be called help. I might have some favors I can call in. We'll see.

"But things are going wrong because the letter's with the wrong person. This city's going a little sideways, and a storm's coming in off the coast. It's gonna be a big one unless you can get that letter from Miss Farnsworth and maybe help her out of the fix she's got herself in."

"Why, what's the big deal about a letter?"

"Just like in Chicago City, the way *Hubris* and *Industry* worked a con to take control of the whole city. They sent Larson around after all the other messengers, disrupting the mail, see? Gods have to communicate to keep things steady. When the mail gets messed up, things don't go right. At first it's just small potatoes. Eventually, maybe a city burns down, or a storm takes it off the map. Let it go long enough, it's the war to end all wars, redux."

"Okay," Aiden said, nodding and feeling the truth of his old boss's words settle into his heart. "I need to read that letter or something bad's going to happen to the city, and Miss Farnsworth's got the letter. So how do I find her?"

"She's working for Bacchus, flying girls around the city while her jazz man plays his horn for them in the gala houses. Just keep going to work and I bet you'll see her soon enough. Was that all you wanted?"

Aiden gave his old boss a look, and the way Mr. Brand's face went slack told Aiden he'd made his point. But he added a few words for good measure.

"Yeah, that's all," he said.

Mr. Brand lifted up the curtain behind him and slipped out of sight, leaving Aiden alone in the tunnel by Mama Shandy's place. Feeling the coins in his pocket, Aiden put a hand on the outline of the passageway in the tunnel wall, and a second later he stood on the street in front of Mama Shandy's house. His jaw fell open and his eyes went wide at the sight.

The windows were blacked out and the porch sagged on one side. The fine paint and polished wood were all chipped and scratched up. All around him, Aiden felt the air like a wet sheet sticking to his skin. A second later, and like it was meant for good measure, a hot wind whipped through the night and turned Aiden's face to the side. At the base of a tree out front of Mama Shandy's, Aiden saw black feathers lying this way and that, like they'd fallen from the angry clouds overhead.

CHAPTER 29

EMMA KEPT ON WORRYING HERSELF ABOUT what Brand had said, and what was in the letter she hadn't opened. She tried to ignore it, but the envelope with her name on it kept finding a way in front of her face. She'd put it in her dresser drawer, with her underthings. The next morning it was on the night table beside her bed, waiting for her when she woke up. She'd stuck it under her pillow and went downstairs only to find the letter on the kitchen counter next to the cutlery block.

Now she carried it in her coat pocket while she walked Eddie to the curb where his band waited in a van. They didn't have any shows lined up this week, he'd said, so they were going to rehearse at the Sun tonight. Emma had planned to go along, but she'd been called up by Bacchus to run the girls to another gala house.

"Be home late tonight, Emma. But don't you worry. Me and the fellas just be playin' our numbers and learnin' some new ones. Supposed to be a big night comin' up soon, so we gotta play good and smooth."

"Maybe I can go with you then," she said, doing her best to make the words sound sincere.

"Yeah. Maybe so," Eddie said, kissing her on the cheek. He stepped into the van and waved before closing the door. She watched the van drive off and didn't even pretend she hadn't heard the whooping and laughter that faded into the night air behind the dimming tail lights.

A warm wind swept through the air, leaving fingers of moisture tickling Emma's face. She wanted to enjoy it, but it just felt heavy and unwelcome. Suffocating, like a hug she couldn't escape.

• • •

An hour later, Emma was on the *Vigilance*, opening the door so the girls could board and take their place at the rear of the cabin. They came in like usual, slow and somber, and a seventh girl had joined them this time. Pretty and dark-skinned, the girl hung back with the chaperone, who gave Emma a mild curtsey as she stepped off the gangway. The new girl looked like she might be sick any minute and the chaperone seemed to hold her close with her eyes.

Emma gave the new chaperone what she hoped was a friendly wave. The woman gave back a half-hearted smile beneath eyes that couldn't decide if they wanted to frown or grimace. Then she seemed to remember something and her face lit up.

"Miss Emma, a pleasure. I'm Lisette Durand," the chaperone said. "A pleasure," she said again, extending a gloved hand.

"You said that twice," Emma replied, simply nodding rather than shaking the chaperone's hand.

"Oh, you're right, Miss Emma," the woman said, retracting her hand to clutch her little bag closer to her bosom. Emma didn't miss the way the chaperone's worried eyes aimed in the new girl's direction.

"I did. My apologies, please. I'm—That is, this is my first time in an airship, you see, so I suppose that's why I'm acting nervous. Do excuse me, please."

Emma nodded and went to close the door. Something smelled funny about the chaperone and the new girl. She didn't know everything about Bacchus's operation, but she knew enough to figure the chaperones had dirty tricks of their own, just like their boss. Still, this was the first time one of them had anything like kind words to share, much less a curtsey of respect. Emma wasn't sure if that meant good or bad for the future, so she gave up, deciding it was wasted time. She was too busy with her own concerns.

Emma had a plan for tonight that would require the chaperone to trust her. If it worked out, she'd get inside the gala house and at least see what it looked like and what kind of "dancing and laughing" went on there. Then she could finally give Eddie the rundown and they could decide if it was time to run off.

Or I can decide all by my lonesome.

"I'll have us to the house in ten minutes, Miss Lisette," Emma said, taking the pilot's seat and radioing the gearboxes to cut them loose.

"Oh, there ain't no rush, Miss Emma. Sure enough, these girls don't need to be getting to that house any earlier than they have to."

The woman's voice quivered as she spoke and Emma felt certain it was from more than a newcomer's anxiety. She let it slide, though.

Working the ballast, Emma got them into the air and away over the French Quarter rooftops. The chaperone had met her at the mooring deck down from her and Eddie's house, another change to the way things usually worked on this gig. Thinking about it now, Emma decided to risk a little conversation. Maybe this chaperone would be up for sharing some details beforehand. Anything that might help Emma prove what she felt sure to be true about the gala houses.

"Say, Miss Lisette?"

"Yes, Miss Emma. What do you need?" the woman asked, standing from where she'd been leaning against Brand's desk.

"Need? Oh, nothing. But I wondered if you could tell me something about the gala house."

"Oh sure thing, Miss Emma. Sure thing. Anything at all, you just ask."

That settled it. Emma knew a sap when she saw one, and this girl was all sap and nothing but. Instead of asking for information, Emma went straight for the throat.

"What's with the rabbit act, sister?"

Emma had hoped that would be the pin that held the floodgates closed, but it turned out to be a stopper in the bottle instead.

"Rabbit—? Now, Miss Emma, I don't know what you mean by asking me that." The woman's voice changed; it dropped lower and picked up some heat on the way down. "Why don't you just keep your eyes on your flying and leave me and these girls be."

"Okay," Emma said, smiling to herself at how the woman's choice of words revealed her anxiety. A little more prodding and Emma would have exactly what she needed to prove to Eddie they were in a dirty business.

"We'll be at the house soon, so you should probably get your girls ready. Don't you think, Lisette?"

That last bit didn't register with the chaperone. Lisette Durand did exactly as Emma suggested, directing the girls to gather themselves up and get ready to step nice "for the guests."

Emma knew for sure she'd found the back door she'd been hoping for. As soon as they were alone, for the return trip, she'd get some questions answered.

• • •

The girls stepped down the gangway, slow and frightened like usual. A pair of toughs in fine suits met them at the bottom and led them into the gala house beside the mooring deck. Lisette stayed on the deck, watching the girls enter the house. This was the fanciest arrangement yet, and part of Emma wished she could join in the fun. Hear the tinkle of ice in her glass. Feel the warmth of a fireplace and the click of her heels on the floor.

The better part of her wanted to take the girls and fly away somewhere. But where would they go? Even if she did get away clean, she could only hide out for a day at most.

The *Vigilance* wasn't the only airship in New Orleans, but Bacchus had a way of knowing where she was. And she'd already seen what the *krewe* boss did to employees who failed to satisfy his demands. Emma shuddered thinking about what Bacchus might do to someone who straight out acted against him.

Lisette stepped back up the gangway after the last girl had gone inside, and now the chaperone stood at the cabin door, one foot still on the gangway.

"You going to stand there all night or should we get on with it?"

"Yes'm, Miss Emma. You right. Let's get on," the young woman said. Lisette stepped into the cabin and worked the door closed. She took halting steps to Brand's desk and fell into the chair with her face in her hands.

Emma got them airborne in silence, but as soon as they were at elevation, she started in on Lisette.

"So you gonna spill now the girls are out of earshot? What's with you? You're not like the other chaperones."

Lisette sniffed from where she sat behind Emma. Then the girl spilled her guts in between sobs and hollers of sorrow.

"My baby girl," Lisette said, sniffling and coughing sad. "My little Juliette gonna get auctioned off with the rest of 'em and ain't nothin' I can do to save her."

A wrinkle of hatred creased Emma's brow as Lisette's words hit home. "Auction?"

Lisette sniffed and coughed some more and went silent. Emma looked back and saw the chaperone staring out the cabin windows, eyes dripping tears down her cheeks and her jaw trembling.

"That's right, Miss Emma. Mr. Bacchus runnin' his debutante auction a few days from now. Them girls, and my Juliette's one of 'em, they all gettin' sold off for that New York money."

Emma's head spun every way at once and snapped back into place just as fast. That man she'd seen on the street that first night out with Eddie. The way the girls looked scared and almost sallow, like they'd be sick any second.

"They're going to be sold? Like cattle?"

Lisette hummed a reply.

"How long has this been going on?" Emma asked.

"The auction? Only jus' started up really. But Mr. Bacchus been trading girls left and right in this town long as I can remember."

"How'd you get mixed up in it? Your daughter. How'd Bacchus get her from you?"

"He didn' have much trouble. When a baby come out, whoever catch her pretty much say where she gon' go. Mother can try to snatch her back, but after you done pushin' and cryin' and gruntin' like it's about to be your last breath . . . Fight goes outta you quick as can be. Mr. Bacchus had the nurse take my baby girl outta the room. Her twin brother, too. Then Mr. Bacchus, he told me how it'd be."

"Why?" Emma asked. It felt so inadequate, so small a question, and it was still the only thing Emma could find the strength to say.

"Man named Otis," Lisette said and gave a short laugh. "Man. He just a boy when I knew him. He went up Chicago City way. Said he'd make some money and then come and get me and the child I was goin' be havin' by him. Course, he didn' know was two of 'em I'd be havin'."

Lisette's face went cloudier still but brightened just a touch, so that Emma figured she'd best hold on to her questions and let the woman tell her tale. The chaperone didn't disappoint.

"Otis, he like to playin' a horn. Trumpet. First time I saw him he just sittin' on his stoop playin' that horn. When you that young, a man playin' music look like every star in the sky.

"He got me with a child, and then he went up that river while I had my baby. Like I say, I had not just one, but two. I supposed to end up like them girls we just put in that house, goin' off to Mr. Bacchus' debutante card games, but a few months before I turned sixteen, me and Otis celebrated, and soon enough the house mother talkin' to Mr. Bacchus about my 'condition.'

"Pregnant girl can't be auctioned off for no kinda money. Them New York men come looking for girls ain't know what it means to lay with a man yet. Mr. Bacchus, he keep me around, though, say I'll pay my way back into his good graces."

"What about your kids?" Emma finally asked, dividing her attention between flying and keeping hold of every word that came out of Lisette's mouth.

"I had my twins. Julien and Juliette. My sweet baby girl, Juliette. Raised them both up with help from Mr. B, and he say I just have to work the Sun hall to pay him back. Well I been doin' that job near sixteen years now, and I'm thinkin' I paid my dues to Mr. Bacchus and his *krewe*. So I went in and ask him last night if we was fair and square."

Emma didn't miss the bit about the 'Sun hall,' but she couldn't let her own worries intrude on the moment. Lisette had the scoop and then some, and Emma wasn't about to let the story get away from her now. "What'd Bacchus say? Last night, when you asked him."

"He said sure enough we was fair and square. Said I could even 'move up in his employ.' Gave me the chaperone job starting tonight. And then I see why he did it. My little girl's standing there with the others, all waitin' on me to take 'em to the gala house for the show and tell."

"How's that?" Emma asked. "What do you mean 'show and tell'?"

"How they do it. Show the men what they biddin' for. Man not gon' pay up his money he don' know what he gettin' in return. I thought you knew that, though, Miss Emma. You been flyin' these girls all round New Orleans, ain't you?"

"Yeah, but nobody told me why," Emma said, feeling the pain of Eddie's lies like a gunshot to her heart.

"Just how they do things here, Lovebird. Girls go out with daddies and uncles. Brothers, too."

"Well, now you know," Lisette said. "I suppose I should say thank you, as you seem nice enough and don' give the girls no hassle. I can' expect you been treated too well by them other chaperones, and I'm sorry for that, Miss Emma."

Lisette went back to sobbing and Emma kept her eyes on the night through the windscreen.

"Sixteen years!" Lisette shouted, startling Emma. "That man been holdin' his cards close. Sixteen years and Mr. B didn't never say nothin' about takin' my baby girl from me. Sonofabitch ain't lost nothin' wasn't his to lose anyway, and he damn sure ain't gettin' nothin' more from me now he killed my Otis."

"Bacchus didn't shoot Otis," Emma said. "It was his man Hardy. The guy who runs his mooring deck out in Metairie."

"How you know this?" Lisette asked. Emma heard the woman stand from Brand's desk and come a few steps up behind her.

"I was there when Hardy did it," Emma said, keeping her eyes on the night in front of them. "Otis came with me and . . . my man. We were flying down from Chicago City. Otis was picked up by a copper named *Wynes*." Emma snarled the man's name and went on to tell Lisette about the lynching and how she'd killed Wynes and helped Otis and Eddie escape along with the Conroys.

As she brought the *Vigilance* in over the neighborhood deck, Emma hoped she'd have no cause to ever share stories about the other things she'd seen that night in Chicago City. And part of her knew that hope was about as misplaced as a white girl flying an airship in New Orleans.

"You wantin' to be helpin' somebody else escape now," Lisette said and came to stand by Emma's side. "I can see it in you, Miss Emma. Way you look out that window. Sure as I'm standin' in this airship, you want to fly away your own self. Somewhere. Anywhere but New Orleans. I'm right, too. Tell me I'm not."

"You're right," Emma said. "But that won't change anything. I'll fly away and you'll still be here. Your kids'll still be here."

"Not if you help us get free we won't."

Emma let the words sink in for half a breath before she nodded. "Okay," she said, turning to look Lisette in the eye. "But we can't just take your little girl and leave the others. We've got to get them all out, and put Bacchus down if we can."

Lisette's eyes went round with fear, but she kept her voice steady. "I don' know about killin' Mr. B, but we gon' get them girls free."

"Damn right we are," Emma said, going back to looking out the windscreen at the night ahead. "You know, Lisette, I think I might need your help with something else."

"With what?"

Emma heard the words in her mind and she saw the scene laid out a film reel. Eddie getting into the van. The other jazz boys laughing and slapping him on the back. The things she'd heard them say about "biddin'" and "seein' what's on the block."

"What you need my help with, Miss Emma?" Lisette asked again, breaking into Emma's thoughts.

She paused before she answered, took a deep breath, then replied, "Sniffing out a rat."

CHAPTER 30

I T TOOK AIDEN TWO LIFTS TO GET UP THE STEPS
and a third to set the mop bucket on the splintered boards of
his new cart.

New.

Aiden sniffed and tugged the bucket closer to the middle of the
cart so it wouldn't spill over the side. His old cart, it'd had a strap
to keep the bucket steady. But this one . . .

When he'd gone into Mama Shandy's place, she had a look on
her face that told him it was a bad day to be asking for anything, let
alone a new clean-up cart. Like the mess outside the house hadn't
already told him enough.

"What you want, Dove?" she'd asked, with her eyes glued to the
wall above Aiden's head. He'd told her about losing his cart and held
out the can he kept his money in. He'd put it on her desk and she
had snatched it before his fingers left the rim of the can.

Without even counting it, she'd told him it wasn't enough for a
new cart. She'd then shooed him out with her fingertips, still staring
up at the wall above the door, her face shaking and eyes red-rimmed

with anger and fear. Aiden had caught a glimpse of the wall as he left. Something dark, like paint, was smeared there, and the shape of a bird. Feathers scattered around it.

And blood. Aiden had smelled it as he left.

A tough outside Mama Shandy's office had taken him by the scruff and pushed him down the stairs. Aiden had kept his feet, but he had still skidded down a few steps and nearly turned his ankle. The tough bird then opened a closet under the stairs and had pulled out this pile of splinters and old twine on four beat-up, old rubber wheels. He'd shoved it across the floor at Aiden, telling him he'd best get to work.

Mama Shandy's voice had come down from above him and Aiden had looked up the stairs to see her tear-stained cheeks and wild, crazy eyes glaring at him.

"Damn dove be workin' a year 'fore he pay off a new cart. Well, that Bonvivant bitch can take it outta his ass. She gettin' nothin' else from me!"

Mama Shandy's words echoed around Aiden's head now. He pushed the cart into the new gala house where he had been told he'd be working. He was careful not to hit the door jamb or the newel post just inside the entry. A hall led into the back, where Aiden could see the kitchen. Doors led off left and right to parlors and other rooms he'd have to clean up, but he couldn't tell what he was supposed to clean. Aiden breathed in the smell of fresh plaster and paint, and he stared at the gleaming brass fittings and polished wood.

"Hey, boy!"

Aiden looked up the stairs and met the gaze of his new employer, the house mother he'd been sold to, or who'd stolen him like he was something to steal.

Mama Sophie Bonvivant. She stood in the glow of an electric bulb set in a wall sconce at the top of the stairs. Her blond hair lit up like a halo, but the heated look on her pale face said trouble was on the menu.

But he'd just got here, and early. What kind of trouble could he be in?

"Y-yes'm," he said, dropping his eyes to the toes of her shoes.

"Up here," she said, coming down the stairs as she spoke. "And leave the damn bucket where it is. I've got a room full of mess upstairs. First one on the right. You'll just need a broom and dustpan."

With her last words she came to the bottom landing. Mama Sophie was about Aiden's height, maybe a little taller. But she carried herself like she was ten feet tall. Her hands framed her hips and her blazing blue eyes added a weight to her slight frame. Aiden knew that she wouldn't think twice before knocking him silly with the back of her hand.

"Yes'm," he replied, standing still and holding his hands in plain sight on the cart handle, like he'd learned to do.

"You all right, boy?"

Aiden didn't much care for the way she called him, but he had to admit it was better than *dove*.

"Yes'm. I'm fine, ma'am."

"The way you're standing there like you don't have work to do, I thought you might be getting the vapors. You aren't, are you?"

"No, ma'am," Aiden said, moving his head side to side nice and slow.

"Well that's good, then. Go on and do your job. Money'll be in the can outside when you're done."

"Yes'm," Aiden said, still not moving because he'd have to go around Mama Sophie to reach the stairs, and he knew as well as any houseboy never to set foot in the path of a house mother or her staff, or pretty much anyone he met in the gala houses.

"Well go on then, boy," she said, stepping to the side.

"Yes, Mama Sophie," Aiden said as he waited for her to leave.

She stopped with her hand on the knob and gave him a look up and down. He could feel her eyes burning into his cheek. "They tell you to call me that when they sent you over from Shandy's pit? Huh, boy? They tell you to call me *Mama*?" She took her hand off the doorknob and came to stand inches away from Aiden. He could smell a hint of gin on her breath as she hollered into his ear.

"Maybe they told you to call me *Mama* because they thought it'd be funny. Well listen up, boy, and listen up right. You see a white woman in front of you, you don't call her your *Mama*. You call her *Mother*. Is that clear, boy?"

"Yes'm," Aiden said, shaking and waiting for the hand that he knew would come up any second and sweep across his face like a storm.

But she didn't hit him. Ma—Mother Sophie Bonvivant stepped back and put her hand on the knob, turning it. Then she clicked her tongue and muttered something about "soiled doves" before going out the front door.

When she had gone, Aiden lifted the dustpan off his cart. Taking the old broom from its clasp he breathed deep and let it out as he made his way upstairs.

The single electric light cast a glimmer around the door to his right. Three more doors stood across the hall, all closed. Nothing but silence came back to him as he listened to the house. The washroom was to his right, just beyond the room he would be cleaning. Past that was another closed door. The far wall was all windows and looked out to the yard behind the house.

Aiden went back to the first room and pushed the door all the way open. He stepped in and stalled with his foot halfway to the floor.

The room was torn apart. Pictures had been ripped from the walls, glass lay around in scattered shards, the bits by the door reflecting pinpoints of warmth from the wall sconce. In the corners of the room, lamps were on their sides, the electric bulbs shattered across the wood flooring. A couch was turned over on its front, like it had been pulled away from the wall and forced out of someone's way.

Rolls of the carpet buckled up from the floor in places, and the corners of the rug were all peeled back, making a sort of basket for all the broken glass. Moonlight slanted through a window in the wall opposite the door, casting crazy shadows with the toppled furniture. A door in the left wall of the room was closed, but Aiden could tell it had been open when the mess was made. Shards of glass had scraped across the floor and under the door into whatever was behind it.

The last time Aiden had seen such a mess he'd been running from the Governor's army in Chicago City. For a second he worried a soldier would come through the closed door with a gat in his hand, ready to plug Aiden in the chest for helping Mr. Brand mess things up for the Great Lakes Governor.

But that was all behind them. It had been over a month with nothing from Chicago City, not even a peep.

Lifting his feet careful around the larger shards of glass, Aiden swept the bits and pieces together. He picked up the corner of the carpet and shook it gently, bouncing the smaller slivers into a pile in the middle. He got the big shards collected by hand and pitched them into the waste chute in the wall. But the house mother hadn't told him how to get the smaller pieces out of the carpet.

He could sweep until the sun came up and not have them all cleaned away.

Since this was a new house, it had to have one of those fancy vacuum systems. Aiden looked around and, sure enough, he spotted a valve set into the wall by the door. So somewhere there had to be a hose to connect to it, and a way to turn it on.

Aiden went to the closed door. The vacuum hose and control box was probably in there. He tried the handle, but it wouldn't budge. It wasn't locked, just jammed with something that stopped it from flipping up or down. He jiggled it again and felt it slip away from whatever had jammed against it. He tugged and the door fell open, pushing Aiden backward.

Something heavy fell out from behind the door, pushing it against Aiden. He heard a thump and felt something hit the floor as he stumbled and went down against the overturned couch. With a quick grab, he steadied himself so he wouldn't land in the pile of glass on the carpet. When he had his feet again he looked at the door and what had come out.

A Negro girl was lying there, half out of the closet that held the vacuum hose. When Aiden went over to her, he recognized her. She'd been at Mama Shandy's place a week back, on the arm of some thick-necked bird, and the both of them were dressed for uptown. The guy was white and had a set of dark eyes like gun barrels.

The girl had been smiling that night, a week ago. But now, Aiden could tell right away she was dead. Her cheeks were puffy and bruised under both eyes, and a scarf was wrapped tight around her neck. The one eye Aiden could see was open and bloodshot.

He reeled back then, knowing what he'd found and knowing good and well he wasn't supposed to have found it, and why Mother Sophie had told him how to do his job.

"You'll just need a broom and dustpan."

But he couldn't just hide the girl's body again. There was no way he could put it all back like he'd never opened the door. They'd find out. The house mother and every man in her *krewe* would know he'd seen the dead girl.

As Aiden stared at the girl's frozen eyes, Mother Sophie's angry voice swept up the stairs like she didn't care who heard.

"I know who he is, Mr. Bacchus. And I know where he's from. He killed one of my girls and he's gonna pay up for it. That fat white cat shows his face in your auction house tomorrow night, I want him in the street. You hear me? *In the STREET!*"

Aiden whipped a hand over his mouth when he heard Bacchus's name. He stayed silent and still and waited for the gangster's heavy voice to reply. He got nothing for his trouble but more silence. Aiden wondered what Mother Sophie meant by "auction house." The words played around in his head like puzzle pieces that wouldn't quite fit together. Then Mother Sophie shouted a curse and kept on.

"I don't care if all of New York City comes down on my head. Sophie Bonvivant doesn't run from any man."

When no reply came again, Aiden figured the house mother was on a radiophone. He hadn't seen one when he'd come in, but the house had to have one. It had a vacuum system.

And a dead girl in a closet.

Aiden nearly shrieked when Mother Sophie's voice sliced the quiet house apart again.

"Well the Birdman owes me for giving him my bitch of a half-sister, doesn't he? When he's done with Shandy and her *krewe*, you get him a message. Tell him Mother Sophie needs to collect."

Aiden heard the clatter of a radiophone in its cradle. He crept away from the dead girl to watch the stairs in case Mother Sophie came up to check on his work. A door opened somewhere downstairs. Aiden craned his neck for a look below the landing, but Mother Sophie's voice rang out of the kitchen and hit his ears like a fire alarm.

"Boy, you about done up there?"

Aiden backed into the room and shouted, "Yes'm!" He kicked at the glass near his feet to make sounds like he was cleaning.

"Good. Get on and finish."

"Yes'm, Ma—Mother Sophie. I will."

"That's your only free one, boy," she yelled up at him. "Mix me up with a *Mama* again, you'll feel the cane on your backside. And don't tell me what you *will*. Just *DO*! And hurry up. I got some more work for you out back, too."

Aiden listened for her footsteps on the stairs, his heart in his throat as he waited. Then he heard the kitchen door close a second time and he stepped fast but careful to the landing windows.

Mother Sophie went down a stone walk to a little shack where two colored men were busy flinging mud all over the outer walls. A white man came out from the shack with a bucket that he filled at a trough where the other men were also collecting mud and who knew what else.

"Got some other work for me, huh?" Aiden said to the empty house. He felt a twitch in his throat and it told him he'd made his last move in the houseboy game. Aiden stepped down the stairs. He went as quiet as could be and unlatched the front door, breathing a silent hope that the stoop wouldn't be guarded. He opened the door and saw the night waiting for him, empty and cold, so he ran into it with all his will, leaving the house and its horrors behind.

CHAPTER 31

AS EMMA PILOTED THE *VIGILANCE*, SHE thought about the letters Brand gave her. They were in his old desk now, where Lisette was sitting. Emma tucked the letters in there as soon as she and Lisette got on board, and she hoped that's where they would stay. They hadn't moved since she put them there. No showing up in the cockpit right when she went to start the motors or radio down to a mooring deck.

Maybe Brand was just playing tricks to scare her. But why would he do that?

As soon as the question hit her mind, Emma swatted it away. Who cared what Brand was up to? If she'd thought the letters were magical before, it must have been the stress of dealing with Eddie and the worry about the job she'd been doing for Bacchus.

Brand was just a crazy old tramp, half drunk, or all the way drunk.

But what if he wasn't fooling? And how could he be with that vanishing act of his.

If one of those letters was for her, then it meant she'd found some way to get the gods' attention, more than before anyway.

But so what? If they've got something to say that's so damned important, why not just say it instead of sending Brand around flapping envelopes in my face!

Emma wiped her eyes and drew in a deep breath, forcing herself to calm down. She had important business of her own tonight, and it was damn sure more important than any old letter handed over by a bum.

"You okay, Miss Emma?" Lisette asked.

"Yeah. I'm fine," she said, not believing a word of it and knowing Lisette didn't, either.

"Sounds like you got more to tell than you lettin' on, but I ain't gon' press you on it none. Not if you don' want to be tellin' me."

Emma knew a bait and switch when she heard one, but Lisette's had to be the smoothest and kindest she'd ever been handed.

"The place where Eddie practices," Emma said and swallowed a laugh that turned into a cough. "He told me that's what he does there anyway. Said it's just a little room where bands go to work up their chops. What do you know about it?"

"The Sun? He call it a practice hall?" Lisette said, her voice betraying the fear and worry that found a home in her just then. Emma did her best to put the woman at ease.

"I get that's a lie. You don't need to worry about shocking me, Lisette. I've seen just about the worst there is in this world."

"If you say so, Miss Emma."

When Lisette didn't continue, Emma nudged her again. "So what do you know about it? Where am I taking us and what am I going to see?"

Lisette kept her tongue for a moment but finally let on. "Sun ain't no little room. It's like to bein' the oldest dance hall in New Orleans. Full name's *the Rising Sun*, and ain't no man go there not knowing what he gettin' into and hopin' he gonna get everything he can."

Emma thought back to Brand's last visit, and the warning he'd given about Eddie. *So what if he did land himself in the street,* Emma thought. So what if he woke up covered in mud with nothing but a banged-up horn in one hand and vomit down his shirt.

So damn what.

Emma flew them on to the deck by her and Eddie's place. She and Lisette sat in the ship, talking while they waited for the night to grow old enough.

"You said they don't get going 'til after midnight."

"That's right, Miss Emma. Usual it's the bands play them gala house shows first. Then they all go to the Sun and kick up a bit. That rum they get from down the Gulf, and that sweet leaf they smoke, makes the whole night feel right as can be."

Emma didn't much care for the way Lisette's eyes went glad as she talked, so she switched up the story fast.

"What're we going to do when we get the girls out? Where can we go? Do you know anywhere that's safe?"

Lisette's face drooped in a heartbeat and she almost went back to shaking and sobbing. With a long slow breath, she held it in.

"Sure I don't know anywhere around New Orleans that's safe if that's what you askin'."

"Well what about farther away? Do you have family anywhere? Cousins? Anyone?"

Lisette shook her head. "We all from down here and the Durand name pretty much all gone now 'cept for a few that don' wanna admit they blood with me and my babies."

"So we go somewhere else," Emma said, mulling over the ideas she'd had since Lisette told her the truth about Bacchus's game. She'd seen the one banker that night she was out with Eddie. And one New York banker was more than enough for her. But she had to be sure.

"They're all from New York?"

"Who?"

"The ones who come down and buy the girls."

"Oh. Yes, that's what everyone always sayin'. New York money this and New York money that. Might be different men spendin' it, but it always the same money."

Emma let it sit. Lisette looked tired. If Emma had to admit it, she was exhausted herself. And she still had to confront Eddie and fly back home afterward, so a little rest seemed the right thing just then.

Lisette leaned herself onto Brand's desk and let out a little sigh as she settled in. Emma thought about grabbing a quick nap in the bunkroom, but as soon as the thought came it went back out. She'd never wake up, and that'd be the end of their big plans. Bacchus didn't have any work for her tonight, so she and Lisette were going on a snake hunt. She just had to stay awake until it was time to fly.

Three hours later, Emma snapped awake in the pilot's chair and glared at the clock set into the control panel. She shook herself and rubbed her face. Lisette stirred behind her and came awake slowly as Emma got the *Vigilance* airborne again.

The Rising Sun sat by the riverside, over in Carrollton. Emma took them there as quick as she could, and they came in too fast over the nearest mooring deck. Emma had to loop back around to approach from a better angle. She breathed deep the whole time, doing what she could to calm her shaking hands. Lisette kept asking if she was all right, but Emma held in every word that clawed its way onto her tongue. All it seemed to do was make her eyes water and her throat burn.

• • •

The walk from the deck was quiet enough, except for the steady *thump-thump* of Emma's angry heart. The sting of Eddie's lies ate away at her from the inside and turned her gut to acid. Halfway to the hall she had to lean against a tree and gulp some air to keep her stomach down. Lisette said she'd stay behind in the ship because people would recognize her out here.

"This where Mr. B had me workin' all these years, while he was raisin' up my Juliette for auction."

Emma had wanted to ask about what to expect, but speaking her daughter's name made Lisette go silent and still while tears dripped from her cheeks. So Emma had left her in the ship and made her way down the street on her own.

When she saw the hall up ahead by the riverside, Emma felt her insides spin again and only just kept them steady with a hand pressed flat against her belly.

Glowing lights from the second-story windows lit up the night around the hall. People standing on the balconies there etched the scene with their laughter and sweet-smelling smoke. That and the foot stomping from inside told Emma everything she needed to know about Eddie's "rehearsals" out here. Even without Lisette's information, she'd had plenty of reason to suspect before. But seeing it with her own eyes stabbed the blade of betrayal even deeper.

Two heavies stood at the doors: white men with jaws that look like they could chew bricks for breakfast. They stood either side of the entrance dressed in the same liveries as Bacchus's other boys, but these two looked twice the fight as any Emma had seen so far. Both men wore a look that said you were welcome only if you meant to have a good time and not cause any trouble. Emma had seen their type back in Chicago City and worked up her best smile, just like she'd done back home when it meant getting into the mayor's speaks without any hassle.

"Evening, miss," one of the men called to her as she approached from across street.

"Hi," Emma said, letting her hips say more than her lips did. "I hear it's girl's night tonight. Is that right, boys?"

The two men chuckled and one came forward, letting his hands fall to his sides.

"If you're here as an invited guest, it can be your night."

Emma almost let her mask slip into worry, but she caught herself in time and let out a giggle instead. "I believe I'm on the list, but my invite is with my man inside. His name's Eddie Collins. I'm sure you know him," Emma said, hating herself for making a mockery of the fire that burned her heart to ash. "Don't you, boys?"

At first she thought she'd overdone it. Both men had looks on their mugs that said they wished she'd told them different, but as the near one reached a hand up to his jacket, the other put a hand out and touched his partner's arm.

"She's with the band. We don't need that kind of trouble," he said and dropped his hand back to join the other one in front of his belt.

"Yeah," the near one said to Emma. "Go on inside."

Emma nodded her thanks and stepped between the two men. As she passed through the wide-open double doors, she heard the men chatting behind her.

"Guess he likes white and dark meat on the grill," the first one said.

Emma swallowed the ball of rage that flared in her throat. She used a thumb to dab the tears that threatened to leak from her eyes and went into the hall. At the back of the foyer, a staircase led up to the next floor. To her left and right, high doorways opened into grand parlors filled with tinkling glasses, laughter, and dancing feet.

A white woman came from the parlor to Emma's left holding a drink in one hand and a silver cigarette holder in the other. The woman wore flapper beads, a feather fascinator, and what looked like half the dress she was meant to be wearing. With a quick flick of her eyes, the chippy took in Emma's plain skirt and simple blouse. In that instant, Emma regretted not dolling herself up in the glad rags Bacchus had given her.

If I hadn't fallen asleep . . .

Emma knew what it felt like to be weighed and measured. She'd had plenty of men send their eyes in her direction before, looking her up, down, and all points between. This wasn't the first time a woman's eyes treated her this way, but it was the first time Emma felt it like a punch to the gut. The flapper's lips and eyes curled into a look that told Emma she'd wandered into a viper's den.

"My, my," the woman said, pausing to puff on her smoke. She let the holder dangle between her fingers like it might fall only to snap her fingers closed around it, trapping it in her grip. Her face hadn't changed any, and Emma waited for the insults to start flying from the woman's ruby lips.

Emma didn't have to wait for long.

"My, *oh* my. What *would* be the occasion?" she said, dropping her eyes to Emma's simple brown shoes and white stockings. The smoking woman had on a pair of jet black sandals with straps that tied above her slender ankles.

Emma figured she had one play, and it happened to be the one she'd been holding in since they got to New Orleans.

"I'm here looking for my man. He's a horn player. Name's Eddie Collins. You seen him?"

The flapper didn't miss a beat in replying, and the steam Emma thought she'd put behind her words escaped from her lips in a gasp of surprise.

"Oh, Eddie? Your man, is he? Well"—the flapper stepped close enough that Emma could smell the cigarette on her breath—"You'll find him around back, I suspect. But you know that saying about fools rushing in. Best if you just hang there by the door and listen," the woman suggested, her lips still doing the same serpent's smile as before.

Emma's hand shot out before she could stop it. The flapper's face spun to the side, driven by the slap like a car that'd been slammed into.

One of the toughs at the door stepped inside with a hand hovering over his lapels.

"Miss June, is everything all right?"

The flapper recovered and waved a hand at the doorman. She said it was all right. That and her eyes told Emma she'd won this round.

"Where is he?" Emma asked. "You said out back. Where out back?"

"In the gatehouse," the flapper said. "But—"

"But what?"

"You don't want to go out there on your own. He won't be the same man you know, and it won't be good for you."

Emma sniffed at that. "Sister, he's not the same man I know and from the look of how this place runs, he hasn't been for a good long time."

"That's not what I mean, honey," the flapper said, her old malice coming back into her voice. "I mean no woman ever goes out there and comes back the same as she was before."

Emma let that sink in. For a second she thought about heading back to the *Vigilance* and just flying out of town, anywhere but here in this hellish den of vice she'd wandered into. Then Lisette's face came to her memory, and Emma's feet took her out the front door and down the stone walkway that led around the building to the gatehouse by the riverbank.

Heavy dark trees lined the walk and Emma kept to the shadows as best she could. She paused when she heard Eddie's voice from around the corner of the house. His deep laugh, the laugh that used to make her smile, echoed between the trees like a whispered warning.

CHAPTER 32

AIDEN SHUFFLED UP THE STAIRS TO HIS AND his ma's apartment, cradling his left arm with his right and keeping away from the wall in case he slipped and had to fall against it to keep his feet. The way his shoulder hurt, he knew he'd scream if it bumped against anything but air.

He'd gotten away from Mother Bonvivant's house. Well enough anyway, even if he wasn't well enough to work for the house mother anymore.

He'd run and kept running, but they'd caught up to him. Two guys from Mother Bonvivant's *krewe* rounded a corner in his path, so Aiden had dodged and made for the other side of the street. An alley opened there, and he was sure he'd get away if he could just make it inside.

One thing he'd made sure to do since getting work as a houseboy was learn the streets. Julien had helped him there, and the alley would have given him a maze to hide in. They'd never have caught him if he'd made it inside.

But two more of the house mother's *krewe* had come right out of the alley and made straight for him. By the time he'd dodged again, the ones behind him had his arms and soon enough the other pair had his legs, too.

"Little dove tryin' to fly. Time to clip your fool wings."

One of them had grabbed his left arm and wrenched it up behind his back hard enough to pop it loose. Aiden had felt a heavy burn shoot straight down his arm and across his chest, a pain like someone had shoved a branding iron against his shoulder and held it there.

The toughs dropped him to the ground and had kicked him a few times in the gut. He'd curled up, holding his good arm against his belly and taking the kicks there. One of them had spit on his face and talked about knocking out some teeth, but another one said they'd done enough, that "Mother Sophie don't want her little dove thinkin' she has no use for him."

"She just say teach this white boy a lesson he don' forget. We taught him, I'd say. What you say, dove? You learnin'?"

They'd all laughed, and one of them had put a foot into Aiden's crotch before they left. Aiden had cried and held his lame arm, fighting the urge to move it but feeling like he had to so it would go back where it belonged. Finally he'd struggled to his feet and swallowed hard as he gripped his left arm and pushed it up. A fire like he'd never felt spread across his chest, down his back, and so deep into him that it brought up his dinner.

He'd made it home right about the time he'd usually get there, but with tears still pouring from his eyes. At the top of the stairs, he'd leaned back against the wall so his arm would rest against his body. Then he'd used his good hand to pull his key out from his shirt collar.

It took a few tries to get himself set right, so his bum arm wouldn't hang wrong and hurt more, but he'd finally got the key in the lock and gently turned the knob with his good hand. With a push from his foot, the door had slowly swung open.

His ma was awake when he came in. And she was dressed, wearing a coat and everything. He wanted to ask her what was what, but she came to him and cradled him against her like she did when he was a little kid. Aiden felt her tears falling on his cheeks, mixing with his own. Even though it felt like his ma was a new person out of the blue, he couldn't pretend he didn't like the way she held him. He'd missed it.

Without any words, she ripped a bed sheet and rigged up a sling for Aiden's arm. Then she went to the little dresser and pulled out a traveling satchel from the bottom drawer.

Aiden's tear-blurred eyes met his mother's.

"We're leaving, Aiden. Now."

She pulled open the first drawer in the dresser and stuffed their clothing into the satchel. "I've been such a fool, Aiden," she said. "You don't have to look at me like that. I'm not blaming you."

Aiden wanted to say something about how it sure sounded like she was blaming him. But before he could get a word up from his throat, she was back at the packing and twice as hard. She went to the sink basin and grabbed up the box of soap chips and a few rags that she stuffed into an old coffee can from a high shelf. Then she leaned on the sink and looked fire at him. Whatever had her acting sweet and kind just then, it looked to be gone now.

"If you'd only found a different job, Aiden. Then *He* wouldn't have to test us this way."

"'He' who, Ma? And what kinda test?"

"The Lord," she said, and some of the fire left her eyes when she said the word. "He's been testing and testing and testing. And we haven't been listening. This whole time, and I've been such a fool not to see it. I've been too worried about the people you've been working for."

"Ma, I . . ." Aiden began, thinking about all the things he wanted to say. But something ate a hole in him. The letter Mr. Brand had had for him, and what he said about Miss Farnsworth needing help. And as soon as her name hit Aiden's mind, he saw his mother shrieking in fright when Mr. Collins had come into the cabin that day they'd flown into New Orleans.

She wasn't just afraid of colored folks. Aiden's ma was terrified of Negroes. She acted like they were the Devil come to earth.

"Did you want to tell me something, Aiden?" she asked, and he felt himself shiver as he leaped out of his memories and back to their little room with her standing there against the sink, still giving him a look that warmed him but felt halfway to burning.

"No, Ma. I-I got nothing to say."

"*Don't have anything*. How many times do I have to remind you, Aiden? Proper speaking will get you where you need to be. But if you keep on talking like a nigger, you'll—Oh, Aiden . . ." She then shook her head and folded her arms across her chest. "Don't you see? This is just another test. For us both. God is testing us, to make sure we know what's right and what's wrong.

"When we first landed and that savage stabbed your father's hand, I thought for sure we'd come down to Hell. But this is just the place of our trials and the only reason we're here is because we're not right with the Lord. But we can be, Aiden. We just have to have *faith*."

"Okay, Ma. But I—There's something . . ." Even as he felt the words forming in his mouth, he knew he'd never get them out. Telling his ma about Mr. Brand and the letters would be about the dumbest thing he could say right now.

"You're confused, Aiden. I know," she said, coming forward to kneel in front of him and look up at him. She put her hands on his and looked him in the eye with a goofy smile on her face, like she wasn't even seeing him. Aiden tried to keep his eyes steady, but he saw something in his ma's face, and it didn't shine like anything holy. It glowed behind her eyes, like gold mixed with oil, a swirling mess of everything beautiful turning into nothing but ugly.

"Aiden, it's all okay now. God has shown us all what we've needed to see. It's okay, Aiden, what those men did to you. God has shown you," she said, touching his hurt arm gently. Aiden wondered how she knew. He hadn't said anything about how he got hurt. For a second, he figured maybe she was in on it, like she'd helped those heavies find him and twist his arm out of joint. Aiden opened his mouth to speak, but his ma was right back at it before he got a word up on his tongue.

"This wounding isn't a reason to fight back. It's a reason to listen, to hear *Him*. He's speaking loudly now, Aiden, because we haven't been listening. At least not all of us. Your father . . . he dulled his hearing so much he couldn't listen if he tried. And that's why he walked out on us to go curl up in the street with the other lost souls."

That was too far, and Aiden had to say something this time.

"Ma, he didn't—"

"Didn't what, Aiden? He didn't love us enough. Didn't love himself enough. He's lost, Aiden. But us, *we* can be saved."

"No, Ma. I mean . . . Pa, he didn't walk out. He got—"

"He got himself into a mess he can't get out of. That is his trial, Aiden. *His* burden. But this has been a trial for *us*, too, for you and me, Aiden. To hear. To listen and to hear. And now this has happened," she said, touching his shoulder softly again, but making him wince and try to pull away from her just the same. Something wasn't right with his ma's eyes.

Something wasn't right with her at all.

"Ma—?"

"Aiden, don't speak. Just listen to me. Listen and trust. Have faith, Aiden. We've been tested, and this wounding you've received, it's the last trial, Aiden. The last one we'll ever need to witness. We can leave New Orleans and all these . . . these niggers and their money. We can leave it all behind. We don't need it anymore."

Aiden didn't know what to say to any of it. He thought to tell his ma that Mother Sophie wasn't a ni— He couldn't even get the word into his mind let alone his mouth. Before he could think of what he should say, his ma had stood and then took the floor again.

"Do you know how they get that money, Aiden? Do you know what they do to earn it? Oh, you can't even call it earning," she said, twisting her mouth into a snarl. Then her mouth went back to the goofy smile she'd had on and she started in on him again. "It's stealing, Aiden. They're thieves and pirates, no better than the rum runners in Chicago City."

"Ma, I . . ."

"Yes, Aiden? What is it, son? Do you need to confess a sin? I can't give you absolution, but we can go see Father James at the—"

"No!" Aiden shouted, before he knew what he was saying. His ma looked funny at him, like she was scared of him for a second. Then her face twisted sideways and her eyes went dark and angry. "Do you want to stay here, Aiden? Do you want to tell me we should stay here? Well, you can forget it. New Orleans isn't our town anymore than Chicago City can ever be our town again.

"There are white communities around here. They're clean and straight, with no *krewes* fighting one another to own the streets. I've been paying a woman I work with downstairs ever since we got here. She says we can stay with her anytime we need to, and she knows people over in Pass Christian who'll take us in."

Aiden's mind spun around what his ma just said. She'd been payin' a sewing lady? Was that what she'd been doing with his money?

His ma went back to the kitchen and opened the cupboards, removing cans and jars and putting them on the table next to the satchel holding their clothes. She worked like one of them fancy gearboxes on the Metairie mooring deck, all practiced and smooth, almost like she'd planned this and was just waiting for the day to do it, and thinking about it now, Aiden figured that was just what his ma *did* have planned.

Aiden looked back at the dresser; the small wooden case appeared smaller now that Aiden felt his world crushing into him from all sides. Everything in the room felt distant, removed from touch and sound, vanishing into the distance and threatening to leave even his memory.

"Ma?"

"What?" she asked as she went to the mattress to fold up the blankets. He still hadn't earned enough to get them a proper bed frame. That was supposed to be his next buy after a visit to the

Ghost's window. But he hadn't been back to see the Ghost since the last time he saw Julien.

That's going on two weeks, isn't it?

Aiden's mind went in circles as he watched his ma work. She pulled a canvas duffel out from behind the mattress and used it to stow the linens after she folded them up. She stopped halfway as she was stuffing a blanket into the duffel to stare at him.

Aiden wanted to say something, anything . . . but the look in his mother's eyes made him think twice, and better. He nodded and went to gather up his things. First he pocketed the little knife and other items he kept on the shelf over the mattress.

His ma went on packing things behind him. He heard more cupboards open, and then a sound like splitting wood.

Aiden stole a look out the corner of his eye and saw his ma using a bread knife to pull up a loose floorboard. She reached into the space and lifted out a Derringer. Aiden knew he shouldn't say anything else, but he couldn't pretend any longer when he saw his mother holding the tiny pistol.

The *krewe*s carried bigger guns than that, and they did it right out in the open, on the street and anywhere else they wanted to go.

"They'll get the drop on you, Ma."

"Just shut up, Aiden. Shut up and get in line for once. For one damned time just do what you should do."

She tucked the little gun into her coat pocket and went to the kitchen to get the last few jars she'd pulled down from the cupboard.

"Honestly, Aiden, if you hadn't taken that job with those savages, we wouldn't be in this mess. You got a job, all right. You got a job and that kept us from going hungry. But you couldn't even get the right job."

That rankled him and Aiden found he couldn't let it go. "C'mon now, Ma, that ain't fair."

Aiden's ears rang with his mother's words.

"You couldn't even get the right job."

But she didn't know why he'd been beat up. Did she? Aiden couldn't make head or tail of it now. His ma seemed to know things she shouldn't and believed stuff he'd never even thought about much less figured his folks had considered.

And she didn't know about the dead girl. The one a white guy from New York had killed.

He was about to explain it all to his ma when she opened her mouth again and let out just about the worst thing he'd ever heard.

"You're no better than them now, Aiden. No better than those filthy criminals. We should have just left you with that awful Farnsworth woman in the airship. She could have set you up with a nice little dark girl and then you'd both be happy with your Negroes." Then, her eyes rounding in anger and fire and hatred, she finished by saying, *"And I wouldn't be here frightened for my life."*

Aiden tried to see his mother underneath all the tears, the rage in her face, but she was gone. Whatever was crawling around behind her eyes had found a way out. All that remained of his mother was a monster. She looked ready to speak again, and Aiden waited for more insults, but she just shouldered the duffel full of blankets and lifted the satchel with her other hand.

"I guess I'll have to carry it all since you're sitting there with a broken wing," she said, surprising Aiden. He thought she'd actually cooled down, but it looked like he was wrong.

His mother warned him with a look as Aiden shuffled across the room to open the door. Tears spilled down his cheeks, but he held in the sobs.

She's been ready for this day all the time. And she didn't tell me about any of it.

"It's about time you started listening to your mother," she said. "It's a good thing those niggers didn't get you acting like them, too. I'd have to leave you behind if that was the case."

Aiden couldn't believe his ears. His ma looked like she was about to say more, like half of her wanted to drop the bags she carried and come over and sweep Aiden into her arms like she did when he was a boy, like she had when he first came home.

But the other half won, and right then Aiden knew this was the last time he'd see his mother.

Her eyes went dark as could be, and all around her the air shook and filled with wisps of memory and thoughts of fear. Fire licked the night around his ma's hair, and flaming ghosts danced all about her, wrapping her in shrouds of smoke and oily black rage. His ma's face went slack, like the part that had been keeping her alive was slowly fading or being sucked out by the ghosts that whipped and swirled around and poured from her mouth.

Her eyes, though. His ma's eyes stayed firm and focused, beady and dark like black pearls. Whatever gold or beauty he'd seen before was long gone now. His mother's face twisted around like some kind of monster and she roared at him.

Aiden stood frozen in place, afraid to move and afraid to stay. His mother had become a nightmare he couldn't escape.

"Get out of my way, boy," she said and reached a clawed hand for his face. Aiden flinched and shrank away from her, but she stepped closer and set her hands to strike. Her fingernails grew out like knives and aimed straight for his eyes.

Aiden ran out the door. He held his lame arm in the sling tight against his stomach as he clattered down the steps. He tore through the alley, down to the end and onto the street. Aiden ran with all his might. He had to make sure he was far enough away. Far enough that none of his mother's ghosts could snake out and touch him.

Down the street and across to another alley. On and on, Aiden ran through the Irish Channel, hunting for safety wherever he could find it. Finally, he pulled up at a park and hid behind a thick tree trunk next to a little bench.

"Mr-Mr. Brand?" he called to the night.

Mr. Brand showed up quick, slipping out of the wall beside the cabin door.

"You needed me?" Mr. Brand asked.

"Yeah, I got a note to send."

"To who?"

"To—" Aiden was about to say his ma's name, but he remembered the way his mother had looked at him and the feeling he'd gotten, like she wanted nothing but to see every dark-skinned man or woman end up dead and gone, and him along with them. "To *Hatred*."

Mr. Brand nodded and stayed hush while Aiden told him what the note would say. When he was done, Mr. Brand put a hand on his pocket and nodded again. "It's there. I'll get it to . . . to her."

"Thanks, Mr. Brand."

"Of course. And, could . . . could you do me a favor, too? I know I shouldn't ask, but . . ."

"What is it?"

"Remember me. Okay?"

It was Aiden's turn to nod and keep his face like a stone even while he felt all the tears he'd ever cried trying to get out at once.

CHAPTER 33

EDDIE'S VOICE DRIFTED OUT OF THE GATE-house and to Emma's ears like it was buoyed by the revelry inside.

"Must be 'bout time they startin'," Eddie said.

Emma heard the gatehouse door slide in the dirt and then slide again. More laughter came from inside, and a little whooping and hollering, too. Emma followed the path around the hall and stopped at the corner of the gatehouse to listen again.

From the crack in the main doors, she heard glass on glass and cheering. A drumroll started. Emma stepped around to the gatehouse's side door and looked in through the window.

She saw a chaperone she recognized, who was surrounded mostly by men with instruments. A few women speckled the crowd, their flapper haircuts and cloche hats making it easy to pick them out. White faces and dark faces filled the room in a ring around the chaperone, who stood much higher than anyone else. Emma thought at first it was because everyone was sitting, but then she saw the girl was standing on a small platform about two feet off the floor.

The chaperone held a cigarette in one hand and a glass of hooch in her other. The drumroll kept up a *pitter-patter-pitter-patter* rhythm for another several beats and then stopped. The girl tipped back the hooch into her mouth and then flung the empty glass behind her. Emma heard it crash against something solid as the crowd roared.

Emma spotted Eddie off in the side of the room, where he stood with another musician and a couple of women, who hovered by each man's elbow.

Eddie put his horn to his lips and blew: "Shave and a haircut."

Everyone laughed and the chaperone let herself fall forward to be caught by a white man, who lifted his hat as if to congratulate himself on the catch. Another woman hopped up to take the chaperone's place and the mock auction repeated itself.

Emma watched while three different women took their turns slamming back hooch and swaying into the arms of whichever Casanova came to the rescue. Finally, Eddie came close enough to the platform that it looked like he'd be playing the knight in shining armor next.

Swallowing her heart, Emma turned around and followed the stone path back to the Rising Sun Hall. She left the scene behind and made her way through the neighborhood streets to the *Vigilance*— the only place of safety she truly had left in New Orleans.

But when Emma got back to the ship, Lisette was gone and a mess of black feathers lay scattered around the street below the mooring deck.

• • •

Emma flew home alone, worried sick about Lisette. She slept in the airship until the sun came up. With a heavy heart, she left the ship and made her way off the mooring deck to head back to *her and Eddie's place*.

When she saw Lisette hiding under the deck, Emma burst into tears and ran to give her a hug. She needed to hold on to someone she could trust, someone who knew what it was like to have your life eaten away in bits and pieces.

Lisette's son was with her, too. She held an arm around the boy and filled in Emma as they walked to the house.

"I seen the Birdman come up the street while I was waitin' on you, Miss Emma. So I ran out and made my way home to get my boy here. Julien, this is Miss Emma. She gon' help us get your sister free and then we gon' fly outta New Orleans."

The boy was about the same age as the Conroy kid, maybe a little older. He seemed ready to buy what his mother was telling him, but only just. He walked with one hand holding hers and the other resting over his heart, ready to snap it into place over his eyes.

"My Julien, he a houseboy for a few years now. Says it's all gettin' messed around with Mama Bonvivant comin' into town recent."

"Messed around how?" Emma asked when they reached her and Eddie's place. She wished she could think of it differently, but it'd always be her and Eddie's place. Until she left it behind anyway.

Emma opened the door and led them inside. Lisette made to answer her question, but her son spoke up first.

"They all talkin' 'bout Dove Conroy," Julien said, and Emma whipped around to look at him, feeling the shock hit her face like a slap.

"Conroy? You mean Aiden?"

"Yeah. Dove Conroy what we all call him. Boy gotta be crazy. He run off from Mama Bonvivant's place. He supposed to be cleanin' a room and he just run off."

"Where'd you hear this?" Emma said.

"Around the street, you know? Other houseboys all sayin' it. Damn fool dove, I tried tellin' him."

Emma sniffed at the boy's use of the word *dove*, and just nodded in reply. She'd heard about the houseboys who came in after everything was over and done with, and cleaned up the gala houses so they'd be pretty for the next night's singing and dancing and drinking.

So Aiden Conroy had been keeping things tidy and clean for Bacchus's *krewe* and the filthiest business Emma had ever heard of.

She figured the Conroy kid didn't know what was going on. He had to be working just to help him and his folks keep a roof over their heads and food on the board. But the way his folks were about Negroes . . .

Brand gave me a letter for him. So he'll be all right. He has to be.

Emma let the worry slip aside. It wasn't anywhere near as strong as the anger she still felt toward Eddie.

"So what we doin' now, Miss Emma?" Lisette asked, breaking into Emma's thoughts about Aiden and his folks.

"We get ready for tonight. We'll fly like usual. I'll pick up the girls and you'll play chaperone since that's how Bacchus wants to do it, right?"

"But the Birdman after us, Miss Emma. I seen him on the street."

"And you've still got both your eyes and I have mine. If he's after us, fine. He hasn't found us yet. Right?"

"That's right," Lisette said and looked at her son who still kept a hand at the ready. Lisette put her arm around him tighter and continued. "Mr. B, he said seein' the auction'd be like to reminding me of how it would've been with me back then. We gonna go pick up your sister, Julien, sure we are. Then we gonna fly on outta New Orleans once we get them girls on board."

"But we need to get some things together first," Emma said. "Clothing, whatever food we can take with us. Cans and jars. There's a small icebox in the ship, but it'll only hold two bottles of milk at best, and who knows when we'll see ice again."

Emma went back to the kitchen with Lisette and Julien following behind. They grabbed whatever they could and brought it back to the front parlor. Lisette and her son went back for more while Emma sorted out what they had.

A few cans of beans, some jars of jam and mustard. A couple more of stewed corn and tomatoes. Emma made to head back to the kitchen for another armload when she heard a soft saxophone note from outside.

She went to the window and looked down the street. There he was, holding his horn to his lips and half stumbling up the sidewalk. So Eddie'd made his way back home somehow, probably in a van with the others Emma had seen at the gatehouse. In that moment, Emma realized she'd truly given up caring about him. He could have died out there, or ended up a tramp like Brand, but it wouldn't have mattered one bit to Emma.

Then Eddie's music found her memories and she fell onto the couch in a heap.

Up the walk he came. She heard him stepping this way and that on the concrete, sometimes coughing and sometimes playing on his horn. He played notes running up and down, spinning in circles then drawing out. He played one tone, long and slow, then another. The haunting sounds moaned through the window to collect around Emma like so many tortured spirits.

Instead of the warm skies and hotter nights Eddie's music once inspired, Emma felt only decay, a rot that infected and spread faster than wildfire through tenement shacks.

Eddie played a fast string of notes again, a melody she knew from the first time she'd heard him play. She shook and sobbed and let the music assault her now, push her back against the cushions and hold her there, frozen and broken and chained.

The playing stopped and the front door opened. She heard him shuffle in and close the door. Then Lisette came from the kitchen with her son, and Eddie seemed to figure he was in the wrong house.

Emma put him straight. She stood up and stormed toward him with her fists at her sides and tears pouring from her eyes.

"Lovebird? What's the matter?"

"You knew!" she screamed, and flung herself against him, shoving him back outside. She beat her fists on his chest, but the anger and fire went out of her the minute she saw his face. Her blows wanted to be a hurricane and landed as nothing more than droplets.

Eddie pushed her hands away and backed up a step.

"The hell's got into you, woman? What happened?"

"What happened, Eddie? What happened?" she said through tears that simply wouldn't stop, no matter how hard she tried to pull them in. "You knew, that's what happened. You knew and you went along with it. This ain't Storyville, but it's only different in name. You knew and you told me it would be okay. But you didn't tell me the score, Eddie Collins. You didn't tell me what the *krewe* bosses and house mothers were doing to those girls.

"You knew all along and you pulled me into it to help them do it. Damn you!" she said, finally summoning the strength to swipe a hand at his face. The slap hit him as a glancing blow because she'd moved so slow he'd seen it coming, and Emma hadn't put enough into it anyway.

"Settle yourself down now, girl," he said, putting a hand up like he'd give it back to her.

"Why? You going to hit me, too, Eddie? How many of those girls have been hit? How many of them have been beat because they wouldn't do what the *krewe* boss or the house mothers told them to? Because no girl, not anybody, nobody should be sold like a slave!"

Emma turned aside and buried her face in her hands. She felt him come up behind her. His hands on her, pulling her to lean back against him.

"Lovebird, I—"

"No," she said, pushing away and spinning to face him with all the fire she could muster. "I'm leaving New Orleans, Eddie. You can stay here for all I care. Play your horn for them, so those girls will dance the way they've been taught. Shimmy and shake for the ones who came down from New York to buy them up. That's what you've been helping make happen, Eddie. And you knew. Goddamit, Eddie Collins, you knew!"

. . .

While Lisette's boy, Julien, stayed downstairs and packed up the foodstuffs they'd collected from the kitchen, Emma and Lisette gathered up the warmest clothes she had. If they managed to get any of the girls out, she'd have to be sure they could keep warm. It'd be colder the farther north they went, and none of her passengers would have any time to prepare for this trip.

Not much different from the last time.

Emma put thoughts of her flight from Chicago City out of her mind. Now wasn't the time to get nostalgic. And memories of Eddie's voice weren't helping much.

"You every kind of crazy there is, Emma. Why don't you settle yourself down, girl? Settle down, and let's talk about this. C'mon."

But she'd had as much as she would take from him or any other man who tried to change her mind. She'd shoved Eddie back out the door and slammed it in his face, then went back to packing. She'd spared a look out the window at him, though, and she let her face tell him good-bye. He waited on the stoop for a full minute of silence, then stumbled away into the morning with his horn.

Emma stood still in their room now, waiting for the sound of Eddie's horn to come again. It didn't, so she tightened her jaw and got back to work. In the closet, she snatched up the hat and coat the gypsies had given her in Chicago City. Lisette had the rest of her heaviest clothes in a suitcase already.

"We ought to be thinking about taking them dresses, don't you think, Miss Emma?"

Emma looked at them, the pretty dresses and their frills and lace and tassels. Beside them was the heavy fur coat Bacchus had given her that other night. Hatboxes were piled on the shelf above. She couldn't bring herself to take any of it. Taking the luggage that Bacchus's money had provided was hard enough.

"You're welcome to 'em," she said and turned to leave. In the corner of her eye, she saw Lisette lift the coat and four of the dresses off the closet rod and drape them over her arm.

In the doorway, Emma looked back at the room she'd shared with Eddie for almost a month. The dark wood of the bed and vanity gleamed in the early morning light from the window. Her shadow extended across the bed and the wall behind it like a ghost, hovering there like a question.

"What happened, Eddie?"

• • •

The suitcase sagged against Emma's hip as she walked, but she forced her feet to keep a steady pace. Lisette trailed a bit behind her, burdened with the heavy coat and dresses she'd insisted on taking. Her son hauled a box in his arms and another one behind him on a rope. The box scraped along the concrete like a rasp across Emma's ears, but she forced herself to let it be.

The airship hung above the silent deck. Emma trudged up the stairs, banging the suitcase against each step. Lisette and her son struggled behind her with the coat and dresses. It took two more trips to haul up the foodstuffs to the deck.

Emma moved to the deck's switchboard to get the gearboxes up and running. The machines clattered to life and shuffled a metallic step down to the mooring winches. Emma paused when she heard a rustle and coughing from the street below. She went to the rail at the edge of the deck and looked over.

A lone figure in a white suit stood beneath the deck smoking a cigar and clutching the dark, struggling mass of a rooster that crowed against the man's restraining hands. The man's pale brown face seemed to glow in a halo of burning light.

The bird's screech cut Emma's ears and she flung herself away from the railing, staggering back a step to lean against the switchboard for support. To her left, Lisette and her son huddled in the gearboxes' little shed. One of the gearboxes drew up and stopped in its tracks. The other kept moving and posted beside the mooring winch at the airship's tail end. Lisette hissed at her from where she and her son hid and shielded their faces with half-raised hands.

"That the Birdman, Miss Emma. That's him down there, I bet my life on it."

Emma whirled around and worked the lever to call back the one gearbox and reset its command cycle. As the automaton retraced its steps, Emma cast frantic eyes around the deck. She didn't dare look below it again, not with the Birdman down there. She still heard the feathers, rustling like sheets of cold, dry paper moving in the midday breeze.

"Go on," she said to Lisette and her boy. "Get in the ship and throw down the sheets from the bunkroom. Make a rope so we can haul these things up."

Lisette nodded. She and her boy hustled across the deck and up the ladder. Emma waited for the gearbox to get back into position and cast a wary glance in every direction she could. She spun on her heel and did her damnedest to keep quiet enough so she could hear the bird or its owner. Not for the first time, and she figured not the last, Emma wished she had a gun in her hand.

Finally, the gearbox reset and marched down the deck. With it posted by the nose winch, Emma searched the deck and listened for movement. After heaving a breath into her lungs, she stepped away from the switchboard, grabbed her suitcase by the handle, and lugged it to the ladder where she kicked loose the airship's retaining pins just as Lisette dropped down a tangle of bedsheets all knotted together.

Emma tied the sheets to the suitcase and Lisette and Julien hauled it up. Emma kept darting her eyes this way and that, fearing any second that the Birdman would come out of nowhere.

When the sheets came down again and touched her on the cheek, Emma jumped and shrieked. She caught her breath and tied a sling around the box Julien had carried. The boy hauled it up on his own while Lisette whispered down to Emma.

"C'mon, Miss Emma. Get yourself up here now. Birdman around. C'mon, please."

Emma grabbed the rope attached to the last box and made to climb the ladder. But the rope slipped from her hands and the box tumbled off the side of the deck. She heard the shattering of glass and the metallic clatter of cans and jars.

Throwing a fast curse at the mess below, Emma went up the

ladder, hand over hand, one foot up, then the next one to follow. She got into the cabin and when no attack came, no wild rooster out of nowhere to screech at her and claw away her eyesight, Emma let herself relax enough to just sit and breathe on the floor. Lisette and Julien sat together at Brand's desk.

"We ought to be gettin' on, Miss Emma," Lisette said, and her boy's face told Emma he was thinking the same thing. Emma leaned against the door housing and looked out into the grim humid morning. That same hard and hot wind shot into the cabin then and Emma felt it against her eyes and mouth. Even though she knew it was just fear that drove her, Emma whipped her head to the side. In a flash, she reached for the lever and brought the cabin door closed, feeling her heartbeat settle as the door latched tight.

She stood and went to the cockpit, letting her gaze rest on Lisette and her son for a moment before sitting down.

"You ready for this?" she asked.

"Yes I am, Miss Emma. Yes I am."

Emma smiled at Lisette. Then she winked at the boy, who still had a hand up near his face. He didn't seem to know what she meant by her gesture, so Emma let her face go stone cold again, figuring he'd know tough talk better than soft.

"Let's go get your sister, Julien. And then let's get the hell out of New Orleans."

CHAPTER 34

THE MECHANIC'S COT IN THE AIRSHIP FELT JUST as close and tight as when Aiden had slept in it back when they were coming down from Chicago City. But it was the only safe place he could remember in all of New Orleans.

He and Mr. Brand spent a few moments in that tunnel, after Aiden ran off from his ma—from *Hatred*. When his old boss left him there to deliver his message, the mud men had showed up and gave Aiden a good run. While he'd run, he'd thought about how they'd started out, his folks and him on the airship with Miss Farnsworth and her jazz man and the other Negro. Then, as he'd run down the tunnel, the door to the airship appeared in the wall and he wound up here in the mechanic's space.

Aiden had no idea where the ship was, or who even owned it anymore. Still, something about the airship felt right, even though just about everything else in his life felt wrong.

What had happened to his ma? She went from angry to goofy to crazy and at the end Aiden figured she'd been all of those things at once.

And a whole lot worse. She'd called me boy, *just like Mother Sophie had.*

Struggling and with his shoulder still aching like hell, Aiden got himself off the cot and went to the hatch. He should find out where the *Vigilance* was berthed. Maybe the ship wasn't the safest place after all. He put his good hand on the hatch clasp. Then his mind went sleepy and the night caught up with him. Aiden settled onto the cot. He slowly wrapped himself up in the blanket he'd left there the last time he'd come to hide in the tight space.

He woke with a start and knew he'd been asleep for a good long while. The engine room felt warmer, like the day had had time to grow. A heavy wind outside buffeted the *Vigilance* and Aiden rocked in the cot with the swaying of the ship.

He heard voices then, from inside the cabin; at least three, and he wasn't able to recognize any of them. He listened and waited. Two heartbeats passed and the engines started up all around him, rumbling and humming heavy and deep.

· · ·

In between working the ballast or the radio, Emma kept her hand in her pocket, touching the envelope and tracing the letters of her name with a fingertip. She'd taken it and the one to Aiden out of Brand's desk in case Lisette or her son got curious.

Brand, you damn lazy bum. I never should have put a hand on those letters.

She'd open hers soon, Emma promised herself. And then she had to figure out some way to get the other one to the Conroy kid.

Just then, Emma startled as she realized she hoped Aiden was close. And that he'd be the same kid he'd been the last time she'd seen him. New Orleans had a way of changing people. Emma knew that better than most, and she knew those changes never really turned out the way you'd like.

Lisette stirred behind her and Emma looked to see the woman helping her son get settled in the corner of the cabin near Brand's desk. Julien had a blanket pulled up tight around his chin. Emma tried to send a smile his way, but she felt it only get halfway up her face.

Turning back to the controls, she focused on the flight ahead. It wasn't more than a handful of minutes before she got them to the boarding house and set down on the deck. Once they'd been moored she suggested they all get some shuteye.

"It'll be a fine thing if we all sleep through the show later, so let's catch whatever winks we can. Lisette, you and Julien can take the big room on the right. I'll be across the hall from you. We'll keep the ship locked up tight just in case, but I don't think anyone'll hassle us here on one of Bacchus's decks."

"You sure about that, Miss Emma," Lisette asked. Her eyes seemed to spin in her head and looked every which way as she spoke. Emma glanced left and right out the cabin windows at the quiet night.

"I don't think the Birdman will come after us. He plays for keeps if he plays at all, at least the way I've heard it. Since we've still got all our eyes in our heads, I think he was just there to scare us. We're setting up like usual to do a job, so if anybody asks we've got plenty to back us up."

Lisette nodded and seemed to accept what Emma was saying. Taking Julien's hand, Lisette led the boy quietly down the hall where they disappeared into the main bunkroom.

Emma was surprised to find that she almost believed her own words, too.

The Birdman was just making a showing for Bacchus. He was just incentive. Encouragement.

That was a word that Frank Nitti had used with her father once. Emma hated herself for thinking it now. She waited a few breaths before going back to the bunk Eddie and Otis had shared on the trip down. She grabbed the pillow there, went back to Brand's desk and folded herself across it. Sleep came in an instant and stayed with her until the afternoon sun warmed the cabin like an oven. When she woke, she felt the envelopes stabbing her in the side, so she pulled them out of her pocket and stuffed them back in the desk drawer.

Who cares who finds the damn things.

A harder wind than before shook the ship and sent currents of heat through every crack and crevice. Emma steadied herself as she stood and went to check the time on the clock in the cockpit.

Just before 7:00 PM. Time to start the show.

Taking a breath to settle her hands, Emma started up the engines and went back to wake up Lisette. The woman and her son came out of the bunkroom as Emma got to the corridor entrance.

"Just about time," Emma said.

Lisette nodded and wiped the sleep from her eyes. She went to the windows by Brand's desk and looked out at the boarding house. Emma rushed to her side when Lisette snapped a hand over her mouth and burst into tears.

"My baby girl!" she cried and crumbled to her knees, sagging against the wall and sobbing.

Outside, on the ground, Bacchus and his torpedoes were leading a girl from the boarding house. They stepped down the walk to Bacchus's sedan, which was waiting at the curb. Another group of girls waited by the front door of the house with the house mother.

As Emma's fury built, Bacchus and his group got into the car and drove away. Emma took Lisette's hand and tried to put some comforting words on her tongue. But all she had to give was rage, and Lisette's heart was the wrong destination.

Julien came up beside his mother then. Emma let the woman's hand go as Lisette held her son close and the sobs shook her. Then the house mother was on the radio asking why the chaperone wasn't down there to collect the girls. Emma and Julien had to coax and pull and finally force Lisette to her feet, all while the house mother screamed at them over the radio. Finally, Lisette had herself together enough to go and do her part.

Emma shooed Julien back into the small bunkroom. Then she undid the cabin door and helped Lisette onto the gangway. She followed the woman with her eyes, waiting at every step for the

Birdman to show up. But the night stayed calm and silent. Except for the grumbling of the house mother from the street below.

As Lisette stepped slow and steady down the mooring deck, Emma promised herself they'd still get the girls out. But she had no idea how they'd do it. Her hand went to her pocket without her even thinking about the letters, and the next instant, Emma was on her feet and backing away from the shimmering wall of the airship cabin.

• • •

Brand stumbles into the *Vigilance* and lets the curtain drop into place behind him. He has the door at his back, and he remember the last time he was in this position.

A thousand feet up with nothing but the Chicago City skyline to break my fall.

Brand doubles over and coughs into his lap. He keeps one hand on his hat so it won't fall off his head. When he looks up, he sees Miss Farnsworth staring him down like a prize fighter ready to land the last punch of the night. Brand almost wishes she would belt him a good one. Anything to shake the sense that he's lost the last bit of hope he had left.

"Miss Farnsworth," he says, tipping his hat now and lowering his eyes to her shoes. She's wearing nicer kicks than the last time he saw her, but nothing so fancy as what he knows she should be wearing.

All the other gods get dolled up in glad rags every chance they get.

But she's not like the others, and he knows it. On cue, she proves him right.

"Brand," she says. "So you're back. And right when it looks like I'll need a helping hand again. Funny how you seem to be here at the right time and still make it feel like the wrong place."

"I'm sorry, Miss Farnsworth," Brand says, still with his eyes on her toes. "I thought about taking a bath, but the other fellas told me not to bother. As much time as we spend in the mud, a guy might as well roll himself in pig slop if he wants to get clean."

"That's not what I meant, Brand, but now that you mention it. . ." She wrinkles her nose at him and steps back a pace, then another, until she's up against his old desk. He eyes the drawer where he used to keep his bottle. It's empty, and he knows it. Even if the bottle was still there, it'd be empty, too. After what's happened to the people who rode this pig down from Chicago City, Brand's surprised they aren't all swimming in the mud like Al Conroy.

"How's the kid? Conroy? Is he okay?" he asks.

"I don't know," she says, folding her arms and softening her face a bit. "I heard he's in trouble with the house mothers, but that's all I know about it.

"the house mothers? Dammit. What'd he do?"

"I said that's all I know about it. Now what are you doing here? What do you want?"

Before Brand can reply, Miss Farnsworth dips a hand into her pocket and pulls out the envelopes.

"You can have 'em, Brand. I don't want them anymore. I don't know where Aiden is and I don't care what you think I'm supposed to be. Take 'em back!"

Brand shifts his eyes left and right, but they keep going back to the envelopes pinched between Miss Farnsworth's fingers.

"I—"

There's a shout from outside, a woman talking sharp and fast. Brand spins around and sees a white lady, one of the house mothers. She's on the mooring deck with her hands on another woman, one with dark skin. That woman has a crowd of girls behind her like ducklings. Brand's seen the house mother before. Just the other day. She was with Bacchus when Brand made a delivery.

Miss Farnsworth whisper at him from across the cabin. "You'd better get out of here, Brand. Go on. Scram."

Brand doesn't waste a second. He lifts the curtain, ducks out of the cabin, and stalks back into the mud tunnels behind New Orleans. He's learned to inhabit the place pretty well since he arrived. Even the guys who moan and groan for a piece of him don't bother him anymore.

"Hi, fellas," Brand says to the mud men that come out of the walls. Their hands reach, but he swats them aside like he's learned to do. They don't really want much. Just somebody to remember them. That'd give them a reason to care enough to wake up every morning and say hello to the day.

Brand has his own reasons, and he just left one of them on an airship with a storm of who knows what coming her way. The other one, though . . .

Conroy. Hang in their, pal. Just give me a call, and I'll come runnin'. Ol' Mitch will be there.

Brand shuffles through the tunnel thinking about Conroy and knowing he can't promise the kid anything. But he wants to, so he says it just the same.

"I'll be there, Conroy. If you can be there for me, too."

• • •

Emma stuffed the envelopes into the top drawer of Brand's desk and went to the cabin door. She crossed her fingers that nobody outside, not Lisette, the house mother, or the girls, had seen Brand. He'd scooted like she told him, but he could just pop back in any second and throw another wrench in the works. Emma figured Lisette had to know about things like gods and monsters, but Brand was somewhere in between and would probably put the woman right over onto her backside if he pulled his jack-in-the-box routine now.

Out on the mooring deck, the house mother gave Lisette two earfuls and then some, just for good measure. Emma waited until the house mother was gone before opening the cabin door. Lisette came into the cabin with a beaten look on her face. Emma had a question on her tongue, but she waited until they'd reached the gala house and Lisette had taken the girls inside.

When Lisette came back, Julien greeted her at the cabin door and stayed by her side as she stepped on unsteady feet. Emma took a breath and went to work on her.

"Are we doing this or aren't we?"

"What you mean, Miss Emma?" Lisette asked, drawing up short in the middle of the cabin. "Doin' what? What we got left to be doin'?"

Before the tears could start, Emma went to Lisette and gripped her by the arms.

"Sister, now isn't the time to go soft in the head. Your little girl is in that house and some New York City fat cat is planning to buy her for a handful of folding money."

Lisette shocked her by knocking Emma's hands aside.

"You think I don' know it?" she yelled in Emma's face. "You think I don' know Mr. B got my baby Juliette in that house and 'bout to put her up on the auction block?"

"I know you know it, and I know you want to stop it. Or you did before Bacchus put our plan out to pasture. So now we need a new one. Fine. Let's figure it out."

Lisette's eyes glistened and her lip quivered, but she held it in and stepped over to Brand's desk where she sat in a rush, like she'd have fallen over if the chair wasn't there to catch her.

"How?" she asked as Emma came closer to her. "How we gon' do this?"

Emma didn't have an answer right away. She took in Lisette's clothes, the standard dress and heels of a chaperone, a bonnet that had come untied with all of the woman's sobbing and shivering with fright or rage or both.

"You got those dresses," Emma said, suddenly seeing the way out of the mess they were in. "The ones from my closet."

Lisette's eyes went round with recognition and she almost let her lips curl into a smile. "Yeah. Yeah, we did get them dresses. So let's go get them dresses on and then we go in there an' get my Juliette. That what you thinkin' Miss Emma?"

"Yeah. That's what I'm thinking, Lisette."

"Okay then," Lisette said. "But it ain' like to bein' easy as that.

We can' jus' waltz on in and out and again. People be seein' us come in and won' go lettin' us out we try an' take Juliette out their hands."

"They won't see us coming, sister," Emma said, her eyes rounding as a rush and drive flooded her chest. "The plan is we get dolled up right. We go in there and make a ruckus somehow. Everybody'll be going this way and that. None of Bacchus's boys will go shooting up a room full of his best paying guests. We get the room going crazy and then we get the girls and run like hell."

Lisette nodded fast and stood up faster. "Yeah. We get my Juliette back. And then we run."

"And the other girls," Emma reminded, putting a note of caution into her voice. Lisette picked up on it and nodded again, but she kept her face firm and cold.

The women each took a dress and got ready in the bunkroom. Lisette helped Emma put her hair right with some extra pins and a brush she had in her handbag. Emma didn't look the part of a proper flapper, but it would have to do. They took turns in the washroom putting on a little of the face paint Lisette carried, too.

"Julien," Lisette said as she and Emma came back into the cabin, "you keep this ship locked up. Hear me? But you keep an eye. When you see me an' your sister comin', you open that door and be ready to close it just as quick. Mr. B gon' have his boys on our tail."

"Yes, Momma," the boy said, his eyes flashing left and right and that hand still hovering around his collar.

• • •

Emma and Lisette got held up at the gala house door, but the one-time chaperone worked her magic with the toughs there.

"Mr. Bacchus say he want me inside," Lisette explained. "My little girl on the block tonight and I'm s'posed to see it. It's Mr. B's parting gift to me, he says. See my little girl off proper."

The tough didn't do more than nod and get out of the way. Emma and Lisette stepped inside and took in the room. In that instant, Emma knew they were sunk. She and Lisette stood at the back of a throng in glad rags all packed in like sardines with that sweet stink of hooch dripping from every tongue.

Emma spun in place as a group came in the door behind her. She ended up face-to-face with the flapper from the Rising Sun.

"Well," the woman said. She took a puff from the cigarette she clutched in one hand. Emma stared at her, thinking the woman held in a mouthful of venom. But she blew the smoke out of the side of her mouth and into the crowd beyond. "I do think you'll want to keep your hands to yourself this time," she said while tossing a nod at the men standing to her left. Emma looked at the bruisers and recognized the two doormen from the Rising Sun.

The flapper and her little group made their way through the crowd and Emma turned to see where Lisette had ended up, but she couldn't find her in the tangle of suits and beads and skirts. All she could see were straw boaters, cloche hats, bobs, finger waves, and peacock feathers. The men all had paddles with numbers on them, and the women all held cigarettes or drinks, or just the arm of the man they were with.

Between two women standing close to her, Emma caught sight of a white suit. A sleek jacket and trousers over a pair of fine shoes, and a white fedora to match up top. The man held a paddle, too. Emma felt a stab of fear when she recognized the Birdman, but then the man turned to the side and Emma spied his eyepatch.

The Ghost turned again, as if he could feel Emma's eyes on him. He put a finger to his hat brim and winked with his one eye above a slim smile that faded as fast as it came.

Emma thought to push through the crowd to catch up to the Ghost. As she stepped forward, she heard Eddie's horn. Her heart skipped before she remembered his betrayal and what he'd been a part of and known he was a part of the whole time.

When she got her thoughts together again, the Ghost had vanished into the crowd that kept pressing around Emma and trapped her where she stood.

Where is Lisette?

• • •

Aiden crept out of the cot and opened the hatch. He slid his good hand down the side of the ladder as he stepped down the rungs to the corridor. Whoever had been in the ship was gone now. The cabin was empty and quiet at the end of the corridor, so Aiden stepped down to see what he could see out the windows.

At the bunkroom door, someone jumped out at him, and Aiden caught sight of a blade glinting in the moonlight coming through the cockpit windows.

"Oh, damn, Dove Conroy!"

Aiden stumbled backward and saw Julien standing in the bunkroom door holding a kitchen knife.

"What the hell you doin' here?" Julien asked. His face was tight and scared. "I almost stuck you like a pig there. What you doin' on this ship? And how you get in without me hearin' you?"

"I was hiding up there," Aiden said nodding back at the engine room hatch. "My ma . . ."

Aiden stepped down the corridor, past Julien, who stayed back in the bunkroom but hissed a warning at him as he went by.

"Don' go out there, dove. They see you, it all gonna go wrong."

Aiden ignored his friend and went to Mr. Brand's desk. He couldn't say why, but he felt like he should be sitting there. So he did and opened the top drawer. Two envelopes sat there mixed in with some of Mr. Brand's old news notes from Chicago City. Aiden lifted out the envelopes and saw one had Miss Farnsworth's name on it. He put that one back and opened the one with his name.

Innocence,

I don't know how to tell you this nicely, so I won't bother. You've been in my way for too long, and now you're going to pay for it. Say good good-bye to Mommy Dearest and get the hell out of New Orleans.

Yours,
Hatred

Aiden's heart did a flip-flop. Then he heard a commotion coming from outside and looked out the window. Miss Farnsworth was in a tangle with two tough guys holding her arms. Aiden felt his heart flip again when he recognized one of the toughs: Theo Valcour. Aiden hadn't seen the older boy since he'd chased Aiden through the streets and into the pile of mud with all the tramps.

So that's where you ended up. Sitting high and fat after you took my money.

Behind Aiden, in the corridor, Julien again hissed a warning, so different from the first time the boy had called Aiden's name outside the Ghost's alleyway. Aiden looked back at his friend and shook his head. Then he reached up, pulled back the curtain of the city, and left the airship cabin.

• • •

Emma bumped and bustled her way through the crowd until she felt a hand on her arm. At first she thought it had to be Eddie, because nobody with dark skin ever put a hand on her there except for Eddie.

But it was some tough guy from Bacchus's *krewe*. He was young, but big, and Emma felt him urge her to leave the room. Then another heavy took her other arm and the two of them hauled her out of the house as the auctioneer started to rattle off his litany and the paddles went up.

• • •

Aiden grabbed Theo Valcour from behind, putting his one good arm to the task. He got the bigger boy by the scruff of the neck and yanked as he stepped back behind the curtain. Theo toppled backward almost coming down on top of Aiden, but with a quick dodge to the side, Aiden was out of harm's way.

"The hell is this?" Theo yelled, scrambling out of the mud and putting his fists up like he was ready to kill. Then he seemed to notice where he'd ended up. And who had brought him there. His eyes went left and right, like a scared rabbit's, but his fists stayed balled.

"You must be ready to die, damn fool dove. Touchin' on a man bigger'n you and stronger'n you. And a man in Mr. Bacchus's *krewe*. You know what he gon' do after I'm done with you? Birdman gettin' your name, dove. He gettin' your momma's name, too. Time your whole family got plucked."

While Theo busied himself talking, Aiden kept an eye out for movement in the tunnel. Sure enough, as Theo stepped up with a fist pulled back and ready to fire, the wall came alive to Aiden's left. He stepped back and Theo moved to follow until a muddy arm wrapped around the bigger boy's mitt.

Theo hollered at first and shook off the mud. Then more of the wall came to life, arms and legs, fingers curled into claws that stained and smeared. And those gaping, moaning mouths that spoke of nothing but hunger and sorrow.

Aiden kept stepping back, flashing a look left and right to make sure the mud men didn't come up on him by surprise. But they seemed content with their prize. Theo struggled and wrestled against the hands that wrapped over his mouth and face now. He howled and roared. And then he screamed and flailed his limbs.

But it was done. Aiden slipped out from the tunnel and back into the airship cabin. Julien stood there at the corridor entrance, mouth open like the mud men, but only with shock and fear on his face.

"Dove Conroy, you—"

"Yeah," Aiden said. He saw Julien's face squeeze up in fright and then the boy's eyes rolled up and down he went.

Just like my ma.

Only Julien didn't go to thrashing in fits.

• • •

Emma felt the man behind her let go, but the other one kept

his hands on her. Then he went stiff and his eyes bugged out like he'd seen a ghost. He let Emma go and fell to the side.

Lisette stood behind the bruiser, holding one of Emma's kitchen knives in her hand. Blood dripped off the blade, long and thick, to the ground where it joined the pool around the man's body.

"Took it when we was in your kitchen," Lisette said, tucking it back into her handbag. "Bet you glad I did. Now come on. They puttin' my Juliette up on that block soon."

They dragged the dead gangster behind a bush. Emma hunted the night for the other man who'd grabbed her, but she couldn't find him anywhere.

Inside, the bidding was going fast and furious, and Emma heard a mess of groaning and moaning from one side of the room. She and Lisette wove their way into the crowd together until Emma saw him: that damn New York banker from the night she was out with Eddie.

The man stood in a group, all New York from what she could see: the cut of their suits and the way they held themselves, big and tall, proud like skyscrapers. The banker and his friends all wore the same ugly look, too.

The auctioneer called out a bid and one of the New Yorkers stuck up a paddle, but just as fast he was outbid. Emma scanned the crowd for the winning paddle. She spotted the Ghost not a few feet away. He stood right in front of the auction block and something in the set of his face told Emma he wasn't here to bid on the same prize the others had in mind. The Ghost's one good eye was bent up like he wished he didn't have to see any of his surroundings.

It's like he wishes he wasn't here. Or that this place wasn't here.

Up on the auction block, Juliette shivered like a puppet with broken strings, all knock-kneed and doing her best to stay upright. Behind her, the other girls who'd all been bid on stood in a row, doing the same frightened dance of standing still and wanting to fly.

Emma turned to Lisette to say something when the room exploded in a storm of black feathers. Everyone screamed and Emma heard a woman's voice cut through the chaos.

"This's for that girl you thought you owned before you paid for her. Damn New York dummy!"

A man from the New York crowd hollered bloody murder and Emma caught a hollow laugh that turned to acid in her ears, like the shrieking of steel against stone. She heard a rustling of dry paper and dead leaves, and then the crowd split apart as a dark shape came rushing at her. She tried to back away, but the people pressed her forward into the coming blackness.

Emma saw at the last minute that it was a rooster being carried by a man wearing a white suit, just like the Ghost, but he had both eyes and laughed like a maniac as he ran at her with the bird in his mitts.

She staggered back and came up against the crowd, and they all pushed her forward again. The rooster came in close and Emma swatted with an arm, shoving the bird to the side. But she felt blood trickling down her arm from where its beak had dug into her flesh. The crowd pushed once more and Emma went down on her knees. She lifted an arm to cover her face and rolled to her left until she felt shoe leather against her back.

Someone shoved with the toe of his shoe, and Emma moved away, still holding her arm up in front of her eyes. The shrieking and crowing of the rooster threatened to split Emma's eardrums. Some in the crowd were cheering, and other laughed. Emma even heard a bet being made as she circled around the small space the crowd had made for her and the crazy man with the rooster.

With her arm up, the best Emma could do was to focus on her shoes and the limits of the little arena that had formed in Bacchus's gala house. If she could spot a gap between two sets of legs, she'd make a break for it. She just had to—

The Birdman's cackling came to Emma's ears again, closer than before, and then she heard the rasping screech of the rooster right beside her head. A hand grabbed her arm and yanked it away from her face, and she smelled the wet stench of a barnyard as black feathers filled her vision.

A gunshot cracked through the air and Emma staggered back.

The Ghost stood beside her with a smoking pistol leveled at the Birdman, who fell to the floor with a hole in his face where his right eye should have been.

"Now we're even, Birdie," the Ghost said, tucking his pistol into his coat pocket. The rooster squawked as it fluttered off to the side of the room. The crowd drifted apart, breaking up the arena and clearing a path for Emma to see Lisette grabbing Juliette's hand and running for the door. Eddie was up on stage with the band, watching Lisette and her daughter go, too.

Another gunshot cracked through the night and Lisette stumbled and landed on her stomach. Juliette screamed. Eddie dashed down from the stage and Emma raced through the splintering crowd to join him. Eddie helped Juliette turn Lisette over while Emma searched for the shooter.

From the middle of the crowded room, Bacchus's footsteps were like thunder on the floor as he crossed in front of the auction block.

"I believe you all have something belonging to my person," Bacchus said. The red mist began forming around him again, pouring from his eyes and mouth, and this time everyone in the room seemed to notice it. They all went hush and still, except for the few people close enough to almost touch the fat gangster with the smoking gun in his mitt. As those guests backed away, too, Emma felt Bacchus's eyes on her, hot and angry, but hungry at the same time.

Eddie gave Emma a look that said *run* as he got to his feet.

"Mr. Bacchus, sir, whatever you want, I'll pay it. I can owe you the money, if that's okay, and I'll just play your shows until it's paid. Just please, let Emma go free."

Bacchus seemed to consider the offer, but Emma felt the scream rise in her throat when the red mist ballooned in the space between the two men and the gangster's face fell like he just couldn't be bothered.

Bacchus raised his gun and shot Eddie in the chest. Emma cried out and went to him as he fell dead on the floor. She huddled over him, crying and knowing they'd lost everything. She and Lisette had bet the house and come up empty-handed.

Bacchus's feet set down beside her in a slow and heavy *one-two*.

"I've long needed a new diversion for myself, and I believe you'll make a fine addition to my . . . menagerie, Miss Emma."

Emma kept her face pointed down. To her left she saw Lisette taking shallow breaths as she lay cradled in her daughter's lap. Emma spied the glint of her kitchen knife then, the one Lisette had been carrying. It was half hidden by Eddie's head. Emma slid a hand across the floor by her knee, like she meant to use it to help her stand up.

Bacchus chuckled and Emma heard him sliding his pistol into a holster under his coat. His heavy hand reached down in offering, like he'd help her to her feet.

"Come now, Little Miss Lily White. We'll have a nice time of it and you can forget all of this."

Emma turned to him, and saw the red mist sucking back into his face, filling his eyes and mouth, and disappearing into his bulk once more. Emma held her face unchanged, keeping her look fallen and stained with tears. She shuffled a knee so she could stand and then rose, clutching the knife and bringing the blade up to thrust into Bacchus's heart.

The big man heaved in a breath and she thought she'd missed, until blood bubbled from Bacchus's lips and he fell away from her. His enormous body shook once, viciously, and the red mist of Emma's nightmares billowed out around Bacchus as he stood there quivering. He lowered his thick head and looked at the knife coming out of his chest. The mist around him grew dense and flooded back into his nostrils and ears.

Bacchus lifted his left hand to grip the knife. Emma rushed forward and slammed all of her weight against the handle, shoving the blade deeper into Bacchus's chest. The man shook again and the mist sprayed out now, filling the room and going in every direction at once. People screamed as a cascade of angry crimson washed through the space.

Emma felt the mist trying to get into her, but something kept it out, like a shield or a wall inside her that wouldn't let even a scrap of Bacchus's vile nature get in. Emma shuddered, but felt her strength return as she fought off the violent mist that seemed to thrash around the room now. The crowd shrank away from it, and some fainted, or just fell down in terror.

Bacchus shook and spit blood, but kept his feet. Then another mist, an oily black one, joined the red. Together, the fogs of horror swirled into pictures of death and mayhem, murder, and violence of every kind imaginable.

Emma felt herself wanting to scream, but her hands wouldn't leave the knife.

Not until it's all out. Not until this place is free and clear of you.

The ghosts of death and crime whorled above the crowd. Emma stepped back from Bacchus, letting go the knife because she knew the blade had done its work.

All around her, the guests and partygoers whimpered or wailed, but the Ghost himself stood in the middle of the space, with the hint of a smile on his lips. The black and red mists tried to get into him, too, Emma saw. But they couldn't touch him, and finally fled the room in a torrent through the open ballroom door.

Emma watched the gods depart. She clutched her arms around herself as they left, remembering the way it felt to have them picking at her, trying to find some way inside her heart. Then the gods were gone, and the room was still. Emma turned back in time to watch Bacchus crash to the floor.

His heavies came from all sides, climbing to their feet or out from behind screens, and all of them with heaters in their mitts. But the Ghost stepped onto the auction block and fired a shot into the ceiling. The torpedoes all lowered their gats and put their hands to their sides like soldiers waiting on orders.

"That's the end of that," the Ghost said. "This auction house is now closed for good."

The crowd murmured and some barked a few words of objection. Over in the corner, the New York contingent huddled around the banker Emma remembered. He was holding a hand to his face and streaks of blood ran down his cheek.

"Ladies and Gentlemen," the Ghost continued, "I did not say it would be the end of the gala houses, only that this . . . *revolting enterprise* was at its end. Y'all can go on drinkin' and dancin' until your feet fall off. It makes no nevermind to me."

Emma waited for the Ghost to say something else, something that told her she could leave. When he did turn to her, he simply winked at first. Then he stepped down from the auction block and walked forward, tipping his hat as he came. Emma saw wispy faces around the man's head. They were colorful in bright reds and blues and yellows, with numbers all around.

Playing cards, Emma thought as the Ghost reached a hand out to take hers and raise it to his lips. He kissed her fingers and let her go with a look of warning.

"I am ever so pleased that you received my note. But now might be a good time to get yourself out of here," the Ghost said. Emma remembered the envelope.

"But I didn't—"

"Not now, Miss Emma. Just be getting on, hey?" the Ghost said. He nodded to the side like he meant to get her attention on something.

The New Yorkers had broken their huddle and moved as if to snatch the group of girls standing behind the auction block.

Emma ran forward, crouched by Bacchus's body, and yanked the pistol from the holster under his beefy arm. She aimed it at the New York men as she stood.

"Hands off, dammit!"

Emma motioned at the girls to head for the door. "C'mon. We're flying out of here."

The girls didn't miss a beat and shimmied their way out the door quick as could be. Emma backed up until she stood beside Juliette.

"Is your mother going to make it?" she asked the girl.

"I-I don't know."

Emma risked a look down, taking her eyes off the bankers, who still had their eyes on her.

Lisette held a hand over her belly where blood pooled under the dress, staining it in a halo around the bullet hole.

"Gon'-gon' be okay, Juliette," she said. "You go with Miss Emma here. She got your brother out in that airship. You go on and get away from this place."

Juliette shook her head and dropped her tears onto her mother's face. Lisette's eyes squeezed tight and Emma could tell the pain was too much as the woman ground her teeth and held a grunt behind her lips.

Then she shook and went still, letting out a breath that rattled and caught at Emma's own heart.

The Ghost's voice came across the room then. "Only so many favors I can call in, Miss Emma," he said. "Best be gettin' on, like I said."

Emma looked at Eddie, dead on the floor, then she and Juliette stood up. They stepped to the door, leaving Lisette and Eddie where they lay.

· · ·

Outside, the airship was already running, and the winds of a storm were blowing in off the gulf Gulf harder and hotter than they had yet. Emma didn't know what was going on with the *Vigilance*, but she'd damn sure soon find out. She raced up the gangway to find the Conroy kid at the controls. He had one arm in a sling, but a half-grin slid onto his mug when he saw her.

"Figured I'd just keep her warmed up for you," he said. The girls all moved inside to stand in the corner by the galley door. Julien was hunkered down in the opposite corner with a knife held out like he'd stab whoever came close first.

Juliette stepped into the cabin behind Emma and Julien's face went soft and messy with tears.

He knows.

Emma went to the cockpit and looked the Conroy kid in the eye.

"Where'd you come from?"

"Engine room. Figured it was the safest place for me after my . . ."

"After your what?"

The kid seemed like he'd give her an answer, but then his eyes went to Brand's old desk.

"There's a letter for you. I opened mine already."

Emma saw the torn-open envelope and a note card on the controls, like they'd been thrown there. She went to the desk and took out the envelope with her name on it. She still couldn't quite get her head around the way it was addressed.

VIGILANCE C/O EMMA FARNSWORTH

While the kid crumpled up his letter and stuffed it down the waste chute beside her, Emma read hers. It was from a god named *Chance*. He was thanking her for her kind assistance in keeping the city of New Orleans on an even keel, and asking if she could go one better by showing up at tonight's event. A grin spread across her mouth as she read the note and she laughed once.

"I guess I can at that, Mr. Chance. And I guess Brand wasn't lying after all," Emma said as she pushed the card and envelope down the waste chute by the desk. She glanced at the gala house through the cabin windows. Bacchus' tough birds held the doors open for the flood of people pouring out and trailing away into the night. Some of the guests seemed almost happy, but most of them staggered along like they'd just come off a battlefield and weren't sure they still had all their pieces.

Emma waved a hand to dispel their memory and went to the cockpit. She came up short beside the pilot's chair when the cabin wall shimmered and Brand stepped into the cabin.

"You again," Emma said, staring Brand in the eyes. "I would have thought you'd push off by now. Your job's done, isn't it?"

"Maybe," Brand said, pawing his tattered hat off his head and holding it over his stomach. "Was . . . I mean, if it's not too much trouble, I was . . ."

"Mr. Brand," Aiden said from behind Emma. He came around and made to shake the tramp's hand, but Brand just scooted back up against he cabin wall like he'd fall through it before he touched the kid's mitt.

"What is it, Mr. Brand," Aiden said. "What's wrong?"

"Nothing's wrong, kid," Emma said with a smile. "He just needs a ride. Right, Brand? Why don't you take the seat at the desk?"

Emma motioned for Brand to take his old seat, and the tramp didn't waste a second. He nodded his thanks and shuffled over to flop down in his old chair. He gave a little smile and pivoted right and left with a quick flex of his legs.

"Just like old times, eh Mr. Brand," Aiden said. Brand nodded again, smiled some more, and then sniffed once before he wiped away what Emma figured had to be tears of joy.

The winds pushed and shook the airship then, rocking it against the mooring lines. Emma told everyone to get settled as she went to the cockpit. Juliette wrapped herself up in a blanket with her brother. Aiden showed the other girls the bunkroom corridor, and told them where they could find blankets for themselves.

"You can take the bunkrooms, too. If you want. I'll be up in the mechanic's cot."

"You got any know-how for fixing this ship, Aiden?" Emma asked while she radioed the gearboxes to set them loose from the deck.

"A little," the kid said. "But Mr. Brand probably knows more. Ain't that right, Mr. Brand?"

Emma gave a sideways glance at the tramp sitting at the desk. He might not be flapping his gums about *What's what* and *All the news that's fit to blab about*, but it was still Brand, sure as sure could be. And the way he held himself and nodded, Emma almost thought he might have what it takes to keep them in the air if something went wrong.

"Fingers crossed you aren't just nodding your head so you can catch a free ride, Brand. This ship's been through a lot already. No telling if she'll get us to our destination."

Brand didn't say anything, but his eyes told her what she needed to know. As long as she was watching out for him, he'd give everything he had to keep her and the others safe.

"Where're we going?" Juliette asked.

"New York City," Emma said. "You and the other girls here are just the first ones to get free. Bacchus had this business going on for who knows how long. There's a lot more work to do."

ACKNOWLEDGEMENTS

Gods of New Orleans would not exist without
the help, support, and encouragement of these wonderful people:

Beta and proofreading

Belinda Sikes, Zoë Markham, John Paul Catton,
John Monk, Alice Kottmyer, Horace Brickley, Sarah
Zama, Mike Harris, and Dover Whitecliff

Formatting by Therin Knite of Knite and Day Design

Cover design and artwork by Eloise J. Knapp

ABOUT THE AUTHOR

I write and edit speculative fiction, primarily in the dark/weird/thriller/sci-fi genres. In addition to my novels, Gods of Chicago and Gods of New Orleans, I've published multiple short stories and have co-edited two anthologies of Steampunk / Alternate-history fiction. When I'm not writing or editing (or picking up after the kids), I'm probably out in the woodshop making sawdust and chips with my grandfather's hand tools.

You can connect with me and find out more about my editing services at www.ajsikes.com

I avoid Facebook like the plague, but hang around on Twitter @AJSikes_Author

Now and then, I blog about woodworking, writing, and editing at writingjoinery.wordpress.com